A STRANGER'S KISS

Devlin threw open the door, scooped a startled Meghan up into his arms, and strode inside the darkened cabin. He closed the door behind him with an impatient nudge of his booted heel, then lowered his speechless burden to her feet. Without any preamble whatsoever, he swept her masterfully against the length of his hard body and brought his lips crashing down upon hers.

Meghan stiffened with shock. Shock was almost immediately replaced by a whirlwind of other emotions, however, as she felt Devlin's arms tightening about her with fierce possessiveness. A strange spark was ignited deep within her, a spark which rapidly flamed into a fire that raged throughout every fiber of her being. She had certainly been kissed before—as the undisputed darling of last year's London season she had been ardently pursued by a swarm of admirers, but this kiss was entirely different. She felt shaken to her very soul, and there appeared to be nothing she could do in the way of ending the fiery enchantment . . .

EXHILARATING ROMANCE
From Zebra Books

GOLDEN PARADISE (2007, $3.95)
by Constance O'Banyon

Desperate for money, the beautiful and innocent Valentina Barrett finds work as a veiled dancer, "Jordanna," at San Francisco's notorious Crystal Palace. There she falls in love with handsome, wealthy Marquis Vincente—a man she knew she could never trust as Valentina — but who Jordanna can't resist making her lover and reveling in love's GOLDEN PARADISE.

MOONLIT SPLENDOR (2008, $3.95)
by Wanda Owen

When the handsome stranger emerged from the shadows and pulled Charmaine Lamoureux into his strong embrace, she knew she should scream, but instead she sighed with pleasure at his seductive caresses. She would be wed against her will on the morrow — but tonight she would succumb to this passionate MOONLIT SPLENDOR.

TEXAS TRIUMPH (2009, $3.95)
by Victoria Thompson

Nothing is more important to the determined Rachel McKinsey than the Circle M — and if it meant marrying her foreman to scare off rustlers, she would do it. Yet the gorgeous rancher feels a secret thrill that the towering Cole Elliot is to be her man — and despite her plan that they be business partners, all she truly desires is a glorious consummation of their vows.

DESERT HEART (2010, $3.95)
by Bobbi Smith

Rancher Rand McAllister was furious when he became the guardian of a scrawny girl from Arizona's mining country. But when he finds that the pig-tailed brat is really a ripe voluptuous beauty, his resentment turns to intense interest! Lorelei knew it would be the biggest mistake in her life to succumb to the virile cowboy — but she can't fight against giving him her body — or her wild DESERT HEART.

CAPTIVE FLAME

Catherine Creel

ZEBRA BOOKS
KENSINGTON PUBLISHING CORP.

ZEBRA BOOKS

are published by

Kensington Publishing Corp.
475 Park Avenue South
New York, NY 10016

First printing: July, 1988

Printed in the United States of America

To the man who has held me "captive" with his love and kindness and tolerant nature for the past fourteen years . . .

Chapter One

Coarse, sea-roughened hands thrust Meghan Kearny into the room.

A sharp gasp escaped her lips as she stumbled forward, tripping over her long tattered skirts while her thick, waistlength hair of burnished gold tumbled riotously about her face and shoulders. She hastily regained her balance and spun about in outraged indignation to confront the man she had mere seconds ago termed—quite accurately— a "black-hearted spawn of the Devil," but before she could hurl further epithets at his unkempt, lice-infested head, the miscreant slammed the door shut.

His evil laughter burned in Meghan's ears, along with the accompanying sound of the outer bolt shooting home. She flew to the door and raised her fists to pound upon its splintered planks, but to no avail. Tears of helpless rage and rising panic stung against her eyelids. Valiantly choking back a sob, she whirled and squared her shoulders in an unconscious gesture of proud defiance.

" 'Twould give them the last laugh indeed if you were to succumb to hysterics *now*, Meghan, me girl!" she murmured to herself, striving to gain courage not only from the' words themselves, but also from the bolstering, wholly Irish manner in which her tongue rolled them forth. It was only in times of great stress, or great joy, that her voice offered such undeniable evidence of her true heritage. And there could be no greater time of stress than the one facing her at this very moment!

Imprisoned within a pirate's harem, she silently reiterated the horrifying truth.

Until now, she had at least been able to glean some small measure of comfort from the company of the other female prisoners. Although from Cuba and therefore possessing no true knowledge of English, the young women had managed to communicate, by means of a few all-too-understandable gestures, their shared predicament to the newest captive.

Meghan's heart pounded fiercely, and she folded her arms tightly across her breasts as though to quell its wildly erratic beating. Wondering why she had suddenly been cast into solitary quarters, she leaned wearily back against the door for support.

"Dear God, what am I to do?" she beseeched aloud. Her wide, sparkling gaze made a swift appraisal of the unfamiliar surroundings, desperately searching for any possible avenue of escape.

The room—in actuality little more than a cell, thought Meghan in disgust—was empty, save for a narrow mahogany bedstead and mattress in the far corner, an ancient porcelain chamber pot only half hidden by the overhang of the bed's stained and torn coverlet, and a spindle-legged washstand with a cracked pitcher and bowl resting serenely beneath the single barred window. The rays of the midmorning sun warmed the closely set iron barriers and cast long, widening shadows on the rough stone floor.

8

Hurriedly crossing to the window, Meghan clutched at the bars and strained upward in an attempt to discern the position of her new chamber in the pirate fortress built high upon a bluff bank. Her eyes, their color a gloriously rich-hued blend of emerald and sapphire, narrowed against the bright sunlight, then grew wide again as they traveled anxiously across the panorama of blue sky and limitless ultramarine waters. There was no sign of the vessel which had brought her to the Bahamian island of Andros three days ago, nor of the two other ships she had spied anchored in the palm-sheltered cove the previous day.

She breathed a heavy, dispirited sigh as she turned away from the window. Crossing her arms snugly against her full young bosom once more, she sank down onto the bed. The ropes creaked noisily beneath her weight. The feather mattress, rife with lumps of a questionable nature, fairly reeked with the tangy odor of the sea, but Meghan was too deep in thought to notice.

Come, now, Verity, we face no danger of being set upon by pirates, she had confidently assured the young woman who had befriended her aboard the "white guineaman" not long after the brig had set sail from England. As was usually the case, the chief, most valuable cargo of the *Bristol Packet* had been human—more than a hundred indentured servants and redemptioners bound for the Colonies.

Meghan's silken brow creased into a deep frown as she recalled her fellow "passengers." Thrown together by the vagaries of fate and the caprice of mankind, the unfortunate wayfarers had included convicts being transported instead of hanged, emigrants hopefully transplanting themselves to a new

9

and better life, rogues, vagabonds, cheats, whores, and brash adventurers of all sorts, and a good many individuals of decent substance who had either been decoyed, seduced, deceived, inveigled—or forcibly kidnapped, like herself. This incompatible mass of humanity, crammed below decks, had endured nearly two months of confinement in the stifling hold with only brief periods in the open air. Men, women, and children had been tortured by seasickness and fever, had prayed frantically for deliverance while under attack by the terrifying perils of both wind and sea. . . .

She shuddered involuntarily as the awful memories of the voyage ran together in her mind. Giving silent thanks once more for the fact that she herself had escaped illness, she drew in a deep, ragged breath and flew back to the window. Her troubled gaze fastened upon the densely wooded landscape below, where the warm tropical breeze whipped the water into frothy waves that went rushing headlong to crash upon the sandy, deserted shore. The pirates had chosen their retreat well, thought Meghan unhappily, for there appeared to be no other inhabitants there on the southern tip of the island. Indeed, the only sign of life she had observed thus far consisted of swallows and hummingbirds soaring effortlessly in and out of the trees. Watching them, she could not help but be reminded of the scornful words spoken to her by the captain of the servant ship.

Aye, 'tis free as a bird ye'll be once ye've served out yer term! he had sneered in response when she had proudly demanded freedom. The blackguard had paid no heed whatsoever to her claims of abduction, and she now realized that he had in all

10

likelihood been in collaboration with the very men responsible for spiriting her away from Ireland.

Raising an impatient hand to sweep the tangled golden tresses from her forehead, Meghan began to pace restlessly back and forth like a caged tigress. Her heart twisted anew as she recalled the painful, shocking events of that fateful day—could it truly have been a few short weeks ago?—when her entire world had been turned upside down . . . .

"I'm sorry, Meghan, truly sorry. But surely you must see how it is. Your father, may the good Lord rest his soul, borrowed heavily against the estate. Even if you were able to sell Rosshaven tomorrow, I fear it would not fetch half enough to settle his debts."

"You were his friend as well as his solicitor, Ambrose O'Donnell," Meghan spoke through her tears. "Why did you not seek to prevent him from—"

"From what, my dear?" the tall, bespectacled older man demanded gently. "From being what he was?" Ambrose gave her a sad little smile while shaking his head. "No, Meghan, it was beyond my abilities as either friend or advisor to do that. Your father was a good man at heart—indeed, there are some who might claim he was generous to a fault— but there was a sickness within him which could not be cured. I pray you will not judge him too harshly, for in truth, he had not the power to change."

Meghan, her eyes burning and her head spinning as a result of all she had just learned, fell silent. She turned toward the fireplace, staring deeply into the dwindling flames which sought in vain to chase the winter's chill from the parlor.

11

The great house at Rosshaven had stood guard over the vast, green-mantled grounds for more than a hundred years, had been the birthplace of three generations of Kearnys, had witnessed war and famine as well as peace and prosperity . . . but never had it suffered the humiliating defeat which now seemed unavoidable. Because of Thomas Kearny's inability or unwillingness—or both—to control the inner demons compelling him to enter into one disastrous wager after another, his untimely death at the age of forty-eight had left his only daughter with heartbreak and indebtedness instead of the restitution he had always meant to make her.

To Meghan, his death had come as more of a blow than she could ever have imagined possible. Rosshaven had not been her home for nearly eight years, not since her mother had suddenly fled with her to London one cold day in November. There had been no explanations, no attempts to make her understand exactly why she was being torn away from her home and her beloved but frequently absent father. It had been as though no one expected a ten-year-old child to have any opinions upon the matter at all. In time, she had of necessity adapted to her new life in England, where her mother's parents saw to it that their beautiful young granddaughter was provided with the very best clothing, education, and friends that their wealth and excellent social standing could obtain.

But she had never truly forgotten Ireland, nor Rosshaven—nor her father. Though she had not seen or heard from him once throughout that time, not even after the death of her mother two years ago, he had remained an integral part of her life, a part buried deep inside, but a part which could not

12

be denied. She realized now that she had never ceased to love him. That was the true reason she had defied her grandparents and come home, the true reason she had felt it necessary to gaze upon Thomas Kearny's face one last time.

"God knows it's the last thing you need to hear, but I'm afraid there is another certain 'difficulty' of which you must needs be made aware," said Ambrose, his deep voice drawing her back to the present. Meghan raised her lace-edged handkerchief and hastily dabbed at her eyes before pivoting about to face the kindly solicitor again.

"Difficulty?" she asked, her heart pounding with dread at the answer. *Dear Lord, what else could there be?* she wondered silently.

"Yes. You see, there is a woman who claims to be your father's lawful wife. She has sworn before witnesses that she and Thomas Kearny were married legal and proper some three months ago." Ambrose O'Donnell, inwardly bemoaning the fact that such unpleasant disclosures were necessary during times of greatest sorrow, adjusted his spectacles and quickly scanned anew the documents he held in one hand before setting them back down upon the desktop. With a frown, he reluctantly pronounced, "The papers appear to be in order. If it is proven that the woman is telling the truth, then she may very well be entitled to a share—perhaps even all— of the inheritance."

"But you have just informed me there *is* no inheritance!" Meghan pointed out, her eyes full of mingled hurt and confusion. It pained her to learn that her father had remarried. She felt a sharp sense of betrayal for the fact that he had never bothered to let her know, but then told herself ruefully that it was completely in keeping with his character that he had maintained his stubborn silence until the very end.

"It is true that nothing remains of your father's holdings," Ambrose confirmed with a nod. His mouth turned up into a faint smile as he added, "However, there is some property in Dublin which belonged to your grandfather—not valuable enough to be of much help in the way of satisfying Thomas's debts, but of reasonably profitable commercial substance all the same. Your grandfather's will stipulated that, instead of following the usual custom of passing directly from father to son, it was to be held in trust for Thomas's heirs. And you, my dear, are the only heir." He paused, his wide brow furrowing once more.

"Unless, of course," he continued a moment later, "we are forced to acknowledge your father's 'widow.' If that is indeed the case, then the two of you will share the inheritance. There is a very real possibility that she will contest your right to it. I have heard she is . . . well, that she is most assuredly not the sort of woman you would wish to claim as your stepmother. Truth be told, she is reported to be an evil, grasping creature who boldly pursued your father, unaware that he was not the rich man she believed him to be. With the proper legal counsel, she might even be able to persuade the court that you, estranged from your father for ten years and since your mother's death the legal ward of titled English subjects, should not receive any portion—"

"I don't want the property," Meghan wearily proclaimed. "If the woman's claim is authentic, she is welcome to all of it. I care only about Rosshaven." There was a telltale quaver in her voice, and she

14

battled a fresh wave of tears as she moved to take a stance at the lace-curtained window near the desk. "If there were only some way I could pay off my father's debtors without sacrificing it."

"Perhaps your grandfather would be willing to help." He was unprepared for the way Meghan suddenly rounded on him.

"*No!*" Her eyes momentarily sparked with a brilliant turquoise fire, and she appeared vastly altered from the tearful, grief-stricken young woman of a second ago. Ambrose O'Donnell found himself gazing down at her with a mixture of surprise and bemusement . . . and more than a touch of purely masculine admiration. There was no denying the fact that her anger only served to heighten her beauty.

"I—I'm sorry, Ambrose," she apologized sincerely, her temper cooling as rapidly as it had flared. "It's simply that my grandfather wishes to eradicate all traces of my former life here. He was violently opposed to my mother's choice of a husband, and he made no pretense about his satisfaction when she finally left Ireland and returned to London. No, I cannot ask him to help me save Rosshaven," she concluded with a sad, resigned shake of her head. She managed a weak smile up at the gray-haired solicitor as she extended her hand toward him.

"You've been very kind, Ambrose. I wish we could have renewed our acquaintance under happier circumstances. You see, I still remember the way you used to toss me high above your head in spite of my mother's laughing protests." Ambrose clasped her hand warmly between both of his and felt his heart stirring as it had not done for more than twenty years.

"If there's anything else I can do for you, Meggie," he said, the old endearment slipping easily into his speech now, "do not hesitate to send word to me. I give you my solemn promise I'll be trying to think of a way to help you keep your Rosshaven. Do not give up hope just yet."

Meghan smiled again and nodded bravely for his benefit. She watched in silence as he gathered up his things and left. Once the door had closed behind him, she sank down onto the bench before the fire. Her troubled thoughts drifted to and fro across the years, remembering bad times as well as good, remembering a childhood that had been both enchanted and full of loneliness. The memories warred with one another in her mind, while outside the twilight deepened into night.

Suddenly, there was a knock at the front door. Meghan started in reflexive alarm, then breathed a long sigh as her tensed muscles relaxed. She waited and listened for the one remaining servant—outspoken but fiercely loyal Brenna Gilmartin, who had been with the Kearny family for the majority of her sixty-odd years—to admit the unexpected visitor, but the old woman did not appear.

Wondering who could be calling at such a late hour, Meghan rose to her feet and started out of the parlor. Another loud knock echoed throughout the dimly lit entrance foyer before she had traveled more than a few steps. With a frown of increasing perplexity, she hastened forward and shivered at the blast of cold air that met her as she opened the door.

"Yes?" she queried, straining to see in the darkness. Before her loomed a tall, cloak-enshrouded fig-

ure silhouetted against the night sky. The person—
male or female, she could not yet be certain—stood
in foreboding silence. Meghan frowned a bit in
growing bafflement. "Who are you? What is it you
want?"

"Be ye Mistress Meghan Kearny?" the mysterious
caller demanded in a low voice that was little more
than a growl.

"I am indeed," she answered with a slight inclination of her head. Suddenly feeling another sort of
chill which had nothing to do with the cold, she
instinctively stiffened and pulled her plaid woolen
shawl more closely about her body. "Who are you
and why have you come to Ross—"

Without warning, the man lunged forward.
Meghan's words abruptly ended on a ragged intake
of breath as a heavy blanket was thrown over her
head. She was lifted bodily and tossed over a broad
shoulder, a burly arm locking her legs and a large
hand clamping roughly down upon her backside.
Though she struggled as best she could beneath the
suffocating heaviness of the blanket, she was quickly
borne away from the house and across the grounds,
borne away from Rosshaven and Ireland and freedom . . . .

It seems more of a nightmare than reality,
thought Meghan as she sank wearily down upon the
bed once more. In the space of that one accursed
day, she had buried her father, had learned that she
was to lose Rosshaven, and had been forcibly abducted. Even then, she mused bitterly, fate had not
yet played its final cruel joke upon her. No, *that* had
come when she had been carried off the conquered

17

English ship by a fiendish rogue of the sea and brought to his "den of iniquity" in the Bahamas.

Who would ever have believed it possible that such an act of piracy would occur in the year 1772? she asked herself again, still shocked and amazed at the misfortune which had befallen the *Bristol Packet*. Once the well-armed brigands had taken control, the hapless crew had been set adrift, the brig ransacked, and the passengers subjected to all manner of rough and humiliating treatment. Strangely enough, however, only two of the more than twenty young women aboard had been taken captive by the pirates when they returned to their own vessel. The remainder of the women, along with all of the men and children, had been left aboard the ship to suffer God only knew what fate.

"Why?" Meghan wondered aloud, rising to her feet again. "Why was *I* chosen? And what has become of the other?" Thinking of the cold, haughty young woman who had refused to speak to her even after they had been thrown together into peril, she frowned. The fair-haired beauty had not been imprisoned with the rest of the female prisoners. Was it because she was obviously a woman of quality and means? wondered Meghan, a bitter little smile tugging at the corners of her mouth as she pondered the irony of that particular thought. *She* was a woman of quality and means, and yet no one would believe as much.

Her ears suddenly detected the sound of the bolt scraping back. She leapt to her feet and moved to the window, an audible gasp escaping her lips when the door was flung open. There, framed ominously in the doorway, stood a man who was all too familiar to her.

Please God, no! Meghan exclaimed inwardly, her hand instinctively flying to her throat. Known simply as "The Wolf," the man was the leader of the pirates. He was also the same sinister yet darkly attractive buccaneer who had seized her after the attack. She had not seen him since that day, but he had been in her thoughts all too often. Indeed, she had been fearing the moment when he would finally come to *claim his prize!*

The Wolf's mouth curled into a faint, derisive smile when his heavy-lidded gaze met the startled roundness of his captive's. He wore a curly, shoulder-length black wig and a black cloth patch over one eye, while his slender but well-muscled frame was encased in a black costume whose severity was lessened only by a waistcoat of red satin.

In spite of the way her pulses raced and her whole body trembled, Meghan retreated behind an air of bravado. She drew herself stiffly erect, her proud and lofty demeanor belying the terror in her heart as well as the dishevelment of her attire.

"Have you perchance come to tell me that I am finally to be released?" she demanded imperiously.

"Release is hardly what I have in mind for you," he countered with another meaningful half-smile. Dismissing the guard who waited obediently behind him, he closed the door and turned back toward Meghan. "My apologies for these rather spartan accommodations," he said mockingly, "but they will at least afford us with the privacy we desire."

"I desire no privacy with *you,* you black-hearted scoundrel!" she proclaimed, her magnificent eyes ablaze. "You have no right to keep me here! What kind of man are you to prey upon innocent women? For your information, sir, there are laws—"

19

"I follow no laws but my own." The harsh, menacing light in his dark eyes lent credence to his words.

Meghan swallowed hard and did her best to conceal her rising panic. Though she considered for a moment trying to dart past him and out the door, she realized such a maneuver would in all likelihood yield nothing but hated physical contact with her captor.

"Why have you brought me here?" She regretted the question as soon as she had given voice to it. A tremor ran the length of her spine when she saw the Wolf smile. It was a slow, predatory smile which obviously boded ill for its recipient.

"For the very reason you suspect," he answered, his gaze raking over her with insulting familiarity. "You should feel honored. I seldom trouble myself with women, other than for the purpose of ransom. As a matter of fact, I have come to tell you that I will be unable to 'trouble' with you until I have completed business in Nassau."

He smiled again, briefly, before informing her, "I must go and arrange ransom for your sister in adversity. It is my good fortune that she has such well-placed connections. Had she been naught but a candidate for servitude—like yourself—I would still seek to rid myself of her. Although she is an attractive creature, she cannot compare to you." His eyes traveled boldly over Meghan once more, and his swarthy features tightened with desire. "I am loath to postpone our long overdue rendezvous, but Mistress Hammond should fetch more than enough to compensate me for the wait."

"You—you are going to ransom her?" echoed Meghan in surprise. Not only was her fellow captive safe, but the woman was actually going to be released. Hope stirred within her breast when the pirate reaffirmed his intention with a nod and a sardonic arch of his eyebrow. "Then why not ransom me as well?" she calmly put to him. "My grandfather will pay you well for my safe return to England!" Her eyes flashed as her suggestion was met with scornful laughter.

"Even if you had a grandfather, he would scarcely be able to afford to buy your freedom. No, my sweet, if that were the case, you would not have spent the past several weeks in the hold of the *Bristol Packet*."

"But it is true!" she cried indignantly. "I am no bondswoman! My name is Meghan Kearny, and I am the granddaughter of Sir Henry—"

"You can call yourself whatever you like, but the fact remains that you are my prisoner. No, not prisoner," he amended, favoring her with a look of such lustful intensity that she gasped and flushed hotly, "my willing slave. Or at least that is what you shall become once I have tutored you. Unless my instincts prove me wrong, you have never known the touch of a man, and certainly not a man such as I."

With that, he finally began advancing upon her with slow, purposeful steps. Meghan furiously commanded herself to stand firm and betray no fear, but she could not help retreating. Her back soon came up against the immovable barrier of the stone wall.

"You are making a terrible mistake, I tell you!" she insisted breathlessly. The blood roared in her ears as her eyes filled with horrified disbelief at what was happening—or rather was about to happen—to her. "My grandparents will have people searching for me! You cannot expect to keep me

21

hidden away here forever! Someone will eventually find out what has become of me, and you will then be made to answer for any mistreatment I have suffered at your hands!"

Appearing totally unaffected by her threats, The Wolf drew closer. His eyes darkened with undeniable hunger, and Meghan inwardly blanched at the sheer, practiced sensuality his body exuded. Though she bit back a scream when his hands reached for her, she did not feel in the least compelled to let him have his way with her. God help her, she would die first!

"*No!*" Laying aside all sense of decorum, she chose to fight with every ounce of strength she possessed. She raised her fists and struck out at the pirate like a magnificent, golden-haired hellion. Caught off-guard by the ferocity of her defense, he ground out a savage oath and angrily hurled his body forward against hers. Meghan cried out in pain as the cool stone bruised her thinly covered back, but she did not waver in her resolve. If anything, she battled with even more determination than before, her arms flailing and her feet kicking wildly.

In the end, however, she was unable to prevent The Wolf from capturing her in his relentless embrace. He laughed in triumph before bringing his lips crashing down upon hers with punishing force. She attempted to twist her head away from his, but to no avail. His mouth ravished hers while she was helplessly imprisoned between him and the wall. Her arms were locked at her sides, and she could only moan in futile protest when his hot, seeking tongue cruelly plundered the virgin sweetness of her mouth.

Meghan fought against the nausea which rose in her throat. Her legs threatened to give way beneath her, and she felt herself growing faint. The pirate's kiss, far from pleasurable, made her shudder with mingled revulsion and terror. *Dear God, please, please don't let this happen to me!* she beseeched in frantic tearfulness.

Miraculously, she found herself released.

Leaning weakly back against the wall as her black-clad tormentor spun away from her with a curse, she brought a trembling hand up to her tender, swollen lips and gaped at him in stunned bewilderment. He wrenched the door open, then wheeled abruptly about to deliver his parting shot.

"When I return in two days' time, my sweet, I shall teach you that it is far better to submit. Only in that way will you spare yourself the sort of pain and humiliation which, I assure you, I am entirely capable of inflicting upon you."

His lips curled into a smile of malevolent satisfaction when he saw the look of wide-eyed horror she cast him. Without another word, he took his leave.

His unsavory warning continued to echo throughout Meghan's brain long after he had gone. Her head spinning, she made her way over the bed and sank gratefully down upon it. Hot tears burned against her eyelids, and she pressed a hand to the spot where her stomach still churned.

There seemed little chance now of her ever being able to escape The Wolf's clutches. While she knew it to be true that her grandparents would do everything in their power to find her, she was forced to concede the fact that their search would in all probability not include her present surroundings. It was doubtful that anyone but The Wolf and his men knew of the fortress's existence; even if the few natives inhabiting the island were aware of their unscrupulous visitors, it was unlikely that they would be able to report anything of consequence. No, Meghan reflected despondently, her only hope lay within herself. But what could she do?

Finally, exhausted by both her efforts to formulate a plan and the after-effects of The Wolf's brutal kiss, she lay down and tumbled off into a deep and dreamless sleep. . . .

The pressure of a man's hand on her mouth awoke her. She inhaled sharply, her body tensing as her eyes flew open to see that it was quite dark inside the room.

Dear God, The Wolf has returned! her mind screamed in stark, paralyzing horror.

Chapter Two

"Be still, my love. It is I—Devlin!"

Devlin? Meghan echoed silently, a shiver dancing down her spine at the sound of the resonant, deep-timbred masculine voice. Relief flooded her entire being as it dawned on her that the person kneeling beside her was not The Wolf after all.

But I know no Devlin! she then realized. Though thankfully not the pirate she had feared him to be, the man was nonetheless a stranger to her. She came to life at the thought and attempted to sit upright in the bed, but he pressed her back again to offer a caution.

"Do not make a sound," he whispered close to her ear. His face hidden by the cover of darkness, he appeared nothing more than a mysterious, shadowy figure—a figure who was inarguably human. Meghan was acutely conscious of his warm, strong hand upon her. "I've come to take you home."

Home? Her heart sang at the word. Suddenly, it did not matter to her that she had never known a Devlin, nor that he probably hadn't the faintest idea where her home was—all that mattered was that he intended to take her away, to rescue her from the despicable clutches of The Wolf. She shuddered anew as an unbidden image of the pirate's dark and sinister countenance swam before her eyes. In that moment, she wouldn't have cared if her liberator were the Devil himself!

Nodding mutely in agreement, she was plagued by a strange sense of loss when the man finally removed his hand. She had no time to ponder its significance, however, as she was suddenly hauled to her feet by two strong arms. A cloak was flung round her shoulders, and the hood yanked impatiently up over her bright curls. The stranger clasped her hand firmly with one of his and tugged her along with him to the door, which had been left slightly ajar to precipitate their escape.

Almost before Meghan knew what was happening, she found herself being pulled headlong down the narrow, torchlit corridor outside her room. She was startled to note that her rescuer's attire looked suspiciously similar to that of the pirates', and she suddenly wished she could catch a glimpse of his face, but there was little opportunity for such indulgence as the two of them rounded a corner and went rushing toward an unguarded door at the end of yet another torchlit corridor.

Meghan suffered a sharp intake of breath as the man she knew only as Devlin drew to an unexpected halt and tugged her abruptly back against the wall with him. The reason for his action became clear to her when, a dangerously brief moment later, she saw two men pass along an intersecting hallway a little more than an arm's length away. She could hear her heart pounding as she literally held her breath in fear of detection, but the pirates were fortunately too engrossed in a vulgar discussion of their

26

latest visit to the harem to take note of anything else.

After waiting for what seemed like an eternity, Meghan and Devlin were once again flying toward the door. They were but a few steps away from freedom when one of The Wolf's cohorts—a veritable giant of a man with the amazing capacity to tolerate nearly an entire keg of strong spirits—strode singing lustily into the fortress through that same door. The rogue's eyes, bloodshot and bleary through they were, fell upon the escaping prisoner and her much taller companion.

"What's this?" he bellowed with a ferocious scowl in their direction. "Where the bloody hell d'ye think yer goin'?"

Meghan froze and felt the color draining from her face. Gasping when Devlin thrust her protectively behind him, she watched in wide-eyed dismay as the pirate jerked his cutlass from its sheath and came barreling toward them with the obvious intention of cutting the other man into a dozen pieces.

Devlin swiftly whipped off his cloak, drew his sword, and hastened forward to meet the challenge. His tall, lithely muscled body poised for action, he appeared to Meghan much like some splendid male animal preparing to defend his mate. She gazed upon him for the first time—and found herself mesmerized by what her eyes beheld.

He was without a doubt the handsomest man she had ever seen. More than six feet in height, he was possessed of a devastatingly virile form. His long, booted legs, taut thighs, and narrow, well-shaped hips were molded to perfection by a pair of close-fitting buckskin breeches. A bright red sash was wrapped dashingly about his trim waist, while his

27

magnificent, broad-shouldered upper torso was encased in a white muslin shirt left open at the neck to offer a tantalizing glimpse of the bronzed, granite-hard expanse of his chest.

Meghan felt her cheeks grow unaccountably warm, and she tugged the hood lower upon her head as she pressed numbly back against the wall. Her eyes traveled back up to Devlin's face, turned in profile to her as he readied himself to parry his opponent's first strike.

Even though danger closed in, she could not ignore the fact that his eyes were of the deepest midnight blue she could ever have imagined, nor that his thick hair was a rich chestnut brown streaked golden by the sun. Gazing breathlessly upon his tanned, chiseled features, she found herself thinking that he appeared more like a mythological god of old than a mere mortal of present day.

Her secret assessment of her rescuer's undeniably masculine charms came to an abrupt end when the pirate growled a blistering oath and finally began the conflict in earnest. He brought his cutlass slicing murderously downward, only to gape in almost comical disbelief as Devlin performed an expert maneuver of defense with his own weapon. The black-bearded giant cursed again and threw his considerable bulk behind his next thrust, but Devlin easily deflected the blow and retaliated with a masterful counter-riposte.

Steel clashed with steel in ever-intensifying fury after that, setting up a terrible clamor that bounced off the stone walls and reverberated in Meghan's ears. She bit nervously at her lower lip and watched in wide-eyed apprehension while the two men fought, uncertain whether she should remain where

28

she was or take flight. Offering up a fervent prayer for Devlin's victory, she was startled to realize that her desire for freedom had become completely overshadowed by her concern for his welfare. A sharp twinge of pain shot through her at the possibility of his defeat. He was a stranger, a man she had known for only a matter of minutes, and yet she could not bear the thought of seeing him harmed.

The battle concluded a mercifully short time later, though not as either participant had expected. There was the sound of a man's ale-slurred voice raising an alarm nearby, followed quickly by a second guttural outcry, then the resounding thunder of booted feet drawing closer and closer as the report of trouble rang out through the fortress.

Cold fear clutched at Meghan's heart, and her eyes instinctively flew back to Devlin. *Please!* she silently beseeched him, frantic at the thought of being seized by the pirates when on the very brink of freedom. She could not face the prospect of such loathsome captivity again—nor could she endure the thought of what would happen to her when The Wolf returned!

Devlin's blue eyes suddenly darkened with a savage gleam. Breathing a curse, he hurled himself forcefully toward his opponent. The pirate was taken completely off-guard by this unusual tactic, and he stumbled heavily back against the wall, his matted head striking the stones at the same time the tip of Devlin's sword buried itself in his shoulder. Crying out like a wounded beast, he slumped to the floor.

"Run!" came Devlin's terse command as he swiftly drew his weapon back and grabbed Meghan's hand. She winced at the discomfort when his fingers clenched tightly about hers, but she uttered no complaint, instead gathering up her skirts and obediently racing along with him to the end of the long corridor.

They were just passing through the doorway to the welcoming darkness outside when the reinforcements, brandishing pistols as well as blades, rushed into the corridor a short distance behind them. The self-appointed leader of the motley, drunken group paused to kneel beside his wounded comrade while the others took off to give loud and vigorous chase.

"Take the wench alive or else the captain'll have your worm-eaten hides!" he roared after them. The words were no sooner out of his mouth when he heard the sound of a gunshot. He swore loudly and leapt to his feet. Telling himself there'd be hell to pay if The Wolf was to come back from Nassau and discover that his precious little doxie had escaped or been killed, he hurried outside to try and prevent either disaster.

Another shot echoed through the night air. A sharp, breathless cry escaped Meghan's lips as the ball struck the ground immediately in front of her. She stumbled and would have fallen if not for the steadying pressure of Devlin's hand upon her arm.

"Courage, my love!" he exhorted, urging her ever onward down the rocky, starlit incline to the spot where a boat awaited their arrival. Three more shots rang out in close succession, but the resulting destruction was far wide of the mark, and The Wolf's men were left with no further use for their stolen, single-shot Moroccan flintlocks.

Meghan, at first relieved when she and Devlin reached the cover of trees which lined the shore, soon found herself faltering again as she was pulled briskly along through the dense underbrush that tangled about her long skirts and threatened to send her tumbling earthward. Devlin, his sense of urgency growing when he heard the pirates plunge noisily into the fragrant greenery behind them, swung about and caught Meghan up in his strong arms. Carrying her as though she were naught but a babe, he resumed his flight at an even more breakneck speed than before. Meghan's arms moved instinctively about his neck, and she held on for dear life as she was borne pell-mell through the last thick grove of palms separating them from the beach.

They reached their destination none too soon, for two of their more fleet-footed—and slightly less intoxicated—pursuers had managed to close the gap considerably by now. Meghan was quickly handed over into the care of a large, craggy-faced man who waited beside the dinghy, while Devlin spun about with sword drawn to engage both pirates in battle.

"Cast off, damn it!" he thundered over his shoulder.

His partner in the daring rescue hastened to obey. Tossing Meghan unceremoniously into the boat and giving it a mighty shove seaward, the burly stranger then scrambled aboard himself to take a seat at the oars. He paused long enough, however, to raise his own pistol and fire a well-aimed shot at one of the cutthroats, sending the fellow crashing to the sand with a hoarse cry of pain and thereby evening the odds somewhat for Devlin. That done, he began to row with all his might.

Meghan clutched at the sides of the boat and pulled herself upright from where she had tumbled headfirst into the watery bottom. Impatiently pushing the wet hood farther back upon her head, she drew in her breath upon a gasp as her searching

31

gaze fell upon Devlin again. His tall outline was growing smaller and smaller in the shadowy distance, but she could see that he was now virtually surrounded by a pack of fierce, cutlass-wielding corsairs.

"Dear God!" she whispered, naturally fearing the worst. *"No!"* Her eyes full of anguish, she grasped at the rower's brawny arm and demanded, "Stop!" We must go back for him!"

"No, m'lady, we'll not go back!" he growled, never ceasing in his efforts to propel the boat around the night-cloaked point to where a ship lay anchored. "The cap'n ordered me to get you to safety, and that's bloody well what I'm goin' to do!"

"But he'll be killed!" she exclaimed in heartfelt panic. Her horror-stricken gaze moved back to the frenzy of swordplay on the beach. Although miraculously holding his own against the encircling throng, Devlin was nonetheless being edged increasingly farther out into the water.

Something snapped within Meghan. She launched herself at the dour, harsh-featured man, grabbing at his arm in a highly spirited but ultimately futile attempt to make him desist.

"I don't care *what* the orders were!" she cried, her eyes flashing and her voice brimming with righteous fury. "You will stop rowing at once, do you hear? We cannot leave him there to—"

"Blast it, m'lady, calm yourself!" the stranger's gruff voice cut her off. Jerking his head around to fix her with a keen look of mingled exasperation, amusement, and begrudging admiration, he allowed the merest glimmer of a smile to cross his weatherroughtened countenance. "As sure as that rascal George sits on the throne of England, you won't be seein' the cap'n put in the ground for another three score years!" To prove his point, he nodded back toward the shore, his smile broadening into an outright grin while his eyes twinkled with surprising merriment. "Looks to be a fine night for a swim, wouldn't you say so, m'lady?"

A thoroughly baffled Meghan followed the direction of his gaze. Her eyes grew round as saucers while her heart leapt anew. There was Devlin, little more than a dark form against the swell of the waves, but nevertheless discernible beneath the softly glowing night sky as he swam toward the boat.

Meghan's startled gaze moved hastily to the shore to see that the pirates were still gathered on the narrow stretch of sand, not a one of them brave enough—or drunk enough—to risk drowning. *He is safe*, she thought, her body flooded with profound relief for the second time that night. She sank wearily back down into the boat and felt a merciful numbness overtake her.

Seconds later, Devlin hoisted himself over the bow in one swift, agile motion. After sparing only a brief glance for Meghan, who sat silent and dazed behind him with the cloak wrapped securely about her, he took up the oars and began rowing in unison with the other man. No one spoke as the boat sliced rapidly through the dark waters. There were only the sounds of the sea and the wind, the steady slapping of the oars, and the angry voices of the pirates growing fainter in the distance.

Meghan shivered beneath the damp cloak while her eyes fastened with a will of their own upon Devlin's broad back. The transparency of his wet shirt offered her a mesmerizing vision of the power-

33

ful, bronzed muscles which rippled and flexed with each stroke of the oars.

Acutely conscious of his proximity, she felt her mind and body begin to come alive again. Another tremor ran the length of her spine, but it was not from the cold.

Who is this man? she asked herself in thoroughly stunned bewilderment. *And why is it he makes me feel both secure and threatened at the same time?*

A pragmatic inner voice declared it foolish of her to be concerned with such matters. After all, it pointed out with sobering accuracy, she had just been rescued from a fate worse than death, had been dragged forcibly down a cliff, had nearly been the recipient of a pistol ball which would at the very least have rendered her incapable of completing her flight, and was now huddled like a drowned cat in a boat with two strange men who might very well turn out to be little better than the scoundrels on shore!

Giving herself a mental shake, Meghan forced her gaze away from Devlin and peered toward the large schooner which had by this time come into view. Three tall masts were visible against the horizon, while the ship's sails glowed eerily in the pale moonlight as they were hoisted to billow in the salt-scented breeze.

To Meghan, those huge white squares of canvas suddenly seemed to represent all that she had prayed for these past two months. She would be safe from The Wolf now, safe from the awful nightmare of bondage . . . and safe from this strange, highly disturbing sensation which made her yearn for the feel of Devlin's arms about her and the sound of his deep-timbred voice murmuring words of comfort in her ear. Yes, thank God, she thought with a ragged sigh, she would soon be on her way home again. *Home*.

Stilling their oars when they reached the ship, Devlin and the craggy-faced man positioned the dinghy below the rope ladder which had recently been tossed over the side. Meghan was once again surrounded by a pair of unbelievably strong arms, swung up to the ladder where her hands were seized by two members of the crew above, and lifted aboard. She looked hastily back toward the boat as soon as her feet met the deck, only to see that her handsome liberator had already scaled the ladder and turned to offer a hand to his burly partner.

"Weigh anchor, Mr. Hobbs!" commanded Devlin, his resonant voice ringing out with well-accustomed authority as the other rower climbed to the deck. The schooner's young first mate, who stood beside Meghan, nodded a silent acknowledgment of his captain's orders and hastened to obey. Within seconds, the deck became a flurry of activity beneath the softly glowing night sky.

Meghan, wet and tired and more than a trifle overwhelmed by what she had just gone through, shivered again as the cool wind swept across her. Almost before she knew it, Devlin's arm was about her shoulders, and he was leading her swiftly across the deck. She did not protest when he propelled her down a narrow passageway to his quarters. Anxious to be offered the opportunity to change into dry clothing and hear her gallant rescuer's explanation regarding his mission, she naturally assumed he intended to fulfill both wishes.

But such was not the case—at least not *precisely* the way she had expected.

Devlin threw open the door, scooped a startled

35

Meghan up into his arms, and strode inside the darkened cabin. He closed the door behind him with an impatient nudge of his booted heel, then lowered his speechless burden to her feet. Without any preamble whatsoever, he swept her masterfully against the length of his hard body and brought his lips crashing down upon hers.

Meghan stiffened with shock. Shock was almost immediately replaced by a whirlwind of other emotions, however, as she felt Devlin's arms tightening about her with fierce possessiveness.

Merciful heavens, this can't be happening! she thought, her head spinning and her eyes sweeping closed against the onslaught of unfamiliar, alarmingly intense sensations. She knew she should be outraged, should pull free at once and deliver the sort of rigorous tongue-lashing for which she had become so well known among her social peers . . . but for some inexplicable reason, she could summon neither the will nor the strength to fight. She could do nothing more than stand meekly within the bold stranger's passionate embrace while his warm, insistent mouth thoroughly conquered the softness of hers.

A low moan of half protest, half excitement rose in her throat when his velvety tongue thrust between her parted lips to explore, with provocative urgency, the never-before-tasted sweetness of her mouth. Though she was aghast at her own actions, she could not prevent her arms from raising to entwine themselves about his neck, could not refrain from swaying against him and straining instinctively upward.

A strange spark was ignited deep within her, a spark which rapidly flamed into a fire that raged throughout every fiber of her being. She had certainly been kissed before—as the undisputed darling of last year's London season she had been ardently pursued by a veritable swarm of admirers—but those properly chaste tokens of affection bore no similarity whatsoever to the wildly intoxicating kiss being "forced" upon her at present. The Wolf's embrace had left her sickened, but not so Devlin's. No indeed, *his* was achieving entirely different results! She felt shaken to her very soul, and there appeared to be nothing she could do in the way of ending the fiery enchantment.

It was Devlin himself who finally broke the spell.

Suddenly, and quite without warning, he lifted his head. Meghan's eyes flew wide when she felt his strong arms leaving her. She took an unsteady step backward in the darkness, then gasped as his hands shot out to close about her trembling arms with what seemed to be punishing force. He bit out a blistering curse before yanking her toward him again.

"Who the devil are you? And where is Rosalie?" he demanded in a tight, angry voice.

Meghan could literally feel the fury emanating from his virile body. She found it difficult to make out the chiseled planes of his handsome face in the cabin, for the only source of illumination was the porthole, where the moonlight did little more than create a pale silvery sheen upon the salt-spotted glass. Wondering dazedly why she had been singled out as the object of this man's displeasure—particularly since only moments ago she had been the object of his desire—she swallowed hard and attempted to keep her voice steady while answering with telltale breathlessness.

37

"My name is Meghan Kearny. I was taken captive along with Mistress Hammond three days ago. We—"

"Damn you, where is she?" he ruthlessly cut her off, his fingers tightening about her arms.

Meghan could sense the way his eyes were burning down into her upturned face. She flushed hotly and felt her own temper rising to a perilously high level.

"Take your hands off me at once!" she snapped. "I'm neither strumpet nor child, and I'll not be treated as such!" Setting up a vehement struggle to free herself from his grasp, she was startled when he released her. Once again, she stumbled backward and managed to steady herself by catching hold of the rounded edge of the massive, map-strewn captain's desk. She could only stare at Devlin in mingled trepidation and bemusement while he spun about to light the lamp. When he turned to face her again, the lamp's strengthening flame cast a warm golden glow upon his rugged features and gave further evidence to his anger.

Meghan held her breath as his piercing, midnight blue eyes raked over her. The hood of her cloak had slipped to her shoulders, baring her lustrous mane of hair and affording Devlin with his first unobstructed view of her beautiful young countenance. In spite of her loveliness, he did not appear pleased by what he saw.

"Where is Rosalie Hammond?" he demanded anew. His deep voice was quite low and full of what sounded to Meghan's ears like deadly calm. She trembled involuntarily before lifting her head and fixing him with a look of proud defiance that belied her inner turmoil.

"As I was endeavoring to tell you before, Mistress Hammond is no longer a prisoner at the fortress. She was taken to Nassau only this morning, to be ransomed for freedom." Somewhere in the befuddled recesses of her mind, it began to dawn on her that she was apparently not Devlin's intended damsel in distress after all. And if that were true, she next realized with an acute feeling of dismay, then neither had she been the intended recipient of his kiss. Why did that particular thought trouble her so? she asked herself with a self-deprecating frown. She was behaving as though she were a woman scorned by a lover, instead of a foolish, overly romantic girl caught up in a simple case of mistaken identity!

"And how is it, *Mistress Kearny*, that you are in possession of such knowledge?" Devlin eyed her with visible suspicion, his already thunderous expression growing even more forbidding. Meghan blanched inwardly at the savage gleam in his eyes, but she forced herself to meet his gaze without flinching.

"I was apprised at her situation by none other than The Wolf himself! He is the blackguard responsible for—"

"I know who he is!" Devlin ground out. "What I want to know is why you did not see fit to reveal your true identity to me before now!" He took a threatening step closer, prompting Meghan to draw in her breath upon an audible gasp and give serious consideration to bolting for the door. She gazed up at him with wide, sparkling eyes while he towered ominously above her in the lamplit darkness.

"Because I . . . I . . . you never allowed me the opportunity to do so!" she stammered weakly, only to feel her temper flaring once more as righteous indignation overcame fear. Two bright spots of color rode high on the silken smoothness of her cheeks, and her eyes took on an angry brilliance that gave them the appearance of matching pools of liquid blue-green fire.

"How dare you interrogate me in this odious manner!" she now furiously reproached, sounding and looking every inch the spirited young lady she was. "May I remind you, sir, that I did not ask to be rescued by you, nor did I ask to be brought aboard this ship and ravished by you in your—"

"Ravished?"

Meghan's eyes grew round as saucers, for it appeared in that moment that he would dearly love to strike her. If such ungentlemanly impulses were truly present, however, he managed to quell them and instead settled for favoring her with a hard, scorching look that succeeded quite well in conveying his disfavorable opinion of her charges. His rugged features tightened, and his lips curled into a faint yet undeniably mocking smile before he remarked in a voice edged with biting sarcasm,

"I have never found it necessary to force myself upon any woman, but if such had indeed been my intent, then I venture to say *you*, Meghan Kearny— if that is in truth your real name—would by this time have found yourself lying atop that bed"—he nodded curtly toward the narrow bunk in the corner—"with your skirts tossed high above your pretty head while I *ravished* you until you begged for mercy!"

Meghan gasped sharply and took an instinctive step backward. Acute embarrassment washed over her at his words, and she almost wished she were back on Andros. Recalling the way she had responded so wantonly to Devlin's kiss, she blushed to the very roots of her glorious golden hair and tried to force her wicked mind away from thoughts of what it would be like to be passionately loved by a man such as the one before her.

"Not that it matters," he continued with a fierce scowl down into her rosy, wide-eyed countenance, "but I believed you to be my betrothed, Rosalie Hammond, when I took you from the pirates and brought you here to my cabin."

"That has already become painfully obvious to me!" she retorted hotly. "Though I fail to see how you could mistake a total stranger for the woman you are to marry!"

Devlin's mouth tightened into a thin line, and his blue eyes spoke volumes, none of which were of a particularly charitable nature. His anger was further fueled by the realization that he himself was to blame for the foolish errors that had been made that night, just as he was to blame for Rosalie's having fled to England in the first place. It had been a stupid, damnably useless quarrel, he recalled darkly, one that had proven far more disastrous than either of them could ever have imagined.

Abruptly turning to set the lamp back down upon the desk with unnecessary force, he was plagued by a sudden, all too vivid memory of the kiss he and his unintentional "guest" had shared minutes earlier. Much as he hated to admit it, her sweetly innocent response had fired his blood more than Rosalie's more experienced embraces had ever done. Damn, but he had been too caught up in the sheer pleasures of the moment to realize the woman he held so tightly within his arms was not his fiancée after all, but rather a sharp-tongued little wildcat

41

who had as yet to express any measure of gratitude for the fact that he had risked his life to save her! He suddenly found himself wondering what would have happened if he had not discovered his mistake before things had progressed beyond a mere kiss. . . .

"I was directed to your room by one of the other women!" he growled as he wheeled about to face Meghan again. Cursing himself for the defensive note which had crept into his voice, he took another menacing step closer to her. "Her understanding of my admittedly fractured Spanish was nonetheless adequate enough—or so I thought at the time—to apprise me of Mistress Hammond's whereabouts. Rosalie's hair is also fair, and the two of you are much the same size and age," he concluded, his gaze sweeping boldly over her once more. His eyes darkened with renewed anger. "But for the similarity in your appearance, I would no doubt have—"

"If you had only troubled yourself to look at me first, you would have been spared this blow to your masculine pride!" Meghan provoked him with all the rashness of her youth and inexperience.

She raised her chin haughtily and folded her arms across her full, thinly covered breasts. Though she deplored the tattered condition of her gown, she had obstinately declined the pirates' insolent offer of new silken finery. She had bathed daily alongside the other female captives, but had refused to attire herself in the same revealing, form-fitting apparel they wore. Clinging to her stubborn pride had at least given her some small measure of comfort, even if it now meant she looked very much like the guttersnipe Devlin had probably judged her to be.

Devil take the man! she raged silently. He had no

right to treat her like some poor, nameless unfortunate who was undeserving of either his swashbuckling heroics *or* his accursedly disquieting attentions!

"Given the circumstances in which you found me, is it any wonder I was so willing to come with you?" she stormed, foolishly paying no heed to the warning light in Devlin's steely gaze. "Why, you . . . you've no idea what sort of humiliating trials and tribulations I have endured these past several weeks! And you, sir, *you* come blithely along and pluck the *wrong woman* from the clutches of those pillaging heathens and then . . . then have the audacity to behave as though it were all *my* fault!"

Battling tears of mingled wrath and emotional strain, she could not keep a telltale catch from her voice as she continued, "I know not who you are, nor how you came to be here this night, but I cannot regret the fact that I am free of that loathsome captivity at last and on my way home! My grandparents will reward you well for any *inconvenience* I have caused you, Mister—" She broke off here and glared up at him with angry helplessness, for it was only his Christian name she knew thus far.

"Montague," he supplied in a low tone, his handsome face still dangerously grim. "Devlin Montague."

"Very well then, Mister Montague, if you will be so good as to provide me with passage back to England, I shall see that you are reimbursed—"

"We're sailing to Nassau, not England."

"To Nassau?" she echoed in wide-eyed disbelief. "But that is where The Wolf—"

"Precisely," interrupted Devlin, sending her a faint, humorless smile. His eyes became suffused with an alarmingly savage glow once more. "In spite of what has occurred, it is still very much my intent to rescue my betrothed."

"But she has surely been ransomed by now!" Meghan ventured to point out.

"Perhaps. In any case, we will reach Nassau at first light. If my investigation there does indeed yield the knowledge of her release, then we'll set a course for Charlestown without delay."

"Charlestown?" A sharp pang of dismay shot through her again. Charlestown was to have been the destination of the servant ship! There, she and her fellow victims were to have been sold into virtual slavery for terms ranging anywhere from two to fourteen years. Dear God, she mused anxiously, was it possible that she would still be forced to honor that unscrupulous captain's contract? The fate of the *Bristol Packet* and its passengers was still a mystery to her; for all she knew, the pirates had murdered everyone and sent the white guineaman to a well-deserved fate at the bottom of the sea. . . .

"But I do not wish to go to Charlestown!" she emphatically declared, her eyes flying back up to meet the gleaming intensity of Devlin's. "I . . . I shall remain in Nassau, where I have no doubt I will be able to procure passage on a ship bound for England." She drew herself stiffly erect and said with an icy composure that would have daunted lesser men, "If you will but advance me the necessary funds, Mister Montague, then you will be rid of me and—"

"No," he startled her by replying.

"No?" she echoed weakly, blinking up at him in stunned disbelief. She grew uneasy beneath the piercing steadiness of his gaze. There was a disturbing air of barely controlled violence about him, and

44

she felt a sudden tremor of fear. "But why not? I assure you my grandfather, Sir Henry—"

"I am well aware of the cargo carried aboard the *Bristol Packet*, Mistress Kearny," he told her with another ghost of a smile, though his gaze smoldered still. "In my efforts to find my fiancée, I learned a great deal, including the fact that Rosalie was the only young female passenger above decks. It requires very little intelligence on my part to deduce that you are one of the bondswomen who passed the voyage down in the hold." He paused and took a step closer, so that his tall, powerful body was mere inches from Meghan's soft, trembling curves.

"You are correct when you accuse me of apparent insensitivity to your plight," he admitted quietly. "For that, I offer you my sincere apologies. You are, of course, not to blame for the situation at hand. And it matters not to me how you came to be banished to the Colonies as an indentured servant— you could have been one of the most notorious murderesses in England for all I care. Your past life is of no concern to me, Mistress Kearny," he insisted in a tight, angry voice, almost as though he were trying to convince the both of them. "But the fact remains that I am responsible for you now!"

"What do you mean, 'responsible'?" she demanded, her bright eyes narrowing mistrustfully up at him. "For your information, Mister Montague— if that is in truth *your* real name—I was not a murderess, nor a pickpocket, nor anything else of the sort! My presence aboard that ship was achieved by the foulest means, for I was abducted by two strange men and forced to become a passenger—"

"Spare me your theatrical protestations of innocence, Mistress Kearny. Not only are they unconvincing, but insofar as I am concerned, they will avail you nothing," he said coldly. His gaze, however, was still anything but cold. It fairly burned with an unfathomable yet clearly dangerous emotion. "Whether I agree with the practice of indenture or not, you are the legal property of another man. I cannot allow you to go free. You will be turned over to the proper authorities once we reach Charlestown, at which time I shall let them settle the question of what to do with you." He spoke this last in a tone of unmistakable disdain, leaving little doubt as to his annoyance at being saddled with her.

Meghan bristled with righteous fury, and her hand itched to slap his handsome face. She had never been so infuriated during the entire course of her young life, had never wanted to strike out at a fellow human being as she now found herself sorely tempted to do. Even the villains responsible for her plight had not prompted her to such all-consuming wrath. *They*, at least, had never questioned her honesty! By all that was holy, she could not and would not remain to be so grievously insulted again!

Something snapped within her in that moment. She was wet and chilled to the bone, tired and aching from head to toe, her nerves strained beyond the outermost limits of tolerance, and she saw her precious freedom slipping away from her once more. If ever she had felt the need to ride like the wind or burst into a flood of weeping, she felt it now. Since she was in no position to do the former, she would find a way to achieve the latter—only *not*, by all that was holy, in Devlin Montague's presence!

Flinging about in a vehement swirl of damp silk, Meghan dashed blindly for the door. Devlin was upon her in an instant, his hand closing like a vise

46

about her wrist. She gasped as he yanked her up hard against him, his unfathomable gaze searing over her once more before he thrust her roughly into a chair. A sharp gasp of mingled pain and outrage escaped her lips when she landed on the uncushioned wood, and she jerked her head up to present a furious, tear-streaked face to Devlin.

"Lay hands on me again, you motherless jackanapes, and you'll regret it to your dying day—*if ever you live that long!*" she threatened hotly, sounding more like a wild Irish princess than a proper English miss. Her fiery, glistening eyes shot invisible daggers at his handsome head while her full breasts heaved beneath the clinging gown.

His mouth curving into the merest suggestion of a smile, Devlin felt his blood racing at the glorious spectacle she presented. Damn it all! he swore inwardly, another dark scowl creasing his brow. Why the devil, if he had to be cursed with the ill fortune to rescue the wrong woman, did she have to be so blasted young and comely? More importantly, he then asked himself, what the bloody hell was he going to do with her while he searched for Rosalie?

"I'll leave you to your feminine hysterics, Miss Kearny," he finally proclaimed with a studied detachment that belied his own inner turmoil. Nodding curtly down at the sea chest on the floor beside the desk, he added, "You'll find whatever you require in there." He strode to the door and paused for a brief moment to toss a deceptively negligent glance over his broad shoulder. "I'd advise you to get out of those wet things without further delay— unless, of course, you wish to arrive in Nassau looking like a drowned kitten." With that last unchivalrous observation, he was gone.

Leaping to her feet, Meghan impulsively snatched off one of her worn kid slippers and hurled it after him. The shoe bounced harmlessly off the closed door and landed with a rather watery thud on the wooden floor. In the next instant, she heard the all too familiar sound of the key being turned in the lock.

Her first instinct was to fly across the cabin and pound vigorously on the door while protesting such treatment, but she was forced to realize that such tactics would avail her nothing. No, there would be no reasoning with the sort of domineering scoundrel her *rescuer* had turned out to be!

"The fates be cursed again and again," she muttered as she flung herself back down into the chair, "I have but traded one prison for another!" She had traded captors as well—The Wolf had been replaced by a man who appeared to be every bit as cruel and heartless, though his methods were different. Indeed, this Devlin Montague might not share the pirate captain's lustful interest in her, but he did display the same unwillingness to believe her tale of abduction, just as he, too, refused to heed her demands for freedom.

Is there truly no justice in the world? Meghan wondered as a choking sob of despair welled up in her throat. She could hold back no longer. With a strangled plea for heaven's mercy, she stumbled over to the corner and threw herself facedown on the narrow bunk. She poured out all her misery upon the soft comfort of the pillow, until, thoroughly exhausted, she fell into a deep and dreamless sleep that would last far into the night.

Devlin, meanwhile, stood beneath the stars, his booted feet planted firmly apart on the weathered deck while he watched the cool night wind billowing the sails. His thoughts were drawn irrevocably back to the bedraggled yet captivating young wildcat he had just left, to the impassioned kiss he had mistakenly pressed upon her sweet lips, and most particularly to the way her soft, damnably beguiling curves had been molded so perfectly against his powerful hardness. He felt a renewed surge of desire, and cursed himself for a traitor.

Rosalie. Her name echoed freely throughout his mind. For some inexplicable reason, however, he was unable to conjure up little more than a blurred image of her beautiful, aristocratic countenance. He told himself it was because they had been parted for so long, but he knew that to be a lie.

Casting a black look heavenward, he moved forward to grip the railing, where his fingers clenched tightly about the smooth rounded wood. No, he acknowledged silently, his memories of Rosalie were dim because of the golden-haired temptress below. The sooner he turned this Meghan Kearny over to the authorities, the better. The better for them all. . . .

"Begging your pardon, Captain, but I trust Mistress Hammond is well?" the young first mate politely inquired beside him.

"No, by damn, Mr. Hobbs, she is *not!*" ground out Devlin, his expression growing even more thunderous. "Neither is she aboard this ship," he then muttered half under his breath.

"Not aboard, sir?" Peter Hobbs asked in obvious confusion. His gaze shifted hastily toward the companionway, and he frowned. "But—"

"The 'young lady' is not my betrothed," Devlin reluctantly supplied, hating like the very devil to ad-

49

mit his mistake but enough of a man to do so anyway. "It seems that Mistress Hammond has been taken to Nassau to be ransomed. With any luck, we'll be able to find her before that cowardly bastard succeeds." He did not add that he also planned to exact a certain bloodthirsty vengeance upon Rosalie's captor should they catch up with him. The Wolf had dared to seize the intended of a Montague, and for that he would pay with his life!

"I see, Captain," the boyishly attractive Mr. Hobbs murmured, though he did in truth not see at all. If the young woman below decks was not Rosalie Hammond, who was she? he wondered. He was not, thank goodness, foolhardy enough to pose the question. Nodding wordlessly at his employer, he marched away to check the *Pandora's* course again.

Devlin was left to scowl pensively down into the dark, churning waters of the sea. It was quite some time before, with a savage oath, he took himself below to speak with his "guest" once more.

He found her sleeping like a babe upon his bed, one arm curled up beside her head while the other rested across her waist. She was still fully clothed, her bright, tangled locks spilling across the tear-soaked pillow, and there was a look of such innocence and vulnerability about her that Devlin felt both a fire in his blood as well as an uncomfortable twinge of guilt.

"Angel or witch—it matters not to me," he insisted aloud, then named himself a fool for doing so. He turned out the lamp and strode from the cabin, only to return mere seconds later.

With another scalding curse directed at himself, at Meghan, and at the whole world in general, he crossed angrily to the sleeping girl again. He managed to strip off her cloak and gown without waking her, then yanked the covers up over her shapely form, now clad in nothing more than a white cotton chemise that reached scarcely to her knees.

Musing that a man of lesser honor would not feel so compelled to pass up the opportunity presented by a half-naked young woman lying atop his own bunk in his own cabin aboard his own ship, Devlin Montague found himself momentarily regretting his noble birth and upbringing. He sighed heavily before bending his tall, muscular frame into a chair. Leaning back, he stretched his long legs before him, folded his arms across his chest, and closed his eyes. . . .

51

Chapter Three

Meghan returned to consciousness an hour before dawn, her eyelids slowly fluttering open as she moved somewhat stiffly upon the bunk. Inhaling a deep breath of air in an effort to throw off the lingering, benumbed effects of sleep, she could not help but be made aware of the aroma of freshly brewed coffee wafting throughout the shadowy cabin.

Coffee? She sat bolt upright in the bed, only to tense and utter a soft moan of protest at the way her head swam. Her eyes swiftly became adjusted to the darkness, and she experienced a moment of sheer panic as her wide, anxious gaze swept the unfamiliar surroundings. In the next instant, however, memories of the previous night came flooding back to hit her full force.

"Devlin Montague," she whispered, his name sounding like a strange cross between a prayer and a curse upon her lips. An involuntary tremor shook her. Her eyes fell toward the bed where she had slept so soundly, and she suffered a sharp intake of breath upon discovering that her clothes had somehow been removed in the night. The thin, lacy undergarment she wore provided scandalously little in the way of covering.

"Sweet Saint Bridget, how could I have slept through *that?*" She blushed fierily from head to toe. Someone had undressed her—that much was certain—but what else had happened while she'd lain helpless? Her cheeks flamed hotter as vivid, shocking images of the various possibilities filled her mind.

With an inward groan, Meghan snatched up the blanket and clutched it to her breasts in an instinctive gesture of maidenly protectiveness. No, she told herself firmly, it was not at all possible that she could have remained asleep through . . . well, through anything more than what she *had* slept through! Even with such rational self-assurances, she still trembled at the disquieting thought of a stranger's hands stripping off her clothes. *Was Devlin Montague himself the one who had done it?* The thought gave her little comfort.

Her troubled blue-green gaze flew to the door, then the porthole, only to travel back to the desk, where she spied a silver tray laden with food and drink. Telling herself quite philosophically that there was no use in wondering how the tray had gotten there, she suddenly realized that she was utterly famished. Her last meal had been less than appetizing, not only for its lack of any real nutritional value, but also because it had been served by a foul-smelling knave who had made repeated overtures of a highly repulsive nature. She shuddered at the memory, giving silent thanks once more for the timely intervention of another pirate who had reiterated The Wolf's orders that his "special" captive be left untouched.

Meghan tossed back the covers, slid from the bed,

and padded barefoot across the short distance to the desk, dragging the blanket after her. Wrapping the soft indigo wool about her supple, scantily clad curves, she lit the lamp and sank down into the chair. There was a fresh loaf of bread and half a round of cheese awaiting her pleasure, as well as a surprisingly elegant silver coffeepot full of the black brew still sending its unmistakable fragrance into every corner of the room.

She quickly ate her fill and washed it down with two cups of the coffee, which was strong and bitter but at least hot. Afterward, feeling considerably better, she performed her morning toilette as best she could with the basin and pitcher of water she found atop the unusual, fold-down washstand nestled in a tiny cubicle off the main cabin. Her eyes continually strayed to the door, and she grew increasingly apprehensive about her captor's inevitable return.

Finished with her ministrations, she hurriedly searched about the cabin for her gown. It was not, however, to be found.

Good heavens, she mused with a frown, she couldn't very well go ashore in nothing more than her shift and a borrowed blanket, not if she hoped to persuade someone to help her escape and return to England. No indeed, she would have to look like the granddaughter of a titled nobleman if she expected anyone to believe her story.

You'll find whatever you require in there, Devlin had said about the sea chest. Recalling his words—and realizing that she had little choice in the matter—Meghan knelt on the floor and raised the lid of the massive, leather-bound trunk. Her eyes widened in pleasant amazement at the sight which met them.

There were easily half a dozen beautiful gowns of rich velvet, shimmering satin, flowered muslin, and hand-painted silk, all in a dazzling array of color. Included among this unabashedly feminine finery were all the necessary accessories and undergarments—shoes, caps, gloves, fans, petticoats, stays, stockings, and chemises. Everything was of the highest quality, and Meghan could not help but feel a twinge of envy toward the woman for whom the wardrobe was intended. That the clothing was a gift was obvious; each item was new and meticulously folded, as though the chest had been packed with loving expertise.

"Mistress Hammond, no doubt," Meghan theorized about the recipient's identity. She was startled at the way the small spark of envy suddenly magnified into a fierce, burning sensation of outright jealousy.

Why should she feel jealous of that woman? From what she had observed aboard the *Bristol Packet*, Rosalie Hammond was thoroughly spoiled and haughty and so taken with herself that there would be little room in her heart for anyone else. She and Devlin Montague were in all likelihood a perfect match!

With a defiant toss of her tangled golden mane, Meghan withdrew the gown of flowered muslin and a pair of dark brown kid shoes, since her own were nearly worn through. She impulsively added a pair of white silk stockings and a fine linen chemise trimmed with spidery lace to her elegant booty, telling herself that if she was to look the part of the lady she was, then she must feel like one down to her very toes. It gave her some perverse sense of satisfaction to know that she would be wearing clothes that belonged to the arrogant Mistress Hammond!

She was already dressed and in the process of

brushing her hair when Devlin flung open the door without warning. With a loud gasp of alarm, Meghan whirled about to face him.

He stood just within the cabin, his tall, virile frame seeming to fill the lamplit room. His handsome features were unfathomable, though there was a telltale gleam in the penetrating blue gaze which fastened upon her with unnerving intensity.

A rosy blush crept up to Meghan's face. Her eyes met his, and she knew in that moment that he had been the one to undress her. There was a certain disturbing, *knowing* look in those midnight blue orbs of his as they flickered briefly but quite boldly over her. The realization made her color deepen, and she was dismayed to feel her entire body tremble.

Have you become such a coward, Meghan Kearny, that you should quiver and quake before the likes of this rogue? she furiously asked herself. Mentally consigning the man before her to the devil, she lifted head proudly and faced him with the light of battle in her flashing turquoise eyes.

Devlin's lips twitched in appreciation at her show of spirit, but he managed to refrain from smiling. All traces of humor vanished in the next instant, however, when he found his appreciation taking an entirely different turn.

He could not help but notice that her appearance had altered vastly. The bedraggled spitfire of the previous night had been transformed into a veritable goddess. If not for the luxuriant golden tresses streaming unrestrainedly about her face and shoulders, mused Devlin, she would look perfectly at home in the drawing room of any of the most fashionable establishments in Charlestown.

Though it was the simplest and least ornamented

gown he had chosen for Rosalie, there was no denying the pale pink costume fit its unintended wearer to perfection. The boned, square-necked bodice, with its hook-and-eye closing in the front, was molded tightly across Meghan's full young breasts as it curved downward to end in a point. The ankle-length gathered skirt, open to reveal a white silk petticoat, was caught up in *paniers* on either hip, while the gown's sleeves reached to just below the elbow, where a wide ruffle of lace fell in graceful folds. A crisscrossed white lawn kerchief—usually referred to as a "modesty piece"—had been tucked by Meghan into the décolletage in order to cover the alluring swell of her bosom. It was there that Devlin's burning gaze lingered before he forced it upward to her beautiful, stormy countenance.

"Since our destination is but a short distance away now, I think it time we came to an understanding," he declared in a low tone, finally closing the door behind him. He moved forward with a leisurely, masculine grace that prompted Meghan to swallow hard. She tilted her head back to face him squarely when he came to a halt before her. Although she met his gaze without flinching, her pulses raced alarmingly and her fingers tightened about the hairbrush she held at her side.

"Well then, sir," she demanded in a lofty manner that belied her disquiet, "may I take that to mean you have come to your senses and changed your mind about letting me go?" Acutely conscious of his proximity and the absolute power emanating from him, she could well remember the way he had so masterfully swept her into his arms a few short hours ago. Never in her life had she been so aware of her own femininity—nor of what it meant to a man.

57

"No." Devlin gave a slight shake of his head while his mouth curved into a faint, mocking smile. "The understanding to which I refer is one whereby you, Mistress Kearny, agree to cause me no further trouble."

"Cause you—" she started to echo in disbelief, then bristled with righteous indignation. "Why, you pompous scoundrel! *I* cause *you* trouble?" She gave a short, humorless laugh while her eyes blazed wrathfully up at him. "In the event your memory fails you, I have not been the source of your 'trouble' thus far—no indeed, Mister Montague, it has been of your own making!"

She brought her arms up and crossed them rigidly beneath her breasts, which had the inadvertent effect of making the rounded, creamy flesh swell even farther above the gown's low neckline. The so-called modesty piece proved woefully inadequate when it came to concealing the full extent of her charms.

Devlin's eyes were once again drawn downward. Every inch a hot-blooded male, he felt another traitorous leaping of his pulses. *Damn, but the little termagent was bloody well playing him for a fool!* Whether it was intentional or not, he could not say, but the fact remained that she was driving him to distraction. He wondered again who she was, what she was, and if there was any man in all of Christendom who would not find himself tempted by such an angel-faced vixen.

"Heed me well," he continued as though she had not spoken, his gaze traveling back up to encounter the fiery depths of hers, "when I tell you that I have neither the time nor the patience to concern myself with you while we are in Nassau. All my energies will be focused on finding my betrothed. The last thing I need on my hands is a young woman bent on escape. Therefore, I give you fair warning that I will not tolerate any attempt on your part to interfere with my plans."

"I have no intention of interfering with your search for your precious betrothed!" Meghan hotly avowed. "As a matter of fact," she added with another defiant toss of her head, "I wish you success, for I am persuaded the two of you deserve one another!"

"Good. Then you agree not to seek your freedom when we go ashore." His words were a statement, not a question.

"Why, I . . . I most certainly do not!" she sputtered, abruptly unfolding her arms. "I will do everything in my power to escape you, Mister Montague! If you had one shred of decency within you, you would release me at once!" Tears sprang readily to her eyes once more, and she could not prevent a note of appeal from entering her voice. "Can you not begin to imagine what a nightmare these past two months have been for me? Have you no compassion at all for my plight? My life is in a shambles, my poor grandparents are no doubt frantic with—"

"You are a consummate actress, Mistress Kearny," Devlin pronounced with a frown. "If I were not aware of your true status, I would no doubt be taken in by your performance." He paused, his gaze raking over her with audacious familiarity. One eyebrow raised in a mocking tribute before he asked smoothly, "What other particular 'talents' do you possess?"

Meghan gasped as though she had been struck. There was no denying the insolent meaning of his remarks. That he believed her to be an indentured servant was bad enough, but that he should think her a . . . a common *doxie* was both humiliating and infuriating!

If there was ever a straw that broke a camel's back, Meghan had just suffered its weight. She did not pause to consider the wisdom of her actions—she simply obeyed the reckless inner voice that told her to seek revenge against the man who had so grievously insulted her. Her hand now tightened about the hairbrush as though it were a club, and she raised her arm to deliver a punishing blow.

Devlin, fortunately, reacted with lightning-quick speed. He first dodged the silver hairbrush aimed at his head, then clamped an iron hand about Meghan's wrist and easily forced the bristled weapon from her grasp. He flung it aside, and it fell to the floor with a loud clatter.

Meghan had no time to escape. A sharp cry of mingled pain and outrage broke from her lips, quickly followed by a startled intake of breath when Devlin suddenly caught her about the waist and twisted her arm behind her back. She raised wide, luminous eyes to his dangerously narrowed ones, his face mere inchers from hes and his hard, muscular frame pressed intimately against her trembling softness. His eyes seemed to bore down into her very soul, and she found herself unable to struggle, unable to offer any protest whatsoever. It was as though she were being held spellbound by his smoldering gaze every bit as much as he was being held captive by his arms.

Then, quite without warning, Devlin's mouth came crashing down upon hers. For what seemed at once like an eternity and a fleeting moment in time, Meghan gave herself up to the sweet madness of his kiss. Her lips were soft and pliant beneath the impassioned force of his, and her free hand slid instinctively upward along the tensed, sinewy hardness of his arm to curl about his neck. A low moan rose in her throat when his velvety tongue thrust between her lips to hungrily explore the moist cavern of her mouth. She felt her head spinning, felt every square inch of her body tingling with the most deliciously wicked warmth . . .

Suddenly, once again without any indication of what was to come, Devlin released her other arm and brought his hand about to snatch the white lawn kerchief from where it was tucked above the alluring roundness of her bosom. Meghan's eyes grew wide, and she gasped against his mouth when she felt his strong fingers trailing a path of fire down across the slender, graceful curve of her neck toward her breasts. Swelling above the low, square-necked bodice, the delectable globes were very nearly revealed in all their silken glory. Indeed, they proferred an irresistible invitation to Devlin as they rose and fell rapidly with each uneven breath.

Meghan shivered at the bold contact of his hand with her feverish skin and tried to pull away, but to no avail. His arm tightened like a band of steel about her waist. A small, breathless cry of protest welled up deep within her in the next instant when, abruptly ceasing its masterful vanquishment of hers, his mouth traveled lower to feast upon her half-naked bosom.

She inhaled sharply and caught her lower lip between her teeth at the first touch of his warm, insistent lips upon her unprotected flesh. His highly intoxicating caresses sent liquid fire coursing through her veins, and she moaned softly again and again as his mouth roamed with dizzying urgency across the tops of her full, perfectly formed breasts. Another gasp escaped her lips when she felt his hand tugging impatiently at the gown's neckline in an apparent attempt to bare her breasts completely.

At that point, reason overpowered passion.

Dear God in heaven, what am I doing? thought Meghan in rising panic. She grew frightened, of herself as well as Devlin, and her fear provided the necessary catalyst to bring about a belated resistance.

"No!" she choked out, shaking her head with such heartfelt vigor that her long golden tresses swirled wildly about both her face and Devlin's. She brought her hands up and pushed at his broad chest with all her might. "No! Let me go!"

Her shrill cries and frantic struggles successfully brought Devlin crashing back to earth. He raised his handsome head and seized her arms in a firm, almost punishing grip. Gone was the man who only moments ago had kissed her with such wildly stimulating ardor, and in his place stood a scowling, arrogant stranger who gazed upon her without a noticeable trace of warmth at all. Instead of offering an apology for his actions, he chose to treat the encounter as some sort of lesson in worldly compartment.

"Never seek to strike a man unless you are prepared to suffer the consequences," he cautioned her tersely, his bronzed features suffused with a dull, angry color and his eyes gleaming fiercely. With a muttered curse, he released her arms as though the contact burned him and spun about on his booted heel. The door slammed resoundingly after him seconds later.

Meghan furiously swept the hair from her face as she glared toward the door. Her cheeks flamed scarlet, while her eyes were virtually spitting blue-green fire. How dare that rogue subject her to such . . .

such *carnal treachery* and then behave as though the incident had been nothing more than a cold-blooded exercise for her benefit! She was so enraged she could scarcely breathe. Never, in the entirety of her eighteen years, had any man dared to do what Devlin Montague had just done!

With a most unladylike oath, she marched to the bunk and sank down heavily upon the rumpled covers, oblivious to the fact that by doing so she only creased her borrowed finery even more than the combined efforts of the sea chest and its accursed owner. She would make him pay, she vowed fervently. Oh yes, she would make Devlin Montague sorry he had ever set eyes on her!

First things first, however, she told herself as she resolutely squared her shoulders, straightened the muslin gown, and tried her best to forget the near painful ecstasy of her tormentor's kisses. Before she could set about getting even with the man, she had to escape him. And that was something she would do—even if it meant she had to pretend to be properly chastened and meekly accepting of her situation.

Heed me well, she silently warned her absent captor, mocking him with his own words, *if it's the last thing I do, I will make you rue the day you tangled with a Kearny!*

The sun had just risen to set the world aglow when the *Pandora* glided into the clear sapphire waters of Nassau's bustling harbor.

Peering anxiously through the cabin's porthole, Meghan was disappointed to see what amounted to little more than a shabby port rambling across a hillside. Her heart sank at the prospect of trying to

63

find a means of escape and safe passage homeward in so small a place. The town appeared to be overgrown with shrubs and trees, and there was a definite look of neglect about the place, in spite of its picturesque setting amid a panorama of blossoming color. Surely this odd collection of mostly wooden buildings and a few colonnaded, vine-covered stone structures couldn't be the same city that had once been the notorious haunt of pirates and rum-soaked sailors?

She had read of this infamous capital of New Providence Island, of how it had been a wildly raucous port full of gambling and bawdy houses, of how it had actually been the headquarters of more than a thousand buccaneers during the early years of the present century. It had been called a "pirate's republic" by some, a "festering hold of debauchery" by others, and the anchorage had once been fairly choked with the tall-masted vessels of these brigands. There had been a time when the likes of Blackbeard, Anne Bonney, Henry Morgan, and Mary Read were content to loll upon its shores in between bouts of wrecking, raiding, and pillaging. They and other bloodthirsty bandits of the sea had preyed relentlessly upon merchantmen in the coastwise and European trade routes for more than thirty-five years, until finally drinking and fighting their way into oblivion.

Not all of them, a tiny voice inside Meghan's head reminded her. She shuddered as The Wolf's image rose unbidden in her mind. Her heart pounded at the thought that he might be in Nassau at that very moment. . . .

"I trust you'll remember what I said." Devlin's splendidly deep-timbred voice startled her from the doorway. She whirled to face him, her cheeks burning and her pulses leaping anew. It was all she could do to refrain from informing him, quite pointedly, where he could take himself and his contemptible threats.

"Of course," she murmured instead, feigning an air of docile obedience. She lowered her eyes and clasped her hands primly before her for effect. Inwardly, however, she fairly seethed with the turbulence of her emotions—resentment at Devlin's authoritative manner, a sense of wounded pride for the way he had so carelessly dismissed their embrace, and an ever-increasing desire for vengeance as a result of his cruel insensitivity toward her plight. If all went as she planned, he would soon be made to pay dearly for daring to so mistreat a young woman of her high station. Her grandfather, with his well-placed connections, would not only see to it that Devlin Montague made a humble apology for his crimes against her, but also that he suffer an appropriate disgrace . . . perhaps even a public flogging? Her eyes sparkled with wholly feminine satisfaction at the thought.

Devlin's brow creased into a frown when he glimpsed the strange little smile playing about Meghan's lips. Wondering what sort of mischief she was plotting, he cursed himself once more for his mishandling of the whole affair. It was enough of an ignominy that he had rescued the wrong woman, but then to allow his baser instincts to get the better of him—he was furious with himself for having lost his head earlier. He had vowed, for his own protection as well as hers, never to lay a hand on her again, and yet he had ended up behaving like a damned, lovestruck fool. Confound it, he swore inwardly, what the devil *was* there about the little spitfire that drove him to such wild impetuosity?

"Come, Mistress Kearny," he ordered curtly, "it's time to go ashore."

"So it is, Mister Montague," retorted Meghan, though she did so with a deceptive expression of somber, wide-eyed innocence.

Devlin's frown deepened as his suspicions grew even more aroused. He watched as she swept forward with all the grace of a duchess, her full skirts and flounced petticoat rustling softly and her bright, securely pinned curls catching the sunlight that filtered through the porthole. She preceded him from the room and through the narrow passageway, taking great—and obvious—care to keep a safe distance between them at all times. His eyes were drawn to the seductively swaying movements of her hips as she climbed the steps leading to the deck, and he muttered yet another oath under his breath before following her up into the cool morning air.

Meghan wondered why she had not simply been left aboard the ship, but she would not allow herself to ask. She held herself rigidly erect while Devlin led her across the deck to where the gangplank was being lowered, and she remained obstinately silent when he took her arm in a firm grip and propelled her down to the quay.

Acutely conscious of the many pairs of masculine eyes fastened upon her, she lifted her head in an unconscious gesture of womanly defiance. Her turquoise gaze swept the surrounding area as she went, making a quick survey of the crowded wharf area. She was pleased at the sight of so many ships, most particularly those which were proudly flying the Union Jack, anchored in the harbor. It appeared that her plan had a very good chance of succeeding after all.

The sights, sounds, and smells of Nassau came

forth to meet her with a vengeance as Devlin ushered her impatiently along. Peter Hobbs followed closely behind. Unbeknownst to Meghan, the young first mate had been chosen to guard her while his captain was making inquiries as to the whereabouts of Rosalie Hammond.

Proceeding along Bay Street, which was the heart of the town as well as its main thoroughfare, the trio passed an intriguing array of buildings. Houses and shops of all descriptions lined one side of the narrow, shore-winding lane, while on the other side was the open harbor. There appeared to Meghan's fascinated eyes to be a vast number of people going about their business—Europeans, Bahamians, and Americans—and the air was alive with the din of voices as well as with the rather overwhelming aroma of food, woodsmoke, and horses. Added to that was the sweet scent of orchids and frangipani, joined by the equally pleasant fragrance of hibiscus and bougainvillea, which was carried on the slight breeze sweeping down from the hill where the wealthy seamen and merchants had long ago built their mansions.

It wasn't until she and her two "escorts" were passing directly opposite an imposing green, single-storied building that Meghan noticed a crowd gathered beneath and all about its arches. She was shocked to hear a man's loud voice boldly detailing the physical assets of a young black woman who stood with eyes downcast high upon a platform. Although Meghan did not know it, this was Nassau's notorious slave market, Vendue House, where human beings had been put on the auction block alongside cattle, fish, pigs, and coconuts for the past three years.

Feeling sickened at the sound of men bidding on

the unfortunate girl, Meghan quickly averted her gaze. Devlin did not fail to notice the sudden paling of her cheeks, nor did he fail to grasp the similarity of her situation to that of the other woman's. She, too, would be put upon the block when they reached Charlestown. She, too, would be subjected to the humiliation of being ogled by a crowd of men who would be lustfully appreciative of her golden-haired beauty.

His blood boiled at the thought. Even though he told himself it was no concern of his, he could not deny the rage that filled him as he envisioned Meghan standing helpless and frightened like the captured African woman being displayed at the present. His eyes flashed and darkened, while his fingers tightened with almost bruising force upon Meghan's arm. Stifling a cry of protest, she settled instead for directing an umbrageous look up at his handsome, strangely thunderous face.

She was relieved when they reached their destination a few minutes later, their route leading them past an assortment of other public buildings that ranged from the simple to the sublime. The two-storied house Devlin finally led her to stood behind a massive limestone wall. Constructed of the same stone in an architectural style made popular in the Colonies, it boasted broad wooden porches with wrought-iron rails and latticework, a wide main entry supported by graceful columns, and a separate kitchen house. There were exotic flowering bushes and trees everywhere, and the whole effect was one of unmistakable charm.

The interior, as Meghan soon discovered, was every bit as impressive. The furnishings were obviously of the finest quality, just as the intricately carved moldings adorning the high papered walls had without a doubt cost the owner dearly. It occurred to her then to wonder precisely who the owner was, and exactly what sort of establishment Devlin had brought her to. Both questions were answered to her satisfaction once she and her captor, after being admitted along with Peter Hobbs by a middle-aged woman wearing a spotless white apron, came to a halt at last and faced one another in the spacious, sun-filled entrance foyer.

"Will you be staying long this time, sir?" the housekeeper asked Devlin respectfully. She smiled and cast a look of mild curiosity Meghan's way before adding, "It's just that the servants were wondering if you and Mistress Hammond might perhaps be—"

"Mistress Hammond is not with me, Mrs. Fairway," Devlin informed her with a slight edge to his deep voice. "I've brought Mistress Kearny instead. She and Mister Hobbs will remain upstairs until I return. See that they are provided with refreshments at once." The woman nodded in silent accordance and dutifully hurried off to do his bidding, at which time he turned back to Meghan and declared coldly, "You may consider my home yours for the moment, Mistress Kearny—so long as you confine yourself to the two rooms I have assigned to you. I have charged Mister Hobbs with the responsibility of your welfare in my absence."

"If my welfare were truly your concern, Mister Montague, you would release me at once!" she retorted with spirit, momentarily dropping the pretense of meek compliance. Devlin merely offered her a wordless, mocking tribute with one upraised eyebrow, then took his first mate aside for a brief discussion. Although the two men spoke together quietly, Meghan was nonetheless able to catch the

69

gist of their conversation.

"Stay on your guard, Mister Hobbs. If she makes one false move, you're to tie her to a chair without hesitation!"

"But surely, Captain, you wouldn't wish me to treat the young lady with such—"

"Yes, Mister Hobbs, I damned well would! Under no circumstances is she to be allowed to escape. Is that clearly understood?"

"Yes, Captain. She'll not escape, never fear."

"It will be your hide if she does. If I've not returned by nightfall, take her back to the *Pandora* and wait for me there. Whether I meet with success or failure, we'll weigh anchor before this day is through."

His steely gaze flickered over Meghan once more before he left her alone with the young seaman. Peter Hobbs, looking decidedly uncomfortable with his role as jailer, cleared his throat noisily and said, "If you please, Mistress Kearny, the captain's orders are that we should repair to the rooms upstairs." His awkwardness visibly increasing, he stepped forward and placed a light hand upon her arm. Meghan, though tempted to jerk free, gave him a dazzling smile and gathered up her skirts.

"Whatever you say, Mister Hobbs. I am, I suppose, completely at your mercy." This she spoke with her eyes modestly downcast, her thick, sooty lashes emphasized against the creamy smoothness of her skin. Peter Hobbs, his boyishly attractive face coloring, swallowed a sudden lump in his throat and released her arm with almost comical swiftness.

Meghan smiled again—to herself this time—and preceded him up the curved staircase with purposeful unhaste. Her mind raced with various schemes as she allowed her hand to trail upon the carved railing. She was more than ever confident that she could manage to charm the first mate and thereby make good her escape. This particular brand of persuasion was not entirely foreign to her, for she had worked her wiles on men before, albeit while in the midst of good-natured repartee at some assembly or house party.

Nevertheless, she told herself that the role of seductress, at least up to a certain point, could not be all *that* difficult. She was a woman, wasn't she? And if Devlin Montague was determined to treat her like an experienced "lightskirt," she mused defiantly, then why shouldn't she use that degrading assessment of her character to her full advantage?

The room Peter Hobbs showed her into was situated only a short distance down the hall from the spindle-balustraded upper landing. Meghan swept gracefully through the wide double doors, her luminous gaze making a quick but thorough scrutiny of the room in order to locate the best possible avenue of escape.

"I'm afraid we've only these two rooms," explained Peter with a sincere air of apology, "but I will, of course, allow you as much privacy as possible. I"—he broke off here and cleared his throat again before continuing—"I shall remain here in the sitting room while you occupy the . . . the other room." Another dull flush rose to his face as he declined to reveal the other room as the bedchamber it was.

"Thank you," replied Meghan. She gazed rather soulfully into his startled eyes for a moment, then crossed to the lace-curtained French doors which led out onto the veranda. Peering down upon the tropical lushness of the walled garden, she decided that she could very well climb over the upper porch's,

71

iron railing and lower herself to the ground if the need arose.

"Tell me, Mister Hobbs," she requested as she turned back to him, her mouth curving into another smile calculated to entrap, "have you ever been to London?"

"To London?" he echoed in surprise. "Why, yes, as a matter of fact, I have." He gallantly waited until she moved to take a seat upon a chintz-covered sofa before bending his slender frame into a massive wing chair nearby.

"Then mayhap you have heard of my grandfather, Sir Henry Claibourne?" she asked hopefully.

"Your grandfather?" He frowned in puzzlement and shifted uncomfortably in the chair. "The name has a familiar ring to it, but . . . you say Sir Henry Claibourne is your grandfather?" It was obvious that he greeted her claim with no small amount of disbelief. Devlin had told him the young woman he was guarding had been bound for the Colonies as a bondservant. How then could it be possible for her to be the granddaughter of an English nobleman?

"That he is," confirmed Meghan. Her beautiful face took on an expression of such heartfelt appeal that Peter found himself wanting to believe anything and everything she told him. "Oh, Mister Hobbs, you must agree to help me! I am not what you think me—I am but an innocent victim in all of this! Your employer refuses to believe me, but you are different. I could tell from the very first that you are a true gentleman. You must help me!" she reiterated, her eyes glistening with tears. She withdrew a silken handkerchief from her skirt pocket and raised it to her face with a trembling hand. Dabbing prettily at first one eye and then the other, she waited anxiously for the man's reaction. She was not

72

disappointed when it came.

"Please, Mistress Kearny, do not weep!" As always, the sight of a woman's tears tugged at the first mate's compassionate young heart. His face paled, his gaze filled with a look of abject misery, and he shot to his feet at though compelled by either pain or providence. He went down on one knee before Meghan, taking her hand in a warm clasp between the both of his. "I will promise to speak to the captain about this, if only you will not distress yourself so!"

"You—you truly will?" she asked, sniffing pathetically. She raised wide, shining eyes to his, and Peter Hobbs knew himself lost.

"Dearest lady, I give you my word!" His fingers tightened almost convulsively upon hers. At that moment, he would gladly have journeyed to the very ends of the earth to grant her request. Never before had he felt such a peculiar combination of yearning and protectiveness, just as he had never before wanted to—*God forgive him*—sweep a woman into his arms as he now found himself wanting to do to the angelic little creature whose hand trembled so stirringly within his.

Meghan suffered a sharp pang of conscience as she glimpsed the warmth filling Peter's gaze. She decided then and there that she found the role of temptress not at all to her liking. Still, she had to escape! Consoling herself with the thought that the young seaman would quickly recover from such a brief encounter, she forced a tremulous smile to her lips and said softly,

"I believe you, Mister Hobbs." She did not seek to remove her hand from his grasp, which only encouraged Peter all the more. His face lit with pleasure, and he rose to take a seat beside her on the sofa.

"If there is anything else you require," he offered eagerly, "anything at all, I would do everything in my power to—"

"There *is* something," she cut him off with another thoroughly bewitching smile. Blushing rosily, she finally withdrew her hand and dried the last of her tears. "I should like above all else to have a bath." She blushed again as her eyes fell before his.

"A *bath?*" Peter Hobbs felt himself grow warm and flushed. He shifted upon the sofa and gave an inward groan at the suddenly wicked turn of his thoughts, but he was helpless to dispel the imaginings of a healthy, red-blooded young male. Clearing his throat with even more vigor than before, he nodded and replied with a telltale quaver in his voice, "Of course. I'll ring for Mrs. Fairway at once."

"Oh please, sir, would you be so kind as to venture downstairs yourself?" appealed Meghan. "You see, I . . . well, I shall indeed require a few moments' privacy beforehand, and even with a door between us, I would feel decidedly ill-at-ease knowing that you are in the very next room."

"But the captain left strict orders regarding—"

"I know, and I am truly sorry to place you in such a position, but surely you don't believe I would take advantage of your generosity? What possible harm can there be in standing guard below stairs for half an hour at the most?" she reasoned.

Her expression was one of such innocence and entreaty that Peter felt himself miserably torn between duty—coupled with fear of Devlin's wrath—and the desire to please the newfound object of his admiration. Meghan, aware of his dilemma as well as the fact that he was wavering with no clear direction, sighed dramatically and drew herself up from the sofa.

"Perhaps I misjudged you after all, Mister Hobbs. On the one hand you proclaim compassion and loyalty for me, while on the other you behave as though you think me unworthy of your trust. I would have expected as much from your employer, but not from you!" she concluded with a highly affronted air and an accompanying toss of her beautiful head. Fixing Peter with a reproachful look from her flashing blue-green eyes, she was rewarded with a prompt decision in her favor.

"Please, my dear Mistress Kearny, forgive me!" the utterly smitten young man pleaded, belatedly rising to his feet as well now. He gazed contritely down into her stormy, upturned countenance and cursed himself for a wretched fool. "I should never have doubted you! I shall go at once!" Pushing aside all thought of what the captain's reaction would be if his disobedience were ever found out, he hastily exited the room. Not all of the duteous caution had been charmed out of him, however, for he did pause to lock the door behind him.

Meghan waited until she heard his footsteps retreating back down the hallway before she whirled abruptly about and flew to the French doors. Opening them quietly, she stepped out onto the veranda and gathered up her skirts, then wasted no time in hoisting herself atop the ornate railing. She swung both legs over, carefully found her footing on the narrow ledge of limestone, and took a deep, steadying breath.

Securing a tight hold upon the iron bars, she proceeded to step off into space, her feet dangling freely as she lowered herself from the upper terrace. Since she was not quite tall enough to reach the safety of the ground, she was forced to let go and fall the last short distance. She landed squarely in the midst of a giant hibiscus plant. Hurriedly extricating herself from the thick greenery as well as from a tumble of muslin and ruffled linen—her skirts having become tangled up about her during the fall—she glanced about to make certain her actions were unobserved. Thankfully, there was no one in sight.

She went scurrying across the garden to a corner of the wall, only to draw up short when she spied a young Bahamian woman sauntering through the nearby side gate with a basketful of fruit perched high upon her head. Meghan concealed herself behind the shrubbery and peered anxiously through the leaves as the woman headed toward the separate kitchen building nestled beneath the trees in back of the main house. She disappeared inside, and the sound of two feminine voices raised in anger could be heard drifting forth from the kitchen immediately thereafter.

Meghan, satisfied that she had remained undetected, raced for the gate the woman had left standing open. She knew she had to hurry, for Peter Hobbs was bound to discover her absence soon. But it was not Peter's face that swam before her eyes while she hastened through the gate and away from the great limestone mansion—it was Devlin's.

I give you fair warning that I will not tolerate any attempt on your part to interfere with my plans. She caught her breath as she remembered, with disturbing clarity, the steely light in his eyes when he had spoken those words. A sudden shiver ran the length of her spine.

"Are you for turning coward again, Meghan Kearny?" she challenged herself in a furious undertone. Even if she *were* afraid of Devlin Montague

76

and what he might do to her if she failed to get away, she would never allow her fear to overpower her determination. Escape she must, or else face the horrible prospect of slavery, for slavery was what it was. No Kearny had ever surrendered without a fight, and she would not do so now!

With a renewed, single-minded purposefulness, she turned her steps toward the waterfront.

Chapter Four

"She *what?*" thundered Devlin. The fierce gleam in his penetrating, deep blue eyes grew so savage that Peter Hobbs blanched and took an instinctive step backward.

"She—she escaped, Captain!" the hapless younger man stammered. Feeling utterly ashamed, not to mention sick at heart, he swallowed hard and hastened to explain. "You see, Mistress Kearny had requested a . . . well, sir, she had requested a bath, and I had gone downstairs to—"

"Damnation, man, do you mean to tell me you left her *alone?*"

"Yes, Captain, I'm afraid I did," Peter admitted sheepishly. "But only for a few minutes! She wanted a bit of privacy, you see, and I thought it could do no harm to grant her request. Mrs. Fairway was already on her way upstairs with refreshments when I came down, so there couldn't possibly have been more than two minutes' time passed between—"

"What the devil does it matter how much time passed? You deserted your post and Mistress Kearny seized the opportunity to take flight!" Devlin tersely pointed out, his handsome visage suffused with an all too visible fury. "It would not surprise me in the least, Mister Hobbs, if you were now to inform me that the young 'lady' achieved her freedom by waltzing through the front door under the noses of my very own servants!" he added with biting sarcasm.

"Why no, Captain, she apparently left the house by way of an upstairs window," Peter willingly supplied, only to find himself the recipient of yet another darkly wrathful scowl.

"How long has she been gone?" ground out Devlin. The other man's obvious reluctance to answer did nothing to cool his rapidly escalating ire. "How long?" he demanded once more, taking a decidedly threatening step forward. Peter Hobbs, owing to the perception gained from several years' acquaintance with his employer, wasted no more time before blurting out the truth.

"Since this morning!"

Devlin swore roundly. His eyes flew to the ancient grandfather clock standing guard at the foot of the staircase, only to reaffirm that it was nearly three o'clock in the afternoon. Battling the powerful urge to hit something—or someone—he settled for spinning about and slamming the palm of his right hand forcibly down upon the mahogany banister. The pain, though inconsequential to a man of his strength and stamina, gave at least some small measure of release to his raging temper. Indeed, his brief outbursts of violence was even more effective owing to the fact that he imagined Meghan Kearny's saucy bottom as the recipient of the punishing blow.

"You have my deepest apologies, Captain Montague," the young first mate offered quietly behind him. "I—I suppose there is no real excuse for my failure to discharge my duties, save for the reasons I have stated. Regardless of my own feelings in the matter, however, I realize I should never have allowed myself to be persuaded into disobedience."

Devlin pivoted slowly about to face him again. He was both surprised and angered by the utter anguish he glimpsed in the young man's eyes, for he knew such misery could not stem from guilt alone. The poor fellow, innocent that he was, had been bewitched.

"I am as much to blame as you," Devlin conceded with a heavy, disgruntled sigh. His mouth curved into the merest glimmer of a self-mocking smile as he clapped a hand upon Peter's shoulder. "In truth, Mister Hobbs, I should never have left a lamb to guard a she-wolf."

Before Peter could protest the comparison—on behalf of Meghan's defense as well as his own—Devlin strode to the door and flung it open. He paused momentarily, and when he turned back to the other man, there was a forebodingly grim look on his face.

"Return to the ship at once," he ordered curtly. "My betrothed is no longer in Nassau. We will set sail for Charlestown as soon as I find Mistress Kearny."

With that, he was gone, leaving his duly chastened first mate to stare after him with a mixture of puzzlement, remorse, and heartache. Peter Hobbs vowed then and there never to be taken in by a pretty face again. He had learned his lesson. Still, in all honesty, he could not blame Meghan for taking advantage of his misplaced trust—whether she was truly an innocent captive, or the sort of woman Devlin believed her to be, it was only natural that she would do whatever was necessary to escape. And as long as he was being truthful with himself, mused Peter as a slow smile spread across his attractive young features, he hoped she made it.

Although she was loath to admit it, Meghan was beginning to lose all hope. It seemed that her fortune was intent upon following the same course as the setting sun, which sank lower and lower into the limitless blue horizon and in so doing set the sky ablaze with color.

Evening had given way to twilight, so that the cool ocean breezes were unleashed to dutifully chase away the heat of the day. Nassau settled into the coming night with its usual aplomb—the respectable folk went home to their families, while the more colorful elements of the port town gathered along that section of the waterfront reserved for the taverns, gaming hells, and other such establishments catering to the hordes of young sailors who sought solace, in either liquid or human form, from their lonely life at sea.

For Meghan, the long day had brought to life her worst fears. She had suffered every insult, had walked until her feet begged for respite, but her efforts had been for naught. None of the captains she had spoken to would agree to take her to England. Obviously skeptical of her story, they had demanded payment in advance for her passage—though some had been "generous" enough to make an offer involving an exchange of her favors—and there had not been a single one of them who would heed her promises of a hefty reward once she was reunited with her wealthy grandparents.

There is yet another way, her mind's inner voice compelled her to reconsider.

"From grand lady to pirate's captive to stowaway," she murmured aloud, her mouth curving into a rueful half-smile while her eyes sparked with a reborn determination. Yes, she would do it!

After all, she reasoned with herself, what other alternative did she have? Either she remained hidden in Nassau until Devlin Montague gave up and sailed away, or she found a means of escaping the town before that unlikely event occurred. And the only means presented to her was the one whereby she sneaked aboard one of the ships bound for England and concealed her presence until it was too late to turn back. It was her only choice.

Standing from where she had been perched atop a wooden crate inside an old, deserted storehouse just off Bay Street, Meghan shook the dust from her muslin skirts and carefully picked her way back across the cluttered, musty-smelling room. It was by far the last place she would have wished to spend an entire afternoon, but its unlocked door had been the only avenue open to her at the time. She had contemplated the possibility of appealing to the local clergy for help, but had quickly dismissed the idea upon realizing that Devlin Montague would no doubt search the most obvious places first.

Her nerves had been on edge the entire day, for she could not help but envision Devlin's handsome face at every turn, and she had as a result taken great pains to conceal her identity. A discarded satin cloak, though torn and dirty, had provided a disguise whenever she found it necessary to go out. She had seldom ventured forth, however, so that both her stomach and her head were now rebelling against the lack of proper nourishment. Giving silent thanks for the child who had earlier taken pity on her at the open-air marketplace and shared his dinner of steamed conch and fresh bananas with her, she knew she must somehow gather enough food to sustain her through several hours—perhaps even days—at sea.

"It would have been easier had I been the guttersnipe he thought me," she remarked to herself, thinking of Devlin yet again. If she had possessed the sort of low character he had accused her of, then she would not have thought twice about stealing something from his house before fleeing. It would have required only a few pieces of silver to barter her way to comfort aboard an English ship. But, she realized with an inward sigh, she could not have turned thief, no matter *what* the circumstances. As always, her indomitable pride would have prevented any compromise of her principles. Ah yes, she mused with a touch of bitterness, she would soon be hungry and uncomfortable in the damp, stinking hold of a ship, but her pride would remain intact!

Darkness was rapidly blanketing the island when Meghan slipped out of the storehouse. She wrapped the cloak securely about her and raised the hood to cover her bright curls, then hurried back down to the waterfront. Her steps unknowingly led her to the very part of Bay Street any decent woman feared to tread after sundown.

The taverns were already overflowing with eager patrons, as were the other pleasure dens that had flung wide their doors to beckon the thirsty men within. Trollops with painted faces, wearing little more than seductive smiles, stood poised in readiness to drape themselves across the young seamen whose pockets would be completely empty come morning. In some ways, it seemed, Nassau had not changed a great deal since those long ago days when piracy had reigned supreme upon its hilly shores.

Preoccupied with the formidable task before her, Meghan was at first oblivious to the raucous activity going on about her. She frowned as it became increasingly difficult to find a path along the crowded boardwalk, and she was shocked to hear herself referred to by a passing group of sailors as a "right fancy little piece." Her eyes flew wide, then made a hasty surveillance of the dimly lit street and the revelers milling about. She was even more startled when she took note of the women who offered a tantalizing glimpse of themselves in nearly every doorway. It was then that the true nature of her surroundings dawned on her.

Her heart pounding fiercely within her breast, she tugged the dirty satin pelisse even closer about her and continued on her way at an even more accelerated pace than before. She did her best to ignore the insolent remarks and bold advances that were offered her as she went, but she found it necessary on two separate occasions to violently wrest herself from the grasp of an overzealous admirer.

Just when she was beginning to be confident of her success in running the gauntlet that was Bay Street at night, a man suddenly caught her up in his big, burly arms and spirited her toward one of the taverns. Meghan kicked and beat at him with all her might, but she found herself carried inside almost before she knew what was happening.

"Put me down!" she cried furiously, pushing at the fellow's massive chest while squirming in his arms. "Help! Please, someone help me!"

The man who held her prisoner was a tall, blond-haired Norwegian who would have been deemed handsome if not for the visible ravages of a childhood bout with smallpox. He flashed his struggling prize a yellowed, gap-toothed smile while he bore her father into the very midst of the boisterous merrymaking.

Men filled every corner of the smoky, grog-and-sweat-scented room, and Meghan felt herself growing faint. Her struggles and pleas for help became increasingly frantic, albeit entirely useless, as she was borne rapidly through the crowd to a table in the far corner. It so happened that the table was occupied at the moment, but Meghan's strapping Nordic captor did not allow such a small detail to stand in his way. He merely dispatched the brawniest of the men with a hard blow to the chin, thereby successfully "persuading" the unfortunate sailor's companions to beat a hasty retreat before they received more of the same.

A sharp gasp broke from Meghan's lips as the blond Viking suddenly bent his hefty frame into a chair and settled her upon his lap. She made a desperate attempt to scramble free, but he clamped an arm about her waist and imprisoned her quite effectively in spite of her violent protests.

"Unhand me!" she breathlessly demanded, still refusing to surrender. She doubled her hand into a fist and brought it up to strike his pockmarked, wolfishly grinning features, but he seized her wrist in a bruising grip just in time. "Let me go!" She tried to pummel him about the head with her other hand, only to have it captured as well. Panic raced through her, and her terror-filled gaze swept the clamorous room in another futile attempt to find someone willing to aid her in her distress. She was dismayed to see nothing but mingled lust and amusement on the faces of the men whose eyes were fastened so avidly upon her.

The disheveled appearance she presented certainly did nothing to advance her cause. Her golden locks were now streaming down about her face and shoulders in wild disarray, while her struggles had loosened the ties of the cloak so that the hood had fallen back and the tattered garment itself hung off one shoulder. To make matters worse, the white lawn modesty piece had become dislodged and now dangled ineffectually from one corner of her gown's low bodice. Gasping sharply to feel her captor's burning gaze upon her unprotected, half-exposed bosom, she renewed her efforts to escape.

"Let me go, you foul-smelling blackguard!" she raged fierily. "How dare you accost me in this evil manner! I am not—"

"By damn, Olaf likes a woman with spirit!" the blond giant interrupted with a wickedly appreciative laugh that boded ill for Meghan. The self-proclaimed Olaf tightened his arm like a vise about her waist, forcing the breath from her body and threatening to crush her ribs. He bent his head closer to hers, and she felt nausea rising within her at the overwhelming stench of his breath upon her face. "But soon, my sweet, Olaf will make you purr like a kitten instead of spit like a tigress!" he prophesied with another chuckle. As if to prove his point, he gave a meaningful thrust and rotation of his lower body upward against Meghan's hips so that she was made painfully aware of his lecherous intent.

"No!" Her voice rising on a shrill note, she was

aghast to feel herself being scooped up into the man's arms once more. He rose from the table and proceeded with his furiously resisting burden toward the narrow, dilapidated wooden staircase which led up to the rooms where it was customary for the tavern's patrons to be "entertained" by its female employees.

Dear God in heaven, this can't be happening! Meghan screamed inwardly. Surely it was not her fate to have her maidenhood stolen by the likes of this man! After all she had been through, to find herself raped in some dirty room above a tavern— no, as God was her witness, she would die before she'd allow it to happen!

In one violent motion, she flung both of her arms about her assailant's head and jerked her body upward. Olaf, caught off-guard, found his oath of surprise muffled against Meghan's breasts as he suddenly lost his precarious balance upon the steps and went staggering heavily backward. His broad back slammed up against the wall, prompting him to groan in pain and momentarily loose his possessive grasp on Meghan.

A roar of drunken laughter from the crowd of onlookers greeted Olaf's disgrace at the hands of his beautiful young captive, who seized full advantage of the opportunity to wrest herself free. Making a desperate attempt to bolt from the tavern, she was vastly relieved to find a path cleared for her. The men cheered her on with laughing, ribald expressions of encouragement as she raced for the door. She had no sooner reached it, however, when a recovered Olaf caught up with her and enveloped her in another bone-crushing grip from behind.

"No!" she cried once more, hot tears of defeat

filling her eyes. "Let me go, damn you!" The blond giant's only response was to fling her about, tuck her securely facedown under one arm, and begin conveying her purposefully back to the staircase.

A still dauntless Meghan, her legs thrashing helplessly and her long hair trailing along the filthy wooden floor, made good use of what her father had once taught her about the vulnerability of the male anatomy. Though she had never found it necessary to employ such drastic methods before, she wasted no time in doing so now. She balled her hand into a fist and brought it smashing up against Olaf's unsuspecting manhood.

A great howl of pain broke from his lips. His prisoner found herself abruptly released as he doubled over, his hands clutching at the front of his trousers. Meghan gasped to find herself hurtling downward to the hard floor, where she landed with such an uncomfortable jolt that she lay stunned for several long moments.

The crowd erupted into loud guffaws and appreciative curses at this latest turn of events, but Olaf was anything but amused. Even though he was temporarily incapacitated, he managed to snake out a burly arm and catch Meghan about the waist just as she scrambled up to her hands and knees. Judging from the furious light of revenge in his eyes, there was little doubt that he meant to make her pay. A choking sob welled up deep in her throat, and she felt her strength rapidly waning.

Please God, please help me! she begged in silent anguish. Unbeknownst to her, the answer to her heartfelt prayer was already at hand.

"Let her go, you bastard!"

The newcomer's voice rang out in curt, authoritative tones above the laughter. Meghan's head snapped up at the sound of that wonderfully deep-timbred voice, for it was one which had become all too familiar to her throughout the past twenty-four hours.

Devlin Montague! her heart sang as her eyes widened in shocked amazement. The most profound relief she had ever known flooded her weary, trembling body. *Devlin Montague had come to save her!*

A startled silence had fallen over the crowd, but it was quickly shattered by the brawny Viking, who jerked Meghan to her feet beside him. His feral, murderously glittering gaze searched the room.

"What man dares to call Olaf a bastard?" he growled. "Show yourself, I say! Show yourself and be damned!"

Once again, the crowd parted. Devlin strode forward with deceptive nonchalance, his handsome face inscrutable and his eyes flickering only briefly over Meghan's pale, breathlessly expectant features. A faint smile touched his lips when his gaze, undeniably challenging, met the blaze of Olaf's.

"Damned I may well be, but you will either release the woman at once or face the consequences," warned Devlin, his voice quite low and deadly. The only real outward evidence of his smoldering rage was provided by the strange gleam in his eyes, those same midnight blue orbs that had held Meghan spellbound from the first moment she had encountered their piercing intensity.

"Consequences?" Olaf echoed with a snort of derisive laughter. A few of the onlookers nervously joined in. "Either you are a very brave man or a foolish one!" he proclaimed, his mouth twisting into

89

a malevolent grin before his pockmarked features became an ugly mask of anger. "The woman is mine!"

Meghan suffered a sharp intake of breath as she was once again subjected to the mercilessly crushing pressure of Olaf's arm about her waist. Her eyes flew back to Devlin's face, and she sent him a look of such desperate entreaty that he felt a sudden, knife-edged pain in his heart. His blood boiled with vengeful fury at the sight of her in the other man's cruel, possessive grasp, but he maintained an iron control over his emotions and measured his words carefully.

"That cannot be so, for she already belongs to me," he contended. "And I claim the right to take her from you!"

"Then you will have to do just that!" roared Olaf. He suddenly thrust Meghan from him and charged forward like a bull on a rampage. Devlin met the challenge head-on, drawing his sword while his opponent did the same. The other seamen in the tavern immediately formed a wide ring about them, prodding the combatants onward to violence with eager shouts and cheers.

Meghan climbed dazedly to her feet from where she had been sent crashing into a table. Clutching the satin cloak about her, she shook her head as if to clear it and impatiently swept the tangled golden tresses from her face. Her throat constricted painfully at the terrible scene being enacted before her.

Devlin was by this time engaged in fierce swordplay with the Norwegian sailor, whose obvious lack of fencing skills was compensated for by his superior brawn. Though he and his adversary were well matched in height, Olaf was the heavier by a good fifty pounds. He fought with a savagery that would easily have routed a lesser man. Devlin, however, successfully parried each attack until the fair-haired Viking began to tire. Employing the tactic of perseverance over power—taught to him many years ago by the most exacting fencing master in all of Charlestown—he managed to wear his wildly thrusting opponent down in a matter of minutes.

Meghan stifled a cry as she watched the two men suddenly lock swords and grapple with one another. Then, Olaf lost his footing. He fell heavily back against a table and chairs, his husky frame splintering the furniture into pieces while his sword went flying harmlessly across the floor. Devlin quickly stepped forward and pressed the tip of his own blade to the other man's throat.

"Do you yield the woman to me?" he demanded harshly, battling the temptation to run the fellow through.

"Yes, damn your eyes!" snarled Olaf. Though he had spoken his surrender, his gaze still shone with a malignant light that promised retaliation. He was allowed to rise to his feet, but the sword's point remained at his throat. His anger at such unaccustomed defeat made him reckless, and he spat bitterly at Devlin, "Take your whore away and be gone! She is not worth the—"

He got no further, for Devlin ground out a curse and pressed the blade closer. Blood trickled from a wound to Olaf's flesh that was painful but by no means as grave as its inflictor would have wished it. Although his sense of honor forbade him to kill an unarmed opponent, Devlin was nonetheless seized with the irresistible urge to give the bullying knave a severe trouncing. He did not pause to ask himself why he should become so enraged at hearing another man term Meghan what he himself had once insinuated; he merely tossed his sword aside and swung back to bring his fist smashing forcefully up against Olaf's chin.

The burly sailor grunted loudly as he staggered back against the wall, but he swiftly recovered and countered with a blow aimed at Devlin's unguarded midsection. Reacting with lightning quick speed, Devlin avoided Olaf's fist and launched another blow to his pockmarked face.

At that point, all hell broke loose.

The crowd of spectators, no longer content to remain just that, suddenly began to fight among themselves. Meghan watched in startled disbelief as men turned upon those who had only moments earlier stood laughing companionably beside them. Someone yelled *"Free fight!"* to denote that the brawl was open to one and all, and then someone else obligingly added *"No bottles or blades, you friggin' swabs!"* Men poured in from the street, filling the tavern to overflowing and prompting Meghan to scramble hastily atop a table in the corner in an attempt to find safety.

Devlin! She forgot her own peril as her wide, sparkling gaze searched anxiously for any sign of him amid the melee. She felt faint with relief when she sighted him across the room, where he and Olaf were still engaged in their efforts to beat one another to a mindless pulp. To her eyes at least, it appeared that her "champion" was winning—his handsome face bore little visible effects of the battle, while his opponent's was bruised and bloodied and grimacing in pain. Devlin finally put him out of his misery with one last blow to his left jaw. The hap-

92

less Olaf crumpled to the floor and lay there in a stupor, oblivious to the riotous fray going on about him.

Devlin spun about to look for Meghan. Their gazes met and locked across the churning sea of men, and Meghan felt a powerful current pass between them. She had no time to contemplate its meaning or significance, however, as two of the brawlers chose that particular moment to come hurtling into the table on which she stood.

Her eyes filled with shocked dismay, and a breathless little scream escaped her lips as she suddenly went toppling downward. Her fall was cushioned somewhat by the jumbled heap of bodies—some unconscious, some not—on the floor. Hastily extricating herself from the tangle of arms and legs, she stumbled to her feet in a daze, only to feel herself being forced abruptly to a halt when her skirts were captured by one of the men lying amid the clutter. She tugged furiously upon the delicate fabric, but the man refused to let go.

"Not so fast, you proud little bitch!" he bellowed above the din. Winding the flowered muslin about his hand, he pulled himself upright and jerked Meghan toward him. He was not nearly as large as Olaf, but he appeared just as wickedly determined to possess her. "Let's you and me get out of here, duchess, and go somewheres we can be alone!" He flashed her a drunken but unmistakably predatory smile and raised a hand toward her arm.

The next thing Meghan knew, her newest assailant was sent reeling by a well-placed fist that seemed to come out of nowhere. Her eyes were round as saucers and full of amazement as she whirled about to see that it was none other than

93

Devlin Montague himself who had saved her virtue once more. Amazement instantly turned to joyful gratitude, and she forgot all about the fact that it was because of him that she had found herself in such a frightful predicament in the first place.

"Thank God you—" she breathed, only break off with a loud gasp as she was suddenly caught up in his powerful arms. He tossed her unceremoniously over his shoulder as though she were nothing more than a sack of grain. "What in heaven's name are you doing?" she demanded a bit shrilly. Devlin's only answer was to clutch her firmly about the legs with one arm and begin making his way through the fracas.

Meghan, hanging upended over his broad shoulder with her thick mass of hair tumbling downward to obscure her view, had little choice in the matter. She gasped to feel herself being swung this way and that as Devlin's free arm masterfully dispatched all those who dared to block their path. Finally, they reached the doorway and emerged into the relative safety of Bay Street.

Expecting to be released now that they were outside, Meghan braced her hands against Devlin's hard-muscled back and raised her head. She frowned in puzzlement when he showed no sign of putting her down. His arm remained clamped about her legs while his long, angry strides led them toward the moonlit wharf.

"You can let me go now, Mister Montague," she protested, squirming in his grasp. "I am perfectly capable of walking under my own power!" A breathless cry of mingled shock and outrage escaped her lips as her rescuer-turned-captor, his blue eyes suffused with a dangerously intense light, delivered a hard whack to her conveniently placed backside.

"Keep still, damn it!" he ground out.

"Why, you—how dare you!" she sputtered indignantly, her cheeks flaming. "Put me down at once!" She punctuated her demand by striking at the broad target of his back with her hand. "Put me down!"

"Keep still, woman, or else you'll find yourself unable to sit for a week!" he warned tightly.

Meghan's eyes flew wide at that, and she felt a tiny shiver of fear run down her spine. She had little doubt that the arrogant scoundrel would make good on his threat. Mentally consigning him to the devil, she ceased her squirming and fell silent.

Moments later, Devlin carried his fuming captive aboard the *Pandora* and gave the order to weigh anchor. Meghan caught a glimpse of Peter Hobbs's solemn young face as she was borne swiftly across the deck, and she experienced another sharp twinge of remorse for the trick she had played on him. All thought of remorse, however, was driven from her mind when Devlin kicked open the door of the lamplit cabin and hauled her inside. Set on her feet with a roughness that literally took her breath away, she started in alarm when Devlin slammed the door and rounded on her.

His expression was quite thunderous, his magnificent blue eyes were smoldering with fury, and he showed a noticeable proclivity toward violence in the way his hands were clenched into tight fists at his sides. Meghan pulled the tattered pelisse about her like a shield and raised her head in a gesture of proud defiance that belied her rapidly growing apprehension.

"You have caused me a great deal of trouble this

day, Mistress Kearny," charged Devlin in a low voice laced with barely controlled rage, "and by damn, I am sorely tempted to take it out of your beautiful, blasted hide!"

"Lay hands on me ever again, Devlin Montague, and I swear I'll see you hanged for it!" she threatened rashly, her own eyes ablaze as she took an involuntary step backward. Her anger provoked her to further impetuosity, so that she added with biting sarcasm, "Pray, sir, if you have been troubled this day, then 'tis your own fault! Indeed, I have done nothing but what any woman in her right mind would do when faced with the disagreeable prospect of spending so much as another hour—nay, another *minute*—in your company!"

"Then I take it you would prefer the company of those pawing ruffians at the tavern?" he countered harshly. "If so, I can arrange it!"

"The only thing I want arranged by is you is my freedom!"

"That was lost to you the moment you committed the offense—God only knows what sort of treachery you're capable of—that resulted in your presence aboard the *Bristol Packet!*"

"I told you, I was an innocent captive aboard that ship!" she reminded him with fiery-eyed vehemence.

"Just as you are innocent of having seduced my first mate into compliance with your schemes?" he parried, closing the gap between them now so that he stood towering ominously above her.

"I did not seduce him!" Meghan hotly denied with a furious toss of her wildly streaming golden locks. Tilting her head back in order to face her accuser squarely, she met his scorching, inexplicably damning gaze with an indignant glare that glistened with tears. "Neither did he comply with my efforts to escape! Whatever I did, I did entirely on my— oh, but what is the use in trying to explain to you?" She spun about toward the porthole and folded her arms tightly across her heaving breasts. "You refuse to listen to anything I have to say, you refuse to acknowledge the possibility of your own misjudgment! You are without a doubt the most thoroughly pigheaded, supercilious man I have ever known! Would to God our paths had never crossed!" she finished tremulously, the hot tears threatening to spill over at any moment.

An uncharacteristic frown of uncertainty crossed the rugged perfection of Devlin's features, but he purposely hardened his heart against the note of despair in Meghan's voice. No, by all that was holy, he vowed, he would not allow himself to be deceived by her! Whoever she was, whatever she was, it would be utter folly to continue letting her rule his every waking thought. . . .

"Would to God indeed," he murmured half to himself, then seized her arm in an iron grip and forced her abruptly about to face him again. Taking natural and highly visible exception to such treatment, Meghan attempted to pull free, but he held fast, his hand closing relentlessly about both of her arms as he disregarded her furious protests and tersely decreed, "It matters not what you think of me—you *will* do as I say until we reach Charlestown! You damned near got the both of us killed tonight, you little fool!" His fingers clenched with near bruising force about her soft flesh, while his eyes flashed and narrowed vengefully, "Blast it woman, if I had not found you in time—"

"I was managing quite well enough without you!"

she rebelliously insisted, though she knew as well as he that it was a lie. Still refusing to be subdued, she brought her hands up to push at the immovable force of his chest. He scowled darkly and yanked her closer.

"The devil you were! It may well be that you're more than accustomed to the likes of such men, but I'll not leave you to their mercy as long as you are under my protection!"

"I did not ask for your protection, Devlin Montague, nor do I desire it! Now take your hands off me and get out!"

"In the event you've forgotten, Mistress Kearny, this happens to be *my* cabin, and I'll not get out until it damned well suits me to do so!"

"Why, you—you pompous bully!" she stormed, her struggles intensifying as her temper flared ever upward. "I've had quite enough of your despicable insults and your loathsome manhandling! You're no different than those ill-mannered rogues at the tavern! Oh yes, they too sought to bend me to their will, to take advantage of the physical weakness bequeathed to me and all others of my sex! Mayhap your precious Rosalie finds such churlish behavior to her liking, but I most assuredly do *not!*" she concluded on a bitter note, her heart twisting painfully at the sudden memory of his deep voice, raw with concern, demanding news of the beautiful, haughty Miss Hammond.

It occurred to her then to wonder if he had been successful in his search for his betrothed, but she was in no mood to ask him. And he, as was immediately apparent with one look at his bronze, tight-lipped features, was in no mood to be asked.

"You dare to mention her name to me?" he

ground out, startling her into wide-eyed silence as he suddenly swept her up hard against him. His fierce gaze burned down into her luminous, frightened one, while his arm tightened about her waist until she could scarcely breathe. "Damn you, Meghan Kearny! Damn you to hell!"

Before she could demand to know what she had done to suffer such ruthless condemnation in his eyes, she found herself locked within the powerful circle of his arms, her supple curves molded with intimate perfection against his tall, muscular frame. Perilously lightheaded all of a sudden, she could not deny the warmth spreading throughout her entire body, a warmth that became a raging fever when his lips descended angrily upon hers.

His mouth, hard and punishing at first, grew more tenderly demanding moments later when she began to kiss him back. Her proud defiance was once again conquered by the man who had provided her with the first real taste of passion's forbidden fruits, and she was soon swept away by the sweet madness that called to her whenever Devlin Montague—a stranger still, a devastatingly handsome but disturbingly enigmatic man she knew virtually nothing about—took her in his arms. It was only the third time her lips had been claimed by his, and yet she felt strangely at home in his embrace, as though she was exactly where she belonged. . . .

The innocent fervor of her response fired Devlin's already blazing desire to such an extent that he groaned low in his throat and knew himself facing inevitable disaster. Once again, Rosalie Hammond was driven completely from his mind. He could think only of the exasperating but thoroughly captivating young woman in his arms, this angel-faced little vixen who had bewitched him as she had no doubt bewitched countless others. Although he could not yet explain how or why, he had apparently become obsessed with her, and it was this mysterious obsession that now prompted him to defy his own conscience, to ignore the warning bells sounding in his brain.

With another inward groan, Devlin tightened his arms about Meghan's pliant softness and kissed her with such provocative urgency that her legs threatened to give way beneath her. His tongue explored the willing sweetness of her mouth, while the heat of his virile, lithely muscled body seared through her clothing to set her own blood afire. Her hands clung weakly to his shoulders, her heart pounding beneath his. She matched his inflamed passion with her own, a passion he himself had awakened with the first touch of his lips upon hers, and she instinctively strained farther upward into the deepening kiss that seemed to be stirring her very soul.

She gave a low moan of protest when his mouth finally relinquished hers, but her sense of loss was quickly replaced by sheer, dizzying pleasure as he impatiently swept aside the satin cloak and pressed his lips to her bosom. The lawn kerchief lay forgotten on the floor back at the tavern, so there was nothing to prevent Devlin from paying tribute to the alluring swell of her breasts with a succession of moist, wildly intoxicating kisses. This time, however, he was not content with claiming only a portion of the delectably rounded globes. Before Meghan was aware of what was happening, his fingers had strayed purposefully to the low bodice of the borrowed muslin gown.

"Oh!" she gasped in the next instant, her eyes

flying wide in shock as the delicate fabric gave way beneath the unexpected force of Devlin's hand. She felt a rush of cool air upon her tingling flesh, then drew in her breath upon another sharp gasp as her beautiful breasts, now completely bared for Devlin's pleasure as well as her own, were subjected to a dual assault of the most sensuously persuasive manner. Shivers danced down her spine, and she cried out softly as his hand closed upon one pale, rose-tipped breast while his mouth fastened about the other.

Her fingers tightened convulsively upon his strong arms as his hot, velvety tongue flicked erotically across the delicate peak. His warm lips suckled as greedily as any babe's, causing Meghan to bite at her lower lip in an effort to stifle the unintelligible cry which rose deep in her throat. Her head fell back, and she closed her eyes tightly against the intense, unfamiliar sensations which held her captive as surely as did Devlin Montague's arms.

She felt her senses reeling out of control as his mouth continued with its rapturous possession of her heretofore unsampled charms. His hand moved beneath each of her breasts in turn to lift their satiny perfection even higher for the ardent, burning caresses he bestowed upon them. He delighted in her breasts, their silken roundness tasting sweet to his lips and their pert nipples beckoning irresistibly for his attentions, and it soon became clear to Meghan that he meant to love them well.

She was powerless to stop him. Never before had she experienced such an overwhelming desire to have a man touch her as boldly as this one was doing now. She found herself yearning for his kisses, longing for his caresses, and though she knew herself damned for it—*God forgive her*—she could not summon the strength of will to resist.

It seemed the natural course of things when Devlin scooped her up in his arms and bore her swiftly across the cabin. His lips claimed hers again as he lowered her to the narrow bed. In that small part of her brain still capable of rational thought, Meghan heard a voice telling her to desist, to pull away before it was too late, but she refused to heed it. Though she was a woman of considerable fire and spirit, she was also a woman of flesh and blood, in truth a passionate innocent whose maidenly inhibitions were being conquered with both tenderness and mastery by the only man to ever succeed in tumbling the barriers she had long ago erected about her heart.

"You beautiful, maddening little witch!" he whispered hoarsely as his lips roamed over the flushed planes of her face. His body pressing hers deeper into the mattress, he tangled a hand in her skirts and began tugging them impatiently upward. The petticoat followed the same course immediately afterward, thereby exposing her shapely, silk-stockinged limbs to the cool, lamplit air within the cabin. Her clothing lay bunched up about her waist, leaving her virtually naked except for the thin cotton chemise which still reached to the tops of her pale thighs.

Although Meghan possessed a very good idea of what took place between men and women when they loved, she was shocked to feel Devlin's strong hand sliding upward along the smoothness of her bare thigh. She moaned softly beneath the returning pressure of his lips, then moaned again when his fingers trailed farther upward along the enticing curve of her hip and delved beneath her to caress

102

the naked roundness of her bottom.

"Oh, Devlin!" she gasped out as his mouth seared a feverish path back down to the enchanting, rose-tipped fullness of her breasts. He shifted his weight above her, his hand gliding from her buttocks to her belly, then downward to the alluring triangle of golden curls at the apex of her thighs.

Meghan started in alarm at the first touch of his hand upon the very center of her femininity. In the next instant, however, she felt a pleasure so intense that it was like wildfire coursing through her, and she cried out at the sensation.

Sweet Saint Bridget, what is happening to me? she wondered in a breathless daze. She could not prevent her hips from straining upward, nor her thighs from spreading wider, and any momentary qualms she might have suffered evaporated as Devlin's skillful fingers began an exquisite torment to her womanly flesh. His lips reclaimed hers in a kiss so imminently compelling that she felt her emotions spiralling out of control. So swept away was she upon the surging tide of passion that she was only vaguely aware of the moment when Devlin's hand moved to the fastening of his breeches. She clung to him as though she were drowning, her head tossing restlessly to and fro upon the pillow while her breath became nothing more than a series of soft gasps.

Then, disaster struck.

The unbidden image of Rosalie Hammond's face suddenly swam before Devlin's passion-clouded eyes. For a moment, he wavered—but only for a moment. Unconscious of the fact that he did so aloud, he defiantly cursed the guilt that crept over him at the thought of his betrothed.

"Damn you, Rosalie!" he murmured, his lips wandering hotly along the graceful curve of Meghan's neck.

To Meghan, hearing him speak another woman's name, and at *that* particular moment in time, had the same effect as a bucketful of cold water being emptied over her head. She came crashing back to earth, her heart aching terribly and her face burning with mingled indignation and shame.

"No!" she cried brokenly, pushing at him with all her might. *"No!"*

Devlin, taken off-guard by her sudden protests and the startling vehemence with which she uttered them, did not demand an explanation until she had already managed to wrest herself from beneath him. She stood to her feet beside the bed, one hand furiously smoothing down her skirts while the other tugged at her bodice in a frantic but ultimately unsuccessful effort to cover her heaving breasts.

"What the devil—" growled Devlin, his hand shooting out to close about her wrist. "Blast it, woman, what ails you?"

"Let me go!" She wrenched her arm free with a vengeance and took an unsteady step backward. Her anger served only to heighten her beauty, and Devlin's eyes glowed with the full force of his desire as he drew himself up from the bed. Meghan did not fail to notice the way his smoldering gaze raked meaningfully over her. She whirled to take flight when his hand once again detained her.

"Where the bloody hell do you think you're going?" He drew her roughly back toward him, his handsome face a mask of white-hot fury. "You'll not get away from me so easily, Meghan Kearny!"

She fought him like a veritable tigress then, kicking and writhing and thrashing wildly until he finally held her locked within his hard embrace with her arms imprisoned behind her back. Gazing down into the stormy, brilliantly flashing depths of her eyes, Devlin was certain he beheld pain as well as outrage. He cursed himself for a fool and demanded tersely once more,

"What the devil sent you flying into a rage all of a sudden?"

"Well you should ask, you—you *libertine!*" she retorted venomously. She winced as his fingers bit into the flesh of her arms.

"Call me that ever again, mistress, and you'll have cause to regret it!" he warned through tightly clenched teeth, then suddenly realized that she had every cause, indeed every right to term him such. He was betrothed to Rosalie, and yet he had very nearly consummated his infatuation, purely physical though it was, with another woman. God damn him to hell, there was no excuse for what he had done, but that did not mean he was willing to let some fire-spitting little termagent take him to task for his inconstancy, especially when she herself was the one who had provoked him to it! Giving her a brisk shake that made her teeth rattle, he offered menacingly, "Either you tell me what occurred to—"

"Save your threats for Mistress Hammond!" Meghan cut him off. Her mouth curved into a smile of bitter, taunting sarcasm as she challenged with a noticeable brogue, "Or perhaps, Mister Montague, you're after confusing me with her again? It appears you cannot keep the two of us straight—*either in your bed or out of it!*"

Devlin's temper, having already flared to a dangerous level as a result of both anger and the most

105

acute frustration he had ever known, exploded at that point. With a savage oath, he flung Meghan back onto the narrow bunk. He subjected her to one last savage, thoroughly scalding glare before he abruptly wheeled about and went stalking from the cabin. The door was opened and closed with such force in the process that the brass hinges rattled in protest.

Meghan lay stunned amid the rumpled covers of Devlin's bed. She expelled a long, ragged breath. For a moment, she had been afraid he was going to throttle her with his bare hands. The murderous gleam in his eyes had certainly attested to his temptation to do so!

Feeling perfectly miserable, she battled a fresh onslaught of tears and pulled herself into a sitting position. Not only did her heart ache terribly, but it seemed every square inch of her body screamed for a respite from the sort of punishment it had received throughout the last hour. Of course, she mused while choking back a sob, not all of the night's events had proven unpleasurable. Thinking of the profound enchantment she and Devlin had shared before the spell had been so grievously shattered, she closed her eyes against the anguish welling up deep within her and collapsed wearily back upon the bed.

"Dear God in heaven, what have I done?" she lamented forlornly, her voice quavering as she continued to fight back tears. "What have I done?"

You have done the inexcusable, Meghan Kearny, her mind's inner voice suddenly answered. *You have lost your heart to a handsome, blue-eyed rogue who loves another.*

"No!" she denied aloud. She came bolt upright

in the bed again and vigorously shook her head. "No, it—it cannot be so!"

But it was, and well she knew it.

Her eyes filled with shocked amazement as she finally acknowledged the truth. She had fallen in love with Devlin Montague. She had lost her heart to a man who could never love her in return, a man who was so unfeeling as to hold her close and wish she were another. The memory of his cruel infamy wounded her to her very soul. Other memories came flooding back to haunt her as well, and she now realized why she had been unable to resist him, why she had been unable to consider anything but the sheer ecstasy of being in his arms.

"God help me, I love him!" she whispered, still feeling thunderstruck at the realization. "I love him, and I am lost . . ."

Pain and elation mingled strangely together within her breast. Burying her face in her hands she wept, her tears pouring forth all the torment and despair bottled up within her as the *Pandora* sailed homeward through the sparkling, moonlit waters of the Atlantic.

Chapter Five

"Aye, Cap'n, and I'll wager you the thievin' bastard's made Jonas Hammond pay ten times the goin' price for that proud-as-a-peacock daughter of his!"

"Keep in mind, you old sea dog, that you are speaking of the woman who will soon become my wife!" Devlin cautioned with a hard glint in his eyes.

"Nay, sir, I've not forgotten it," the other man replied amiably. His craggy features split into a broad, unrepetant grin when he added, "though I thought mayhap *you* had."

"And just what the devil do you mean by that?" demanded Devlin, his fingers tightening about the ship's smoothly varnished railing as his gaze shot back to his burly companion.

"Only this, Cap'n," Malachi Flynn went on to explain with a bluntness that was the privilege of lifelong acquaintance with the young master of the *Pandora*. "It seems you've had a bit of trouble recallin' much about your betrothed ever since the other lass came aboard. Not that I can blame you none— from what little I've seen of Mistress Hammond, she hasn't the pluck this one has," he opined with a significant nod toward the opposite end of the deck.

"Since your knowledge of Mistress Kearny was gleaned from a scant ten minutes spent with her in a blasted rowboat, I fail to see how you can dare to make any comparisons at all!"

"Why, Cap'n, you know as well as anyone that I've always had a sharp eye for the ladies," Malachi offered with a low chuckle. He was not the least bit intimidated by the fierce look Devlin sent him. More friend than retainer, he was well accustomed to the younger man's scowls. "But now that Mistress Hammond will be waitin' for you in Charlestown, you'll have the pleasure of makin' the judgment yourself." Directing a negligent glance overhead at the billowing white sails, he settled his cap lower upon his black-maned head and observed wryly, "Aye, there'll be hell to pay and plenty of it when your ransomed Rosalie finds out about the little wildcat you've been tamin'."

"You talk too much!" growled Devlin. With a muttered curse, he spun away from the railing and strode angrily across the sun-warmed deck toward the passageway leading below.

At that same moment, Meghan was emerging from the cabin. Surprised to discover the door unlocked, she had found herself wondering where Devlin had spent the night. That he had not returned to the cabin she was certain, for she had lain awake until dawn. The pallor of her beautiful countenance and the faint, shadowy circles beneath her eyes testified to her lack of slumber, just as the heaviness of her heart testified to its cause.

Drawing in a deep, steadying breath, she gathered up her skirts and resolutely climbed the steps to the beckoning, salt-scented warmth above. She reached the deck and raised her eyes just as Devlin drew to an abrupt halt mere inches away. A loud gasp escaped her lips, and she felt her head swim at the unexpected sight of his tall frame looming above her.

To her, he looked every inch the dashing sea captain, his handsome features appearing tanned and rugged above the open-necked whiteness of his linen shirt. The hard, powerful leanness of his lower body was encased in fitted dark blue breeches, while the black leather knee boots he wore gleamed beneath the sun's golden rays. It was more the undeniable air of command about him, however, that prompted her to swallow hard and feel her knees weaken.

His piercing blue gaze raked over her with such bold familiarity that her cheeks crimsoned. She had thought herself prepared to face him—but she had been wrong. Though her entire body was aquiver and her pulses raced alarmingly, she managed to give at least the semblance of composure. She schooled her features carefully to prevent any indication of her inner turbulence, then forced her bright gaze to meet the glowing intensity of Devlin's without flinching.

"I thought to breathe the fresh air for a change," she explained in a low voice that was scarcely audible above the roar of the wind and sea.

"So I see," he countered with an unrelenting frown. He silently cursed his traitorous body for tensing and warming at the sight of her, just as he cursed his heart for the way it leapt within his breast as though he were some lovesick stripling instead of a seasoned man of six and twenty.

With a will of their own, his eyes traveled hungrily over her once more, darkening with renewed passion in spite of his resolve to guard against wanting her at all costs. He noted vaguely that she was clad in yet another of the expensive gowns he had bought for Rosalie—she had chosen a highly becoming *robe à la*

110

française fashioned of light, lustrous pink silk—but what caught and held his stormy thoughts was the recollection of those silken curves now molded to such beguiling perfection by the gown and how they had trembled beneath his touch the night before. The memory burned in his mind still; it had haunted his dreams throughout the long night and refused to grant him peace.

Meghan flushed beneath his disquieting scrutiny and battled the temptation to beat a hasty retreat. She did her best to ignore the wild fluttering of her own heart, but she could not keep a certain telltale quaver from her voice as she inquired,

"How long will it be before we . . . before we reach Charlestown?" She raised a hand to sweep a wayward curl from her face, but the wind, playing havoc with her skirts as well as her hair, tugged mischievously at the thick, upswept golden tresses and rendered futile any effort on her part to safeguard her coiffure.

"Two days if the weather holds. The *Pandora* knows the course well," he remarked with a pensive frown, recalling how swiftly he had made the journey to Nassau upon learning of his beloved's peril. "With any luck, our arrival will follow Miss Hammond's by mere hours," he predicted, his frown deepening.

"Then she was indeed ransomed?"

"She was."

"Oh, then . . . then I am glad for her sake." *But not for my own,* she added silently. Her skirts flapped about her legs with increasing vehemence, and she was forced to clutch at the frame of the passageway as the ship suddenly pitched to one side before riding high upon a massive swell.

Devlin resisted the urge to reach out and steady her, for he knew it to be utter madness to touch her

111

again. When the ocean calmed moments later and the deck no longer rolled, Meghan looked back to him and asked,

"Why do you call your ship the *Pandora*?" She was surprised at the faint smile which touched his lips.

"In tribute to the insatiable curiosity of the gentler sex," he revealed, his eyes glimmering with a hint of sardonic amusement. She waited for him to elaborate, but he quickly sobered again instead. "If you've any intention of taking a turn about the deck, Mistress Kearny," he told her with inexplicable sharpness, "make certain you hold tight to the railing—and keep a safe distance from my men. I don't want them forgetting their duties should you go tumbling down with your skirts about your head!" Hot color stained Meghan's cheeks, and her blue-green eyes flashed with indignation.

"I can assure you, Mister Montague, that I shall manage to prevent such a disaster!"

"See that you do." With a curt nod and a narrow, perplexingly fierce look down at her, he took himself off. Her eyes followed him, taking note of the way he strode across the swaying deck with that easy, masculine grace of his, and she felt her stomach do a peculiar little flip-flop.

She had hoped that the morning would bring a return to sanity, that she would find her romantic notions fled with the night. But such was most definitely *not* the case. No, if anything, she had discovered her love to burn brighter than before. In spite of telling herself over and over again that it was impossible to lose her heart to a man she had known a scant twenty-four hours, she could not deny that she had done precisely that.

She had always believed that when she fell in love,

it would be with an eminently suitable, well-connected young man deserving of her affection as well as the approval of her grandparents. Like any girl, she had often fantasized about a handsome, splendidly chivalrous knight on a white charger who would sweep her into his manly arms and carry her off to live in everlasting bliss with him in a castle high upon a hill. She had put such silly dreams aside quite some time ago, and it was a good thing she had, she now mused with an inward sigh, for here she had gone and toppled head-over-heels in love with a man who was neither the noble knight of her dreams nor the proper swain of her intellectual choosing. Fate had instead cast her way an arrogant, hot-tempered, domineering rogue by the name of Devlin Montague.

There was nothing to be done about it, she concluded disconsolately, other than to hope and pray she could somehow manage to fall *out* of love with him. . . .

Releasing another heavy sigh, she gathered up her skirts again and made her way unsteadily across to the nearby railing. She gazed out upon the rocking waters of the sea for a moment, then lifted her face gratefully toward the sun's benevolent warmth. The feel of the wind and salt spray upon her skin was not at all unpleasant, and she soon became lost in her thoughts once more, unaware of the way a pair of glowing, midnight blue eyes were fastened upon her with such fiery intensity.

Feeling the need to stretch her legs a short time later, Meghan shook herself out of her reverie and began to wander toward the ship's bow. She held fast to the railing as Devlin had instructed, though she did so with a touch of inner defiance. Her steps led her to where one of the crewmen was setting the rigging. So preoccupied was he with his task that he did not immediately notice Meghan's presence beside him. When he did notice it, it was too late.

Without warning, the rope slipped from his hands. The boom swung toward Meghan, striking her a glancing blow on the shoulder that sent her reeling. A breathless cry of alarm broke from her lips as she fell, and her hands grasped futilely at the dangling ends of the rope. She landed on her side atop the hard planks of the deck, while her skirts—true in part to Devlin's prophetic warning—went flying up about her knees. To her stunned and humiliated eyes, it appeared that every man aboard ship turned to gape at her exposed limbs.

Thus, in spite of the throbbing pain in her hip, she hastily scrambled into a sitting position and smoothed down her skirts. Scarcely able to believe that the very disaster she had vowed to avoid had befallen her, she sat there in stunned astonishment, her face aflame and her eyes sparkling with unshed tears. She recalled Devlin's angrily spoken words of caution, and it occurred to her in the benumbed recesses of her mind that it was almost as though he had actually *willed* her misfortune.

The next thing she knew, he was sweeping her up in his strong arms and bearing her mercifully away from the avid stares of the crew. His actions startled her, for she had not seen the way he had raced across the deck in a belated attempt to prevent the accident, just as she had not seen the sharp look of dread which had crossed his handsome countenance at her impending danger. She clung gratefully to his hard warmth as he carried her below and into the cabin.

He set her on her feet, though his hands retained a grip upon her silk-covered arms, and frowned down at her in what she perceived to be annoyance but was in actuality a very real concern. She colored anew and felt her skin tingle beneath his hands.

"Are you in pain?" he asked in a low, resonant tone that set her heart to pounding. She looked up, only to catch her breath when she glimpsed a disturbing light in his steady, unfathomable gaze.

"No, I—it's nothing," she murmured, her eyes falling before his. She felt an acute sense of loss when his hands suddenly relaxed their grip on her arms. Unaware of the great effort it cost him to release her, she told herself bitterly that he could not bear to touch her after the way she had thrown herself at him the night before. Her bold, unpardonably wanton behavior had very likely served to convince him one and for all that she was not the lady she claimed to be.

"Damn it, woman, did I not warn you against the hazards of walking about the deck?" he demanded tersely. Meghan's temper flared at the injustice of his reproach.

"How could I possibly have known something like that would happen?" she retorted, her eyes filling with their magnificent blue-green fire. "I was taking every precaution, but there was no way I could have foreseen—"

"That is precisely my point!" snapped Devlin. "You did not see because you were too blasted busy flaunting yourself before my crew!"

"*Flaunting?* Why, I—I did no such thing!" she denied hotly.

"In the future, Mistress Kearny, you will remain below decks until I give you permission to do otherwise. I trust I make myself understood?"

"Indeed you do, Mister Montague!" She raised her head proudly, oblivious to the fact that her hair

115

was tumbling down about her face and shoulders in disarray, and declared in a voice edged with resentment, "But I trust I make myself understood when I say that I have no intention of passing the next two days imprisoned within the stifling confines of this cabin—*your* cabin, as you so pointedly reminded me last night!" she finished, regretting these last words as soon as they were out of her mouth. With an inward groan of dismay, she lamented the accursed looseness of her tongue, for she had vowed never to speak of their wildly passionate encounter again.

"I see," Devlin ground out, doing his best to maintain an iron control over his own emotions. His anger with her, smoldering as it had done from the first moment he had discovered she was not Rosalie, was fueled by her careless mention of the previous night's folly. "Then you leave me no choice but to treat you like the prisoner you are!"

Before she could indignantly demand the meaning of such a remark, he had flung about and left her standing alone in the midst of the sun-filled room. As usual, the door closed resoundingly after him. Meghan heard the key being turned in the lock on the other side of the door, then heard Devlin's deep voice thundering an order to some unsuspecting member of his crew.

Two days, she reflected with a heavy sigh, her own anger evaporating as quickly as it had come. Two days until they reached Charlestown. How on earth was she going to bear it when she and Devlin parted for good? Never to see him again, never to feel his arms about her again . . . oh, how could fate be so cruel?

Swallowing a sudden lump in her throat, and determined to shed no more tears, she wandered over to the porthole. Her gaze clouded with thoughts of a future that appeared bleak and full of heartache, a future that would not include Devlin Montague.

Meanwhile, above on the quarterdeck, the object of her hopeless regard stood at the wheel, his expression undeniably grim and his eyes glinting like cold steel. So forebidding did he look that no man dared to approach him—no man save Malachi Flynn, that is.

"Surely, Cap'n, you're not meanin' to keep the poor lass below 'til we drop anchor?" Malachi asked with a lazy grin that belied his true misgivings about the situation. There was trouble ahead, he told himself. That much was for certain. And come hell or high water or even a grasping female by the name of Rosalie Hammond, he'd not stand idly by while the son of William Montague needed his help, even if that "help" was in the form of outright meddling.

"It's no concern of yours, Flynn!" Devlin shot back, his fingers tensing about the weather-smoothed wheel until his knuckles turned white.

"Aye, sir, maybe not," allowed the burly seaman with a respectful nod, "but I was thinkin' you might give a thought to the young lady's health."

"What the devil are you getting at?" Though Devlin's voice was gruff, it was brimming with noticeable affection for the older man.

"Only this, Cap'n," explained Malachi with an irrepressible twinkle in his eyes, "while I can't lay claim to any true understandin' of womenfolk—what man still breathin' can?—I've seen enough of them in my time to know they tend to sort of brood and sicken when shut away from the world."

"We'll be home in two days' time," Devlin reminded him, his mouth twisting into a wry half-smile.

117

"Aye, sir, that we will, Lord willin'. But two days can seem like two years to a lass of bloom and spirit—a lass like Mistress Kearny." He was satisfied when Devlin's smile broadened.

"Very well, you old pirate! She can venture above as much as she likes, so long as *you* keep an eye on her."

"Me, Cap'n?" replied Malachi in surprise. He had meant to do a good turn, not win himself the job of woman-watcher!

"Yes, you," reiterated Devlin, his own eyes alive with sardonic amusement now. "After all, you're the one who's worried about her health. You can damned well keep her entertained while you're at it—you know, take a turn about the deck with her, show her the workings of the ship, whatever else comes to mind."

"Aye, Cap'n," the crusty old sailor mumbled in reluctant acknowledgment of his orders. He scowled to himself as he turned away, his gaze darkening at his own folly.

Devlin's humor quickly faded when thoughts of Meghan seized control of his mind once more. He knew it was wrong to blame her for what had happened on deck a short time ago, just as it was wrong to blame her for the sum of his troubles . . . but ever since she had come into his life, nothing had gone as he had either wished or expected.

At least Rosalie was safe and on her way home, he reflected with another frown. He would soon be home as well, home at Shadowmoss where he belonged. The plantation always suffered whenever he was away, in spite of his trusted overseer's best efforts. It would soon be spring harvest time again, and he was still hoping to see the renovations to the main house

118

completed before he and Linette made their customary move to Charlestown for the summer season.

His thoughts turned to his lively, flame-haired sister for a moment, prompting a tender smile to tug at
the corners of his mouth. Linette, younger by nearly
ten years, was at times more like a daughter to him.
The loss of their parents to an outbreak of smallpox
several years ago had left the two of them no other
family save one another, so that they shared a special
closeness rarely seen among the wealthy planter society to which they belonged.

But that closeness had been sorely tested since his
engagement to Rosalie, he then recalled unhappily.
Whether the difficulty between the two women owed
its origin to sisterly jealousy or the intense, mutual
dislike Linette had termed it, he could not be sure.
Whatever the case, the fact remained that Linette had
declared it impossible to accept Rosalie Hammond as
her sister, while Rosalie had expressed similar doubts
regarding her own ability to live beneath the same
roof with Linette. He was confident of his success in
bringing harmony to his household once he and Rosalie were married, but it was in actuality a confidence
borne of stubborn determination and little else.

What would Linette think of Meghan Kearny?
something prompted him to wonder all of a sudden.
It struck him that the two of them were really very
much alike in more ways than one. They both possessed a fieriness of spirit that made any attempt to
reason with them a sore trial indeed, he mused with
an inward smile of irony, and they were of an age,
though Meghan was possibly a year or two older.
Linette would no doubt find the angel-faced wildcat a
more compatible companion than Rosalie, whose nature and interests ran not at all in the same vein as her

own.

Following the natural course of his present, unusually impulsive train of thought, Devlin found himself comparing Rosalie to Meghan. Although their size and coloring were remarkably alike, that was where all similarity ended. His betrothed was a woman of incredible taste and sophistication, a veritable goddess whose aristocratic features and flawless, impeccably clad figure drew admiration from everyone.

He had sworn to have Rosalie Hammond for his own the first time he danced with her at a friend's ball. More than three years had passed since then, and yet she had only consented to be his bride six months ago. The long wait had been frustrating, but his patience and persistence had ultimately paid off. At year's end, he and Rosalie would finally be joined in marriage. He was a man well-accustomed to getting whatever he set his mind to, and his future wife had been no exception. She was precisely the sort of woman he had always wanted, the sort of woman who would grace both his drawing room and his bedroom with beauty and elegance, and well-bred charm.

Meghan Kearny, on the other hand, he observed as her face swam defiantly before his gleaming blue eyes once more, was still a mystery to him. Although he did not for one moment believe her wild tales of a patrician bloodline and a melodramatic abduction, he could not deny that there was a certain intriguing quality about her. Her speech was that of a proper young Englishwoman, except when anger released evidence of a fierce Irish temper, and her mannerisms bespoke a training obtained by either foul means or fair—he could not say which.

She was beautiful, but in an entirely different way than his betrothed. There was a fire in her heart, a fire reflected in those flashing turquoise eyes of her, and it was this damnably captivating vibrancy that distinguished her from Rosalie. . . .

"Shall I instruct the crew to trim the sails, Captain?" It was Peter Hobbs who came to stand beside Devlin and in so doing drew him out of his disturbing reverie at last. The young first mate, encouraged by the visible softening of his employer's previously dour expression, had finally deemed it safe enough to approach. He waited for Devlin's response in deferential silence, eager to remain in the other man's good graces after the disaster in Nassau.

"Yes, Mister Hobbs," agreed Devlin, his rugged features tightening while his gaze darkened anew. "Give the order at once. We'll damned well make this ship fly if that's what it takes to speed us homeward!"

The next two days passed in relative harmony for all those aboard the *Pandora*. An unspoken truce of sorts had arisen between Devlin and Meghan, a truce that did not extend to their rare private moments together, but a truce nonetheless.

Whenever Meghan was up on deck, she was either strolling along the rail or sitting beside Malachi Flynn near the schooner's bow. Her reluctant escort spoke little, for which she was glad most of the time, and he appeared generally uneasy in her presence. She pressed him once or twice for information about Devlin, but he displayed no inclination whatsoever to satisfy her curiosity. When he did allow himself to be drawn into conversation, their talk almost always centered about the fascinating and unusual sights Malachi had seen during his life at sea. That it had been a colorful, highly adventurous life was undeniable, and Meghan listened with rapt attention to his tales of faraway peoples and places.

Devlin, on the other hand, made it a point to avoid her. He rarely addressed her when she was above, though she caught him staring at her now and then. His eyes would be fastened upon her with disquieting steadiness until the moment she met his gaze, at which time he would either make her a mocking salute with a nod and an accompanying half-smile, or look away entirely.

The only occasions she had to be alone with him occurred at night, after she had eaten the meal brought to the cabin by none other than the ship's first mate. Peter Hobbs acted strangely distant whenever he came in, and in spite of her attempts to apologize for the trick she had played on him back in Nassau, he would merely set the tray atop the desk, bid her a cordial goodnight, and leave the room in all haste. What she did not know was that Devlin had charged him with this particular duty as a stern reminder never to allow himself to be tempted into disobedience again. It was not meant to be cruel, but rather to be effective, which it was.

The first night Devlin entered the cabin, after startling her by actually pausing to knock first, it was to coldly inquire if she was well and being treated properly by his crew. Meghan was surprised by his concern, impassively offered though it was, and it was all she could do to stammer out an affirmative response. She was left feeling both confused and achingly disappointed when he turned to go after a few brief words regarding the ship's progress. Once the door had closed behind him, she sank wearily down into a chair and fixed her anguished gaze upon the maps and charts strewn across his desk. It was quite some time before she sought the loneliness of her bed.

The second night, however, proved to be a tremendous change from the first.

Meghan was curled up on the bunk, reading one of Devlin's books by lamplight. She had discovered the volume of plays by William Shakespeare when her restlessness had driven her to wander about the cabin as the twilight deepened outside. Somewhat surprised to see the varied collection of books perched on the cluttered shelves in one corner, she had decided that reading might be just the thing to take her mind off her troubles.

She had read extensively from the age of five, when her mother's teaching of such skills had opened up a whole new world to her. Until fate had so cruelly wrenched her from all that she held dear, she had often found it preferable to escape within the pages of a book than to spend time in the company of friends. Then, as now, reading had provided a solace rarely found elsewhere.

So engrossed was she in the timeless—not to mention appropriate—story of Romeo and Juliet's tragic love, that she started in alarm when a knock sounded at the door. Her heart leapt within her breast and her eyes shone with anticipation, for she knew that it was Devlin who stood waiting in the narrow passageway. Scrambling off the bed, she set the book atop the desk and hurried across to the door.

When she opened it, her spirits plummeted. It was indeed the ship's dashing young captain who stood there, but the look on his handsome face was hard and the light in his eyes dull.

"I thought it might interest you to know we'll reach Charleston before dawn," he revealed quietly. In spite

123

of his resolve, his gaze traveled downward to rake over her damnably alluring curves before returning to her beautiful, softly flushed countenance. "Take whatever clothing you desire from the chest."

"I want nothing other than what I am wearing," she murmured, her words indicating the same pink silk gown she had worn ever since they had sailed from Nassau. Her eyes fell before Devlin's, so that she was unaware of the way his features softened for a moment before he hastily schooled them to an unyielding stoicism again.

"As you wish." Nodding wordlessly down at her, he started to turn away, then stopped and surprised himself by saying, "I'll do what I can to see that you are treated fairly by the authorities."

"Will you indeed?" Meghan retorted with bitter sarcasm, her eyes suddenly ablaze as they shot back up to his. "Pray, Mister Montague, do not concern yourself on my behalf! I'm quite sure I shall be able to convince at least one man among them of my innocence!"

"Why the bloody hell must you continue with this ridiculous charade of yours?" he ground out, provoking a sharp gasp from her lips as his hands seized hold of her arms. "Why not dispense with your lies and admit—"

"Because I have nothing to admit!" she adamantly proclaimed. She wrested herself free from his burning grasp and took several unsteady steps backward, her breasts rising and falling rapidly beneath the clinging silk while her blue-green eyes flashed in mingled pain and anger. "But what should any of it matter to you? You will be free of me come morning! Yes, you will be free of me and back in the arms of the haughty, beautiful Rosalie Hammond, a woman who will never love you the way—the way you—" She broke off and spun abruptly away, a heartbroken sob welling up deep within her as she once more envisioned him kissing his betrothed as he had kissed her.

"Who are you to speak to me of love?" Devlin challenged in a low, harsh tone brimming with fury. He closed the distance between them in two angry strides and forced her about to face him again. "What would you know of it?" he demanded, his eyes glinting savagely now. "I'll wager you've captured many a poor, unsuspecting fool in your web of deceit, bewitched them until they were ready to forget all else save holding that soft body of yours in their arms and tasting those sweet lips that promise your passion but hold back your soul!"

His fingers tightened upon the thinly covered flesh of her upper arms until she winced. She opened her mouth to speak, but no sound issued forth. Her eyes glistened with tears as they met Devlin's again, and she could have sworn that she beheld an answering pain in those fiery, midnight blue orbs before they narrowed vengefully down at her.

"Damn you, Meghan Kearny," he cursed her hoarsely, "you'll not count *me* among your victims!" Then, as if to prove his point, he caught her up forcefully against him and brought his lips crashing down upon hers.

Meghan's head spun dizzily, and she moaned softly as she pressed her supple curves even closer to his taut, lithely muscled hardness. She clung to him as though she were drowning and he the only means by which she could be saved, returning his fierce, wildly impassioned kiss with all the love in her heart. . . .

Without warning, it was over. Meghan found herself released as abruptly as she had been seized. Her eyelids fluttered open, offering her the distressing sight of Devlin's broad back turned toward her. She could only stand and watch in stunned disbelief while he strode from the cabin, leaving her alone and full of such utter misery that it was almost beyond bearing.

"Dear Lord, *why?*" she whispered brokenly. "Why did you let me love him when I may not have him?" There followed no divine enlightenment, no lessening of her anquish, and she told herself it was because she had been wicked enough to want a man who belonged to another.

It might have eased her pain, at least a little, if she had known of Devlin's.

Never in the entirety of his twenty-six years on earth had Devlin Montague desired a woman as strongly as he did the golden-haired young temptress aboard his ship. What troubled him the most, however, was the undeniable fact that his feelings for her went far beyond a mere physical attraction. He literally burned for her, whether asleep or awake, and thoughts of her filled his mind to such an extent that he found it difficult to concentrate on anything else. Worst of all, Rosalie's face had grown increasingly dimmer in his memory since this exasperating, tempestuous little vixen had come into his life, so that it was now scarcely more than a blur.

He knew he would never forget the look on Meghan's face when he had forced himself to leave her. Only by calling upon every ounce of iron will he possessed had he been able to tear his lips from the willing sweetness of hers and relinquish his possessive hold upon her pliant, beguilingly formed curves. Had he stayed, had he allowed the madness to go any further, he would have found it impossible to stop until he had made her his in the truest sense of the word.

And that, he told himself as he released a long, pent-up sigh into the gathering darkness of the seaswept night, would have been his downfall, for he knew with a certainty that, once he had possessed Meghan Kearny's body, *he would have demanded her soul as well. . . .*

Chapter Six

"Charlestown." Meghan repeated the name of her fateful destination aloud. Her wide, luminous gaze swept across the southern colonies' leading port city, its awakening prosperity illuminated by the soft, pinkish-orange rays of the rising sun. The *Pandora* was rapidly closing the distance, and Devlin was at the wheel to guide her past the town's natural defense against invasion by sea—a potentially treacherous sand bar at the busy harbor's entrance. He handled the task with ease, his eyes alight with determination as well as impatience to be home.

Meghan's own eyes, sparkling with curiosity, were drawn to a lighthouse standing its benevolent guard nearby, then back to where the city itself, situated on top of a narrow peninsula, lay snuggled between the Ashley and Cooper Rivers. Like Nassau, Charlestown's appearance was not what she had expected, but for vastly different reasons. She could not help but he awed by the sights unfolding before her fascinated gaze, if for no other reason than this was her first glimpse of the country governed by England but increasingly ruled by itself.

Shivering as a sudden gust of wind whipped across

the deck, she pressed closer to the railing and drew her cloak more securely about her. Her heart was heavy, and she felt drained, both physically and emotionally, as a result of the long, sleepless night she had spent—her last aboard Devlin's ship, she mused disconsolately. However, in spite of her unhappiness and apprehension at what was to come, she soon became engrossed in a critical scrutiny of the nearing city.

She was already aware of the fact that Charlestown's powerful economy had been founded on rice, indigo, and slavery—or "black ivory" as it was sometimes termed—and that it was reportedly home to the richest and most cosmopolitan people in all America. Several among her acquaintances back in London had kinsmen living within the city's boundaries, or along one of the many tidal creeks lacing the rather swampy peninsula. There were close ties to England in more ways than one, and many of the port's ten thousand residents were descended from the first British settlers who had founded Charles Towne, as it had initially been christened, nearly a hundred years earlier.

There was no denying that it presented a stirring view for the rest of the world, thought Meghan, her gaze traveling over the wooded green landscape dotted with an impressive array of homes, shops, churches, and warehouses of every conceivable size and composition and architectural style. A profusion of crowded wharves stretched out like long fingers into the harbor, where the blue waters were choked with sloops, brigantines, and schooners from abroad, as well as canoes and "pettiaugers"—relatively small boats that could be propelled in turn both by sails and oars—from the interior.

The holds of the outward-bound ships carried rice,

the prime export of the low country, along with a bountiful cargo of tar, lumber, pitch, tallow, tobacco, beef, pork, corn, and other such items that left the port town by way of thousands of barrels, tubs, bushels, casks, and boxes each year. The names of the vessels themselves indicated the owners' determined pursuit of wealth and status, and often their participation in the growing nationalism—*Enterprise, Success, Endeavor, Good Hope, Merchant's Adventure, Fair America*, and at least a dozen bearing the defiantly significant name *Liberty*. A faint smile touched Meghan's lips when one of these proudly independent ships went sailing past.

Her smile faded as the crew of the *Pandora* made ready to drop anchor. She turned to see Devlin striding toward her, and she felt a sudden lump rising in her throat at the same time a knot tightened painfully in her stomach. Until this moment, she had not really believed he would be so heartless as to condemn her to years of virtual slavery. She had not wanted to think he could let her go so easily. The reality of his intent hit her full force now, causing her face to pale and her eyes to fill with renewed anguish.

Devlin, cursing the sharp twinge in his own heart, paused before her and searched for the right words with which to tell her of his regret for what he was about to do. Finding none, he stared long and hard down into the solemn, upturned loveliness of her countenance. The misery in her eyes was clearly discernible, as was the pallor to her usually glowing skin, and his handsome features visibly tensed at the prospect before him. It struck him, not for the first time, that releasing her into someone else's custody was among the most difficult tasks he had ever faced.

But face it he must, he realized as his lips compressed into a tight, thin line and his eyes glinted with evidence of the iron will upon which he prided himself. His honor demanded it. Meghan Kearny was a bondswoman. By law, she belonged to someone else. No matter what his own personal feelings upon the matter, no matter how distasteful he found the entire system of selling one human being to another for a period of time determined by the very same men who stood to profit most—a system which necessity had forced even *him* to utilize—he must relinquish her into the hands of those who had arranged for her presence aboard the ill-fated servant ship.

Thus, without so much as a single word, he took her by the arm and began leading her toward the lowered gangplank. She was only dimly aware of the angrily sympathetic look on Malachi Flynn's craggy visage as she allowed herself to be led away without resistance. Peter Hobbs watched her go as well, and it was all the tenderhearted first mate could do to refrain from calling out to his captain to desist. A number of others among the crew of the *Pandora* appeared equally tempted, for the young golden-haired lass—true lady or not—had not won their begrudging admiration during the past two days at sea.

Devlin and Meghan stepped down onto the wharf, which was among the largest and boasted more than a dozen warehouses as well as a market. Making their way through the center of the dock's already bustling activity, they passed groups of men who were either engaged in the loading and unloading of ships, in spirited discussions of the price and actual worth of a cargo, or in heated conversation about something as mundane as whether or not there would be rain that afternoon.

There were people from every corner of the world to

be seen along Charlestown's waterfront—newly arrived slaves from the coast of West Africa; seamen from Barcelona, England, the West Indies, New York, Philadelphia, and other major ports wherein flowed a variety of goods from South Carolina; men, women, and children who, like Meghan, had been torn from their European homelands, transported to the colonies, and found their new destinies as "white slaves" in the households of wealthy plantation owners.

As in Nassau, a multitude of smells mingled together to form a somewhat overpowering odor that assailed Meghan's nose with a vengeance as she walked along in a daze beside Devlin. Combined with the tangy, ever-present scent of salt water were the distinctive aromas of recently cut lumber, strong spirits, horses, woodsmoke, tar and turpentine, cattle and poultry, and the food that was either being cooked or sold fresh at the markets situated amid the other buildings on the long wharves.

As she soon discovered, Charlestown's main waterfront thoroughfare was also called Bay Street, though it was a good deal wider and more prosperous-looking than Nassau's had been. She caught a glimpse of a wooden, hand-painted sign proclaiming a merchant's office as bearing the address of Number Twenty-eight Bay Street. Her eyes quickly left it behind, however, as Devlin urged her relentlessly onward with the firm pressure of his hand upon her arm.

He led her down yet another crowded wharf, until they came at last to the building which housed the shipping offices he sought. Meghan's heart filled with such trepidation that she instinctively hung back when Devlin swung open the door. He rounded on her with a look of such raw fury—a fury that was in truth directed at the situation and not at Meghan—that she immediately gathered her courage about her again and pulled free to sweep inside the building with her beautiful golden head held proudly erect.

"Wait here," commanded Devlin, his wonderfully deep-timbred voice brimming with a fierce emotion she could not name. She watched as he disappeared into an adjoining room, leaving her there in the dimly lit confines of the outer office with no other soul about, save for a brightly colored parrot who stared dispassionately back at her from within his gilded cage.

"We have much in common, you and I," she murmured to the bird, her mouth curving into a faint smile of bitter irony. There was a noticeable catch in her voice, and she closed her eyes tightly as a silent prayer for help rose within her mind.

For a fleeting moment, she was strongly tempted to turn and run. She was puzzled as to why Devlin had left her alone and unguarded. Surely he had known she would seize any opportunity to escape, had realized she would rather risk taking flight in a strange city again than submit to the sort of cruel enslavement fate had planned for her. . . .

They why haven't you done just that? that small, perennially intruding inner voice of hers demanded. *Why are you standing here as meekly as a lamb being led to the slaughter?*

"Why indeed?" she whispered, her eyes growing very round. She told herself she had been a fool to put her trust in Devlin Montague. In the innermost reaches of her heart, she had held fast to the hope that he would somehow manage to rescue her as he had done twice before. He had been the knight of her dreams, after all—both at the pirates' fortress on Andros and then again at the tavern in Nassau. And she, desperately in love with him as she was and would always be, had believed he would find a way to save her before it was too late. But it was too late *now*, she thought, and the only help she could count on was her own!

Her turquoise gaze sparkled with determination and the proud, dauntless spirit her beloved Irish father had bequeathed to her. She hesitated no longer. Gathering up her skirts, she flew back to the door. Her hand closed anxiously about the brass knob— and a familiar voice reached her startled ears.

"My thanks to you, Whitman." Devlin took the other man's hand in a firm grip and nodded curtly. "I'll have my solicitor contact yours without delay."

The man known as Whitman, a slender fellow with graying black hair, gave an answering nod and replied that he was glad he could be of assistance. His eyes strayed toward the young woman in question, and he was dismayed to feel a warm flush stealing over him at the sight of her unexpected beauty. Devlin Montague had told him only that the girl was young and in need of a kind master. Kind master indeed! he mused to himself, his heart filling with both admiration and wholly masculine envy directed toward the other man.

Meghan, after starting in guilty alarm at the first sound of Devlin's voice, whirled back around just in time to see him bearing down upon her with a strange, unfathomable expression on his handsome face. She raised a trembling hand to her throat and struggled to regain control of her sharply erratic breathing.

"You would not have gotten far," he assured her in a resonant undertone, his deep blue eyes aglow with wry amusement as he paused to tower above her. Meghan's cheeks flamed while her own eyes bridled with indignation.

"I would have," she stubbornly insisted, "if you had but tarried a moment longer!" Then, shooting a brief, resentful glance toward Whitman, who still stood watching her from the opposite side of the room, she asked Devlin in a slightly tremulous voice, "I suppose *that* is the man to whom I am now to be surrendered?" The pain she felt at this, the final moment of parting, threatened to make her fling herself upon his broad chest and beg for deliverance.

"It was," he answered with a strange light in his eyes.

"Was?" echoed Meghan in bewilderment. She was thrown into further confusion when he suddenly cast her a mocking half-smile. "What are you talking about? Am I not to be—"

"Come," he directed, taking hold of her arm again and opening the door. "There are several other matters requiring my attention."

"But . . . where are you taking me?" she asked weakly. Almost before she knew it, they were outside and on their way toward the end of the wharf. "I don't understand! Where are we going?"

"Back to the *Pandora* first, then home."

"Home?" She drew to an abrupt halt and wrenched her arm from his grasp. "Whose home?" she demanded, her voice rising on a shrill note.

"Mine, of course." His sun-kissed brow creasing into a frown, he reclaimed her arm and began propelling her impatiently forward with him again. "You belong to me now."

"To *you?*" she breathed in stunned disbelief, her wide, luminous eyes flying back up to his face.

"What do you mean?"

"Exactly what I said!" he snapped, his steely gaze darkening. "I purchased your contract from the owners of the *Bristol Packet*. You are now my legal property."

"Your *property?*"

"Damn it, woman, must you repeat everything I say?" he ground out. His own emotions were still in utter turmoil, and he wasn't at all certain what he was going to do with Meghan now that he had taken responsibility for her—a responsibility that was to last for the next three years, according to the terms of that blasted document of indenture he had just signed.

"No!" Meghan exclaimed with fiery-eyed vehemence, pulling at her arm again. "I cannot be any man's property, Devlin Montague, for I belong only to myself!"

Though her heart sang at the thought of being with him, her mind told her there could be no happiness in it. She would be little better than a slave to him. Rosalie Hammond would be his bride, but *she* would be his chattel. Once again, fate had dealt her a cruel blow—it had granted her the gift of Devlin's company, while at the same time ensuring that she could never take pleasure in it.

"Would you rather I had allowed Whitman to auction you off to the highest bidder?" Devlin challenged fiercely.

No, by damn, he mused while his teeth clenched, that was something he could never allow! When it had come right down to it, he hadn't been able to bear the thought of Meghan Kearny under another man's rule—*any* man's. He knew it was tempting fate to take her with him, but he had no choice. Although he could not deny she had proven an accursedly profound distraction to him these past few days, he told himself that things would be different once they were at Shadowmoss. There, he could take pains to make certain their paths crossed as little as possible, just as he would do everything in his power to resist any and all temptation to show her preference above his other servants.

And once he was married to Rosalie, he concluded with a grimness that was in sharp contrast to what one was *supposed* to feel when pondering such a happy event, there would be absolutely no question of his fidelity.

"I would rather you had bargained for my freedom!" Meghan's voice broke in on his turbulent reverie. Muttering a curse, he drew her quickly over to the only privacy available to them at the moment, a narrow alleyway between two warehouses. His hand finally relaxed its grip on her arm as he met her stormy gaze.

"That was never an option," he declared in a low, deceptively level tone. "Even if it were, do you think me fool enough to turn you loose in a strange land with naught but the clothes on your back?"

"But I needn't be in this strange land at all!" she retorted, the went on with conviction, "You could lend me the funds I require to book passage on a ship bound for England! As I've tried telling you before, my grandfather will gladly reimburse you for—"

"Blast you, Meghan!" he ruthlessly cut her off.

She gasped and instinctively retreated a step, for it appeared to her that he was sorely tempted to strike her. So acutely conscious was she of the savage gleam in his eyes, that she did not take note of the fact that this was the first time he had ever addressed her—or rather cursed her—by her given name alone.

"We will discuss this no further at present," he continued in a calmer manner, though his gaze smoldered still. "For now, the only thing you need know is that *I* am your master."

"Never!" she hotly denied, giving such an adamant shake of her head that her thick, lustrous curls were in peril of escaping their pins. Her eyes blazing with defiance as well as hurt, she told him, "In truth, Devlin Montague, I would have thought you different from the sort of men who deal in this barbaric practice of—of peddling human lives! But it seems you are no different at all! Very well then, I shall return to speak to this Mister Whitman myself! Perhaps *he* will prove sympathetic to my cause once I have explained the circumstances to him!" She turned to do just that, but found herself abruptly detained when Devlin's tall frame blocked her path.

"For the last time, *Mistress Kearny*, you are coming with me!" he decreed in a tight voice laced with undeniably menacing intent. "Either you do so under your own power, or I will damned well toss you over my shoulder and convey you there myself!"

For an instant, Meghan considered forcing the issue with further defiance, but then wisely decided that it would be far better to go with him than to risk suffering the ignominy of being carried all the way back to the *Pandora*. Besides, she consoled herself, she would have time to contemplate her next course of action later. Her mind was in a dizzying whirl as a result of all that had just transpired. There was so much to think about, the most important matter being how she was going to escape from Devlin Montague again.

Holding herself stiffly erect, and casting her "master" a look of spirited rebelliousness, she reluctantly

138

nodded her capitulation and set off down the wharf with him again. They returned to the ship, where Meghan was given over into the care of a much surprised Malachi Flynn. That done, Devlin took his leave with the announced intention of returning within the hour. Meghan's heart was heavy indeed as she watched him stride away, for she correctly surmised that he was going to search for his betrothed.

When he returned in even less time than he had calculated, his handsome countenance was inexplicably grim. It wasn't until much later that Meghan learned the reason why.

Tarrying at the *Pandora* just long enough to exchange a few words with Peter Hobbs, Devlin took his newly acquired servant to a waiting boat, one of the round-bottomed "pettiaugers" she had noticed earlier. His strong hands encircled her waist and swung her down into the keeled vessel as though she weighed no more than a babe. Then, lowering himself from the wharf to the boat as well, he pulled her down onto a wooden seat beside him and gave instructions to the young, able-bodied man who stood ready to cast off. Within moments, the three oarsmen were rowing the pettiauger across the bustling harbor to where the Ashley River led inland.

"Why are we traveling by boat?" asked Meghan. She was painfully conscious of Devlin's hard warmth close beside her, but she sternly cautioned herself to try and put such wicked—and forbidden—things from her mind.

"It's faster," he stated simply.

"Then your home is on the river?"

"Yes."

"How far is it?"

"Ten miles," he answered, obviously reluctant to

139

talk.

"Oh," she murmured, reflecting with an inward, dissatisfied sigh that such a great distance would make her efforts to escape all the more difficult. She turned her bright, troubled gaze upon the passing ships and other boats, then glanced overhead toward the cloud-dotted early morning sky. Her eyes traveled back to Devlin's inscrutable face, and she impulsively questioned, "Did you find Mistress Hammond well?"

"I did not find Mistress Hammond at all," he replied, his expression suddenly growing quite thunderous.

"You didn't?" Meghan echoed in wide-eyed astonishment. She felt a sharp pang of guilt for the pleasure his announcement gave her. Several long seconds passed, during which time she waited for him to elaborate, but he did not speak again. She finally grew impatient and demanded, "Well? Was she not ransomed after all?"

"Henceforth, Meghan Kearny, you will concern yourself only with things that truly *are* your concern!" he startled her by prescribing darkly. Then, to add to her surprise and confusion, he practically flung his muscular body to the seat behind hers, snatched up the only unmanned set of oars, and began rowing in cadence with the other men.

Meghan, not knowing what else to do, sat rigidly upright—no easy feat, considering the rocking motion of the boat—and fastened her own stormy, resentful gaze upon the sweeping blue horizon. Once the pettiauger had been maneuvered safely through the harbor, the sail was hoisted and Devlin exchanged places with the man occupying the seat immediately in front of Meghan's. She was then presented with the disturbing sight of his broad back and lean hips,

140

though she did her best to keep her eyes from straying in his direction. Her best, however, soon proved woefully insufficient. . . .

For what seemed to her like an eternity, they traveled up the river in silence, most of their journey shadowed by huge cypress and live oak trees that were dripping with thick, gray Spanish moss. The air was cool and sweet along the waterway, and Meghan inhaled deeply of the fresh scent of magnolias, sweetgrass, oleanders, and wisteria. More than once, she caught a glimpse of some of the homes lining the river's banks as the boat sliced through the slowly coursing waters, but her view was often obstructed by the same trees that prevented the sun's blazing warmth from making the trip uncomfortable.

Even at that early hour of the day, they passed half a dozen other vessels on the river—one of them a long barge whose stylish, city-bound passengers sat upon awninged seats in the stern; two of them "fall boats," which were used to float produce to town from the back country, and each boasting of a small cabin in the center; and three larger versions of the pettiauger in which Meghan rode. For this low-lying, semitropical region interlaced with navigable creeks and rivers, transportation of freight and people alike relied largely upon the abundant waterways.

They had traveled several miles from Charlestown when Meghan began to notice a significant change from the types of houses she had observed thus far. The simple, single-storied structures had now given way to immense, sprawling plantation homes that appeared much like palaces in some sort of wilderness fairyland.

Shrouded in the perennial Spanish moss and lovingly embowered by massive trees and cultivated gar-

141

dens, these princely colonial mansions faced the river that provided their main link to the outside world. From what Meghan was able to see, the architectural fashion of each house varied greatly, though the style followed most often appeared to be either Gothic Revival or Italianate. In that respect, she mused with a sudden twinge of homesickness, this land called South Carolina was not so different from England after all.

Finally, just when she was beginning to think the journey would never end, the pettiauger glided toward a large, noticeably well-constructed landing which jutted out into the river from amid a profusion of cattails and other bulrushes at the water's edge. As soon as the vessel was alongside the landing, one of the men jumped out to secure it with a rope, while the other two young boatmen remained seated and waited for Devlin to disembark.

He swung himself up onto the landing with practiced ease, then reached wordlessly down for Meghan. After only a moment's hesitation, she surrendered her hand to be clasped within the warm strength of his and felt herself being hauled swiftly upward. She was relieved when her feet came to rest on the weathered planks, for she had been sitting upon the hard bench so long that her backside was numb. Resisting the urge to smooth her fingers across her aching flesh as sensation returned with a vengeance, she allowed Devlin to lead her up the double-tiered steps of the river dock toward a wide, immaculately trimmed and cleared path winding through the trees.

The sun's rays, filtering down through the gently rustling leaves, lit Meghan's way with a patchwork of gold and green as she walked up the sloping rise in the land beside Devlin. He broke the silence between them at last, a silence he had imposed for reasons known only to himself.

"I have a sister," he unexpectedly revealed, his handsome features still quite solemn. His eyes glittered coldly down at her when he added, "Linette is very young and very impressionable. I'll not have you filling her head with wild tales of abductions and pirates and the like."

"Not even if they're true?" she retorted archly. *A sister*, her mind echoed. Strange, but it was difficult to imagine him as brother to anyone. . . .

"Especially if they're true!" he shot back. His fingers tensed about her arm, and he quickened the pace until she was hard pressed to keep up. Her blue-green eyes flashed with resentment at his purposely disobliging treatment of her.

"If you will but slow down, Mister Montague, mayhap you will not find it necessary to explain to your young and impressionable sister why your newly purchased *slave* has arrived in such obviously ill-used condition!"

"You are an indentured servant, Mistress Kearny—not a slave. And the blame for any ill usage you have suffered must be laid at your own blasted feet!"

"My own blasted feet are precisely what I am referring to!" she parried caustically, trying her best to hang back so that he would be prompted to slow his long, angry strides. Her efforts did not meet with success, however, and she was forced to practically run beside him. She winced now and then as her feet, inadequately protected as they were in nothing but flimsy leather slippers, flew over the uneven ground. Her gaze flinging invisible daggers at the man who blithely dragged her along with him, she reflected

143

that it was just like fate—which apparently bore a grudge against her—to make her lose her heart to such a scoundrel.

"How can you possibly say with any shred of good conscience," she indignantly challenged him in the next instant, "that I am to blame for the misfortune that has befallen me?" Her silken skirts were threatening to become tangled about her legs, while her hair finally broke free of its restraints to come tumbling riotously downward. "If I *were* to blame for having been captured by The Wolf, then would it not follow that Mistress Hammond is equally at fault? Yes indeed, she was a willing passenger aboard the *Bristol Packet,* and—"

"You are never to mention her name to me again, do you understand?" ground out Devlin, stopping so suddenly that she gasped and collided with his hard, implacable body. Her face flamed as he swore beneath his breath and roughly set her away from him. The light in his midnight blue eyes grew almost savage. "I had thought to give you some time to become accustomed to your new life, but I now see that a clear explication of your position in my household cannot wait!"

"And what, pray tell, might that *position* be?" Meghan demanded bitterly.

"You will remain under my jurisdiction for the next three years," he informed her with studied equanimity. "It is your duty to serve me well and faithfully during that time, in whatever capacity I desire. You will, in turn, be provided with food, drink, clothing, and shelter during the term of your service. You will *not,* under any circumstances, be allowed to assume a level of superiority above the other servants here at Shadowmoss, nor will you ever again speak of your

144

former life—whatever it was! In short, Meghan Kearny, you may do nothing without my consent, neither leave nor have any contact with outsiders *nor*, by damn, marry!" he finished in a voice brimming with raw, inexplicable fury. Meghan's own flaring temper, however, kept her from being intimidated.

"It is a cruel, unpardonable system of which you speak, Devlin Montague, and well you know it!" she avowed hotly. "But I shall find a means to get away from you! Sooner or later, justice will win out!"

"I'm quite certain it will," he surprised her by agreeing, his mouth turning up into the ghost of a smile. Meghan cast him a look of wide-eyed bemusement. She did not resist when he took her arm and began leading her up the path again.

It wasn't until they had reached the very summit of the hill that Meghan had her first view of Devlin's plantation—and what a view it was. She caught her breath at the sight, and her eyes, filing with awe, grew enormous within the delicate oval of her face. Never would she have expected to find such landscaped splendor in this young, upstart country. . . .

The main house itself, like the others she had glimpsed from the boat, stood facing the river. It was a magnificent, two-storied Palladian mansion built entirely of locally made brick, its marble pillars upholding a wide double portico. There were two flankers that had obviously been added later, and the entire, sprawling structure was surrounded by cultivated English gardens highlighted by well-trimmed hedges, aromatic rose beds, and brilliant oleander.

Her fascinated gaze made a broader sweep, taking note of the rice swamps and indigo fields, as well as the imposing expanse of open lawn which spread out over acres upon acres of land bordered by live oaks and tall pines. She could see a number of outbuildings, among them three large barns, the carriage house, the plantation stableyards, the spring house, and the sugar cane mill. There was also a smokehouse, a rice mill, a white clapboard house belonging to the overseer, a neat row of wooden slave cabins, and the servants' quarters, which lay a short walk from the main hall.

Amid the terraced lawn were also a number of small, ornamental lakes, where majestic swans glided peacefully through still waters. Intricate walks led through vast plantings of camellias, azaleas, roses, crepe myrtles, and magnolias. A flock of sheep could be seen grazing contentedly beside one of the lakes, while a number of bright-plumaged peacocks either strutted proudly about or sunned themselves on the low brick walls surrounding the greensward.

The whole effect was one of utter enchantment, and Meghan felt her heart stirring at the prospect of living in such a place—if only until the time when she managed to escape. She was scarcely even aware of the fact that Devlin was still leading her impatiently onward, since her attention was now drawn to the people in the near distance who were going about their work on the plantation.

She saw men and women alike, and even a few children, but what surprised her most was the sight of the black slaves toiling in the fields and at other locations throughout the grounds. The institution of slavery was not unknown to her—loving the written word as she did, she had read much about the barbaric practice—but she had somehow never connected it with Devlin Montague.

But then, she thought ruefully, *I was about and paid for just as they were.*

146

It was not yet known to her that the man she loved was an exception to the rule when it came to the plantation owners she had read about. For now, her mind told her he was no different or better . . . yet her heart told her he *must* be.

Several people, white and black alike, now came hastening forward to welcome home their young master. Meghan stole a look at Devlin's face, only to see that his grim, rugged features had actually relaxed into a smile. He acknowledged his workers' greetings and deftly waved aside their questions, saying merely that he would speak with them all later. They stared curiously at the beautiful albeit disheveled young woman at his side, and one man was heard to remark to another—in what he mistakenly believed to be an undertone—that if this was the young lady who was to be their new mistress, they'd better see what they could do about putting a little meat on her bones.

Meghan, hiding a soft smile of irony at what she'd overheard, swept the wayward golden tresses from her face and went along with Devlin toward the main house. They traveled up the wide front steps, where an older, liveried black man with salt-and-pepper hair spoke a quiet word of welcome from his position within the open doorway.

"It's good to see you back safely, Master Devlin," he said, then told Meghan, "Welcome to Shadow-moss, Mistress."

"Thank you," she replied with a tentative smile, while at the same time bitterly musing that it was hardly as a guest this man or anyone else would treat her once the truth was out.

Her eyes were suddenly drawn to the spot above the door where a carved pineapple had been hung. Unaware that this was the traditional symbol of hospitality in the Southern colonies, she cast it a slight frown of puzzlement before Devlin urged her forward again. Upon moving inside the spacious entrance foyer, he released her arm and turned back to their dignified greeter, who had closed the massive, elaborately framed oak door and now stood waiting for his master's instructions.

"Is my sister at home, Noah?" Devlin queried with a brief, obviously preoccupied smile.

"Yes, sir, the young mistress is upstairs."

"Then go at once if you please and tell her I am awaiting her presence in the drawing room."

"Yes, sir, Master Devlin."

"Oh, and Noah?" added Devlin at a sudden thought, his deep voice effectively detaining the man who had already turned away to do his bidding.

"Yes, sir?" Noah asked with an air of indulgent, oft-tried patience.

"Be so good as to caution her that if she is not in the drawing room within two minutes' time, I will bloody well come up and fetch her myself!" he decreed with a mock scowl of ferocity.

"Yes indeed, Master Devlin," agreed Noah, his own previously solemn features splitting into a broad grin. Meghan observed the look of unspoken understanding that passed between the two men. She was a bit taken aback by this amiable exchange, for she would not have thought it possible for a master and his slave to be on such good terms with one another.

Her bright turquoise gaze followed Noah as he obediently crossed to the staircase, which was without a doubt one of the most unique she had ever seen. Known as a "cantilever" or "free flying" staircase, it appeared to rise upward of its own volition, spiraling broadly roundabout as it reached—with no apparent

148

means of support—to the second floor.

"Come," Devlin bid quietly. He started to take her arm again, but apparently thought better of it. Settling instead for giving her a gentle nudge, by virtue of his hand at the small of her back, he directed her toward a pair of sliding wooden doors to the left of the entrance foyer.

Meghan looked curiously about as they went, noting with mild interest the gleaming heart-pine floor and expensive, raised cypress paneling. Her eyes happened to fall upon another unusual feature of the Montagues' stately mansion—a very large Flemish hall seat of rich mahogany with the artist's rather pixieish likeness carved right into one of the top posts.

"It's a hideous-looking thing, isn't it?" Devlin surprised her by remarking. Glancing up at his face, she saw that his gaze held a touch of wry amusement as it flickered briefly over the hall seat.

"Yes, I'm afraid it is," she murmured with an uneasy smile, then looked back to the offending object and confided, "It reminds me of those dreadful gargoyles which always stare so fiendishly down at one from atop great stone palaces." She did not see the way Devlin's lips twitched at her comparison, nor the way he quickly schooled his handsome features to impassivity once more.

They continued on their way into the drawing room, where Meghan's eyes surveyed the elegant surroundings at some length before she finally took a seat on a wing chair upholstered in a fine silk brocade. She gracefully settled her skirts about her as Devlin, crossing to a century-old walnut lowboy nestled in the opposite corner, proceeded to pour himself a glass of brandy.

Meghan watched him for a moment, then sighed inwardly and returned to her idle scrutiny of the cozy, sunlit room. Her eyes strayed continually back to Devlin, however, as they traveled about. Fielded paneling adorned the walls, the ceiling was high and beamed with naturally finished pine, and the stone fireplace featured an exquisite mantle of rare Italian marble. The furniture was beautifully appointed but not at all overpowering, while the pale yellow, floral damask draperies added considerably to the room's feeling of warmth and comfort. A handsomely detailed painting—which Meghan could tell possessed a good deal of age—in a gilded frame hung above the fireplace. Its subject were a young couple whose likeness to Devlin could not be denied, and she correctly surmised that the dark-haired man and auburn-haired woman were his parents.

"Oh Dev, you're back!" came the sound of a feminine voice from the doorway. While Meghan looked curiously on, a petite redhead in an apple-green gown went flying across the room to launch herself at Devlin.

"Am I indeed?" he quipped in a voice full of mingled pleasure and amusement, catching her up against him in a warmly affectionate embrace. The girl responded with a soft laugh and an enthusiastic kiss on the bronzed ruggedness of his cheek, before being set firmly away for a critical inspection at arm's length. "Have you been behaving yourself, you little termagent?" he demanded with a narrow, deceptively stern look down at her.

"No, dearest brother, I have *not!*" she retorted, then laughed again and added with an saucily unrepentant air, "You know how unbearable I become whenever you are not around!"

150

"I pity the poor, besotted fool who takes you to wife someday," he declared with another mock scowl. He gave her a little shake before releasing her, and his gaze met Meghan's. Appearing a trifle uncomfortable at the fact that she had witnessed the loving reunion with his sister, he frowned in earnest and reluctantly announced in a low voice edged with disgruntlement, "Linette, this is Meghan Kearny. Mistress Kearny, may I present my sister, Linette Montague."

Linette, having finally become aware of the other woman's presence shortly before her brother's curt introduction, subjected Meghan to a brief but nonetheless thorough scrutiny. Though a faint flush rose to her face, Meghan lifted her head proudly and made a swift visual examination of her own. What she saw was a very pretty young woman of perhaps seventeen, with lustrous, dark red curls and a figure that was slender yet beguilingly formed, as well as a creamy, flawless complexion. Her tightly laced *polonaise* gown bespoke impeccable taste and an expert dressmaker, while the light in her blue eyes, which were only a trifle less brilliantly hued then her brother's, gave evidence of her irrepressible, vivacious nature.

"Dev, you've done it, haven't you?" Linette suddenly exclaimed, her face lighting with inexplicable joy. She hurried to Meghan's side and slipped an arm warmly about her shoulders, then startled Devlin and Meghan alike with, "You have come to your senses at long last and found someone else to marry!"

"No, by damn, I have *not!*" Devlin hastened to deny in a tight voice. His gaze darkened as it raked across the wide-eyed loveliness of Meghan's countenance. Furiously dismayed to feel the wild leaping of his desire, he turned back to pour himself another stiff drink of brandy. "It so happens that Mistress

151

Kearny is a bondswoman," he revealed quietly.

"A bondswoman?" echoed Linette in surprise. Her eyes grew round as saucers as they shifted from Meghan to Devlin and back again.

"Your brother speaks the truth, Mistress Montague," confirmed Meghan with a bitter little smile. She rose to her feet and in so doing moved away from the now tensed pressure of the other woman's arm. "He speaks the truth, yet he will not allow me to do the same!" Her eyes flashed their magnificent blue-green fire in his direction. He retaliated with a smoldering look full of unmistakable warning.

"What do you mean?" Linette asked, her youthful brow creasing into a frown of bewilderment while she glanced back and forth at the two of them again.

"As can be expected, Mistress Kearny is not entirely happy with her situation," Devlin answered in a low and level tone. His gleaming, midnight blue eyes silently dared Meghan to elaborate, just as they promised dire retribution if she was foolish enough to do so. "But she will soon learn to accept it."

"Yes, of course," murmured Linette, appearing decidedly ill-at-ease. The air was heavy with tension, and she could well see that there was something not quite right between her brother and the young woman who stood so proudly defiant before him. Not knowing what else to do, she smiled weakly at Meghan and offered, "If you will please come with me, Mistress Kearny, I will take you out to the kitchen. You must be tired and hungry after the journey, and I daresay Jolene, our cook, would be happy to make your acquaintance. Perhaps my brother means for you to be her new assistant?" she finished with an inquisitively arched eyebrow at Devlin.

"I have not yet decided what Mistress Kearny's duties will be." Downing the last of his brandy, he lowered the snifter back to the surface of the lowboy with a trifle more force than was necessary. He did not look Meghan's way again before his sister led her from the room.

When Linette returned a few minutes later, it was only to find him staring out the window with a noticeable air of preoccupation. He took no note of her presence until she spoke and thereby forced him from his troubled thoughts.

"Devlin Montague, how could you?" she demanded indignantly, her eyes full of sisterly reproach. "How *could* you bring that poor girl all the way from Charlestown and then behave as though she were of no more importance than one of your blessed horses?"

"Because, blast it, she isn't!" he ground out, wheeling abruptly about to confront her. "She is an indentured servant, Linette, a woman who indeed means nothing more to me than whatever value I am willing to place upon her!"

"Why, that—that's the most ridiculous thing I have ever heard you say! You, of all people, dare to stand there and insist that the worth of a fellow human being is to be determined by you and not by God above . . ." Her voice trailed away as she searched for adequate words with which to describe her outrage. She apparently found them, for she continued in the next instant, "You never used to be so pigheaded and mean-spirited!"

"On the contrary, my dear sister," he dissented with a mocking smile, "you have termed me 'pigheaded' on a number of occasions."

"That still leaves mean-spirited!" she obligingly pointed out. "And since when have you found it nec-

153

essary to indulge in such questionable 'purchases'? Why, you know as well as I that we already have more than enough household servants, and—"

"Do not press me for an explanation, Linette, for I will not offer it. Suffice it to say that Mistress Kearny is here because I wish it. She will remain in our employ for the next three years, so I would advise you to refrain from befriending her to such an extent that you forget she is naught but a servant."

"*I* am not the one in danger of forgetting it!" she countered with a significant, smugly challenging expression. She then found herself the recipient of a scorching glare from those fiery blue orbs that were so much like her own.

"Just what the devil do you mean by that?"

"Come now, brother mine, do you really think me so naive as to believe you brought her here for no other reason than to wash our clothes and fluff our pillows? She is young and beautiful, is she not? I daresay you were swept away by her charms the moment you set eyes upon her, and you thereupon decided you must be her master, no matter what the consequences!" she concluded with a dramatic sigh.

"I ought to take you over my knee for that!" growled Devlin, his eyes gleaming dangerously.

"Why? Because I know you better than you know yourself?" Linette retorted with a superior little smile. Heaving another sigh, she placed a conciliatory hand upon her brother's arm and gazed earnestly up at him. " I would be the last one to call you to task for wanting whatever is your heart's desire, but you know it cannot be. Even if you were not betrothed to Rosalie, Mistress Kearny is exactly what you said—a bondswoman. She is not the sort of woman a man in your position marries, nor do I think her the sort to

154

grace your bed with no thought to her own circumstances."

She was startled when he suddenly threw his head back and laughed. Perceiving his amusement to be at her expense, she bristled and demanded, "What, pray tell, do you find so humorous?"

"You," he stated simply. "On the one hand you roundly berate me for declaring her to be my property, while on the other you tell me I cannot have her because she is precisely *that!*"

"You may well laugh about it now," Linette observed with sobering candor, "but how do you think Rosalie Hammond is going to react to the news of our beautiful new servant? I doubt very seriously if she will find this particular matter to be in the least bit humorous!"

She watched as Devlin brushed past her and crossed to the walnut lowboy again. Never given to excessive drinking before, he now appeared determined to obliterate his troubles with the aid of brandy. His devoted sister, however, was equally determined that he should face up to them. Her skirts rustled softly as she moved to his side, and her auburn curls danced about her head when she nodded down at the crystal decanter in his hand and said, "That is not the solution, and well you know it! Now tell me, Dev, what are you planning to say to Rosalie?"

"Do you realize, Linette, that you've not yet asked me if I was able to find my beloved and bring her back?" he noted, the ghost of a smile playing about his lips while his eyes glowed dully.

"Well, for heaven's sake, I naturally assumed you had!"

"You assumed incorrectly."

155

"What? Do you mean to say she is still in the clutches of those bloodthirsty cutthroats who attacked her ship?" For a moment, her mind filled with wicked pleasure at the thought of Rosalie Hammond as the slave of some evil, foul-smelling pirate king.

"No, but my mission to rescue her was a failure." He downed the glass of brandy with amazing swiftness before revealing, "Her ransom had already been arranged by the time I arrived in Nassau. There was nothing left for me to do but sail homeward and pray that the transfer had gone smoothly."

"And did it?"

"It did. Rosalie is now safely ensconced in the loving bosom of her family." There was a discernible note of bitterness in his voice, and Linette frowned at the way his features suddenly tightened.

"Then what is troubling you? Surely after you spoke with Rosalie and saw for yourself that—"

"I have not spoken to Rosalie Hammond since the day she sailed for England." He reached for the decanter again, only to release it with a muttered curse and stride back to the window. Linette followed closely on his heels, anxiously waiting for him to tell her the rest. When he did, her own emotions grew turbulent.

"I called at their house in the city as soon as the *Pandora* docked this morning. It was not Rosalie who met me at the door, but Jonas Hammond, who kindly informed me that his daughter was much too overcome by her ordeal to see anyone—least of all me! He went on to declare that he holds me fully responsible for all her misfortune, that it was because of me she was driven to England in the first place, and that if I had been anything other than a selfish bastard I would have begged her forgiveness before it was too

156

late!''

"Why, that hateful, pompous, loathsome old bag of wind!" Linette declared, outraged that anyone would be so cruel to her brother. That it was the father of her future, unwanted sister-in-law only made her sense of indignation run that much deeper. "It is through no fault of yours that she was captured by pirates! How could you have known a simple lovers' quarrel would turn out to have such disastrous consequences? *Oh!* I only hope this malicious behavior leads you to realize once and for all that his daughter is not the woman—"

"Don't say it, Linette," Devlin cautioned in a low, resonant tone that prompted her to fall silent and swallow hard. She knew just how far she could push him—and the limit had been reached. "Whatever has happened, whatever will happen from this day forward, Rosalie Hammond *shall* be my wife."

"That may well be," Linette begrudgingly allowed, then pointed out with incorrigible temerity, "but you have still not addressed the matter of Meghan Kearny!"

"Nor will I. Not to you, my dearest sister, and damned well not to anyone else!" he vowed tersely, his expression growing thunderous once more. "What I do is my own affair, and I'll not answer to any man—or *woman*—on the face of this earth!"

Without another word, he strode from the room, leaving his "young and impressionable" sister to stare after him in stunned, breathless confusion. She heard the front door open and close, and after that the sound of Devlin's wonderfully deep voice, taut with anger, calling out to one of the men to saddle his horse.

Linette Montague released a long, pent-up sigh

and wandered slowly over to the fireplace. Raising a hand to the cool slab of marble above it, she stared wistfully up at the painting of her parents.

"Our Dev has made an unholy muddle of things, hasn't he?" she murmured. She peered closely at their faces for several moments longer, before whirling about with renewed determination. "Then I must see what I can do about putting them to rights again!" she declared aloud, her steps leading her back to the window.

She watched as her brother set off across the grounds on horseback, riding like the very wind. Recalling fondly that Devlin had always ridden to cool his temper or settle his mind whenever something was troubling him, she turned away again and cast one last glance up at the painting. Then, humming softly to herself, she strolled from the room.

Mistress Meghan Kearny might just hold the key after all, she reflected as she made straightaway for the kitchen. She would have been much satisfied if she had known the accuracy of her speculation, just as she would have been greatly surprised to discover that her brother's present thoughts followed a course very similar to her own. . . .

Chapter Seven

Meghan's first day at Shadowmoss proved long and difficult for her, though not because of either the nature or amount of work she was given to do. In truth, Linette Montague had gone out of her way to make things easy for her brother's "protegé," issuing strict orders that the new servant was to be treated with kindness and leniency. Jolene, the middle-aged woman who had served as the Montagues' cook for a number of years, was only too happy to comply with her young mistress's wishes, for she remembered all too well what it had felt like to take her place in a strange household.

As Meghan soon learned, there were five women and one man working in the main hall. The women, four of whom were black and not much above the age of twenty, served in the capacity of housemaids and cook's helpers. Noah was the lone male, and he had been with the Montagues for the greater part of his life. Jolene, who along with her family had emigrated to South Carolina from northern Europe when she was but a young child, had first come to Shadowmoss as the bride of a man hired to tend the late master's impressive herd of thoroughbred horses. Widowed within three years, she had remained to serve the family as both cook and housekeeper.

She was a good-natured woman of forty, with thick brown hair and green eyes that held a perennial sparkle. Most cooks were usually given to plumpness, but not so Jolene. She was slightly above medium height, and her figure, though undeniably well-rounded, still retained its youthful appeal. Meghan warmed to the cook immediately—so much so that, in spite of her inner turmoil, she found herself consuming a generous portion of the dish the woman told her was called "hopping John." A combination of rice, cow peas, and ham, it was seasoned with a good deal of pepper and served piping hot. To Meghan, who had eaten little else but bread and cheese for the past several days, the food tasted almost like manna from heaven.

The person to blame for her disquiet throughout the day was, naturally enough, her new master. She did not see him again until much later; nor did anyone mention him to her. In fact, it seemed that her fellow servants displayed a remarkable lack of curiosity, but she was honestly glad for it, as the last thing she wanted was to be subjected to a barrage of embarrassing questions concerning how she came to be Devlin Montague's indentured servant. She knew no one would believe the truth, just as she knew she would risk suffering Devlin's wrath if she dared to proclaim it.

As soon as she had finished her meal in the separate kitchen, one of the housemaids, a pleasant and almond-eyed young woman by the name of Naomi who wore a crisp white apron over her dark blue cotton dress, appeared and announced that she would show Meghan to her room. The servants' quarters were located a short distance away from the main house down a tree-shaded stone path, and the two women walked along in silence while the sounds of men's voices and children's laughter drifted on the wind about them.

Naomi led Meghan into a small but comfortably furnished room at the far end of the rectangular, gambrel-roofed brick building. Lace curtains hung at the single window, while the narrow bed was covered with a handsewn coverlet of multicolored fabric squares. "Floor cloths" of coarsely woven, stencil-painted wool lay scattered about the bare wooden floor, a washstand and attached mirror stood in one corner, and a nice touch had been added to the floral-papered walls by way of several framed pieces of embroidery, each one a sampler featuring a few choice lines of scripture embellished with fancy borders.

"This room used to belong to the woman who taught school here on the plantation, but she's been gone for a long time now. She married herself a farmer," Naomi disclosed with a small note of envy in her voice. She heaved a sigh and confessed, "I've got it in mind to marry a man who works in the stables, but he says he hasn't the time for a wife."

Before Meghan could reply, the young housemaid frowned and turned her attention to another subject.

"It's forbidden to ever have a man in your room, and there's to be no sashaying about in the altogether unless the shade's been pulled and the curtains drawn. We're allowed a tub bath three times a week, which is twice more than most folks get, and we're required to go to church every Sunday. Saturdays are ours to do with as we please—after breakfast, that is—and we'll be celebrating the spring harvest soon with a big feast and a lot of dancing. It's lucky you came this time of year."

"Yes, I suppose it is," Meghan agreed quietly, though her blue-green eyes were brimming with ironic amusement. It occurred to her that, if all went as she hoped, she would be well away from Shadowmoss before the harvest even began.

"Well then, since Mistress Linette said you were to rest for a while, I'll leave you alone. We follow the usual custom of dinner at three o'clock, and you'll be expected to—"

"Three o'clock?" echoed Meghan in disbelief. Why, in London, she recalled silently, they had seldom dined before nine o'clock in the evening!

"That's right," Naomi confirmed amiably. "And as I was saying, you'll be expected to help with the food as well as seeing that it stays hot when you take it in."

"You mean I shall actually be serving at Dev—at the Montagues' table?"

"Of course." The young housemaid eyed her dubiously for a moment. "Haven't you ever served before?"

"No, I . . . I'm afraid I haven't." She had certainly never expected to learn, either—especially not with Devlin Montague's eyes upon her!

" 'Tis likely you'll learn with no trouble," Naomi assured her with a smile. "All you have to remember is that you stand to the left, you hold the tray steady, and you must never move away until you're certain they've taken all they wish."

Smiling again, the woman took her leave and returned to the house. Meghan closed the door of her new living quarters and sank wearily down upon the bed. Her turquoise gaze, clouding with a number of emotions, absently swept the confines of the room before drifting to the window. She stood bolt upright to her feet again as a sudden thought took flight and deepened into a resolution.

Tonight, she decided, her heart pounding and her lips compressing into a tight, thin line of determina-

162

tion. *I must get away this very night!*

There was no sense in postponing the escape, she told herself, for nothing but more heartache could come of it. She could not bear the prospect of remaining so much as a single day longer in Devlin's company; she realized that now. Living there at his home, seeing him and yet not being able to speak to him, watching helplessly while he married another woman . . . no, all those things would prove intolerable for her.

Hot tears stung her eyes as a sharp pain twisted like a knife deep within her. Torn between the desire to be with the man she loved no matter what the cost, and the instinctive need to prevent her own undoing, she knew she really had no choice.

"Tonight," she whispered. A plan would have to be devised, a plan that would ensure she was able to return to the city, and she would have to find a means of getting aboard a ship once she made her way to the waterfront. She had been prepared to stow away in Nassau; she would do exactly that in Charlestown if the need arose. Somehow, she would succeed!

Feeling exhausted as the effects of the morning's startling events—particularly the long journey up the river—descended on her full force, she sighed and lay back down upon the bed. Her eyes swept closed. She soon drifted away into merciful unconsciousness, oblivious to the sounds of the plantation, to the sunlight spilling into the room . . . and to the tall, grim-faced master of Shadowmoss who paused briefly outside her window before striding away with her unspoken name on his lips.

She was awakened sometime later by Naomi, who brought her a dress and apron, new shoes and under-

163

things, as well as a kettle of hot water for washing. Once she was alone again, Meghan hurried to bathe and change. She was glad to discard her borrowed silk gown. The image of its owner's face rose up to taunt her as she drew it off, thereby prompting her to crumple it into a ball and toss it to the floor with a vengeance. Though she scolded herself for such childish behavior, she could not deny that it had given her some small measure of satisfaction, and her mouth curved into an unrepentant smile as she hastily stripped off the rest of her clothing.

Pouring the hot water into the washbowl, and taking up a cake of lavender-scented soap, she scrubbed at every inch of her skin until it was pink and glowing. She rinsed as best she could and then, wishing she could wash her hair but realizing it would have to wait, she dried herself with a length of fluffy cotton toweling and set about getting dressed.

She donned the clean chemise and petticoat, then the gown that was like those worn by the other female servants, with the exception of Jolene. Although it was simple and relatively unadorned, the dress of soft blue cotton was nonetheless fashionable. The laced bodice was tight and long-waisted, coming to a point in front, the skirt was very full, and the neckline was low and squared across the bosom. She had been provided with a bit of ruffled lace to tuck across the décolletage, while a starched white apron covered the front of the gown from just below the top edge of the bodice all the way down to the skirt's hemline.

Completing the ensemble were a pair of sturdy, square-heeled shoes that were almost a perfect fit, black cotton stockings gartered at the knee, and a ruffle-edged white cap that she settled atop her thick mass of hair, which she had pinned up in a rather severe manner softened by a few loose tendrils curling over her ears.

Casting a critical eye upon her reflection in the washstand mirror, she mused that she looked very much like the young women who had served in her grandparents' household. Gone was the elegant young lady who had not so long ago been the toast of the London season, and in her place stood a prim serving girl. Oh well, she told herself, at least the costume was of good quality, and it would prove very useful indeed for the long voyage home to England, as it would in all likelihood be her *only* wardrobe during that time.

Her mind racing to formulate a plan for the night's adventure, she swept from the room and headed back to the kitchen house nestled within the shadow of the main hall. A covered walkway, or "dog run," connected the two buildings, which were separated owing not only to the threat of fire, but also to prevent the heat and smoke from the cookfire—kept burning day and night—from filling the rooms occupied by the master and his family.

The warmth and delectable aromas came forth to greet Meghan as she stepped through the kitchen's open doorway. Jolene was bustling about to prepare the meal, while Naomi and another of the housemaids sat at the worktable in the very center of the room, peeling the sweet potatoes which had already been boiled. These would be mashed with milk, cream, eggs, and butter, then flavored with cinnamon and sugar to make a baked custard called a *gâteau-patate*. Smoke rose from a silver platter laden with smoked ham and rice croquettes that sat waiting atop another table nearby, and the cook was just putting the finishing touches on a fruitcake flavored with plenty of rum.

"Meghan, would you please take the ham and rice

165

to the dining room?" asked Jolene with a quick smile in her direction. "The soup has already been served, and Master Devlin will be wanting what he calls 'real food' soon enough!"

"Of course," replied Meghan, though she was sorely tempted to whirl about and race back to the safety of her room. A knot tightened in her stomach at the thought of seeing Devlin again, just as her heart twisted painfully at the realization that it would be the last time. *The last time.*

Moving on legs that seemed unduly heavy, she crossed to fetch the platter, then headed off through the narrow passage leading to the main house. It didn't occur to her until she was inside that she hadn't the faintest idea where the dining room was located, but she found it readily enough when the familiar sound of Devlin's voice drifted out into the hallway—as though beckoning her to her doom, she mused ruefully.

He was sitting with his back to the doorway, so that the first indication he had of her arrival came from Linette. The animated young redhead occupied the seat to his immediate right, and she was in the process of relating to him the whimsical tale of her dearest friend Sally's attachment for the new schoolmaster Sally's father had brought back from a recent trip to the city—when Meghan came marching into the spacious, luxuriously furnished confines of the chandelier-lit room with her head proudly erect and her hands betraying her only a little as they sought to keep the platter steady.

Linette stopped talking in midsentence, prompting her brother to cast her a mild frown of puzzlement. Although the topic of her discourse had been of admittedly dubious interest to him, he had nonetheless lent it half an ear. He took note of the sudden widening of his sister's eyes, and of the way they literally danced with mischief. It was a look he knew all too well.

"Good afternoon, Mistress Kearny. I trust your first day here at Shadowmoss has not proven too difficult for you?" Linette queried with a purposeful, congenial smile at Meghan. Her irrepressibly twinkling gaze traveled back to light upon her brother. Closely studying his reaction, she was delighted to view the way his beloved features tensed. She also discerned a slight narrowing of his eyes, which had now filled with a strangely intense, unfathomable light.

"No," Meghan answered in a low tone that was scarcely audible, then forced herself to add, "Thank you." She set the silver platter atop an elaborately carved, wheeled serving cart she spied near the table. Pleased to find that Jolene had thoughtfully placed the ham and rice on separate china plates, she took up the first of them and balanced it on the palm of one hand as she had seen done before.

She could feel Devlin's eyes upon her. In spite of her love for him, it stung her pride that she should have to wait on him like any other servant. They were more than just strangers, she reflected with a touch of righteous indignation. By all that was holy, she had very nearly *given* herself to him the night they had sailed from Nassau! That he had apparently found it so easy to dismiss her from his mind, to relegate her to an equal status with his other slaves . . . it made her all the more determined to escape. Not for the first time, she took refuge in her anger. It did not help ease the pain in her heart, but it did allow her to face him without shattering into a thousand pieces.

She moved wordlessly to Linette's side and presented the plate of smoked ham with an expertise that would make one think she had done it all her life. Her flashing gaze traveled with a will of its own to Devlin, and she caught her breath at what she saw.

His manner of clothing was quite different from what he had worn these past few days. The dashing sea captain had been replaced by a wealthy colonial planter. His face looked particularly bronzed and rugged above the plain white neckcloth of his Holland linen shirt. He had chosen a single-breasted, black frock coat that was at the same time elegant and unpretentious, with tight black breeches fastened just below the knee, and a deep red satin waistcoat—a sleeveless garment that was little more than a vest— providing the only bright touch to his otherwise somber attire. Instead of the usual buckle-fastening shoes affected by others of his class, he wore top boots of polished black leather.

To Meghan, he had never appeared more devastatingly handsome. She felt a warm flush stealing over her, and tried to avoid meeting his eyes. She could not. Once again, her gaze was drawn compellingly to his.

Devlin stared back at her with seeming indifference. His magnificent blue eyes, however, smoldered with raw passion, just as she had seen them do that night on board the *Pandora*. Her blood suddenly raced like liquid fire through her veins, and a delicious shiver ran the length of her spine. . . .

"Merciful heavens!" breathed Linette.

Blushing guiltily, Meghan tore her eyes away from Devlin. She looked down to find that she had unknowingly tipped the plate of ham to one side and thereby sent its entire contents sliding into the young redhead's satin-covered lap.

"Oh, I—I'm so sorry!" Meghan apologized in breathless mortification, hurriedly scooping the ham back onto the plate. She was startled to hear the sound of the other woman's soft laughter, and she straightened to peer down at Linette in wide-eyed bafflement.

"That's quite all right, Mistress Kearny!" Devlin's sister hastened to assure her. Her eyes alight with mischievous good humor, she merely repositioned her linen damask napkin across the front of her skirts and said, "This is certainly not the first time someone in this house has been involved in an unfortunate tangle with their food—nor I wager, will it be the last!" She looked to Devlin now and smiled archly. "Why, my own dear brother once nearly fought a duel with one of our most distinguished guests over a handful of buttered grits, didn't you, Dev?"

"Did I? I don't recall," he lied smoothly, reaching for his goblet of wine.

"Why, of course you do!" insisted Linette. Her sparkling gaze moved back to Meghan. "It was during one of those dreadful political meetings, or rather during the adjournment they had called for cooling tempers, and Dev had brought all of the participants here to the dining room for coffee and refreshments. Anyway, one of the men happened to be Sir Harry Longmont, who was an older and notoriously ill-tempered member of the Council, and Sir Harry had expressed a desire for a plate of Jolene's buttered grits. They were brought straightaway, by Jolene herself, and it was only a short time afterward that I entered the room to pay my respects to the gentlemen." She paused here and cast a meaningful glance toward a strangely silent Devlin before returning to her subject.

"Sir Harry was seated at the opposite end of the table from my brother," she went on to explain, "eating those accursed grits, when the two of them suddenly took to exchanging heated words about something—I never did understand exactly what it was. The room was so noisy, you see, what with all those men arguing and 'discussing' at the same time. Well, before anyone could guess what would happen, Dev and Sir Harry had both shot to their feet.

"Dev reached the other end of the table before Sir Harry could travel far beyond his chair. A sudden hush fell over the assembly when Sir Harry gave my brother a violent shove, causing him to take such an abrupt step backward that he came up hard against the table. The plate of grits, unfortunately, went toppling right down onto Sir Harry's shoes. That ridiculous man got all in an uproar at that point, bellowing that Dev—*Dev*, mind you—would be made to pay for his clumsiness. Then, without warning, he dealt my brother a stinging blow across the face!"

Meghan, trying not to look at Devlin, waited in silence for Linette to continue. She mused inwardly that it felt strange to be listening to a bit of personal reminiscence about the man who had revealed so little of himself to her, the same man who now sat with his piercing blue gaze fixed with unwavering intensity on the half-empty goblet in his hand.

"What followed was a remarkable display of hospitality triumphing over impulse, I can assure you!" declared Linette, obviously taking great delight in the telling. "Dev didn't move so much as a muscle for the longest time, until Sir Harry actually had the audacity to lay hands on him again! I'm sure everyone in the room thought the infamous Montague temper would explode, but it did not."

"In quite the calmest manner I have ever seen, my dear brother simply strolled over to ring for Jolene to bring another plate of grits. Then, with a rather odd little smile, he turned to the startled assembly and announced that it was time they resumed the meeting. Sir Harry hadn't the courage to do anything else, especially since most everyone had broken into laughter by that time. He beat a hasty retreat, poor man, and we've not had the pleasure of his company here at Shadowmoss since that day!" she finished at last, tossing a supremely smug look toward her brother. "Dev has never been known for backing away from a fight. There was little doubt in anyone's mind that he could have very well beaten that nasty old Sir Harry to a veritable pulp, and yet he chose to exercise the most amazing self-control. Self-control can be a wonderful virtue to possess, don't you think so, Mistress Kearny?" she queried, her eyes still brimming with a significant liveliness.

"That it can, Mistress Montague," replied Meghan. An involuntary smile tugged at her lips, but it quickly faded when she sensed Devlin's penetrating gaze upon her again. She stiffened and started to turn away from the table, murmuring, "I shall inform Jolene we'll be needed more ham."

"More ham? Nonsense!" pronounced Linette. She gave a vigorous shake of her head that sent her titian curls bouncing, then took up her fork and stabbed a large piece of the meat to convey to her plate. "I can assure you my gown has not tainted it in the least!"

"Perhaps not, but it has in all probability grown stone-cold by now," Devlin opined dryly, referring to the length of her narrative. He was rewarded with a playful, haughty look of sisterly defiance. Linette remained the focus of his attention for only a fleeting moment, as Meghan had arrived at his side by then with the plate of ham.

He cursed the way his eyes strayed to the beguiling curve of her breasts when she bent ever so slightly forward to enable him to take what he wanted. It would have both pleased and distressed her to know that *she* was what he wanted. He gave no outward indication of his desire, however, as he forced himself to select a generous portion of the ham. Meghan accidentally brushed up against his arm when she drew the plate back, and the contact, though brief, sent a current of sensation pulsing through them both. She drew in her breath upon a soft gasp and felt hot color stain her cheeks, while he groaned inwardly and clenched his fingers about the knife he had just taken up.

None of this was lost on Linette. She was an avid witness to the scene, smiling to herself when she watched Meghan spin hastily away from the table and Devlin attack his ham with a knife and fork as though it were still alive. Her blue eyes glimmered with secret satisfaction, and she told herself that her initial assessment of the situation had not been so far off the mark after all. There *was* something between Devlin and the beautiful young bondswoman, and she was going to find out exactly what it was! Mayhap it was something that would eventually help rid their lives of Rosalie Hammond . . . if so, she silently vowed with all the heartfelt conviction of her youth, she would do everything in her power to encourage it!

Meghan was relieved to be able to escape soon thereafter. She hurried back through the house and along the passageway, arriving in the kitchen out of breath and with her color much heightened. Naomi and the other young housemaid were mercifully absent by now, which left only Jolene to stare at her in surprise and demand with a frown of genuine concern,

"What is it, Meghan? What on earth has happened?"

"Nothing," lied Meghan, though not very convincingly. She quickly managed to regain her composure, but there was nothing she could do about the telltale, rosy flush tinting her countenance. "I—I'm afraid I wasn't very good at serving," she offered lamely.

"Oh, is that what's bothering you? Well then, there's no need!" the cook sought to reassure her. She motioned Meghan toward the worktable and sank down into one of the banister-back chairs with a seat woven of split hickory. Meghan did the same.

"Land's sake, child," said Jolene with an indulgent smile, "no one here expects you to perform your duties to perfection the very first day, least of all Master Devlin and Mistress Linette. You may trust me when I say they are without a doubt the most pleasantly natured employers one could ever wish for."

"But I am not an employee," Meghan pointed out. She heaved a sigh, her silken brow creasing into a frown and her eyes filling with minged hurt and confusion. "I am an indentured servant—a *white slave!* My life will not be my own again until three years have passed. By then, my grandparents will have given me up for dead, and I will have become naught but a faded memory to my friends, and I daresay even my cat will have forgotten me!"

"I've no wish to pry, my dear," the older woman declared gently, "but is it possible that you are in some sort of trouble?"

"Indeed, it is more than possible!" confirmed Meghan with a soft laugh of irony. "Though, to tell the truth, my trouble is not with the people back home in England, but rather with—"

She broke off as though she had already said too much, leaving Jolene to stare inquisitively across at her. Meghan was tempted to pour out the whole truth to this kind woman, but she sensed that it would avail her nothing. It was obvious that the cook was fiercely loyal to Devlin, and as such would never consider aiding in the escape of one of his slaves.

"I'm sorry, Jolene," she apologized, her eyes shining earnestly, "but I do not think it wise of me to burden you with my problems." She forced another smile to her lips before adding, "I'm sure you have enough of your own. As a matter of fact, it cannot be easy preparing all of the meals while at the same time overseeing a house this large. You must go to bed exhausted every night."

"Many a night I do," the other woman admitted with a laugh of her own. She rose to her feet and hurried across to the brick oven to check on the progress of her baked custard. "But this life and I have been accustomed to one another. It was God's own gift to me when my husband died. 'Tis no secret around here that I nearly went out of my mind with grief. If it had not been for my work, as well as the kindness of the Montagues, I would very likely have fallen into hard and fast ways. Instead, I am well and happy, and not too lonely—leastways not when the pastor comes to call."

"The pastor?" echoed Meghan, then glimpsed the faint blush which rose to the cook's attractive face. "Oh, I see," she murmured. She could not help feeling a twinge of envy, for her own heart had been lost to a man who must never know it.

"Mind you, he is not yet aware that I will be his wife, but *I* am!" Jolene drew the custard from the oven and slid it inside the warming shelf. When she turned back to Meghan, her eyes had grown soft and full of a wisdom only life can give. "It is not easy for a woman to find a men who will love her as she wants to be loved, which is all the more reason she should tread lightly until he comes around to her way of thinking."

"And what if she does not 'tread lightly'?" Meghan could not refrain from asking.

"Then she might as well prepare herself for defeat. Men as a rule do not marry the sort of woman who value themselves too cheaply. From what I've seen, it's the thrill of the chase that ensures the chance of a woman's success!"

The thrill of the chase, Meghan repeated inwardly. Was that why Devlin Montague had found it so easy to pretend she was another that night aboard his ship, because she had been ready to surrender without a fight? Had Rosalie Hammond ever surrendered without a fight? she then wondered bitterly. Had Rosalie Hammond ever surrendered at *all?* The possibility that she had provoked such a floodtide of jealousy within Meghan's breast that she found herself wishing she had dumped the plate of ham—and the rice croquettes and the baked custard and anything else handy—into Devlin's lap instead of his sister's.

"Would you care to give it another try?" Jolene suggested, holding the *gâteau-patate* aloft. "I've sent Naomi down to the spring house to fetch some fresh milk, and Mary's gone to feed her new son, so I'm afraid that leaves just the two of us to finish with dinner." Taking note of Meghan's hesitation, the cook flashed her an understanding smile and said, "I'll take it in. You can set the water on to boil for your bath."

"Bath?" echoed Meghan, her voice full of so much pleasure that Jolene laughed.

"Yes—bath! I thought we could bend the rules a little, since it's your first day. We usually do our bathing on Saturdays, Mondays, and Thursdays, but you're no doubt feeling the need for a good scrubbing now, what with the long trip from the city and all. So then," she concluded, arranging the custard neatly upon another silver platter, "I'll be back in a moment to show you where we keep the tub."

Meghan wasted little time in following the cook's instructions. She filled two large iron pots with water and lifted them, with considerable difficulty, to the "back pole" at the fireplace, which allowed them to be swung inward over the flames without risking incineration. That done, she hurried back to the pump to fill two more pots with water that would be used to cool the bath to a comfortable temperature.

Her troubles were momentarily forgotten as she untied her apron and began unlacing the front of her bodice. Since her new gown featured built-in stays, there was no need to wait for help, so that she was already standing ready in her chemise and petticoat when Jolene returned to the kitchen.

The tub was a metal hip-bath that was kept beside one of the cupboards in the storeroom. Jolene dragged it out, placing it before the fire, and smiled at Meghan's obvious impatience.

"At least you'll not have to worry about catching a chill. In the winter, there's many a day too cold to risk plunging yourself into water, even if it is hot enough to boil a potato!"

"The cold would not keep *me* from it," insisted Meghan with an answering smile. She withdrew the last pin from her hair and shook her head, sending her long, luxuriant tresses of burnished gold cascading freely down about her. "I was accustomed to bathing every day until"—it had been on the tip of her tongue to say *until I was abducted*, but she hastily amended it to—"until I left England."

"Were you now? Well, most of the gentry think it unhealthy to bathe with any frequency, but I'm happy to say that Master Devlin and his sister are different." Jolene swung the pots back from the fire and tested the water with one cautious finger. Apparently finding the temperature satisfactory, she emp-

176

tied the contents of the first pot into the tub while Meghan hastened to do the same with the other. "Of course, who can say what changes will be made once he takes Mistress Hammond to wife?" she pondered with a sudden frown.

"And when . . . when will that be?" faltered Meghan, her momentarily lifted spirits hurtling back to earth. She hid the renewed anguish in her eyes by dropping them toward the steaming hip-bath.

"Not 'til Christmas. Unless Master Devlin grows impatient and persuades his future bride to move the wedding date ahead—which, in my estimation, is quite likely to happen," remarked the cook, sighing as she placed her hands on her curvaceous, calico-skirted hips. "Whatever the case, we'll soon have to get used to serving a new mistress here at Shadow-moss."

Meghan wanted to press her for more information about Devlin and his betrothed, but she dared not. The bath was ready for her after Jolene added a bit of the cold water, and she quickly peeled off her chemise and petticoat while the other woman moved consider-ately away to busy herself at the hollowed-out stone sink nearby.

Easing her body down into the tub, Meghan closed her eyes and released a long sigh. The water cradled her within its soothing warmth, while the flames dancing in the fireplace radiated more than enough heat to effectively chase the chill away from the upper portion of her nakedness. She was content to rest against the high metal back of the tub for a time, before finally bestirring herself to take up the cake of soap and the sponge Jolene had thoughtfully pro-vided for her.

After washing and rinsing her body, she climbed from the tub and quickly wrapped her silken curves in a generous length of toweling. She knelt on the floor, then bent over the water to wash her hair—never easily accomplished, due to its considerable length and thickness. By the time she had finished, Naomi had already returned with the fresh milk and left again, Jolene had taken herself off to the main house to deliver the fruit cake and coffee, and neither of the women had taken care to close the outer door until it latched securely.

And so it was that Meghan, standing before the fire in nothing but a knee-length piece of fluffy white toweling with her wet curls streaming down about her naked shoulders, felt a sudden rush of cool air upon her damp skin. Her brows knitted into a slight frown of puzzlement, and she turned to see that the sweetly scented afternoon breeze had teased the door open. Clutching the edges of the thirsty cotton and pulling it tightly about her, she hurried to regain her privacy.

She paused at the threshold and leaned cautiously outward in an effort to grasp the knob—and came face to face with Devlin Montague.

Her eyes grew enormous within the delicate oval of her face, while she blushed fierily from the tip of her bare toes to the very roots of her long, dripping hair. She stood as if transfixed, unable to speak or move or do anything other than stare, spellbound and breathless, up at the man she loved more with each passing day.

Devlin, who had abruptly left the dinner table with the announced intention of riding again, stared back at Meghan as though he could never get enough of the sight of her. His eyes, aglow with the smoldering passion she never failed to arouse in him traveled with fierce hunger over her adorably clinging tresses and her trembling, scantily clad form. His longing to possess her, body and soul, grew more damnably intense than ever before. . . .

Throwing all caution to the winds, he ground out a savage oath and swept her up against him. Meghan had no time to react, no time to struggle—even if such had been her intent—for he bore her with amazing swiftness just beyond the doorway into the seclusion of the abundant, trellised shrubbery that reached all the way up to the roof. Almost before she knew it, she was being thoroughly kissed in the very midst of that cool and fragrant bower, her body molded with intimate perfection against the hardness of Devlin's while his strong, possessively encircling arms threatened to cut off her breath.

She bit at her lower lip to stifle a soft cry of pleasure when his lips set to wandering ardently over her face, down along the graceful curve of her neck, then lower to where her breasts swelled seductively above the top edge of the cotton fabric that was still wound tightly about her body.

Her senses reeled and her pulses raced as she gave herself up to the exquisite, nearly painful torment only he could create within her. She clung feverishly to him, her lips offering a warm welcome for the returning pressure of his. He drank deeply of her willing sweetness, his raging passion becoming hers while his hot, velvety tongue virtually ravished the moist cavern of her mouth. Unable to prevent a low moan from sounding deep in her throat, she swayed even closer against him and felt herself branded by the undeniable evidence of his desire.

Then, as had happened twice before, she suffered the sudden and unexpected loss of his fiery embrace. His arms released her with such abruptness that she went staggering back against the wall of the kitchen house. Pale and shaken, she clutched hastily at the toweling, which had loosened to such an extent that it was in danger of baring her altogether, and gazed in stunned bewilderment toward the spot where mere seconds ago she had been clasped within the strong circle of Devlin's arms.

She looked up, and her round, luminous gaze caught sight of him through the thick foliage. He was heading for the stables, his long strides carrying him across the yard and away from her as though spending so much as another second in her company were the least desirable prospect in the world.

Slowly shaking her damp, tousled golden head in wonderment, she mused that she would never, *ever* understand Devlin Montague. Sweet Saint Bridget, one moment he was practically devouring her in the bushes, while in the next he was tearing off like a man possessed!

She drew in a ragged breath and raised a trembling hand to her lips. The memory of Devlin's burning kiss brought a new rush of color to her cheeks, as well as a sharp resurgence of the warm, deliciously pleasureable sensations that being held in his arms never failed to provoke.

But, all too soon, reality intruded once more. Reminding herself sternly that what she wanted could never be, Meghan turned and made her way back inside on legs that were still not quite steady. She closed the door, then stood leaning heavily back against it while she sought in vain to bring some semblance of order to her emotions. At first too preoccupied to notice that she was not alone in the kitchen, she started guiltily when Jolene's voice reached her from across the fire-warmed room.

"Merciful heavens, child, what were you doing outside like *that?*" The cook set the tray of recently cleared dishes beside the sink and favored the younger woman with a frown of mingled surprise and disapproval. Meghan, dismayed to feel her face turning crimson, instinctively tightened her grip on the length of toweling and hurried back to where she had left her clothing.

"The door was ajar. I went to close it," she explained in low, measured tones that belied the difficulty with which she spoke. She wasted little time in drawing on her undergarments and gown, all the while acutely conscious of Jolene's eyes upon her.

"The strangest thing happened when I took the fruit cake in a short time ago," Jolene remarked conversationally a few moments later. She busied herself with the dishes, yet still managed to toss a curious glance Meghan's way every now and then. "Master Devlin, who as a rule possesses one of the healthiest appetites this side of Charlestown—no, this side of *London,* I daresay—suddenly up and declared he was off for a ride. His sister looked as much surprised as myself, and I could have sworn she mentioned something about you."

"Me?" echoed Meghan, startled, her fingers abruptly stilling in their efforts to lace up the front of her gown. She cursed the telltale rosiness which stained her cheeks. Feigning disinterest, she perched on the edge of a chair and bent down to retrieve one of her black cotton stockings. "I fail to see why Mistress Montague should mention me in connection with her brother's lack of appetite," she spoke ever so casually as she rolled the stocking up over the bare smoothness of her leg. "Unless, of course, she was referring to my disastrous serving of the ham."

"No, she said nothing of that."

"Well then, perhaps you were mistaken," suggested Meghan with a faint smile. She gartered the stocking above her knee and took up the other one, casting a surreptitious look at the other woman as she did so.

She was satisfied to watch Jolene's mouth curve into an answering smile.

"Perhaps I was," murmured the cook, turning back to her work. *And just perhaps, my dear girl,* she added silently, *you are troubled by a great deal more than memories of home.* Being not in the least mean-spirited, however, she never for a moment suspected Meghan of anything truly improper. She simply wondered if the younger woman's relationship with their employer was not quite as it should be.

When Meghan stood fully dressed once more, she pleaded a sudden headache and asked Jolene if she might be allowed to retire to her room for a time. The cook readily agreed, saying that one of the other housemaids would be along soon to finish up with the cleaning. She bade her new charge to rest well and not to worry about returning to the main hall until her headache had completely fled.

The headache was all too authentic by the time Meghan reached the sanctuary of her small room. Several conflicting emotions warred within her breast, while a chaotic jumble of thoughts waged their own battle in her mind. . . .

Devlin was similarly besieged as he rode like the very devil across the fertile, green-manteled land that had been his father's before him. His mood was black indeed, as black as the magnificent stallion thundering beneath him, and it showed no sign of improving. Nor would it, he realized, not until he managed to rid himself of this damnable, moonstruck obsession for a woman who was—*blast it all to hell*—a woman who was not Rosalie!

And rid himself of it he must. What happened that day could never be allowed to happen again. Any plantation owner worth his salt did not go about dragging his female servants into the shrubbery to assault

182

them, he mused with a combination of self-directed fury and ironic humor. Not even when the female servants in question were as beautiful and desirable as Meghan Kearny. . . .

He swore roundly, his eyes darkening until they appeared like two matching pools of brilliant blue fire. Horse and rider flew over the ground as if one, while the sun blazed overhead and the moss-draped trees beckoned them to a welcome respite.

Chapter Eight

Seizing advantage of the moon's silvery luminescence while at the same time cursing its illuminating brightness, Meghan stole across the plantation grounds from the servants' quarters to the stableyard.

She had encountered no trouble at all in leaving her room unobserved, for the doors to the other rooms had been closed and the young housemaids on the other side of them long since asleep. The hour was late, nearing midnight, and Meghan was confident that the entire population of Shadowmoss would be slumbering peacefully by now.

Of course, her thoughts centered with a will of their own upon one particular member of the population. Try as she would, she could not force them away. Memories of her several tempestuous encounters with Devlin Montague returned to haunt her with a vengeance as she quickened her steps. This desperate flight to leave him provoked nothing but pain and sorrow within her breast, yet still she persisted. She told herself that she had to get away before it was too late, before—

No! her mind cried. She must not think of that. If she did, all would be lost! She had to remain strong, to keep her wits about her, and dwelling on what might have been would only breed failure.

Her eyes flashing in a burst of renewed determination, she reached the back door to the stables and carefully eased it open. Darkness cloaked the interior, but the shaft of moonlight streaming inside through the doorway enabled her to find a lamp and light it with the pistol tinder hanging on a hook beside it. Closing the door, she turned back to quickly survey the double row of well-kept stalls. A few of the horses whinnied softly at her presence. She held the whale oil lamp high, its flame allowing her to peruse the animals with a critical eye.

She was not her Irish father's daughter for naught—being an excellent judge of horseflesh, she found her gaze almost immediately drawn to the tall black stallion nibbling at hay in the largest stall. She mentally cast aside the other animals and hurried toward the chosen one, the one she was certain would carry her to freedom. Catching up a bridle, she slipped it over his head, soothing his restlessness by murmuring gently to him and rubbing a light hand down his silken nose. A saddle, she decided, would not be needed; she could travel faster without one.

Leaving the lamp balanced atop one of the posts, she took a firm grip on the loose reins and led the horse from his stall. He continued to snort and whinny softly as if to protest his part in her escape, but she merely threw up the latch on the wide double doors and pushed them open. Then, realizing that her intended liberator stood much too tall for her to mount him without assistance, she led him back to one of the stalls again and gathered up her skirts to climb to the second railing.

She swung her right leg over the horse's broad,

sleek back while at the same time hoisting herself upward. Her skirts and ruffled petticoat flew up about her knees, but she cared nothing for modesty at the moment, her only thought being to ride with all the speed and ability her father had bequeathed her.

Murmuring one last word of encouragement to the majestic stallion that was as black as night, she urged him forward with a firm nudge of her heels against his sides. His response startled her, for he suddenly shot out of the stables and into the yard as though she had put spurs to him instead of the soft leather of her shoes. She gasped in alarm and pulled forcefully on the reins to halt his wild flight, only to find herself holding on for dear life as he stopped dead in his tracks and reared up on his hind legs.

"Easy, boy, easy!" she whispered hoarsely, trying her best to calm him. He let out a loud, shrill cry that echoed throughout the moonlit darkness, and Meghan's apprehension increased tenfold. Fearing that she would be discovered if she did not make good her escape without further delay, she relaxed her grip on the reins and sought to persuade the inexplicably raging animal back down to all four of his immense, hoofed feet by smoothing a hand along his neck.

It worked, but not in the manner she had expected. He pawed furiously at the ground, swung his head to and fro with alarming vigor for a moment, then reared up again. His movements were much more violent this time, and Meghan experienced a sharp pang of very real terror. She clutched almost frantically at the reins, but to no avail. In the next instant, the stallion lunged forward without warning, spilling her from his back.

A breathless, unintelligible cry broke from her lips as she went toppling sideways from the horse. Certain

186

that she was about to hit the ground and be trampled beneath the animal's sharp hooves, she closed her eyes against the impending disaster—and suddenly felt her fall broken by two strong arms that materialized as if by magic to catch her. She was already being borne away to safety by the time her eyes flew open, and she turned their incredulous, glistening blue-green depths upon the man who held her close to his heart while he carried her into the stables.

"Devlin!" she breathed in stunned disbelief, not even aware of the fact that she had addressed him by his Christian name.

"Were you expecting someone else!" he retorted mockingly, though his fathomless blue eyes held no trace of amusement. His expression was decidedly thunderous, and Meghan could feel the foreboding tenseness of his tall, muscular frame before he set her roughly on her feet. "A new conquest of yours, perhaps!" he suggested in a voice that was whipcord sharp and edged with fury. "Some poor fool you bewitched into helping you steal away with my horse?"

"I was expecting no one!" Meghan denied hotly. "Bewitched or otherwise! And I did not know the horse was yours!"

In spite of her spirited display of bravado, she watched in growing trepidation as Devlin, pausing momentarily in order to allow the entrance of the now calm-as-a-kitten stallion who headed straightaway into the stall, closed the doors and set the latch. He rounded on her in the next moment, and the look on his handsome face prompted her to move hastily back toward the center of the lamplit building filled with the sweet yet pungent aroma of hay. The horses were all strangely quiet now, as if hearing their master's familiar voice acted like a balm to their easily strained nerves.

"I've no idea why, but I had assigned more sense to you, Meghan Kearny!" he began, advancing on her with a dangerous purposefulness that sent a shiver of fear dancing down her spine. "It would have been folly enough to try to escape at all, but to attempt it in the middle of the night—"

"How did you know what I intended?" she broke in to demand indignantly. "Why, how on earth could you possibly have suspected what I was about?"

"Give credit where it is due, wildcat," he replied with a brief, sardonic smile. "You attempted escape once before, did you not? It required little in the way of intelligence to deduce that you would do so again."

"So you turned spy, is that it? You were lying in wait for me, weren't you? And I walked right into your despicable little trap!" she stormed accusingly, her eyes ablaze.

"The trap was of your own making. I was merely taking a turn about the grounds, keeping a vigilant eye on what is mine," he told her, placing a significant emphasis on this last, "when I heard the commotion in the stableyard. It's lucky I did, for Ulysses could damned well have killed you!"

"To be sure, Devlin Montague, there's never been a horse yet that a Kearny couldn't ride!" she declared with haughty defiance. She gave an accompanying toss of her head, which only served to bring even more of her golden locks tumbling willfully out of their pins.

"Well now, it seems *this* particular Kearny has finally met her match!" he was unchivalrous enough to point out, nodding curtly down at her as he took a step closer. He loomed menacingly over her, his powerful, hard-muscled frame making her feel both incredibly small and perilously light-headed at the same time. "Where the devil did you think you'd go, you little fool? To travel overland back to Charlestown would take the better part of a day—*day*, mind you, not *night*—and even then over roads so rough and tangled they defy description!"

"I could have made it!" She edged backward a bit and tried not to let him see how disturbed she was by his proximity.

"Indeed?" His mouth twisted into a mile of obvious disbelief. "And what if you had? What would you have done then, Mistress Kearny? You've no money, no friends, and I'll wager you hadn't even given a thought to what you'd do once you reached the city."

"I most certainly had! I was planning to strike a bargain with the captain of a ship, or if all else failed, I would have stowed away!" she confessed as though it were something to be proud of.

"Then you'd have found yourself at sea with a shipload of woman-hungry sailors who would not have hesitated to sample the delectable charms of their uninvited guest!" he bluntly observed, his eyes smoldering and his blood boiling at the thought. Meghan gasped at his meaning, and hot color flooded her face.

"Do not seek to judge all men by yourself, Devlin Montague!" she fumed rashly.

"You'd be in little danger if that were the case," he countered with another faint smile of irony tugging at his lips. "But there's no use in arguing over hypothetical circumstances, since the fact remains that your harebrained scheme did not succeed. In the event you have forgotten, you are mine now, mine to do with as I will. Blast it, woman, I *own* you, and I'll not have you trying to run off every time the impulse seizes you!"

"*No!*" She shook her head in furious denial. "It—it's wrong for one person to claim ownership of another!" she insisted. "It's cruel and it's wrong!" Tears started to her eyes, but she angrily blinked them back and lifted her head to meet his piercing gaze squarely.

"Perhaps it is," Devlin startled her by conceding. His rugged features became quite grim, while his eyes glittered like cold steel. "But it's the way things are here, Meghan. The way they are and they way they'll remain for only God knows how long. All of us, myself included, must do what we can to make the situation tolerable. You can have a good life here at Shadowmoss if you choose." His sun-kissed brow creased into a dark scowl when he added, "It's bound to be superior to the one you had back in England!"

"And how can you be knowing that, Devlin Montague?" she challenged, planting her hands on her hips and shooting him a look charged with angry reproach. "You've no idea what sort of life I had, no idea at all, because you refuse to listen to the truth!"

"The 'truth,' as you call it, is nothing but a pack of lies, and I'll be damned if I'll lend credence to anything told to me by a woman who just tried to steal my horse!"

"I was not stealing him! I was merely going to borrow him for a time!"

"Is that so? Tell me then, if you please—when the bloody hell were you planning to bring him back?"

"Why, I . . . I would have found someone to return him to you!" she stammered with a guilty blush.

"Damn the horse!" he suddenly ground out, his hands seizing her arms in a punishing grip. His fiery gaze burned down into the alarmed roundness of hers. "Do you realize that, under the law, a man has the right to punish his bondservants for attempting to run away? I would be perfectly within my rights to lengthen your term of servitude, or even to beat you!" Meghan blanched at the savage gleam in his eyes, but she forced her head to remain set at a proud angle and her gaze not to fall beneath the fury of his.

"You cannot keep me here forever! And if you dare to strike me, as God is my witness," she vowed in a low, fervent tone, "I swear I shall make you suffer a like fate!"

"How?" retorted Devlin, a glimmer of amusement playing across his face now as he released her. "By sending word to that nonexistent grandfather of yours to come and avenge you?" He gave a slight shake of his head while his mouth curved into a strangely tender smile. "No, my dearest vixen, there is no one to champion you. However, you may rest assured that I have no intention of punishing you. But should there ever be a repetition of tonight's foolishness, be equally assured that you would be made to regret it."

His threat, though mildly spoken, sent another involuntary tremor of fear coursing through Meghan. She folded her arms tightly across her breasts, which rose and fell rapidly beneath her low-fitted bodice, and she turned her head away to escape the unsettling, midnight blue intensity of Devlin's gaze. A sudden lump rose in her throat as she faced the fact that she would in all probability never have another opportunity to escape.

It seemed that Devlin had read her mind, for in the next moment he decreed in that splendidly resonant voice of his, "You will no longer occupy a room in the servants' quarters. From this day forward, you will sleep in the main hall." He paused briefly before delivering the most startling edict of all, "In my bed-chamber."

"What?" she gasped, whirling back around to face him. Her beautiful, wide-eyed countenance displayed mingled shock and incredulity. "Good heavens, surely you cannot mean—"

"I meant exactly what I said," he told her in a cold, clear tone that belied the wild leaping of his own pulses at the thought. His gaze flickered briefly over her damnably enchanting curves before returning to her angelic-looking visage. "It is common practice for a valued servant to be required to sleep at the foot of her master's bed. Henceforth, that it is precisely what you will do."

"I will *not!*" she protested most adamantly. Her eyes kindled with outrage, and she stalked forward to confront him with a countenance more befitting a tigress than an angel. Balling her hands into fists, she planted them on her hips again as she stormed, "I will allow neither you, Devlin Montague, nor any other man to treat me like some . . . some *dog* to be kept in chains at night!"

"It is not for you to 'allow' anything!" he reminded her tersely, his own eyes aglow with an unfathomable light. A tiny muscle twitched in the rugged smoothness of his left cheek, giving outward evidence of the battle he waged against his swiftly rising temper. It occurred to him once more to wonder why this little wildcat standing so proud and fierce before him was capable of firing his anger—and a host of other emotions—as no other. For a man who had always prided himself on the ability to control his reaction to any given person or circumstance, he was at a loss to comprehend why that ability was now forever being tested by a woman who was not only a good seven or eight

192

years younger than himself, but who also continued to display an intriguing combination of naiveté and passion.

"Come, Meghan," he commanded quietly. "The night is half gone already, and there is much work to be done tomorrow."

He reached for her, but she flung away from him and bolted for the back door. It was useless to run from him, and well she knew it, but she could not surrender herself to this humiliation without a fight. She may have lost her heart, she thought bitterly, but she still had her pride, and she would not be worthy of the name *Kearny* if she did not offer resistance every step of the way!

But in the end, of course, it *was* useless. Devlin was upon her before she reached the door. Easily conquering her resistance by tossing her over his broad shoulder, he conveyed her thus from the stables, extinguishing the lamp's flame on his way out and leaving the silent equine witnesses to resume their interrupted sleep.

Although Meghan squirmed and kicked to her best abilities, she was carried inside the house and up the stairs with amazing swiftness. She thought of calling out for assistance, but realized it would avail her nothing. After all, she mused furiously, she was Devlin's bondswoman, she was within the confines of Devlin's house, and there would be no one to respond to her calls for help but Devlin's servants and Devlin's sister. *Blast it!* she swore silently, employing one of Devlin's favorite maledictions, *why did I have to go and choose the one horse that a Kearny could not ride?*

By the time she was set on her feet in the midst of the darkened bedchamber, her head was spinning dizzily. She waited in mutinous anticipation while Devlin moved to a small table beside the doorway and struck fire to the wick of a candle supported by an ornate silver holder. The flame flickered and quickly gained strength, bathing the room in a soft golden glow and bringing shadows to life upon the half-paneled, half-papered walls.

Meghan subjected her new surroundings to a hasty but thorough examination. Her sparkling, blue-green eyes first took in the sight of a wooden floor almost entirely covered by costly Oriental rugs, then traveled across the massive pieces of furniture—made mostly of the deep, rich woods of walnut and mahogany—which appeared quite at home in a gentleman's bedroom. What caught her interest and held it, while her heart pounded erratically in her breast, was the bed itself.

It was quite the largest one she had ever seen, its four massive, carved posts supporting a canopy called a "tester." There were matching curtains of a luxurious, blue and cream patterned brocade for drawing about the feather bed to surround the occupant during slumber. The high four-poster was particularly unusual in that it was not short like most, but rather long enough to accommodate nearly the entire length of a man as tall as Devlin. To Meghan, who stood with her face flushed and her body atremble, the bed seemed as overwhelmingly masculine as its owner.

"Get undressed," she was startled to hear Devlin command in a low, slightly husky tone behind her. She inhaled upon a gasp and wheeled to face him, her disheveled golden tresses swirling wildly about her face and shoulders.

"Un—undressed?" she stammered. Her trepidation increased tenfold when she watched a slow, mocking smile spread across his handsome face.

"You've slept in your shift before, Mistress Kearny, so strip down to it and get into bed." Sauntering past her, he began drawing off his shirt.

"Into bed?" she now choked out, unable to believe what she was hearing. Dear Lord, surely he didn't mean to—

"Have you suddenly grown deaf as well as obstinate?" he demanded with exaggerated patience as he turned back to her. His midnight blue eyes glistened down at her with amusement as well as something else she dared not name. Another faint smile touched his lips. "You do me an injustice, wildcat. I have no intention of sharing the bed with you. I will catch what sleep I can in the chair."

"But you . . . you said I was to sleep at the foot of your bed!" she reminded him, her head awhirl with a chaotic jumble of thoughts.

"So I did," he admitted. His dark brows drew together in a sudden frown before he abruptly presented his back to her again. "But I've changed my mind—something which is also a master's prerogative."

Meghan, thrown into complete and utter confusion by this unexpected development, found herself at a loss for words. She could only stand and watch dazedly while Devlin pulled off his shirt and took a seat on the edge of the bed to remove his boots.

A delicious warmth spread throughout her body as she viewed in fascination the sight of his bared upper torso. Those strong, manly arms which had held her with such possessive mastery were smooth and bronzed, as was the magnificent set of broad, powerful shoulders which had borne her weight all too often. The hard-muscled breadth of his chest was covered with a light furring of richly hued brown curls that tapered downward into a thin line and disappeared into the waistband of his breeches. Meghan blushed fierily at her wicked pondering of where that dark path of hair led. . . .

"Blast it, woman!" Devlin ground out, unable to bear her gaze upon him any longer. "Either take off your clothes and get into bed or else be prepared to have me perform the honors!"

Her eyes flew wide in alarm. Scurrying across the room to the other side of the bed, she reached up and modestly pulled the curtains closed before starting to undress. She was painfully conscious of Devlin's presence in the shadowy, candlelit room as she unlaced her bodice and drew off her gown. Once she had untied her petticoat and stepped out of it, she perched on the feather mattress and hurriedly removed her shoes and stockings, then slipped between the covers.

She could hear Devlin moving about the room as he prepared to make his bed in the upholstered wing chair in front of the fireplace. He had already drawn the curtains on the opposite side of the bed, leaving her to wonder if he was perchance wearing anything at all by now. Since she had never had occasion to watch any gentleman other than her father retire for the night, she did not know if it was customary for other men to wear a nightshirt or not. Somehow, though, she could not envision Devlin Montague's tall, virile frame encased within the long folds of a white cotton garment such as her father had worn.

Although she was tempted to peek through the curtains and thereby satisfy her curiosity in the best way possible, she did not—at least not right away.

She lay wide awake for quite some time after Devlin had settled himself in the chair. Her heart ached for him, her very soul called out to his in forlorn silence, and yet she staunchly forbade herself to stir from her lonely position in the center of the massive bed. It was very warm and very dark in the midst of those brocade curtains, however, and she began to grow increasingly uncomfortable. Throwing off the covers, she tossed and turned restlessly, causing the ropes which were laced back and forth across the frame beneath the mattress to creak softly in protest. Finally, she defied her better instincts. She scrambled to her knees upon the bed and cast open the curtains.

Devlin came out of the chair like a shot. Since he was a man whose impulses were trained to react to the first sign of danger—or, in this case, trouble of a different nature—the sound of the curtains being flung wide prompted him to readiness.

The room was illuminated only by a tiny sliver of moonlight intruding from a gap in the heavy draperies at the window. Meghan could scarcely make out Devlin's form in the darkness, but she was made acutely aware of his approach in the next instant, for he traversed the distance with lightning-quick speed and in doing so crossed the beam of pale silvery light.

She inhaled sharply as her eyes caught the sudden flash of movement, and her heart leapt crazily when she realized that Devlin stood before her in all his naked, masculine glory. Even in the darkness, she could tell that his eyes raked with searing boldness over her scantily clad body, and she was helpless to prevent her own startled gaze from straying downward to where his manhood sprang from a cluster of dark curls. She swallowed hard and felt her face flaming, and she hastily closed her eyes against the shocking yet strangely thrilling sight of his undeniable masculinity.

"What the devil do you think you're doing?" he ground out. Unmindful of his nakedness, he could think only of the possibility that she had tried to escape again. "Damn it, Meghan, were you planning to steal away while I slept?"

"No, I . . . I was . . ." Her voice trailed away into nothingness, and she could not recover it quickly enough to offer a defense before Devlin's hands shot out to close about her arms. She gasped and opened her eyes to find him glaring down at her in all too visible fury.

"What will it take to make you realize you can never escape me?" he demanded in a harsh tone brimming with raw emotion.

Meghan could offer no response, other than to stare up at him in dazed, breathless anticipation. She trembled as his gaze bored relentlessly down into hers, and she would have collapsed back upon the bed if not for the fact that he literally held her there with her knees perched on the very edge. The heat emanating from his magnificent, perfectly formed body seemed to burn through her clothing and set her skin to tingling.

Her awareness of the highly volatile situation was nothing compared to Devlin's, however. He groaned inwardly at the sight of her captivating dishabille—the luxuriant mass of shimmering golden hair tumbling down about her shoulders, the full, firmly rounded breasts whose rosy peaks were thrusting so provocatively against the thin white fabric of her chemise, and the face that was turned expectantly up to his, its enchanting loveliness holding him captive while a pair of beguiling, blue-green eyes offered an unspoken promise of heavenly passion and earthly fire.

"Devlin," whispered Meghan at last, fearful of what might happen and at the same time hoping that something *would.* "Devlin, I—"

The sound of his name upon her lips shattered Devlin's perilously wavering resolve. With a low groan, he gathered her to him with breathtaking fervor and brought his lips crashing down upon the parted sweetness of hers. She melted against him, shivering as her thinly covered breasts made electrifying contact with the hard warmth of his bare chest. Her arms came up to entwine about his neck, and she kissed him back with all the answering fire and passion her eyes had unknowingly pledged.

His strong hands roamed with an intoxicating urgency across the slender, graceful curve of her back before moving lower to curl possessively about her delectably rounded buttocks. The chemise provided a woefully inadequate barrier against the arousing pressure of his fingers, and Meghan felt as though she had been branded wherever they touched her. She strained upward against his hot, virile nakedness, pressing her silken curves into even bolder intimacy with the man who never failed to make her feel this sweet madness whenever he took her in his arms.

Meghan drew in her breath upon a soft gasp as his throbbing hardness swept against her lower body, and she gasped again when he held her close and expertly maneuvered them both down upon the feather mattress. He rolled so that she was atop him, his hands returning to the firm mounds of her bottom and urging her upward so that his mouth could trail a fiery path downward to her breasts.

She moaned and threaded her fingers within the dark, sun-streaked thickness of his hair as his lips captured one of the rosy peaks and drew it within the moist warmth of his mouth. He suckled her breast gently through the thin fabric, his tongue flicking erotically back and forth across the nipple. The sensation was one of unbelievable pleasure, and Meghan felt herself being borne away on the gossamer wings of desire once more.

Oh, she mused through a glorious haze of fleshly delight and heartfelt yearning, *to be able to share this enchantment with Devlin every night for the rest of my life. . . .*

Suddenly and without warning, there swam before her eyes a painfully clear vision of what her life would be like as the mistress of Devlin Montague.

Not only would she have no rights or privileges other than whatever it suited his fancy to give her, but she would forever remain exactly what she was now—a slave. She would be trapped by her love for him as surely as any other slave was trapped by the circumstances of the plantation system itself. There was little doubt in her mind that, once she had given herself so completely to him, she could never bear to leave him.

But he would never be hers. And worst of all, she would be forced to share his attentions with his wife. *His wife*, her mind echoed numbly. That was something she would never be. Recalling what Jolene had said about women who value themselves too cheaply, she wondered if he would have married her even if he had believed the truth of her identity. But no, she reluctantly acknowledged, he would not have done so, for he loved Rosalie Hammond. And God help her, she was selfish enough to want *all* of him!

Once again, she reflected bitterly that the only thing left to her was her pride. She could not and would not surrender that as well. Whatever else the future held in store for her, she knew she must face it with her self-respect intact. Otherwise, she would

200

have nothing, nothing at all.

Her pride conquering her passion with merciless vigor, Meghan pulled away from an unsuspecting Devlin and rolled off the mattress. She wasted no time in putting some distance between herself and the man who let fly with an ear-singing curse at her abandonment.

"What the devil is it *this* time?" he roared, sliding from the bed and flinging her a look that would easily have throttled her if such a thing had been possible. A trembling and crimson-faced Meghan quickly spun away from the sight of his distressingly well-remembered nakedness.

"You are to be married soon, remember?" she told him in a breathless, quavering voice. Trying valiantly to conceal her heartache, she added, "To proceed with—with what we were doing would bring us nothing but pain and guilt, Mister Montague, and I for one do not intend to suffer the pangs of either!" As if to lend credence to her defiant proclamation, she hurriedly lit the candle again.

She was thrown into a quandary by the silence that followed her words. Unable to refrain from tossing a glance over her shoulder, she was surprised to see that Devlin still towered beside the bed. She was further unsettled to glimpse the strangely unfathomable expression on his face. It was impossible to tell what he might be thinking, just as it was impossible to predict what he would do next. When he did speak, his deep-timbred voice held a noticeable trace of the anger and frustration he was trying to subdue.

"I could take you against your will, Meghan. I could damned well take you and be done with it!" He paused for a moment, obviously still torn between reason and desire, then swore beneath his breath and

201

reluctantly conceded, "But you are correct when you say that naught could come of our union but unhappiness. To betray the trust of my betrothed would be bad enough, but to do so with one of my own servants would be unforgivable."

"Why?" challenged Meghan, stung by what she perceived to be his condescension. She rounded indignantly on him, only to whirl back around when her stormy gaze lit upon his powerful nakedness once more. "Because I am so far beneath you? Because you consider me worthy of your lust but not your regard?" she demanded with biting sarcasm. Hot tears gathered in her eyes, and she suddenly wanted more than anything in the world to feel Devlin's arms about her again—but she knew that was something she must avoid at all costs.

"No, damn it! I—" He broke off with another blistering oath and glared across at Meghan's rigid back. The candle's soft glow taunted him by silhouetting her supple, alluringly rounded curves beneath the chemise. Dismayed to feel his desire flaring again, he mentally berated his traitorous male flesh and snatched up the quilted coverlet from the bed. He flung it about his lower body, then stalked angrily across to where Meghan stood stiff and unyielding before the chair that had recently held his tall frame.

"Get back into bed!" he ground out between tightly clenched teeth.

Meghan spun about to confront him, only to feel very real alarm grip her as she viewed the savage gleam in his eyes and the dark, rather murderous look on his face. Drawing in a ragged breath, she opened her mouth to speak, but no sound came. She noticed that his fierce, penetrating blue gaze had fastened upon her bosom, and she looked hastily downward to see that the chemise, wet from the loving attentions of his mouth, clung to her breast with virtual transparency. The delicate, rose-tinted peak grew taut beneath the searing intensity of his eyes, and Meghan colored hotly at so visible an indication of her body's response to him.

"Good night, Mister Montague!" she declared shakily, darting past him. She flew back to the massive four-poster, hurriedly scrambling up to the mattress and drawing the curtains. Tense and breathless, she sat waiting in the midst of that darkened seclusion, but the only sound she heard was that of her own heart pounding in her ears.

Devlin flung himself down into the wing chair and shot yet another blazing look toward the bed.

Damn you, Meghan Kearny! he swore inwardly. *Damn all women!*

He could not in all honesty deny that he was just as much to blame. If he hadn't insisted upon bringing her to his room . . . but she had given him little choice. He was responsible for her, and he damned well couldn't allow her to go running off in the middle of the night. The thought of her lost somewhere out there in the wilds—or even worse, encountering the sort of unscrupulous bastards who prey upon young women alone and without protection—made his heart twist painfully and his blood boil. She belonged to him now, and he would kill any man who sought to do her harm!

He shifted restlessly in the chair and ran a hand through his thick brown hair. This accursed madness cannot go on, he told himself with a heavy sigh. He was only flesh and blood, and what mortal man could endure such torture without eventually reaching the breaking point? For him, that breaking point loomed closer with each passing day.

It had taken every ounce of self-will he possessed to refrain from sweeping her into his arms again and carrying her back to the bed. She fired his blood at every turn, provoked him far beyond reason . . . he literally burned for her. If he did not conquer this obsession soon, he mused fierily, he would either go out of his mind, or find himself tossing Meghan Kearny's skirts over her head one day and damn the consequences!

Rosalie. His betrothed's name suddenly echoed throughout the turbulence of his mind. Yes, of course, he told himself, his eyes aglow with satisfaction now. Once he saw Rosalie again, once he gazed upon her cool, refined beauty and held her in his arms, he would be cured of this temporary insanity Meghan Kearny had brought him. Rosalie was all he desired, all he truly wanted. If not for the fact that they had been separated too long, he would never have reacted so strongly to another woman's presence in his life. He had certainly been no saint before his engagement to Rosalie Hammond, but he had done nothing to be ashamed of since she had agreed to become his wife—*nor would he!*

With that fierce determination burning within him, he drew the coverlet up about his bare chest and tried in vain to find a comfortable position in the chair.

In the bed, meanwhile, Meghan finally stretched out upon her side and rested her head atop her bent arm. Her other hand idly traced repetitive patterns upon the pillow while her glistening turquoise eyes stared disconsolately into the darkness. When she finally drifted off into a troubled sleep, it was with the sweet yet forbidden memory of Devlin's kiss upon her lips . . . and the renewed certainty that he was the

only man she would ever love.

Chapter Nine

"Would you care to accompany me about the grounds this morning, Mistress Kearny?" offered Linette, lingering in the doorway as Meghan and Naomi cleared the table of the breakfast dishes.

"Why, I—I suppose so, Mistress Montague," stammered Meghan uncertainly. She caught the inquisitive look Naomi shot her from across the table.

"Please, may we not employ the use of one another's Christian name?" the petite redhead suggested with a dimpled smile. "After all, you and I are of an age, are we not? And I daresay my brother would approve of the arrangement."

Meghan was tempted to ask her what she meant by this last remark, but she held her tongue and watched as Linette sailed away with the airily spoken promise to meet her in the kitchen in half an hour's time. Naomi frowned once their mistress had gone and theorized,

"I'll wager she wants to ask you about last night!"

"Last night?" echoed Meghan, pretending ignorance. Her eyes fell hastily toward the dishes in her hands, and she was dismayed to feel the telltale color staining her cheeks.

"I went to your room to wake you this morning," the other woman revealed gently. "When I saw you were not there, I ran to tell Jolene. Mercy me, the whole house was nearly turned upside-down before Master Devlin came out of his bedchamber and said you were asleep within. You can imagine our surprise, can you not?" Naomi favored her with another searching look. "The master's never done that before—require one of the servants to sleep in his room, I mean. I wonder why he saw fit to do so now?" She waited expectantly for Meghan to supply the answer, then was sorely disappointed to realize that none was forthcoming.

In truth, Meghan did not know what to say. She had hoped that no one else would learn of what had transpired the previous night, and she felt mortified to think that everyone, including Devlin's sister, was now privy to the fact that she had spent the night alone with him in the privacy of his bedroom. She groaned inwardly at the thought of what they must all be assuming.

As she soon discovered, however, she need not have troubled herself on that score. Devlin, molding a portion of the truth for the benefit of them both, put it about that the young bondswoman had injured herself in a foolish attempt to ride his horse. Upon seeing the light in the stables, he had gone to investigate, and had then thought it wise to tend to her in his own chambers. If there remained any shadow of disbelief in the minds of his servants, none of them dared give voice to it. Although their master was a kind and just one, his temper was a thing to be feared, and it would be sheer folly to invite the sort of tongue-lashing he invariably delivered on those rare occasions when he became truly incensed.

Recalling how she had awakened to find Devlin gone, Meghan heaved an inward sigh and lifted the tray to convey it from the dining room. She had hurried downstairs earlier that morning and dashed around to the rear door of the kitchen, hoping that she would not be too late to help with breakfast. Jolene had said nothing about what she had already learned from Devlin, nor had she behaved in the least bit differently toward her new young charge. Only Naomi, who was by her own admission a bit flighty, had remarked upon Meghan's heightened color and air of preoccupation. Her words had made little sense to Meghan—until now.

"It's not like Master Devlin to miss his breakfast," observed the housemaid as they moved back through the passageway to the kitchen.

"Is it not?" murmured Meghan, who had dreaded the prospect of facing him again under the watchful eye of his sister. But he had not put in an appearance at the table, leaving her to wonder where he had gone and if he was still angry with her.

"No indeed. I don't believe I've ever seen him so troubled." A mischievous smile lit her dark, attractive countenance when she added, "Mayhap his appetite will improve again once he is wed to Mistress Hammond."

Tempted to retort that it would be better for everyone to spend less time worrying about the state of *Master Devlin's* appetite and more time concentrating on their own affairs, Meghan frowned and tightened her hold on the tray. She and Naomi reached the kitchen at last, at which time Naomi took herself off to help Mary and the other housemaids with the cleaning. Meghan had been assigned to help Jolene. The cook usually left the washing up to the younger women, but she sensed that Meghan would be glad of her company at the moment.

"Harvest time is almost upon us, you know," Jolene remarked as she stoked the fire and swung the kettle over the strengthening flames. She turned back to Meghan with a smile. "It's been nearly a year since I met Parson Trimble. He came to pay a call on Master Devlin and ended up seated right here in my kitchen with his bare feet stuck in a tub of hot water!"

"Truly?" asked Meghan, her own mouth curving into a soft smile. "And how, pray tell, did that come about?"

"The poor man was trudging about the rice fields, deep in conversation as well as mud, while speaking to the master about a new roof for the church to which he had just been assigned. He was rewarded not only with the promise of the necessary funds, but with a chill as well." The comely widow chuckled and shook her head in fond remembrance. "Master Devlin gave him into my care. There suddenly stood before me a tall, dignified-looking man, a bit on the thin side, with hair not much darker than mine and eyes that were more gray than blue. He was not the handsomest man I had ever seen, but my heart came to life at the sight of him," she recalled, her eyes shining brightly.

"So you believe it possible to fall in love with someone you have only just met?"

"Why should it not be? There are those who spend a lifetime together, only to learn that they never truly loved at all. There are others who recognize their heart's mate right away. So it was the first time for me, and so it was the second. This past year has only confirmed what I felt in the beginning."

"But what about Pastor Trimble's feelings? Has he spoken of them to you?"

"No," Jolene admitted with a sigh. She crossed to stand beside Meghan at the sink. "As I said before, he has not yet acknowledged what I have known all along. Men can be very stubborn, child, especially when it comes to love. Sometimes, it seems the whole world realizes the truth before they do. And being the last to know doesn't always set well with them, you see. But I am a firm believer in fate, and if two people are destined to be together, then nothing short of death can keep them apart!" she concluded with a decisive nod.

Meghan did not know whether to feel comforted or disheartened by the cook's words. She lapsed into a thoughtful silence as she set about scouring the dishes, her gaze focusing with unaccountable fascination upon the soap bubbles that clung to the heavy, glazed china plates.

It wasn't long before Linette swept inside the kitchen to collect her for their planned excursion. If Jolene considered it a trifle unusual for the young mistress to take such an interest in one of the servants—it *was* unusual—she said nothing of it and merely wished the two women pleasure in their walk.

"I thought you might enjoy a brief tour of the plantation," explained Linette as they strolled away from the kitchen house. She looked particularly fetching that morning, with her upswept, flame-colored locks bouncing beneath a plumed picture hat. The hoopless riding costume she wore consisted of a deep blue velvet jacket with matching skirt, a white linen blouse with a ruffled front, and a pair of dark brown leather boots. Her eyes, so much like Devlin's that Meghan found it difficult to look directly into them, sparkled while they made an encompassing sweep of the magnificent, sunlit grounds. "My father chose this spot nearly thirty years ago when he came here from France. He was the black sheep of a wealthy, highly respected family," she recalled with a soft laugh. "He envisioned Shadowmoss as a glorious symbol of the new life he and other 'radical thinkers' had carved from the wilderness. I think he would have been proud to see what Devlin has accomplished, don't you?"

"Dev—your brother is responsible for its success?"

"Yes. Mind you, my father built the house and started the plantation, and it became quite successful indeed, but it was Dev who brought about the changes that were necessary for it to survive these past few years." Linette smiled half to herself now. "Father insisted that Dev go to school in England—most of the planters send their male offspring abroad for an education, you see, while the daughters must settle for either boarding schools in Charlestown or sour-faced old schoolmasters at home," she detoured for a moment to reveal, then continued with her original train of thought, "Anyway, as a result of that Dev was absent from Shadowmoss for a considerable length of time. He studied law, of all things, but upon his return home he let it be known that he had every intention of becoming a planter."

"Was your father pleased at the news?" asked Meghan, finding it difficult to imagine what Devlin must have been like as a very young man. It was even more difficult to envision him taking orders from anyone, even a father.

"Not at first, I don't think. But he soon became accustomed to the idea. It wasn't long before he and Dev were running the place on an almost equal level

211

of responsibility, which turned out to be a good thing, of course." She paused briefly, her expression growing somber and her eyes clouding with remembered pain. "My brother and I were quite naturally devastated by the death of our parents, but Dev did not allow himself to grieve for long. He literally immersed himself in his work, though he never failed to provide me with the affection and solace I needed, and he guided Shadowmoss into even greater prosperity—as the evidence before your eyes will attest."

Linette fell silent for a time after that and led her companion toward one of the many brick-paved walks lacing the terraced lawn. Although glad of the other woman's confidences, Meghan wondered why she had been chosen to receive them. She was, after all, only an indentured servant in Linette's eyes, and as such could hardly be considered worthy of any personal revelations. Perhaps she had misjudged Devlin's sister, she mused idly, or perhaps there was a hidden purpose to these overtures of friendliness. Whatever the case, she was anxious to hear more about anything concerning Devlin, and she did not wait long before pressing Linette for further information.

"Was your mother from France as well?" she inquired as they strolled along a path flanked by a veritable jungle of greenery ablaze with fragrant color. The air was filled with the fresh, vibrant scent of springtime blossoms and the sounds of bustling plantation life.

"No," answered Linette, "she was a descendant of one of the first families to settle in Charlestown. They had come here from England, after a brief sojourn in Barbados, and eventually met with great success as merchants. There were some who said my father chose her as his bride because of the riches she brought to the marriage."

A soft smile tugging at her lips, she reached up to pluck one of the huge white magnolia blossoms from the midst of the shrubbery. She brought it up to her nose to inhale lightly of its potent sweetness. When she spoke again, her voice held more than a touch of wistfulness.

"But that was far from the truth. My parents loved one another deeply, so much so that one would have been lost without the other. In a way, we were glad their deaths were separated by so short a period of time. My father would have found life unbearable without my mother, and she without him. It was really much kinder for them both, the way things turned out." She looked at Meghan and asked, "Are you parents still living?"

"No, they . . . they are both gone," faltered Meghan, the memory of her father's recent death flooding back to fill her heart with sadness again.

"Oh, I am sorry," Linette earnestly declared. She stopped and lifted a hand to Meghan's arm. "It wasn't very long ago, was it?"

Meghan shook her head wordlessly, prompting the young redhead to gaze upon her with compassion as well as curiosity. In the next moment, Linette startled her by asking, "Is that how you came to be indentured, Meghan? Because you parents were dead and you had no one to turn to for help?"

"*No!*" she impulsively denied, shaking her head again but with more vigor than before. "No, I—" She broke off when it dawned on her that she was perilously on the verge of spilling the truth.

"Then what was it that forced you into bondage?"

"I cannot say," Meghan evasively murmured, turning away to stare toward the small lake which lay just ahead at the end of the path. Linette, however, refused to be put off.

"Why? Because my brother does not wish it?" Upon receiving no reply, she goaded her unwilling subject by demanding, "Are you truly so frightened of him that you dare not speak to anyone?"

"Indeed I am *not!*" exclaimed Meghan with a flash of spirit.

"Then why not tell me—"

"Because it would do little good!"

"How can you know until you have tried?" persisted Linette, her curiosity piqued more than ever. Still met with nothing but silence, she tried another tactic. Her blue eyes literally danced with the mischief she was so fond of creating. "You were trying to escape on Ulysses last night, weren't you?"

Meghan flushed guiltily at that. She knew it was useless to deny what had happened, for it was now painfully clear to her that Linette Montague was as unaccustomed to being thwarted in *her* pursuits as her brother was in *his*. The two of them were more alike than she had imagined! she concluded darkly.

"Yes, as a matter of fact, I was!" she confessed, her head lifting in that gesture of proud defiance that had never failed to both infuriate and intrigue Devlin. Her blue-green eyes flashed across at the other woman as she added quite vehemently, "And I shall continue trying until I am successful!"

"But why?" the petite, titian-haired girl countered in bemusement. "Does the prospect of living here seem so repugnant to you that you will risk such danger?"

"The prospect of remaining in bondage does!"

"To anyone—or just my brother?" retorted Linette, satisfied to glimpse the startlement crossing Meghan's

214

face.

"What an absurd question!" Meghan pronounced bluntly, forgetting for the moment that she was supposed to be subservient to the little minx who was interrogating her with such relentless determination.

"Come now, Meghan, I should like to be your friend," Linette told her with a conciliatory albeit unrepentant smile. "Won't you please consent to tell me how you came to be . . . well, to be 'owned,' if you will, by my brother?"

"Why not ask *him?*"

"I have," Linette admitted with a sigh. Her youthful brow creased into a frown, and she tossed the magnolia blossom to the ground. "He refused to tell me anything other than the fact that your contract was purchased by him in Charlestown yesterday morning." She fixed Meghan with a long, searching look before heaving another sigh and proclaiming with all sincerity, "If you are in some kind of trouble, why not tell me so that I may know how to help? I am not blind, you know—I can see that there is something amiss between you and Dev. Tell me what it is and allow me to be of assistance!" she reiterated.

"You cannot help me, Linette," insisted Meghan, "because to do so would require you to betray your brother's trust! But if you truly want to know how I came to be in this unenviable position, then I will tell you!" She no longer cared if Devlin found out, no longer worried about incurring his wrath. Each day in his presence brought her only more heartache. Sweet Saint Bridget, she was so desperately in need of someone to talk to, even if that someone was Devlin's own sister!

"You and Dev had already met before yesterday, hadn't you?" Linette asked in order to confirm her growing suspicions. Not at all surprised when Meghan nodded, she then mused aloud, "But where could it have been? He has been nowhere of late, save either Charlestown or Nassau . . ." Her voice trailed away for a moment, and her face suddenly brightened with realization. "It was in Nassau, wasn't it?"

"Not exactly," Meghan replied with a sigh of her own. She wandered a trifle farther along the shaded path before turning back to her wide-eyed and expectant companion. "In truth, Linette, your brother rescued me from a pirate's harem on the island of Andros. It was a mistake—that is, he meant to liberate the other young woman who, along with myself, had been taken captive when our ship was attacked."

"Rosalie Hammond!" the petite redhead declared triumphantly.

"Indeed, she was the one he intended to bring back with him. But she had already been ransomed by the time he arrived, and—well, in short, I am the one who sailed home to Charlestown with him."

"But that does not explain how you came to be his indentured servant!" Linette hastened to point out. A shadow crossed Meghan's face, and her eyes glowed dully.

"That resulted from a misfortunate series of events your brother refuses to believe!" she lamented in a voice brimming with indignation and resentment. "You see, I was abducted from my father's home in Ireland, spirited across to England, and thereupon taken aboard a white guineaman bound for the colonies. That is how Mistress Hammond and I came to be aboard the same ship. And that is how I came to be the *property* of your brother!"

"Good heavens," breathed Linette, obviously wavering between amazement and disbelief. She looked

216

at Meghan as though she did not know whether to tender her profound sympathies, or deliver a stern lecture about the damnation one could expect to suffer for uttering such blatant prevarications.

"Precisely," agreed Meghan, her mouth curving into a faint smile of bitter irony. "I warned you, did I not? Even if you believed my story, it would change nothing. I am not so foolish as to expect you to help me escape, nor am I certain it would not serve me better to trust only in my own resources. Either way, I am more determined than ever to return to my grandparents in England!"

There followed several moments of highly charged silence. Linette was obviously still uncertain on the score of what to think. Meghan reflected somewhat despondently that she felt no relief for having spoken the truth; only a prevailing sense of uneasiness.

Finally, Devlin's sister took a deep breath and forced a smile to her lips.

"Shall we continue with our tour of the grounds, Meghan?" she suggested unexpectedly.

"You mean you—you still wish to show me about?" Meghan stammered in surprise.

"Of course! However you came to be here, the fact remains that you *are* here and I should still like very much to help you feel at home." With that astonishing bit of optimism, she set off down the walk again. Meghan, hesitating only briefly, followed after her. The subject of her startling tale remained closed for the time being, and she soon found herself relaxing a bit in Linette's animated company.

They traveled around the lake, then across a bridge arching over a stream, until they reached the spring house. Built of stone, it was a quaint, rectangular structure standing two stories high. Its upper floor, explained Linette, had been used as a school for the slave children at Shadowmoss for the past twenty-five years. Below, the natural spring water flowed through compartments where dairy products were kept cool.

Next, they visited the rice mill and sugar cane mill, each an important feature in the plantation's ability to produce its own food. Shadowmoss, as Meghan learned, was in actuality a self-contained, self-sustained community made up not only of field slaves and house servants, but also carpenters and blacksmiths and bricklayers, as well as seamstresses, washer women, and a host of others. Aside from salt and such imported luxuries as coffee, tea, and spices, the land provided all of the necessary raw materials for building, for heat and light, and for food and clothing.

"Of course, Dev complains that I still spend entirely too much money whenever we go into Charlestown," Linette disclosed with an irrepressible twinkle of her blue eyes. "He insists that if I need anything, it can be found here at home. I pay him no mind, however, and purchase whatever I please. Like all men, I suppose, he finds it difficult to withstand the blandishment of feminine tears and wounded silence!"

Meghan could not help smiling at that. One thing she had noted clearly—Devlin Montague adored his younger sister. Her smile suddenly faded and her throat constricted at the thought that she would never know what it was like to be the recipient of his heart's affection. She envied Linette for that, just as she envied her for having a brother at all. Her own life, she mused with an inward sigh, would not have been so lonely if she had been blessed with siblings. While it was true that her grandparents had always doted on her, it was also true that they had not quite been able to make up for the lack of a companion near her own age.

"Since you've already became familiar with the stables," said Linette, her eyes positively dancing now, "I think we'll proceed to the spinning and weaving room, and after that I'll show you where the women make our pottery."

Meghan soon found her spirits lifted again as she accompanied the young mistress of Shadowmoss to the various buildings inside the sprawling compound. She was able to relegate her troubles to the back of her mind, for a time at least, and she even managed to give her full attention to whatever bits of information Linette willingly passed along to her. It was fascinating to view the inner workings of the plantation, but she was interested most of all in the people themselves.

She smiled to see the children laughing and playing beneath the trees while their mothers kept a watchful eye on them. They all gazed curiously at her as she moved past with Linette, who greeted them by name and offered comments about the school that would be starting up again after the harvest.

Although Meghan was unaware of it, the education of the slaves at Shadowmoss was another very pointed exception to the general rule of ownership, one which Devlin's father had insisted upon in spite of strong objections by his friends to the contrary. Most of the plantation owners deemed it advisable to keep their workers ignorant; it would, they claimed, ensure greater loyalty and less chance of revolt. But there had never been any true stirrings of trouble at Shadowmoss, and the slaves there could boast not only of the ability to read and write, but also of more practical skills which they employed about the plantation. Instead of creating the predicted discontent, education had brought about an increased efficiency in work and more satisfaction in leisure.

Meghan's gaze traveled about the beautiful, terraced grounds as she and Linette left the row of cabins behind. She looked toward the barns, watching as the men and older boys tended the stock, made repairs, and did the hundreds of other things required to keep the plantation running smoothly. Elsewhere, she saw men and women working in the gardens, and her eyes finally drifted to the fields in the near distance, where the all-important crops of indigo and rice were being readied for harvesting.

"Did you know that the slaves were actually the ones who taught the planters here how to cultivate rice?" supplied Linette, noting the direction of her gaze. "They had been growing it for centuries in their homelands. It's rather ironic to think that they are in truth the ones responsible for these 'kingdoms built on rice,' isn't it?"

"Yes, it is," agreed Meghan with a thoughtful frown.

"As you can see, they're draining off the water from the fields now, which means they'll soon be cutting the straw. It's quite exciting, really, to watch it being threshed and winnowed," the young redhead went on to observe, gaining satisfaction from being able to impart such impressive knowledge. It was usually the other way around. "Of course, indigo wasn't introduced to the colonies until a mere thirty years ago. A woman named Eliza Lucas was responsible for its being brought here from the West Indies. Ever since Parliament granted a special bounty to encourage its production—as you no doubt know, it is the source for the blue dye so very much in demand by the English textile industry—my father insisted that we make it our second staple crop."

Meghan was only dimly aware of what Linette was saying, for her turquoise gaze had suddenly lit upon one particular man in the rice fields. Although she told herself it was impossible, she could have sworn it was Devlin who stood bare-chested in the midst of the billowing waves of the nearly ripened grain. It was difficult to tell for certain, given the fact that she and Linette were too far away to make out the faces of the workers.

In the next instant, however, her suspicions were confirmed when the woman beside her exclaimed, "Oh look, there's Dev!" Her eyes alight with pleasure and her mind awhirl with thoughts of how she could make use of the situation, she grabbed Meghan's hand. "Come along!"

"But I don't think—" Meghan protested weakly, only to fall silent as Linette began pulling her down the grassy slope.

Devlin was too preoccupied with the task at hand to take note of their approach. He had been discussing the upcoming harvest of the rice with his overseer, who had exercised the right to disagree on a small matter concerning the way the straw would be cut. The handsome master of Shadowmoss had thereupon stripped off his shirt and taken his place in the muddy field right alongside the slaves. He was in the process of demonstrating exactly what he wanted the still unconvinced overseer to comprehend, when Linette came breezing complacently forth along the boardwalk at the edge of the marshland with a reluctant Meghan in tow.

"For heaven's sakes, Dev, is it really necessary for you to parade about like *that* in the middle of your own fields?" Linette challenged with a playful archness.

He leisurely straigthened to his full height at the sound of his sister's voice and turned to face her. The sardonic smile playing about his lips quickly faded when he saw that Meghan stood there as well. There followed a sudden tensing of his rugged features, and the look in his eyes became guarded.

"Take yourself and Mistress Kearny back to the house, Linette," he commanded quietly. "The fields are no place for women, and well you know it." Without waiting for a reply, he ungallantly presented his back to them again and continued his discussion with the overseer.

Meghan, vexed by the fact that he had spared what amounted to little more than a passing glance for her, could not prevent her kindled gaze from traveling over that broad expanse of gleaming, bronzed muscles as he bent to his task once more. She grew warm at the vivid recollection of what his skin had felt like beneath her hands, and she cursed the weakness that gripped her when her eyes moved lower to where his lean hips and taut, powerful thighs were molded beneath the tight covering of his breeches.

"Come now, Dev," said Linette blithely, not the least bit intimidated by him, "what harm can it do to allow us to remain for a moment? After all, I have been showing Meghan around, and I daresay even *you* will agree that the fields are among the most enthralling sights here at Shadowmoss!" Her voice brimmed with unmistakable amusement, and she cast Meghan a conspiratorial smile.

"Do as I say, Linette," Devlin reiterated as he straightened again. It was obvious from the tone of his voice that he was in no mood to brook interference.

The overseer, a young man near his employer's age who was all too accustomed to that particular tone of voice, hastily excused himself now with a solemn "good day" to the ladies and a judicous promise to Devlin that he would follow his instructions regarding the harvest.

Once he had gone, Linette drew Meghan forward and suggested to her brother, "Perhaps you would care to complete the tour for me? You see, I promised Sally I would ride over after breakfast, for I am ablaze with curiosity to see her new schoolmaster for myself—she has pronounced him the most divinely handsome! It is beginning to get quite late. So, Dev, if you would be so kind, I shall leave Meghan in your very capable hands and be on my way!"

"Blast it, Linette, can you not see I'm busy?" he ground out. His burning gaze raked over a flushed and thoroughly discomfited Meghan before returning to his sister's face. He was about to tell her that she could damned well postpone her ride—but he never got the chance.

No sooner had he opened his mouth than the saucy little redhead gathered up her skirts and whirled about to go racing determinedly back up the hill.

"Linette!" he thundered after her. She flew defiantly onward to the stables. *"Linette!"* Forced to admit defeat, he muttered an oath and flung the starchy grains in his hand back down to the muddy earth.

"You need not trouble yourself on my account," Meghan declared stiffly. She was angry with both Montagues for making her the object of their battle of wills, but she was especially infuriated by Devlin's cross-tempered behavior toward her. "I am perfectly capable of seeing myself back to the house!" She pivoted about with the intention of marching proudly away, but Devlin's hand shot out to detain her.

"Wait, damn it!" he curtly decreed. She turned a stormy countenance upon him, then was surprised when he released her arm as abruptly as he had seized it. Frowning, she followed the direction of his piercing blue gaze to see that his hand had left a muddy imprint of itself upon the sleeve of her gown. Her eyes flew reproachfully back up to his.

"Now see what you've done!" she observed with an accusing glare.

"I own the gown as well as its wearer," he pointed out in a dangerously charged undertone. "I will bloody well get you another one! Now, will you please lower your voice?"

"Why? Because you do not wish everyone to know what an overbearing, insensitive—"

"Enough!" He stepped lithely up to the boardwalk and retrieved his shirt, his booted feet leaving a trail of mud as he stalked forward to confront his fiery-eyed, far from chastened bondswoman. His handsome face grew inscrutable while he stood towering above her, but she did not fail to glimpse the way his own gaze smoldered with a barely controlled fury. "Let us dispense with this nonsense, Mistress Kearny, and speak of things that *do* matter!" He paused for a moment to bring his temper under control, then startled Meghan by proclaiming in a cold, clear voice, "I want it understood that what happened last night will never happen again."

Meghan, stung by his words, gazed up at him with wide, luminous eyes that were filled with a mixture of perplexity and pain. She believed him to be speaking of their brief but wildly passionate encounter in his bedroom. Unable to think of a suitable reply, she looked away and battled the temptation to take flight as Linette had done.

"I won't ask you for your word never to attempt another escape," continued Devlin. The merest flicker of amusement played across his face when he noted, "I do not believe you would give such a promise, nor do I believe you would honor it even if you did." All traces of humor vanished, and his expression grew disturbingly grim. "Therefore, I am left with little choice other than to insist that you continue spending your nights in the main house."

Meghan was torn between pleasure at the prospect of being alone with him every night, and utter consternation at the thought of what might happen if she *were*. She took a deep, steadying breath and met his gaze squarely when she asked, "Does that mean I will still be required to share your bedchamber?"

"No. That was a mistake," he admitted with a faint, crooked smile. He glanced down at the white linen shirt in his hands as if he had just remembered that he held it.

Meghan watched in breathless silence as he slipped it on, oblivious to the fact that the two of them were standing before so many onlookers. A sudden gust of wind sent her skirts and petticoats whipping about her ankles, and she raised a hand to steady the ruffled cap atop her upswept mass of rich golden curls. It was strange, but she felt almost as though her former life had never been, as if the man before her had always been such an integral part of her life.

"I have decided that you will move into the room adjoining mine," Devlin informed her with a frown. "Both doors will be locked at night, and I will see to it that the window is secured." It suddenly occurred to him that he was doing exactly what he had vowed never to do—setting her above his other servants. After all, he had never found it necessary before now to move one of them into the house. The housemaids had always slept in separate quarters; only Jolene and Noah occupied their own rooms on the lower floor of the main hall.

"Of course, the arrangement will be a temporary one," he saw fit to add. "Once I am wed, my bride will naturally occupy the room."

"I see," she responded in a voice that was scarcely above a whisper.

"But until then, I want you where I can keep an eye on you." A shadow of indecision crossed his face for a fleeting moment, and Meghan was almost certain she glimpsed a spark of inexplicable longing in his eyes. "There will not, I assure you, be a repeat of my unpardonable actions. In other words, Mistress Kearny, I will not touch you again."

"No. Of course not." She drew an uneven breath as she looked away again.

"Do you believe me?" he startled her by demanding. Her widened eyes flew back up to his face.

"Believe you? Why, I . . . I suppose so." *Was he trying to convince her—or himself?*

"Good." He nodded solemnly down at her, then turned as if to leave. Meghan, possessed of the sudden, desperate need to prolong their conversation, searched for the words to make him stay.

"Will you not at least allow me to send word to my grandparents that I am well?" she asked, only to realize that she had not chosen wisely at all. She was not surprised by the dark scowl he turned upon her.

"Why must you persist in this nonsensical playacting of yours? Can you not at last admit that you were aboard the *Bristol Packet* for the same reasons as

226

your fellow passengers below decks?"

"I can admit nothing because there is nothing to admit!"

"What did you do, Meghan?" he demanded unexpectedly, his low, resonant voice bringing warm color to her cheeks as it washed over her. He stepped closer and raised his hands toward her, but caught himself and lowered them back to his sides. His gaze held a strangely vulnerable light, and his rugged features appeared to soften with an emotion Meghan could not name. "Was your life truly so painful that you found it necessary to invent another? Where do you come from? And what happened to put you aboard that cursed ship?"

"Why should any of it matter to you?" she countered wearily, her eyes falling beneath the searching intensity of his. She released a melancholic little sigh and said, "I have told you the truth from the very beginning. If you still refuse to believe me—so be it." She looked up at him again, her beautiful face taking on an earnest, imploring expression that affected him more than he cared to admit. "But what harm can there be in allowing me to send word to my family back in England? Whoever I am, whatever I have done, should I not still be granted the right to inform them of my whereabouts?"

Her eyes filled with sudden tears, but she resolutely blinked them back. It dismayed her to realize that she, who had always despised weepy females, now seemed ready to burst into tears at the slightest provocation. Not only had her life been turned upsidedown these past several weeks, but it seemed that she herself had been transformed into someone quite unrecognizable.

Devlin felt his heart stirring anew at the sight of

her distress, and he told himself, not for the first time, that she could not be guilty of any serious crime. It was difficult to believe that a young woman who looked so angelic and exhibited such a peculiar innocense of the world was blameworthy of anything other than a minor infraction of the law . . . but then, he mused with an imperceptible narrowing of his eyes, if he found it impossible to think her capable of the sort of offense that would condemn her to bondage, would it not also serve that she was speaking the truth about everything else as well?

"I will take the matter under consideration," he finally relented enough to promise, his own emotions in a state of perpetual, wholly uncharacteristic turmoil. *As they have been from the moment a certain, golden-haired spitfire came into your life,* an inner voice noted deliberately. It perturbed him even more to realize that Rosalie had never prompted such a loss of control.

"Thank you," murmured Meghan. Although it was not what she had wanted to hear, it was at least a start. "I must be getting back to the kitchen," she reluctantly announced. "Jolene will begin to wonder—"

"Are you being treated well by the other servants?" he asked on sudden impulse as he took another step toward her. In spite of his insistence that he would be the one to decide her position in his household, he had not yet done so. Strangely enough, he found himself unable to issue any orders concerning her duties.

"Yes. Why should I not be? I am, after all, one of them." Her senses, as always, were sent reeling at his nearness. She caught her breath at the way he was looking at her, for his steady gaze held an undeniable warmth. "I . . . I must go," she reiterated in a small voice.

Hesitating no longer, she gathered up her skirts and made good her escape. And escape it was, she thought as she went scurrying back up the hill, since she had been perilously close to surrendering to the temptation to raise her hand and touch the rugged smoothness of his cheek.

Devlin stared after her, his gleaming, midnight blue eyes reflecting all the mingled confusion and yearning in his own heart. He continued to watch her until she had disappeared from view, then frowned to himself and strode purposefully away toward the other fields.

Later that same day, when the sun hung low in the cloudless afternoon sky and the animals grazing peacefully beneath its brilliance sought out the cool shade of the trees, Devlin received an unexpected visitor.

He was seated at his father's tall, multicompartmented "plantation desk" in what had traditionally been the game room. A former sanctuary wherein the gentlemen retired to talk, smoke, or drink and play cards, he had converted it into a study for his own use two years ago. There were no windows to light it, but one wall featured a set of wide glass doors, opening out into a breezeway, through which enough of the sun's rays spilled to keep the room from being too dark.

Engaged in the process of going over the account books, the handsome young master of Shadowmoss scowled frequently and cursed the fact that his beloved sister found it necessary to spend so much on feminine fripperies and household luxuries. He knew, as Linette did, that he could not remain annoyed with her for long, but it nonetheless gave him some small measure of satisfaction to complain.

On that particular day, however, the monthly ritual did nothing to improve his mood. He was in a dangerously ill humor, so much so that even Noah wisely kept his distance. The morning's physical labors had provided him with far less of a release than he had hoped, and his chance encounter with Meghan shortly before dinner had only made things worse.

His eyes kindled anew at the memory of how she had come flying around the corner of the kitchen on her way to the spring house. Precisely why his steps had led him toward the kitchen, he could not—or would not—say. Whatever the reason, he had found himself watching as Meghan turned to respond with a warmly lit smile to something Jolene called out after her. Her smile froze on her face when she saw him, and she had appeared considerably taken aback by his scrutiny before murmuring something unintelligible and hurrying on her way again.

He had never seen her smile like that before. It had been a smile of genuine pleasure, one which had made her look more radiantly beautiful than ever before. The memory of it seemed to have been stamped indelibly on his mind, for he could not rid himself of it no matter how hard he tried to forget it and go on about his business. He realized that Meghan had been given little cause to smile throughout these past several days; he also realized that he himself was to blame for a goodly portion of her unhappiness. . . .

"Damn!" he muttered when his gaze drifted down to fall upon the drop of ink spreading across the page of columns. He blotted the spill and returned the feathered pen to its resting place atop the desk, then stood and wandered over to the doors. He stared pensively toward the gardens behind the house, while his eyes took on a faraway look and his brow creased into yet another frown.

Suddenly, a familiar voice spoke his name. He stiffened, and his features displayed surprise as well as an emotion suspiciously akin to disappointment when he turned to face the person who smiled across at him from the inner doorway.

"Devlin!" the visitor spoke even more dramatically than before. "Oh my darling, we are reunited at last!"

Chapter Ten

"Rosalie!" Her name sounded strangely foreign to his ears. Seized by an inexplicable detachment, Devlin stared across at her as if transfixed. *The woman you love stands before you, and yet you do nothing?* his mind's inner voice prodded him.

He mentally shook himself and hastened forward to greet her in a manner befitting their status as long-parted lovers. His tall, lithely muscled frame fitting easily through the doorway that was too narrow (purposely so) to accommodate a woman's hoopskirt, he gathered her close and kissed her with such forcefulness that she swayed weakly against him.

The kiss may have been thrilling for Rosalie, but it was anything but that for Devlin. He knew almost the very moment his lips touched hers that it would not compare favorably with what he had shared with Meghan; indeed, he had made note of that disturbing truth the first time he had kissed his beautiful, unwitting guest aboard the *Pandora*. Still, he was determined to regain the spark of desire he had once felt for his betrothed, and it was to this end that he continued to kiss her until she fairly swooned beneath the splendid mastery of his embrace.

"Oh, Devlin!" Rosalie Hammond murmured huskily when she was finally released. Her wideset gray eyes were very round and glistening with passion. Her mouth curved into a slow, inviting smile as she stepped back and sent Devlin a look that issued a silent yet undeniably bold challenge.

She raised a hand to her meticulously arranged blond curls in order to repair any damage done to her coiffure, then gracefully smoothed the skirts of her exquisite, lace-scalloped gown of pale blue satin. Her figure was impeccable, her demeanor one of complete self-assurance, and her cool, aristocratic beauty the sort for which men fought duels and penned sonnets—and other women envied to such an extent that they were willing to put themselves through all manner of torture in an attempt to achieve a parallel guise.

"I was so afraid you would be angry with me for coming," she disclosed with an effective sigh. "My father told me what he said to you when—"

"I do not blame you for that," Devlin reassured her quietly. He was dismayed to realize that he actually felt ill-at-ease and uncertain now that the moment he had anticipated for so long had finally arrived. Telling himself it was because they had been apart for a number of months, he reached to take her hands within the firm grasp of his.

"Thank God you are safe!" he declared earnestly, his deep voice brimming with emotion. "When I heard you had been taken captive, I nearly went out of my mind!" His eyes gleamed with a savage light, and his features tightened when he demanded, "You *are* well, are you not? If that black-hearted bastard harmed you in any way—"

"No, no, I was not harmed!" Rosalie hastened to

233

proclaim, her face coloring and her eyes falling before the violence of his. "As a matter of fact, I was treated with surprising courtesy . . . I suppose because The Wolf had decided from the very beginning that I would be ransomed," she finished in a strained, tremulous voice.

"Forgive me, Rosalie," said Devlin, his expression softening and his eyes full of contrition. "I did not mean to distress you further." Drawing her close again, he enveloped her within the warm circle of his arms and held her against his strangely unaffected hardness for several long moments. His thoughts drifted with a will of their own to make a startling and highly troubling comparison.

The woman he held was only a trifle taller than Meghan, as well as being nearly three years older, and the resemblance was such that it was easy to see how he could have confused the two—especially given the conditions under which he had first set eyes on Meghan. But whereas Rosalie's coloring and size could be termed similar, her features were decidedly sharper, her eyes of a far less brilliant hue, and her hair lacking the burnished radiance of Meghan's.

It was beyond comprehension, but now that he had seen her again, he did not find Rosalie Hammond quite as devastatingly attractive as he once had. And if truth be told, he went on to admit to himself with extreme reluctance, his heart did not come alive for her as it did for—

No, damn it! he swore silently. He was betrothed to Rosalie! She was the woman who would be his wife. No matter what his feelings were for Meghan, he could not allow them to interfere with the plans he had made. Honor demanded that he quell this accursed desire for another woman and concentrate on thoughts of his future life with Rosalie.

Honor may demand it, but it is not honor who will share your bed, that roguish voice deep inside him pointed out.

"Come, my darling, let us retire to the drawing room," decreed Rosalie, calmly slipping from his embrace and moving to his side. If she had noticed anything amiss in his behavior toward her, she said nothing of it. She curled a possessive, perfectly manicured hand about his arm and began leading him down the hallway. "We have much to talk about. Now that I am home again, I shall waste precious little time in making all of the arrangements for our wedding!"

It struck Devlin that she seemed none the worse for her ordeal; quite the contrary. If outward appearances could be believed, she was fully recovered and ready to take up exactly where they had left off before the quarrel which had sent her to England those many, endless weeks ago.

"My father does not know I am here, of course," she confessed as they entered the drawing room. "I told him I felt an urgent need to get away from the city for a time, and he agreed to let me visit Cousin Janine. How very convenient it is for us that her husband's plantation lies within so short a distance of Shadowmoss!" She smiled to herself as she recalled how she had persuaded her older cousin to aid her in her scheme. With Janine's assistance, it had been easy for her to travel down the river to see Devlin as soon as her father had gone safely on his way back to Charlestown.

She took a seat on the chaise and settled her skirts about her. With a pensive frown creasing his handsome brow, Devlin closed the doors and faced his serenely complacent fiancée.

"Why did you not send word to me? I would have come to you without delay."

"Oh Devlin, I could not bear to wait any longer! After all that has happened, after all I have endured . . ." Her voice trailed away for a moment while she appeared to be searching for the appropriate words to express her understandably distraught feelings. Devlin crossed the room to bend his tall frame down onto the chaise beside her. He took her hand, his eyes aglow with genuine concern as he gently pressed her to continue.

"Tell me of it, Rosalie."

"I am afraid there is very little to tell. One moment I was taking a turn about the deck of the *Bristol Packet*, on my way home to you, and the next we were under attack!"

"What of the pirate leader, the one who took you captive?"

"The Wolf?" she provided, her eyes suddenly growing very wide. The pirate's dark, rakish image flashed across her mind, causing her to take a shuddering breath and hastily avert her face from Devlin's searching gaze. "I can tell you even less about him. He only paid me a visit on two occasions, and we spoke of nothing but the details of my ransom," she lied with remarkable equanimity. She had often rehearsed what she would say, so that now the moment was here, she was able to successfully affect the mien of a woman who had been terrified by her captor. *Devlin must never know the opposite was true!* she vowed anew to herself.

"While I am relieved to hear you were not ill-treated by him, I must nonetheless make certain he is made to suffer for what he did to you and—" He caught himself before speaking Meghan's name, and instead vowed harshly, "I will not rest until he is brought to justice!"

"Please, Devlin," Rosalie entreated, "I beg of you not to pursue this matter any further!"

"I must," he ground out, standing abruptly to his feet and moving to take a stance before the fireplace. When he thought of Meghan in the clutches of those cowardly brigands—*Meghan*, not *Rosalie*—his eyes glittered fiercely and his whole body grew taut with vengeful fury.

He braced a hand against the mantel, his fiery gaze drifting briefly upward to the portrait of his parents before returning to the flushed countenance of his betrothed. Her discomfiture did not go unnoticed by him, but he merely attributed it to a natural reluctance on her part to recall what had no doubt been a harrowing experience. Still, it was not Rosalie's face which rose in his mind at every turn. . . .

"I know this is difficult for you," he allowed in a low, slightly hoarse tone, "but surely you must see that he cannot be allowed to go unpunished for his crimes!"

"Is vengeance all you care about, Devlin Montague?" the aristocratic blonde countered reproachfully. Her eyes sparkled with tears, and since she was one of those rare women whose beauty is not diminished by crying, she made no effort to compose herself. "Of what import is anything else, so long as you and I are together again?" She rose to her feet as well now and glided across to plant herself before him with an appealingly provocative expression on her upturned features. "I pray you, my darling, let us put these past few months behind us! Our separation has been long and painful for us both, and I do not intend to ever be

237

parted from you again!" To seal her promise, she lifted her hands to his shoulders and strained upward to seductively brush his lips with her own.

Suddenly, the doors were flung open. Linette breezed lightly into the room as if she were completely unaware of the fact that she was interrupting the reunion of her brother and the woman she had always considered an insufferable, calculating female.

"Why, Rosalie Hammond!" she exclaimed innocently, stopping dead in her tracks when she stood in the very center of the room. "For shame, Dev!" she then scolded her brother with mock severity. "Why did you not tell me we had a visitor?"

"How did you know I was here?" demanded Rosalie sharply. She drew away from Devlin and turned to fix the impish redhead with a keen, decidedly unamicable look.

"I know a great deal more than my brother suspects," Linette retorted with an enigmatic little smile at the two of them. Her flowered dimity skirts rustled softly as she sauntered across to the same chaise Rosalie had just vacated. She took a seat upon it and cast a sly glance toward a still silent Devlin before returning her perceptive gaze to the haughty blonde. "I must say, Rosalie, that you look none the worse for wear."

"And just *what* do you mean by that remark?" demanded the other woman, her face suffused with a dull, angry color.

"Why, only that you appear remarkably well for someone who has only recently been delivered from the midst of a band of pillaging cutthroats," she answered with another wide-eyed, deceptively guileless expression.

"*I* was not subjected to the sort of humiliation suffered by the other captives!" Rosalie hastened to proclaim indignantly.

Devlin, who was all too accustomed to such exchanges between the two women in his life, suddenly thought of Meghan again. What sort of humiliation had *she* suffered? he wondered, his temper flaring to a near explosive level at the possibility that she had been lying when she claimed to have been spared the "attentions" of her captors.

"Indeed?" murmured Linette with a significant cocking of her delicate auburn eyebrow. Her blue eyes filled with a purposeful light as she watched Rosalie move stiffly forward to take a seat in Devlin's favorite chair. "Were you aware of the fact that my brother risked his life to rescue you?"

"What on earth are you talking about?" Rosalie demanded with a frown of mistrustful bewilderment. She darted an inquisitive look at Devlin, who scowled darkly and favored his sister with a speaking glare that warned her to say no more.

"It is of no importance," he told Rosalie in a low and level tone.

"Oh, but it *is!*" his sister defiantly protested. "He was like a man possessed when news of your capture reached us, and he set sail for Nassau without a moment's delay!"

"That is enough, Linette!" Devlin cautioned tersely, his gaze darkening and his hand clenching into a fist atop the mantel.

"Is it true, Devlin?" Rosalie questioned in disbelief. Her cool gray eyes shifted from him to Linette and back again. "Did you really attempt to rescue me?"

"He did!" Linette confirmed for him. Disregarding the warning light in her brother's eyes, she took

239

pleasure in revealing to his visibly stunned betrothed, "Not only that, but he actually succeeded! Well, of course, he *would* have, if not for the fact that you had already been ransomed," she amended very matter-of-factly. "The irony of it is that he rescued another woman in your place!"

"Another woman?" echoed Rosalie, eyeing the petite redhead quite warily before looking to the elder Montague again. Devlin, telling himself that she was bound to discover the truth sooner or later, cursed inwardly as he met Rosalie's narrow, suspicious gaze.

"A young woman by the name of Meghan Kearny," he supplied with an ill grace, his deep-timbred voice edged with anger. "She was also a passenger aboard the *Bristol Packet,* and she claims to have been taken prisoner at the same time as you."

"Yes, and what's more," Linette was obliging enough to add, "she happens to be an indentured servant in this very house!"

"*What?*" breathed Rosalie, her face paling and her gaze bridling with extreme displeasure. She shot to her feet and rounded on Devlin with, "Why did you not tell me of this before?"

"I had not yet had the opportunity to do so," he pointed out in a cold, clear tone. "Besides which, the matter does not concern you."

"It most certainly does!" Drawing herself regally erect, she uttered in a voice brimming with a mixture of jealousy and scorn, "I remember Mistress Kearny well! She is naught but a prodigiously bold and forward little guttersnipe who wasted precious little time in seeking to ingratiate herself with our captors by offering them her favors in return for—"

"That is a blasted lie, and well you know it!" Devlin startled both Linette and Rosalie by thundering. His magnificent blue eyes ablaze with what seemed to be an inordinate amount of fury at his betrothed's contemptuous accusations, he slammed his fist down upon the cold marble of the mantelpiece and spun about to command in a voice that was laced with steel, "You will not speak of her that way again, do you understand?"

"What is she to you that you jump so readily to her defense?" demanded Rosalie, unwisely provoking him further. She raised her head in a haughty gesture of supreme confidence and reminded him, "I am the woman who will be your wife, Devlin Montague—the future mistress of Shadowmoss—and as such I have every right to question you about anyone who will be serving in this household once we are wed!" She calmed herself somewhat and offered in a more conciliatory manner, "Would it not be wiser to rid yourself of a woman who will always serve to remind us of events best left forgotten?"

"Would it not be wiser still," countered Devlin, "to forget this particular quarrel of ours? For you see, Rosalie, I intend to keep Mistress Kearny in my employ for the duration of her three years' indenture."

"I fail to see why you found it necessary to purchase her contract at all! Once you had rescued her, could you not have simply relinquished her into the care of the proper authorities at Charlestown?" she asked, unaware that he had intended to do just that. "She is an attractive enough wench to fetch a decent price, I daresay, although there is no way of knowing precisely *what* sort of treachery she is guilty of. After all, she was one of the convicts kept below in the hold, so she must naturally be a low and vile creature who—"

"*Enough!*" ground out Devlin.

"You are mistaken about her, my dearest Rosalie," Linette observed at this point. Her timely intervention was motivated by more than a desire to taunt her future sister-in-law, for she had become genuinely fond of Meghan in spite of the initial reservations she'd had about her. "Meghan Kearny is not like that at all. She is obviously well bred, and her comportment is such that I would not be in the least bit surprised to learn she was aboard that ship by mistake!"

"By mistake?" Rosalie Hammond laughed softly in derision. "What a child you are, Linette! Mistakes like that are simply not made. And even if they were, would it not hold that the woman would do everything in her power to rectify her situation once she reached a place of safety? No indeed, if she were an innocent victim, she would not be here now, no doubt hoping to insinuate herself into this household and thereby enjoy a life much easier than the one she left behind!"

Devlin and Linette exchanged looks of a mutually ruminative nature. Rosalie's words had given them both a considerable amount of food for thought—especially Devlin.

Linette rose with the announced intention of ringing for tea. Her brother, meanwhile, battled the temptation to tell his betrothed exactly what she could do with her opinions. For some unaccountable reason, the longer he remained in her company, the more restive and irritable he became.

"Come, Devlin, let us have an end to this," said Rosalie, her mouth curving into a smile calculated to charm. She approached him again and slipped her arm through his. "Is it really so much to ask that you sell the woman to someone else? Call it a gift to your bride, if you will, but please do not disappoint me by refusing."

"You are not by bride yet, Rosalie," he reminded her with a deep frown. He was about to say more, but was prevented from doing so by his irrepressible sister.

"If Dev were to sell her now," Linette opined thoughtfully as she moved back to the chaise, "then I am afraid everyone would say he had done so because he is ruled by the whims of a jealous fiancée."

"I think it is time, Linette, that you left us to our privacy again," Devlin instructed with a sudden tensing of his rugged, sun-bronzed features.

"But I have just rung—" she started to protest, only to fall abruptly silent when she glimpsed the warning light in a pair of midnight blue eyes that never failed to convey their owner's meaning to her. Once again, she realized his limits of brotherly tolerance had been reached. "Oh, very well," she capitulated with a heavy sigh. "I can see there's little use in remaining, for I know the two of you would only bore me to tears with your talk of undying love and devotion!"

"Perhaps you find it boring," ventured Rosalie with a knowing smirk, "because you have yet to experience anything beyond a childish infatuation with that eager, freckle-faced son of the cabinetmaker's."

"Better that than the ongoing flirtation you maintain with nearly every man in Charlestown!" Linette retorted hotly. Aware that she was about to receive a sharp reprimand from Devlin, she defeated his intention by declaring with dramatic loftiness, "Do not trouble yourself, brother dear, for I shall gladly retire to the chaste confines of my room and there remain until Mistress Hammond has gone!"

She whirled about to leave, only to draw up short when Meghan suddenly appeared in the doorway,

243

bearing a tray fully laden with tea and cakes. Jolene, anticipating the need for refreshments as soon as she heard of the unexpected guest's arrival, had already begun the preparations by the time the summons came from the drawing room.

"Meghan!" breathed Linette. Her eyes grew round as saucers before coming alive with renewed mischief. "Why, you are the very person we wanted to see—is she not, Dev?" she challenged, turning back to him with a saucy grin.

Devlin's gaze smoldered with the force of his own emotions. He said nothing, but it was painfully apparent to Meghan that she had arrived at a very inopportune moment. Her luminous, blue-green eyes traveled swiftly from the beloved planes of his face to the woman at his side.

"Mistress Hammond!" she whispered in stunned astonishment. Her heart twisted at the sight of the woman's hand resting upon Devlin's arm, and she suddenly felt so weak and lightheaded that she feared her knees would buckle beneath her.

Dear Lord, no! she cried in anguished silence. She had known this moment would come, and had thought herself prepared for it, but such was most definitely not the case. Her entire body trembling, she forced herself to walk across the room to set the tray on the table.

"Well, well, if it isn't my betrothed's new bondswoman," remarked Rosalie in a tone laced with discernible antagonism. Casting a narrow look up at Devlin, she tightened her hold on his arm and revealed pointedly, "I have just heard of the circumstances which brought you here, Mistress Kearny. It seems you were fortunate indeed in your choice of a rescuer!"

"I . . . I had no choice, Mistress Hammond," Meghan faltered in a small voice, bemoaning her inability to staunch the overwhelming pain in her heart. She tried to arrange the silver tea service and china cups and saucers more neatly upon the tray, but found them blurring before her eyes.

"Did you not? Well then, you should be grateful for the fact that I had already been taken from the fortress before Devlin arrived. Otherwise, I daresay you would still be a member of The Wolf's harem!"

"Harem?" echoed Linette, her gaze widening at the sheer excitement of it all. "You were actually in a *harem?*" she asked Meghan with a touch of awe.

"Leave us at once, Linette!" ordered Devlin in a brusque, authoritative voice much like the one he used aboard ship.

Although she appeared to give serious thought to mutiny, the lively young redhead shot him a scathing glare and took herself off at last. Meghan, admitting defeat in her attempts to restore order to the tray, turned to leave immediately after Linette. She found herself unwillingly detained, however, when Rosalie demanded, "Were you terribly ill used by those cruel ruffians, you poor creature?" Her meaning was quite clear to all.

"Blast it, Rosalie!" swore Devlin. Pulling angrily away, he subjected her to a fierce, scorching look of reproval before transferring his gaze to a flushed and visibly perturbed Meghan. He suddenly felt like throttling his future wife. "Mistress Kearny owes you no answer to such a damnably preposterous question!"

As always, Meghan's indomitable spirit enabled her to bear whatever trouble fate tossed her way. Her anger at the other woman's intentionally hurtful remarks overshadowed her other feelings, and she hesitated no longer before lifting her head in a gesture of proud defiance and meeting Rosalie's malicious gaze squarely.

"I was not 'ill used' at all, Mistress Hammond. Any discomfort or humiliation I suffered at the hands of The Wolf is nothing compared to what I am now facing."

"What the devil do you mean by *that?*" This came from Devlin, who crossed the room in two long, furious strides to stand towering ominously above her. "You said yourself that you are being well treated here!"

"Well treated, yes, but the fact remains that I am still a slave!" she retorted, her eyes flashing resentfully up at him. "Perhaps now that your 'ladylove' has returned, you will consider setting me free so that I may go back to England where I belong!"

"You belong where I bloody well say you belong!"

"Is that so, *Master Devlin?* Then maybe you'll be telling me why it is you're so afraid of letting me send word of my whereabouts to anyone!"

Rosalie, taking great exception to the fact that the two combatants had apparently forgotten her presence in the room, wasted no more time in making them aware of the oversight. She gathered up her pale blue skirts and marched forward until she formed the third side of a very turbulent triangle.

"How dare you speak to him in that manner!" she hissed at Meghan. "You have forgotten your place, you insolent little strumpet!" She next turned to Devlin and imperiously demanded, "Why in heaven's name are you allowing this mockery of convention? Mistress Kearny is a *bondswoman*," she reiterated, pronouncing the term as though it signified the lowest form of life on earth, "and I fail to see why you should grant her the privilege of addressing you—"

"By damn, woman, do not interfere!" he virtually snarled, prompting the coolly elegant blonde to blanch and instinctively retreat a step.

"Why, you—you have no right to treat me thus!" accused Rosalie in breathless outrage.

"I have every right, since I am to be your husband in a few months' time!"

"Not if you persist in this sort of behavior!" she countered pompously.

Meghan, feeling utterly wretched as her gaze traveled from a scowling Devlin to a highly affronted Rosalie, wanted nothing more than to escape. If it had been possible, she would have gained a certain degree of satisfaction from having been the cause of trouble between the man she loved and the woman he would marry—but it was not possible, for the simple reason that she could not bear to remain in the same room with them any longer.

Murmuring an unintelligible excuse, she wheeled about and hurried to the doorway. She heard Devlin call her name—*Meghan,* not *Mistress Kearny*—but it did not forestall her desperate flight from the room. Hot tears threatened to blind her as she retraced her steps back through the entrance foyer to the passageway, and it was not until she paused on the bricks of the covered walk that she realized how dangerously close she had come to telling Rosalie Hammond that she had spent the previous night in Devlin's bedchamber.

Indeed, she mused with an inward groan, it had been on the tip of her tongue to respond to the spiteful woman's calling her a "strumpet" by retorting that a true strumpet would not have hesitated to lure a man—especially a man like Devlin Montague—into her bed when the opportunity to do so presented itself!

"Dear God, what am I going to do?" she beseeched aloud. She released a long, ragged sigh and reached up to tug the ruffled white cap from her head. Then, with her heart heavy and her mind racing to formulate yet another plan of escape, she headed back to the kitchen.

Meanwhile, Devlin and Rosalie were still closeted in the drawing room. The air was heavy with tension, the tea sat untouched and getting cold, and the appointed time for Rosalie's return to her cousin's plantation loomed closer with each passing minute.

"Are you telling me that you absolutely *refuse* to get rid of her?" she demanded icily, the color riding high on her cheeks while her gray eyes glittered with a hard light.

"What I am telling you, Rosalie, is that I refuse to let you dictate to me what I will or will not do," replied Devlin. He had regained control over his temper, though his thoughts continued to be preoccupied with the woman who had just bolted from the room. His dark brows knitted into a frown, and his piercing blue gaze became unfathomable. To Rosalie, he seemed more like an aloof stranger than the man who had asked her to share his life. "We have been through much these past few months," he noted quietly. "Perhaps it would be better if we postponed any wedding arrangements for a time."

"Surely you are not serious?" she questioned in stunned disbelief. "Why, you were always the one who said our engagement would be unbearably long!"

"I know. But . . . things have changed." He had

248

not planned to speak these words, but now that he had begun, he could not turn back. "I think, under the circumstances, it would be foolish to rush into marriage."

"What you mean is that you have taken that shrewish little trollop to your bed and want to prolong the slaking of your lust!" Rosalie charged venomously. "Do you truly think me such a fool, my dearest Devlin, that I cannot read the evidence before my own eyes?"

"And what evidence is that?" he asked in a voice of deadly calm, his handsome face inscrutable.

"Why, 'tis perfectly obvious that your relationship with her is far beyond what is proper between a master and his slave!"

"She is not a slave."

"Perhaps not, but the fact remains that I could literally see the sparks flying between the two of you! And where there is fire, Devlin Montague, there is passion! Yes indeed, it is easy to see why you could not part with her, why you saw fit to bring her back to Shadowmoss instead of leaving her where she belonged! Do you dare to deny it?" When he did not even favor her with a reply, she grew increasingly reckless. "I will speak to my father of this, you may rest assured! If I cannot make you see reason, mayhap *he* can!"

"Do you think I give a damn what Jonas Hammond thinks?" he ground out, causing her to gasp as his hands shot out to close tightly about her arms. His eyes were suffused with an almost savage light, and Rosalie felt a very real tremor of fear shake her. "Tell him whatever you please, for it won't make any difference! My life is my own, Rosalie, and I'll be hanged if I'll let you or anyone else run roughshod over me!" He released her again, as though the contact had suddenly grown distasteful to him, and added in a low tone brimming with scarcely controlled rage, "In a few days' time, when our tempers have cooled and you have set aside these idiotic accusations of yours, we will talk again. Until then, I bid you good day!"

Rarely did Devlin Montague ever disregard the strict rules of hospitality handed down by his father, but he did so now. He paused only to nod curtly down at his breathless, openmouthed fiancée in an obvious gesture of dismissal, before pivoting about on his booted heel and striding from the room.

Rosalie sank heavily down into a chair. She compressed her lips into a tight, thin line of anger as she heard the unmistakable sound of the front door closing behind Devlin. A bright, inimical glow suffused her gray eyes, and her face twisted into a mask of vengeful fury.

To her mind, Meghan Kearny and no one else was to blame for what had just happened. She was convinced that she could easily have persuaded Devlin to hasten their marriage, if not for the other woman.

You will be made to pay, Mistress Kearny! she silently vowed, her body fairly quaking with the force of her hatred. It infuriated her to no end to think that Devlin would prefer that little guttersnipe to her, and a near murderous rage seized her in its grip when she envisioned the two of them entwined in a lover's embrace.

No, damn it, she seethed inwardly, Devlin Montague was hers! He was hers because she had willed it so, because she had employed every feminine wile she possessed to make it come to pass. She had chosen him for many reasons, foremost of which was his splendidly masculine beauty. He was not the wealthiest of her suitors—some had been among the richest in the colonies—but none of the others had made her burn with desire as he did.

The Wolf's face suddenly swam before her eyes again, provoking a rush of mingled shame and passion. She recalled all too vividly how she had surrendered herself to him. A delicious shiver ran the length of her spine, and she caught her lower lip between her teeth as she remembered the feel of his hands upon her naked skin, the warmth of his hard body pressing her down into the bed, and the boldly erotic pleasures he had introduced her to throughout those two nights aboard his ship. . . .

"Dear me, I thought you had gone," Linette drawled lazily as she strolled into the room.

Rosalie Hammond started at the sound of the girl's voice. Coloring guiltily, she stood to her feet and faced Linette with an expression of pure antagonism. She offered no pretense of civility; now that the two of them were alone, she did not feel compelled to hide her true feelings.

"I give you fair warning, you little fool," she spat viperously at the petite redhead, "If you continue to interfere between Devlin and me, I will be forced to take drastic measures against you!"

"Drastic measures?" echoed Linette breathlessly, feigning wide-eyed horror. In the very next instant, her features relaxed into a smile of impertinent humor. "Oh pooh, Rosalie! You do not frighten me," she scoffed. "I am not in the least bit deceived by you, you know. You are becoming quite desperate, are you not? I daresay even my brother is beginning to realize you care only for yourself!"

"How dare you!" fumed Rosalie, sweeping angrily

forward. She reached out and seized Linette's arm in a punishing grip. "You despise me, Linette Montague, and I despise *you!* But I will not allow you to ruin—"

"Let go of me, you steely-eyed witch, or else I'll afford myself the pleasure of laying you flat!" threatened Linette, leaving little doubt that she meant every word.

Rosalie, growing positively spleenish, nonetheless snatched her hand away. Favoring Linette with one last poisonous glare, she flounced from the room in a high dudgeon. Noah, who stood waiting at his post for the visitor to leave, offered a polite bow as he opened the front door for her.

"Good day, Mistress Hammond," he said, his brown eyes twinkling with secret amusement.

"Good day!" Rosalie ground out between tightly clenched teeth. She stalked out into the warm sunshine and down the steps, uncaring of the fact that the young black woman who had accompanied her down the river—and who had obediently waited outside all this time—was forced to run in order to catch up with her.

Noah chuckled and shook his head to himself as he closed the door again. He had seen a good many people come and go during his numerous years at Shadowmoss. A good many. But never before, he mused with another low chuckle, had he seen anyone in such an all-fired hurry to leave. If what he had overheard—unintentionally, of course—was any indication, there was every likelihood they'd not see Mistress Hammond again anytime soon. He could not help but be cheered by the thought.

Devlin had not witnessed his betrothed's hasty departure. At the same moment Rosalie was furiously settling her skirts about her in the boat, he was tossing the saddle onto the broad sleekness of his horse's back.

He had never allowed anyone else to care for Ulysses, save for a young man by the name of Nathaniel who had a special way with animals, and that was the main reason the magnificent black stallion could be ridden by no other. Master and horse had shared much together throughout the past several years; indeed, as everyone at Shadowmoss had come to know, a day never went by without him racing Ulysses over the rolling, green-mantled countryside as though man and animal were one.

"Easy, boy, you'll run soon enough now," he murmured to the softly whinnying horse. Ulysses tossed his head in response, gave a loud snort, and pawed with what seemed to be impatience at the hay-strewn ground.

"If you please, Dev—Mister Montague, I should like to have a word with you," Meghan declared rather tremulously behind him.

He spun about at the sound of her voice. She had slipped quietly into the stables through the back door, just as she had done the previous night, so that she now stood outlined against the fading afternoon light. To Devlin, she had never looked more beautiful . . . nor more sweetly desirable. He cursed the fire in his heart and determinedly schooled his features to betray nothing of his inner turmoil.

"Yes?" he prompted in a low, resonant tone that sent a warm flush to Meghan's cheeks. She drew in her breath sharply and clasped her hands together in front of her.

"It concerns what happened in the drawing room."

"Does it?"

"Yes. I think you must realize, as I most certainly do, that my presence here will only continue to make things difficult between you and your betrothed."

"That it will," he agreed tightly, his eyes darkening.

"Well then, I . . . I propose that you follow her suggestion and sell me to someone else." Not that she had any intention of staying put wherever she was sent, she mused silently. No indeed, she would seek escape at the first available opportunity!

"What the devil are you talking about?"

"Either sell me to someone else, or give me my freedom!" she demanded stubbornly. "It is quite clear that Mistress Hammond and I will never be able to coexist peacefully within fifty miles of one another! Once the two of you are wed—"

"No!" he virtually roared at her. "I will hear no more of this blasted, asinine suggestion of yours! You belong to me, Meghan Kearny, and I'll not let you go!" Then, making it apparent that he considered the matter closed to any further discussion, he abruptly presented his back to her and went on with the saddling of his mount.

Stunned, Meghan stared with eyes full of confusion at the rigid, unyielding form of the man she loved. She had not expected him to give in to her demands without a struggle, but neither had she thought he would react with such bewildering fierceness.

"Why?" she questioned, marching forward to take an indignant stance on the other side of Ulysses. Since her head came only to the stallion's back, she was forced to shift her position of attack to a more effective one in front of the stall. "Why do you want to keep me here? I am nothing to you! If Mistress Hammond does not want me here, and I do not want me here, then why not get rid of me?"

"Don't tempt me!" he muttered, pulling the cinch tight and trying, none too successfully, to keep his eyes from straying to Meghan.

"And just what do you mean by *that?*" she stormed, her eyes ablaze with glorious, blue-green fire.

"Only that I may bloody well wring your neck if you do not get out of here and leave me in peace!"

"That is precisely what I am trying to do!" she shot back. Planting her hands on her hips, she gave a furious, defiant toss of her head. "I am perfectly willing to leave you in peace—*permanently!* If you will but give me my freedom, or arrange for me to serve in another household, then you will never be troubled by me again!"

"Damn it, Meghan!" he ground out, flinging about to take hold of her arms.

His fiery blue gaze burned down into the wide, sparkling depths of hers while his strong fingers tightened almost painfully upon her soft flesh. As had been the case from the very beginning, he could not seem to keep his hands off her—whether in anger or tenderness, he always found himself seized by the accursed desire to touch her.

"You are mine!" he reiterated in a voice brimming with raw emotion. "I will *never* let you go!"

"You shall!" she dissented hotly. "Even if I do not find the means to escape you before then, my term of servitude is for three years and no longer!" She took a deep, unsteady breath and appealed, "Please, can you not see that this is proving disastrous for everyone? You should never have brought me here, you . . . you should never have . . ."

Her voice trailed away when she became aware of

the strangely intense light in Devlin's eyes. His smoldering gaze raked hungrily over her, as though—*heaven help her*—as though he could literally devour her! She swallowed a sudden lump in her throat and felt her whole body coming alive with passion. Her heart cried out to his, her skin tingled beneath the hard, unrelenting pressure of his hands, and her pulses raced in anticipation of what she believed to be coming.

But it did not come.

Instead of surrendering to the urge to sweep Meghan into his arms and kiss her until she begged for mercy, Devlin set her firmly away from him. She could not know the effort it cost him to do so; she knew only that she had practically begged for his embrace and had been rejected. Pain, disappointment, and mortification washed over her, and she blushed fierily as she averted her face from Devlin's penetrating gaze.

"I will hear no more, Mistress Kearny," he decreed in tight, clipped tones, his eyes glowing dully. "You are mine, and mine you will be until I say otherwise."

He ached to hold her, to taste those sweet lips of hers and feel her heart beating against his, but he forced himself to turn away. Too much had happened that day already. As a result, his emotions were in utter chaos, his well-laid plans had all gone awry, and he still did not understand what the devil it was he felt for the angel-faced vixen standing so pale and silent before him. He *did* know, however, that his feelings for Rosalie had undergone a startling transformation. There was much to consider, he concluded as he stole one last look at Meghan, and he knew it was impossible to think clearly whenever she was around.

Meghan watched numbly as Devlin led Ulysses

from the stables and out into the yard. She remained quiet and motionless until she heard the sound of hoofbeats thundering away into the distance. Then, belatedly lamenting the fact that she had not remained adamant in her demands, she released a heavy sigh and took herself back to the house.

Thick gray clouds had now begun to gather in the sky overhead, signaling the storm which would come in the night. In more ways than one, nature was providing a symbolic glimpse of what lay ahead. . . .

Chapter Eleven

Rain continued to descend from the heavens with a vengeance the following morning. The weather did nothing to improve Devlin's dark mood; nor did it serve to lift Meghan's low spirits, either.

The night had seemed endless to them both. While the storm had raged outside, sending flashes of lightning to crackle across the sky and a constant rumble of thunder to split the air, they had lain awake in the loneliness of their beds and thought of one another.

The room assigned to Meghan was being redecorated for the new mistress of Shadowmoss—a fact she had not been able to forget for a single moment. Workmen had only to finish hanging the rosebud wallpaper for the undertaking to be complete. The elegant furnishings were as delicate and feminine as Devlin's were solidly masculine. The bed was also the antithesis of its counterpart in the adjoining room, for not only was it a good deal smaller, but it was swathed in a canopy and curtains of fine Belgain lace instead of heavy brocade.

When Meghan had awakened after finally drifting off into a troubled sleep just before the rain-cloaked dawn, she had been plagued by a feeling that something of great importance was about to happen. She could not say whether it would prove beneficial or disastrous. Like her Irish grandmother, she possessed a certain sense of impending events, but she could by no means lay claim to the ability to predict the future. No indeed, she mused with a wistful sigh, if she could do *that*, she would use her powers on her own behalf.

She frowned when memories of the night came flooding back to her again. Devlin had done nothing more than bid her a curt goodnight before locking her in. She had stared longingly at the door which separated them, acutely conscious of his every move in the next room. Although she had secretly yearned for him to break down the door and carry her off to his bed, she had been relieved when he did not, for she knew herself to be woefully incapable of resisting him.

Now, as she stood before the fire in the kitchen with her eyes fixed unwaveringly upon the flames, she was only dimly aware of the other womens' presence. Jolene and Naomi were in the process of tidying up after breakfast, while Mary was seated at the table with her infant son at her breast. The two remaining housemaids had already begun their work upstairs.

"We could use that hot water now, Meghan," the cook prodded kindly.

"Oh!" breathed Meghan, a guilty blush rising to her face as she was startled out of her reverie. She swung the kettle back from the fire and hurried to convey it across to the sink.

"I'll wager the storm kept everyone awake last night," offered Naomi. She cast an enigmatic smile at Meghan.

"Not me," denied Mary, gently rocking to and fro as her son nursed to his utter contentment. A year or two older than Naomi, she was a solemn young woman who spoke little. "I slept almost as soundly as the babe."

"Whatever the case," Jolene opined with a swift glance of appraisal toward the window, "I daresay we're to have at least another day's worth of this blessed downpour."

"Which means both Master Devlin and Mistress Linette will be in an ill temper," remarked Naomi, heaving a disgruntled sigh.

"You should not speak of them thus, Naomi," Mary reprimanded her with an unusually stern frown.

"But 'tis true!" the other housemaid retorted defensively.

"True or not," Jolene prudently intervened, "we've work to do and no time to stand about gossiping." She reached for the heavy clay pitcher on a shelf above the sink and thrust it into Naomi's hands. "I'll be needing more milk for the custard."

"But it—it's raining to drown the very devil out there!"

"Take the cloak hanging beside the door and cover yourself with it. You'll not drown," insisted the cook. Still looking far from convinced, Naomi reluctantly turned to do Jolene's bidding. Meghan, compelled by a sudden unaccountable impulse, stepped forward to offer,

"Wait, Naomi. I will go."

"You will?" The young black woman blinked her almond-shaped eyes in surprised disbelief.

"Of course," confirmed Meghan. She crossed to the door and took the pitcher from the housemaid's gladly relinquishing hands. "I am well accustomed to rain." Naomi gave her a smile of gratitude and helped her settle the hooded garment over her shoulders.

"Thank you, Meghan."

"Are you sure you remember the way to the spring

house?" asked Jolene. At Meghan's wordless nod, she added solicitously, "Keep to the path. And mind that you take care when crossing the bridge."

"I shall." Pulling the hood up over her head, she opened the door and ventured out into the midst of the torrent drenching the earth.

Her boots sank down into the mud as her steps inadvertently strayed off the brick walk, but she quickly regained her footing and went scurrying down the path. Cool raindrops stung against her face, but the tightly woven fabric of the cloak prevented her clothing from getting soaked. She hastened her flight across the grounds, soon arriving at the spring house and slipping gratefully into its dark, damp-smelling shelter.

Back at the main hall, meanwhile, Devlin was greeting yet another unexpected visitor—normally a rare occurrence at Shadowmoss. The determined man had braved the foul weather and traveled to his friend's plantation in the relative comfort of a "fall boat," all the while giving thanks that his ancestral home lay within only half an hour's journey along the river. He presented himself, water pouring from his greatcoat and tall beaver hat, at the front door of the house just as Meghan was setting off on her errand.

"Good morning, Noah!" the adventurous caller declared cheerfully.

"Why, Mister Charles!" responded Noah, his timeworn features reflecting mingled pleasure and astonishment at the sight of the tall, water-logged guest on the doorstep. "Please, sir, come in out of the rain!" he bid, swinging the door wide.

"That I will, you old rascal!" the younger man agreed with a laugh. Once inside, he quickly shrugged out of his coat and swept the hat from his head, then withdrew a handkerchief to mop the cling-

261

ing drops of moisture from his brow. "I trust your master is at home?"

"Yes sir, Mister Charles," answered Noah, taking the wet things from him. "He and the young mistress are in the drawing room."

"Thank you. I'll announce myself!" Oblivious to the fact that his muddy boots were leaving a trail along the polished floor, he sauntered away with the easy familiarity of a frequent visitor. He paused in the doorway to the drawing room, his twinkling green gaze surveying the domestic scene before him as he stood waiting for his presence to be noticed. Linette was the first to see him.

"Charles!" she burst out. "As I live and breathe, it's Charles Deverill!" She leapt to her feet and flew across the room to launch herself at him. It was her usual custom of greeting those she loved best.

"Hold on, Minx!" he chuckled. He was a glad recipient of her highly enthusiastic embrace, and he kissed her soundly on the lips before his eyes met Devlin's over the top of her head. "For heaven's sake, Dev, can you not teach her some manners?" he complained with a broad grin.

"I have abandoned all hope," Devlin replied dryly. He now came striding forward as well and took his young, raven-haired friend's hand in a warm and hearty clasp. "What the devil brings you out on a day like this?" he demanded, his eyes alight with genuine pleasure while his mouth curved into an affectionately taunting smile. "I thought you were still in England!"

"I was—until two days ago. I would have been to see you sooner if not for the fact that my mother refused to part with my company until now!" Another boyish grin tugged at his lips when he admitted, "Actually, she does not know I have taken myself off.

She believes me to be safely ensconced within the four walls of my room, poring over some dull, hackneyed volume of poetry while she sits below with her knitting!"

"You are beyond belief, Charles Deverill!" pronounced Linette with a look of fond rebuke. "You are a man of four and twenty, and yet you behave as though you were still in leading strings!"

"I pray you, Mistress Minx," he retorted teasingly, "don't start raking me over the coals until I've had the chance to dry out a bit!" He moved past her to stand before the fire, leaving the vivacious young redhead to make a highly expressive face behind his back. That done, she hurried to ring for some refreshments. Devlin returned to his own position in front of the comforting blaze.

"Your business in England went well, I hope?" he asked Charles. The two of them had formed a close friendship many years ago, while still half-grown boys roaming freely over the countryside, and were now like brothers to one another.

"Well enough," the other, slightly shorter and more slender man answered with a noncommittal shrug of his shoulders. He held his hands out to the fire's warmth and frowned idly down at the mud caking his boots. "To tell the truth, Dev, I doubt very seriously if I shall ever return there again. It isn't the same as when we were in school. Things are changing—*we're* changing, come to think of it—and you know as well as I do that this latest dispute over trade is going to lead to further trouble."

"There are some in Charlestown who are opposed to controversy of any kind," Devlin noted grimly. "They fear it will endanger commerce between the colonies and the Crown." He stared deeply into the flames, the firelight playing across the solemn, rug-

263

ged perfection of his countenance. "But soon, even they will be unable to close their eyes to what is happening."

"I can assure you that the growing discontent upon these shores is commented upon with great frequency in London," revealed his friend. "Indeed, it is being said that the king himself includes in his prayers each night a plea for divine guidance in dealing with us 'wild Americans'!"

"Do they really call us that?" Linette piped up from her seat on the chaise. She smiled to herself at the thought. "I consider that something of a compliment, don't you?"

"It wasn't meant as such," observed Charles.

"Was it not?" Linette parried with deceptive innocence, her eyes fairly dancing with amusement. "You must tell us all about your trip, dearest Charles. I will listen to practically *anything*, so long as you and Dev leave off with this tiresome discussion of politics!"

"I daresay you would not find it at all tiresome, Minx, if you had naught but rice in your pretty little head!" he was ungallant enough to remark. He was rewarded with a glare of mock indignation, which caused him to chuckle and reflect inwardly that it was good to be back where women were not always required to be docile, impeccably behaved creatures.

"What of your family there?" questioned Devlin, steering the conversation back to England. "Did you pay a call on your uncle as you had planned?"

"Yes. He and my aunt held a ball in my honor while I was staying in their home. I'll wager they invited every simpering miss and matchmaking mama in all of London!" he recalled with a groan as he finally moved to take a seat.

"And did you find yourself caught in any particular girl's trap, dearest Charles?" Linette challenged mischievously.

"How could I be?" His gaze was full of merry humor as he declared, "You know very well I have been pining away for *you* since that day you peeled off all your clothes and dove naked into the lake."

"I was not naked!" she denied, blushing furiously at the memory. "You are a shameless liar, Charles Deverill!"

"Well, you were almost naked," he relented enough to allow. "And since you were only ten years old, what difference does it make? Of course, if you ever take it in mind to repeat the incident, I for one should find it vastly more entertaining if you made certain you were properly undressed."

"Why, you . . . you . . ." sputtered Linette, finding herself at a rare loss for words.

Flashing her an unrepentant grin, Charles looked back to Devlin and sobered before saying, "Yes, well, my trip to the 'mother country' yielded a bit more than I'd expected. You see, I happened to hear the most amazing piece of news while I was at my uncle's. It seems there is an elderly kinsman of mine—Sir Henry Claibourne by name, a second cousin twice removed or something like that—who claims that his granddaughter has been kidnapped. From what I was told, the girl is not only beautiful, but remarkably spirited as well. I gather that she was much admired among her peers. But she has not been seen or heard of in a number of weeks now, and they say her grandfather is nearly out of his mind with worry. There is no way of knowing if she is alive or dead."

"Oh Charles, that's dreadful!" Linette proclaimed with a shudder, her eyes clouding with horror.

"Yes, and the worst of it is," he continued, "Sir Henry supposedly has reason to suspect the girl's stepmother was involved in her abduction. I remember something being said about the girl's late father, and the fact that the man's solicitor, an Irishman, came to London with the story of the girl's disappearance."

"You mean to say her own stepmother might be responsible?" asked Linette in disbelief. She glanced toward her brother, then grew puzzled when she saw that his face had taken on a strangely inscrutable look. He was staring intently into the fire again, his gaze dark and unfathomable.

"That is apparently a very real possibility," confirmed Charles. "The last I heard before I sailed for home, Sir Henry was off to Dublin with the solicitor to see for himself what to make of the situation." He paused here and released a somewhat disgruntled sigh before disclosing, "The devil of it is, I promised to make inquiries in Charlestown on this distant cousin's behalf."

"Does Sir Henry have cause to suspect that his granddaughter may be here?" This came from Linette, who had begun to wonder at her brother's continued silence. The truth had not yet dawned on her as it had him, so that she was baffled by the sudden grimness of his features.

"I don't know," replied Charles with a frown, "but my uncle charged me with the task of putting the word about. I've not yet had the time to pursue the matter properly, but I intend to do so when my mother and I travel into the city on the morrow."

His words were followed by several long moments of silence, during which time only the crackling and popping of the fire, as well as the rain drumming on the roof, could be heard in the cozy warmth of the room. Linette's bright, inquisitive gaze traveled back to Devlin, while Charles sat and pondered the task before him.

"What is the young woman's name?" Devlin finally asked, his deep voice quite low and resonant.

"Whose?" Engrossed with thoughts of his impending business in the city, Charles looked to his friend with an expression of mild bewilderment written on his face.

"Sir Henry's granddaughter, of course!" Linette supplied impatiently.

"Oh. It's Kearny. Meghan Kearny."

"*What?*" the lively redhead burst out, leaping up from the chaise. "Are you—are you certain of that, Charles?" she asked breathlessly, her eyes round as saucers and full of shocked amazement as they flew back to her brother.

"Quite," Charles assured her as he rose to his feet in a more leisurely manner.

"Oh Dev!" gasped Linette. Rushing to his side, she gazed up at him in stupefaction while a number of conflicting emotions played across her face. "So she was telling the truth after all! Good heavens, Dev, Meghan was telling the truth!"

"How did you know of it?" her brother demanded with a sharp frown.

"Why, she—she told me herself! The poor girl said she had been abducted and put aboard a ship, then taken captive by pirates, then—"

"Pirates?" Charles broke in to exclaim. Thrown into utter confusion by what he was hearing, he turned to Devlin for an explanation. "What the devil is going on here? Who is this Meghan you keep talking about, and what does she have to do with . . ." The sentence was left unfinished as realization struck him, too. He stared across at his friend in stunned disbelief, his face paling a bit and his eyes growing very wide. "Surely it—it isn't possible that *your*

267

Meghan is *Sir Henry's* Meghan?"

"It's possible, Charles," Devlin revealed tersely, his magnificent blue eyes aglow with a fierce light. "It's bloody well more than possible!"

"This is absolutely incredible!" breathed Linette, making her way dazedly back to the chaise and sinking down upon it. "To think that one of our servants should turn out to be the granddaughter of an English lord—and Charles Deverill's kinswoman!"

"My *what?*" ejaculated Charles.

"It's true! If she is the same Meghan Kearny being sought, then she is most assuredly your cousin!" Linette pointed out.

"But how the devil did she come to be here at Shadowmoss?"

"Dev rescued her from a pirate's harem and brought her here as his bondswoman!"

"The hell you say!" His gaze shot back to Devlin again now, anxiously seeking a denial. "By all that's holy, Dev, tell me none of this—this blasted poppycock is true!"

"I cannot," Devlin muttered tightly, his own thoughts and emotions in an upheaval. "Meghan Kearny is an indentured servant in this household. I rescued her—*by mistake*—from the island of Andros, where she was being held captive by a pirate known as The Wolf."

"What do you mean you rescued her 'by mistake'?" demanded Charles.

"Precisely that, damn it! Mistress Kearny and Rosalie Hammond were taken prisoner when their ship was attacked. Unbeknownst to me, Rosalie was no longer at the pirates' fortress when I arrived to free her. But Meghan Kearny was," he recalled, his gaze darkening again. "And it was she who told me that my betrothed's ransom had already been arranged. I returned to Nassau in an attempt to find Rosalie, but I was too late."

"Yes, and our *dear* Mistress Hammond is now safely back home again!" offered Linette, adding a moue of disgust.

"But that still does not explain how Sir Henry Claibourne's granddaughter came to be your bondswoman!" Charles told Devlin, visibly perplexed by what he had just learned. "Did she not apprise you of her true identity? Is she perchance trying to hide from her grandfather for some reason? Confound it, Dev, is this part of some elaborate jest of yours?"

"Yes. No. And no," Devlin answered each of the questions in turn while his mouth curved into a faint, mocking smile. "Mistress Kearny has maintained her innocence from the very beginning."

"Then why the deuce didn't you *do* something about it?" the other man challenged quite emphatically. "You could have seen that she was returned forthwith to England, or at the very least sent word to her grandfather that she was safe and in your keeping! Why did you do neither of these things?"

"For the simple reason that I did not believe her."

"Come now, Charles," Linette interjected reasonably, "surely you must admit that her story would sound a trifle farfetched to someone who did not know it to be the truth. Why, I myself doubted the credibility of what she told me!"

Charles lasped into meditative silence and sought the support of his chair once more. Linette's eyes returned to Devlin, who had resumed his intense scrunity of the flames. The air was charged with an almost visible tenseness, and it was into this volatile atmosphere that Naomi came with a tray of refreshments a few moments later.

"Good day to you, Mister Deverill," the young

housemaid proclaimed a trifle coquettishly when she caught sight of him. He murmured a preoccupied greeting to her as she ambled across the room to set the tray on the table. "Will there be anything else, Master Devlin?" she asked, favoring her employer with a dutiful smile.

"Yes, Naomi," he replied gravely. "Would you please tell Mistress Kearny that I wish to see her?"

"Meghan? Why—why, certainly, sir," Naomi stammered in surprise. "I'll tell her just as soon as she returns from the spring house."

"The spring house? What is she doing out there?"

"She's gone to fetch some milk for Jolene, sir."

"In this downpour?" he demanded with a scowl. Naomi's brown eyes widened at his displeasure, and she nodded quickly.

"Yes, Master Devlin. Jolene was just saying how she should have been back by now."

"How long ago did she leave?" His voice was edged with noticeable impatience now, and his eyes were filled with a harsh light.

"Well, I . . . I suppose it's not been more than fifteen minutes, sir."

Muttering an oath, Devlin strode purposefully from the room. Naomi stared after him in astonishment, while Linette and Charles exchanged looks of mutual perplexity.

Jolene was startled when she looked up from her baking to see Devlin's tall, muscular frame suddenly filling the kitchen's inner doorway. Since he rarely saw fit to pay a visit to the kitchen, his appearance was all the more unexpected. The cook hastily rubbed her hands on her apron and bustled forward to inquire, "Is there something amiss, Master Devlin?"

"Has Meghan not yet returned?"

"Meghan? Why, no sir, she has not." She watched

as he crossed wordlessly to the back door and flung it open. "Surely you're not going out there without a—" she started to protest, only to break off when, apparently heedless of the fact that he would soon be soaked to the skin, he disappeared outside. " 'Tis a dangerous combination," she murmured to herself, heaving a sigh as she turned back to her work. "To be stubborn and impetuous at the same time can prove quite dangerous indeed."

Plagued by visions of Meghan either drowned or escaped, Devlin reached the spring house in record time. He conducted a swift and thorough search of both floors, but Meghan was nowhere to be found. His mind racing to think of where to look next, he set off in the rain again, turning his steps toward the stables. He had traveled but a short distance across the rain-swept grounds when his ears detected the sound of a woman's voice raised in what he believed to be a cry for help.

"Meghan!" he whispered. Spinning about, he raced in the direction of her voice, his heart twisting painfully at the thought of her in danger.

He was both profoundly relieved and hotly infuriated when, upon reaching the same bridge he had crossed on his way to the spring house, his eyes beheld the sight of Meghan kneeling on the sodden grass in an effort to retrieve Jolene's cloak from the lake. She cried out in frustration again as she reached for the garment and came away with only a handful of twigs and leaves stripped from the trees by the night's storm.

"Meghan!" thundered Devlin, causing her to start in alarm. He covered the distance between them in half a dozen long, angry strides while she blinked numbly up at him through the rain. His hand seized her arm in a furious grip and yanked her upright.

"Damn it, woman, what the hell do you think you're doing?"

"What does it *look* like I'm doing?" she shot back, bringing her other hand up to angrily sweep the wet hair from her face. "I twisted my ankle on the bridge, and I dropped Jolene's cloak in the lake, and I've been trying to get it out of that blasted water ever since!" she informed him in a thoroughly exasperated rush.

"Of all the idiotic—" he ground out, then suddenly bent and scooped her up in his strong arms.

Meghan gasped, her features growing stormy and her eyes flashing with indignation as she demanded, "Put me down!"

"I ought to wring your neck, you little fool!" he growled, his arms tightening about her while he carried her back along the path toward the kitchen. The rain beat mercilessly down upon them, the water streaming down their faces in swift rivulets before increasing the already sodden condition of their clothing.

"But I have done nothing wrong!" Meghan vehemently protested, then demanded, "What about the cloak?"

"To hell with the cloak!"

Bearing her into the kitchen, he set her roughly on her feet. A startled Jolene, taking one look at Devlin's thunderous expression, wisely held her tongue.

"Get her into some dry things at once!" he directed the cook. Meghan bristled at being treated like a child.

"I am perfectly capable of getting *myself* into them!" she retorted, her eyes ablaze with angry defiance as she stood glaring up at him. Puddles were forming on the floor beneath them, but they were much too provoked with one another to notice.

"Then do it *now*," he ground out, "for there is someone here to see you!" Alternately tempted to either shake her or kiss her, he settled for subjecting her to a scorching look from those fiery, midnight blue orbs of his.

"Someone to see me?" she echoed, her eyes growing enormous within the delicate oval of her face. Her wet hair was plastered about her head, while her clothes hung in soppy clinging folds upon her supple curves. Devlin, drenched as well, found himself thinking that she looked damnably adorable.

"Yes, blast it!" he confirmed in a voice that was whipcord sharp. "I shall expect to see you in the drawing room in ten minutes—no more!" Wheeling about, he stalked from the room, leaving a trail of water and two stunned, breathless women in his wake.

Nine and a half minutes later, Meghan presented herself in the drawing room. She had changed into another gown, and had fashioned her damp tresses into a single long braid which hung down her back. Pausing just within the doorway, she saw that Devlin stood before the fire, his sister sat nearby, and a young gentleman whose identity was a mystery to her sat opposite Linette. The raven-haired stranger rose to his feet when he caught sight of her, and Meghan could have sworn he flushed in embarrassment.

Her eyes were drawn back to Devlin. He sported dry clothing as well, his simple attire of fitted black breeches and open-necked white linen shirt making him look both rakish and incredibly appealing. The firelight set his thick, chestnut hair aglow and glistened upon the polished leather of his boots.

"Come in, Mistress Kearny," he commanded in a low voice. She followed his bidding without argument, her pulses racing at the strangely foreboding gleam in his eyes.

"How do you do, Mistress Kearny," said the young gentleman as he came forward to politely introduce himself. "My name is Charles Deverill."

"How do you do, Mister Deverill," she murmured, unable to prevent a slight frown of puzzlement from creasing her brow.

"Please, Meghan, do sit here beside me," entreated Linette, smiling warmly. With a graceful gesture of her hand, she indicated the empty spot on the chaise.

Meghan obediently sank down, her apprehension growing with each passing second. She had certainly not known what to expect. Devlin had told her that someone had come to see her, but she had been unable to think of anyone who would do so. Since it appeared that this attractive young stranger was her caller, she was thoroughly bewildered as to what the purpose of his visit could be.

"What is this about?" she asked Devlin.

"I will allow Mister Deverill to tell you," he replied evasively, his handsome visage quite solemn.

"Of course," Charles agreed, though he did so with a conspicuous air of reluctance. "I—I suppose it's best if I get straight to the point." Sitting down again, he shifted a bit uncomfortably in the chair and appeared to be searching for the right words. Meghan read the consternation in his eyes when he looked at her and announced, "You see, Mistress Kearny, I have just returned from England."

"From England?" Hope leapt wildly within her breast. Her turquoise gaze shifted instinctively back to Devlin once more, only to see that he was staring at her with a strange, unfathomable expression on his face. His own eyes glowed fiercely, and she was almost certain she beheld a spark of something akin to regret in their piercing blue depths.

"Yes," confirmed Charles, "and while there, I was apprised of a most amazing story. My uncle was the one who gave me the news. It seems a kinsman of mine is searching for his granddaughter, who mysteriously disappeared while in Ireland."

"Then my grandfather sent you?" she demanded breathlessly, her head spinning at the realization that her ordeal was over with at long last. With wide and luminous eyes, she clasped her hands tightly together in her lap and waited for Charles to verify her hopes.

"Not exactly." His brows knitted together into a sudden frown, and he hesitated before asking uneasily, "If you please, Mistress Kearny, would you mind telling me your grandfather's name? You see, we—we must be certain of your identity."

"My grandfather is Sir Henry Claibourne, Mister Deverill. He resides in London, with my grandmother, and I have lived with them for the past several years," she stated with deceptive composure.

Inwardly, her emotions were thrown into utter chaos. It had suddenly struck her that, instead of being joyful and relieved at the prospect of going home, she felt only bitter anguish. Her heart ached terribly when she thought of leaving Devlin forever. Now that the moment had finally arrived, she was overwhelmed by a sense of desolation more profound than she had ever known. *Dear God, how shall I bear it?* she mused numbly.

"We knew it must be so the minute Charles told us the story!" exclaimed Linette. She reached over and took Meghan's hand in an excited grasp. "Oh Meghan, is this not beyond belief? You are actually cousin to our dearest friend! How fortunate that he happened to be visiting England at the same time the news of your disappearance was being spread round!"

"Linette and Devlin have told me of how you were abducted and taken aboard the *Bristol Packet*, Mistress Kearny," Charles revealed quietly. "And also how you were captured by pirates, then rescued by Devlin. Your grandfather will no doubt be overcome with happiness when he learns you have been found."

"I am so terribly sorry we did not believe you, Meghan," Linette offered with heartfelt sincerity. In the next moment, however, she laughed softly and added with a twinkle in her eyes, "But think of what your friends will say when they learn you have experienced such high adventure! I daresay they will be absolutely pea-green with envy! I almost wish *I* were the one who had been abducted! Yes indeed, you will no doubt cause quite a sensation when you return to—"

"Meghan will not be returning to England," Devlin suddenly declared. Three pairs of startled eyes flew to his face.

"Wha—what did you say?" faltered Meghan.

"Why, Dev!" gasped Linette.

"I say, old boy, what nonsense is this?" demanded Charles.

"Meghan will not be returning to England," Devlin obliged the trio by reiterating. His fathomless, midnight blue gaze fastened upon Meghan as he decreed in a low and level tone, "She will remain here at Shadowmoss."

"*What?*" Meghan stood abruptly to her feet and faced him with an expression of shocked disbelief. "Do you mean to say you still refuse to accept the truth?" She was both hurt and indignant at the thought. Her eyes flashed across at him as she lifted her head in proud defiance. "Well, it no longer makes any difference what you believe, Devlin Montague! I am free at last!"

"No, Meghan, you are not." His manner was one of deadly calm. "You belong to me."

"Surely you're not referring to that ridiculous contract you purchased?" asked Charles, incredulous at his friend's behavior. "Why, she was sold into bondage by mistake! I would have thought *you*, of all people, would seek to rectify this injustice without delay!"

"Do you truly intend to keep her as an indentured servant?" Linette demanded of her brother. "For heaven's sake, Dev, she is a gentlewoman, the granddaughter of a lord of the realm, and—"

"Precisely," he agreed with a mocking half-smile. "Which is why her reputation must be considered. You see, my dearest sister, Mistress Kearny had been thoroughly compromised. Sir Henry Claibourne would be the first to agree that amends must be made at once."

"Please, do not continue to discuss me as if I were some sort of—of *object!*" stormed Meghan. Her mind awhirl with angry confusion, she folded her arms tightly across her bosom and sat back down. She shot a narrow, resentful glare at Devlin. "And I fail to see why you should be in the least bit concerned with my reputation, since you are the one responsible for my being here instead of in England where I belong!"

"Dash it all, man," Charles remarked to Devlin, "are you saying that you and she . . . that you . . . that the reason . . ." He left off when proper words failed him. A dull flush rose to his face, and he darted a hasty, embarrassed glance in Meghan's direction.

"Why, Charles, you are perfectly correct!" pronounced Linette, her face alight with sudden understanding and purpose.

"I am?" he asked, thunderstruck to think that his wicked suspicions were, in fact, reality. "I say, Dev!" he burst out, turning a look of stern disapproval upon the other man.

Linette, her lively blue gaze moving to and fro between her strangely complacent brother and a speechless, wide-eyed Meghan, smiled a smile of utter devilment.

"Yes," the mischievous redhead told Charles with a significant arching of her delicate auburn eyebrow, "and if it should ever get about that the two of them actually occupied the same bedchamber in this very house—"

"*What?*" He rounded on Devlin in righteous indignation. "That cuts it all right to the core, Devlin Montague! You had no right to take an innocent, gently bred young woman like Mistress Kearny and . . . and force your will on her!" Warming to his subject, he grew visibly more outraged. "You were right when you said amends must be made—and *you*, my dear fellow, will damned well be the one to make them!"

"This is absurd!" cried Meghan, shooting to her feet again. She swept forward to confront the two men, her eyes ablaze with brilliant, blue-green fire. Drawing herself rigidly erect, she tilted her head at a proud angle and declared first to Charles, "For your information, Mister Deverill, there is no reason for amends to be made! Dev—Mister Montague has done nothing to me that would require restitution of any kind!" She turned her fiery gaze upon Devlin now. "Why don't you tell him the truth? Tell him I have suffered naught but wounded pride at your hands!"

"It would make no difference," Devlin insisted quietly, his own eyes holding a touch of wry amusement.

"You see, Meghan, society would still be inclined to believe the worst. Neither of us can deny that we have shared intimate quarters—nor can we deny that we have shared considerably more."

"We have *not!*" she hotly contested. Her face crimsoned beneath the bold possessiveness of his gaze, and she felt perilously lightheaded all of a sudden. "Why—why are you saying these things?" she stammered in confusion.

"Because they are true," he replied with bewildering equanimity. It seemed to her that he was displaying a remarkable lack of concern over the matter. Indeed, she mused in a daze, it was almost as though he was enjoying the whole, precarious situation.

"In that case, there is but one remedy for the situation!" proclaimed Charles. He gave Meghan a bolstering smile as he informed her with an air of great importance, "Since you are my kinswoman, it falls to me to see that the family honor is upheld."

"The family honor?"

"Yes. We are cousins, are we not? Surely you must see that it is imperative that we act before word of your predicament reaches London."

"Predicament?" she gasped. "There is no predicament! Nothing has occurred to create one! I have simply been residing here as any other servant for the space of two days and—"

"I'm sorry, Meghan," Linette saw fit to interject at this point, "but that isn't quite the way of it. My brother has never before required a servant to spend the night in his room. And do not forget the fact that you were aboard his ship without benefit of a chaperone for several days en route between Nassau and Charlestown."

"But there were a number of crewmen aboard the *Pandora!*"

"I am afraid, my dear," the other woman responded with a dramatic sigh, "that they simply do not signify."

"The only thing to be done," Charles solemnly decreed, "is for you and Devlin to be married at once."

Meghan stared at him as if he had suddenly taken complete and utter leave of his senses. Linette positively beamed in delight at the turn of events, for they meant she would be spared a lifetime of Rosalie Hammond. Devlin, meanwhile, remained deceptively cool and indifferent to it all.

"This cannot be happening!" Meghan whispered brokenly, her eyes very round and sparkling with several conflicting emotions.

"Oh Charles, you have hit upon the perfect solution!" exclaimed Linette, hastening across to lay a hand upon his arm. "A wedding will solve everything! No one would dare cast dispersions upon Meghan's good name once she is married to my brother!"

"No!" breathed Meghan. "Dear God, no!" She shook her head numbly, all the while telling herself that she must be lost in the midst of a nightmare. She loved Devlin Montague with all her heart, but she didn't want him *this* way. If she could not have his love, then she would not have him at all!

"I know you find it impossible to believe," Devlin finally spoke to her, his tone perfectly reasonable and his rugged features betraying none of his true feelings, "but I place honor above all else in my life. Charles is right. The only thing to be done is for us to marry."

"But . . . but what about your betrothed?" she faltered weakly.

"Mistress Hammond has nothing to do with this."

"Oh, but she does!" she protested quite vigorously.

"She is the woman you love, the woman you chose to be your wife and—"

"Everything changed the moment I discovered your true identity."

"Sweet Saint Bridget, have I not been *telling* you who I really am these last several days? I fail to see why anything should change because of what Mister Deverill has revealed to you!" she insisted in another burst of fiery-eyed vehemence. "You cared not a fig for my reputation before, so why should you—"

"I accept full blame and responsibility for my actions," he told her, his deep voice now possessing a discernible edge. "No one has ever been able to say that a Montague does not own up to his mistakes."

"Mistakes? So then, you wish to marry me for no other reason than to salvage your accursed masculine pride, is that it?" she demanded, her color high and her eyes kindling with bitter resentment at the thought.

"My reasons do not matter," was his only reply.

Meghan wanted to strike him. Her every nerve ending felt twisted and raw, as though she had been wrung inside out. Musing wrathfully that fate was playing yet another cruel trick on her, she fairly quaked with the force of her outrage. Never in her wildest imagination would she have believed it possible to be standing here before witnesses, receiving a proposal of marriage from Devlin Montague. It pained her to her very soul to realize that his offer had been prompted by nothing more than some cold, misplaced sense of duty.

"Well, I say, if you really are going to marry her," Charles intervened at this point, turning to Devlin with a broad grin of mingled relief and satisfaction, "then I will not, thank God, be obliged to call you out! I rather dreaded the prospect of fighting a duel with you, old boy, particularly since you are by far the better swordsman. My mother would have been deuced unhappy to learn I had been cut to ribbons."

"Your mother would be deuced unhappy to learn you had done anything without her permission!" Linette retorted dampeningly, then turned to her former servant and asked in genuine pleasure, "Oh Meghan, isn't it wonderful?" Beaming her a warmly lit smile, she slipped an arm about her waist and gave her a quick, affectionate squeeze. "I've always wanted a sister!"

"No!" cried Meghan in heartfelt defiance, adamantly shaking her head as her wide, anguished gaze met the smoldering intensity of Devlin's. "I will not do this! I do not wish to marry you, Devlin Montague! Indeed, I would not wish to marry *any* man who offered to do so out of guilt or . . . or moral obligation!"

"You have no choice," replied Devlin evenly, neither confirming nor denying her accusations.

"But this is preposterous! You hold no affection for me, you love another!" she pointed out in desperation. Turning to Charles, she appealed to him for help. "I'm quite sure, Mister Deverill, that my grandfather will not care if my reputation is damaged or not, so long as I am returned to him! He would never press me to wed for the sake of propriety!"

"I am afraid, dearest cousin, that he would do precisely that," Charles dissented in a kindly manner. He was in truth baffled by her continued resistance. Given the circumstances, he told himself, she should be grateful for Devlin's willingness to do the right thing. He said nothing of his puzzlement, however, merely explaining to her, "You see, I have no doubt whatsoever that, were he here himself, Sir Henry would demand that you and Dev marry without delay. There is no other way to prevent a scandal. You would never be accepted in polite circles if it were know you had . . . well, that you had passed the night alone in a gentleman's company without benefit of matrimony."

"Charles is right," seconded Linette. Her blue eyes shone earnestly when she told Meghan, "*We* know you to be entirely without blame in this affair, but there are others who would be quick to condemn you on the basis of the evidence before them. Not only have you been compromised as a result of my brother's misjudgment of you, but there is also the matter of your captivity among the pirates," she pointedly recalled. "And it is not at all difficult to imagine how intolerable your life would be with your reputation in shreds. No, my dear, your grandfather would want you to avoid such a fate at all costs. He would not only want to spare *you* the humiliation, but himself and your grandmother as well. Think of how they would be affected if you were to become an outcast among—"

"Enough," commanded Devlin, his deep-timbred voice brimming with impatience. "The wedding will take place tomorrow."

"There will be no wedding!" Meghan passionately maintained, her eyes blazing with stubborn defiance. "I will not marry you!"

"You will," he insisted in a low and dangerously charged tone. His burning, midnight blue gaze moved with studied unhaste over her trembling curves before returning to her stormy countenance. "Either you become my wife, or else you remain my bondswoman."

"You . . . you cannot make me stay here! Once my grandfather finds out where I am he will come and take me home, and there is nothing you can do about it!" she challenged rashly.

"I beg to differ," he answered with a faint smile. "Your identure is valid, Meghan, whether you are a highborn lady or an ignoble strumpet. Either way, you belong to me. The law is very clear on that subject, as you will soon discover if you refuse to marry me."

In that moment, Meghan knew with a certainty that she had lost the battle. She recognized the inevitable for what it was—a dubious future as the wife of the man she loved, the man who did not even want her for herself but for reasons she still could not comprehend.

Seized by a sudden, overwhelming need to escape, she shot Devlin one last rebellious glare before whirling abruptly about and leaving the room. Hot, bitter tears threatened to blind her as she flew up the stairs to the newly redecorated bedchamber which would soon be hers in actuality.

"Oh Dev," sighed Linette, her face reflecting considerable misgivings as she looked to her brother. "Do you really think this is best?"

"It is," he reassured her with complete aplomb. His magnificent blue eyes gleamed in anticipation of what was to come. "It is indeed."

Chapter Twelve

It was a very pale and somber Meghan who sat beside Devlin's sister in the hickory-springed "cheer" the following afternoon on their way to the nearby parish church. Devlin and Charles, who had presented himself at Shadowmoss a short time earlier, rode on horseback ahead of the light, two-wheeled conveyance driven by Linette and drawn by a single roan mare. The rain had mercifully ceased at daybreak, but the ground was still quite muddy and dotted by a multitude of puddles which glistened beneath the sun's rays. Smelling sweet and fresh after the storm, the air was also pleasantly warm and filled with the sonance of birds singing their own melodious praises of the Carolina spring.

Meghan's troubled gaze absently scrutinized the tall, moss-draped live oak trees flanking the drive which led from the plantation's wrought iron gates to the main road. Nearly three quarters of a mile long, the imposing "avenue of oaks" had been planted by Devlin's father many years ago to frame the approach to his new home. The result was unequivocally enchanting, and she could not help but be charmed by it, in spite of her preoccupation with other matters.

The impending ceremony loomed before her. She would soon be mistress of Shadowmoss, the wife of Devlin Montague, the former Meghan Kearny . . . *Meghan Montague*. The sound of her new name echoed throughout her brain, prompting her to frown and clasp her hands tightly together in her lap.

"It's perfectly natural for a bride to feel apprehensive on her wedding day," Linette offered consolingly. "I daresay I shall be just as nervous when I am wed. And that time may not be so very distant," she added with a secretive little smile.

"Do you mean to say you are already betrothed?" queried Meghan in surprise, momentarily drawn from her disquieting reverie.

"Not yet," the petite redhead confessed. Her eyes glimmered in wholly feminine determination. "But I have plans to remedy that particular oversight without delay."

Though tempted to ask her future sister-in-law to elaborate, Meghan held her tongue and turned her attention back to the passing scenery. Her slender, beguiling curves were encased in yet another gown originally intended for Rosalie Hammond. Fashioned of a pale cream, rose, and green floral silk, it was exceedingly elegant and featured a front-hooking, boned bodice with a low neckline above which the ruffles of a delicate, white lawn chemise showed. The sleeves were very full, ending in a flounce of lace at the elbows, and the gathered skirt was divided in front over a white satin petticoat.

Linette, who looked radiant as always in a ruched and lace-trimmed gown of peacock blue dimity, had insisted upon arranging Meghan's thick golden curls into a more elaborate style than she usually affected.

Brushed upward, her long hair had been wound about into a loose plait, then allowed to fall in one luxuriant tress upon her left shoulder. She and Linette both wore bonnets—or "dormeuse" caps—whose ruffles encircled the face and tied under the chin.

Meghan's brow creased into another slight frown as she raised a hand to touch the cameo worn round her neck on a band of black ribbon. Devlin had given it to her just prior to their departure. He had tied it on himself, telling her that it had belonged to his mother, and she had shivered when his warm fingers had brushed her skin.

Was theirs to be a marriage of convenience—or not? she wondered again, her pulses quickening at the possibility of the latter. It was a question which had haunted her dreams throughout the long night.

She had remained shut away in her room following the turbulent scene in the drawing room, and had refused to venture forth even when Linette had entreated her to come down for supper. Devlin had made no attempt to speak to her again, a fact for which she had been conversely relieved and discontented. When she had finally gathered the courage to face him again—at breakfast in the dining room that morning, where she had by her future husband's decree assumed the role of guest instead of servant—he had calmly informed her of his plans for the day, plans which included among them an informal wedding in the small parish church with only Linette and Charles in attendance as witnesses.

Recalling how her thoughts and emotions had battled fiercely with one another while she had agonized over her decision, Meghan released a sigh and shifted uncomfortably on the padded leather seat. Her eyes clouded with renewed confusion as she looked ahead to where Devlin rode astride Ulysses.

You must not do this! the voice of her conscience protested with ever-increasing vigor as the fateful moment drew closer. But she truly had no choice! she told herself defensively. She could not deny the truth of the arguments she had heard yesterday; nor could she deny what was in her heart. Though she had vowed never to accept less than *all* of Devlin Montague, she had finally acknowledged her inability to resist having him on any terms. She loved him more than life itself. He was willing to make her his wife. For whatever reasons, they would share a life together. Heaven help her, but she was only human after all—how could she *not* accept marriage with the man she loved?

Of course, she mused wistfully, there was always the possibility that he would learn to love her. Hope stirred within her breast when she recalled their times alone together. If physical attraction counted for anything at all, she thought as a rush of warm color stained her cheeks, then there was certainly reason to hope.

So there it was, she concluded with another soft sigh. She was marrying Devlin Montague. Her reputation would be saved, her grandparents would not face embarrassment on her behalf, and she would be remaining at Shadowmoss instead of returning to England. Her spirits lifted somewhat, and her gaze filled with a newfound resolve as it traveled longingly over Devlin's broad back.

I shall make your forget Rosalie Hammond! she vowed in silence. *As God is my witness, I shall do everything in my power to make you love me!* Once again, her indomitable Irish pride served her in good stead, for she could not bear the thought of surrendering to defeat without a fight. . . .

They reached the church a short time later. Linette pulled the horse to a halt before a charming, slate-roofed stone building set back from the road amid a profusion of shrubbery and trees. Boasting of a whitewashed, wooden bell tower and an adjoining cemetery with flat-topped tombs enclosed by a brick wall, the parish church had been attended by the same loyal worshipers for many a year.

The interior was distinguished by stained glass windows, pews with high walls or curtains, and a boxlike pulpit set at an impressive height on a pedestal. Each family had its own pew—in many cases, quite elaborately fitted out—while there were separate galleries across the rear wall and transepts for the servants and slaves, most of whom were required to attend Sunday services along with their owners.

Devlin and Charles, who had long been members of the congregation themselves, dismounted and moved to assist the ladies from the carriage. Charles escorted Linette inside, leaving Meghan alone with Devlin for a few moments.

"Pastor Trimble is expecting us," he told her. Though his handsome features were solemn, his eyes glowed with an inexplicable warmth. "I have told him only that you have been visiting from England. There is no need for him to know more."

"Why?" she demanded with a frown, her own eyes bridling with sudden resentment. "Because you are ashamed to admit to the fact that you are marrying an indentured servant?"

"No," he denied honestly. "The news will find its way about soon enough. I merely sought to delay its journey until after the public announcement of our marriage had been made."

"Oh, I . . . I see," she murmured, her gaze falling beneath the unnerving intensity of his.

289

She was acutely conscious of his proximity, of the power and heat emanating from his tall, forcefully masculine body. He was dressed in a well-fitted black coat and breeches, the simplicity of which only served to accentuate his muscular physique. His face appeared wonderfully tanned and healthy above the collar of his white linen shirt, while the sun's rays falling upon his head lit the dark, slightly waved thickness of his hair with gleaming touches of gold. Her skin tingled wickedly and her eyes glistened at the sudden, all too vivid memory of what it felt like to thread her fingers within his hair while his warm lips caressed her naked breast—

Meghan caught her breath upon a soft gasp when he reached for her hand and drew it possessively through the curve of his arm. Her luminous eyes flew back up to his face, only to find that he was looking at her with what she could have sworn was a combination of tenderness and desire. Fervently wishing that it could be so, she walked with him inside the church.

Upon emerging again a scant quarter of an hour later, they were lawfully husband and wife. The ceremony joining them in marriage had been short but nonetheless binding, and it was only now beginning to dawn on Meghan that Devlin had solemnly promised to love and cherish her for the remainder of their lives. Indeed, she mused dazedly, he had spoken the vows as though he had truly meant them, as though he had not been reluctant to do so at all.

Sternly cautioning herself not to place too much trust in what she had heard—nor in the sweetly compelling kiss he had pressed upon her lips afterward—she stole a look at him from beneath her eyelashes. She was surprised to see that he did not appear in the least bit like a man who had just been forced into marriage. His deep blue eyes gleamed with an unfathomable light as he met her surreptitious gaze, and she hastily averted her face in confusion.

Linette caught up her new sister-in-law in an affectionate embrace, while Charles shook hands with his friend and offered his warmest congratulations.

"I don't mind telling you, Dev," he remarked with a low chuckle, "that I feared you might change your mind at the last minute and thereby force me to fight that blasted duel!"

"You know me better than that, Charles," drawled Devlin, his own mouth curving into a smile of wry amusement. "I never turn back once I've set my mind to something."

"Yes, I remember all too well how deuced stubborn you can be!" He now turned to Meghan and brushed her cheek with his lips. "I am very happy for you, my dearest cousin. It is with great pleasure that I look forward to having you for a neighbor!"

"Thank you, Charles," she responded, smiling up at him in genuine warmth. A quick glance assuring her that Devlin was engaged in conversation with his sister for the moment, she added in a low voice, "In spite of my . . . my initial objections, I want you to know I am grateful for your support. My grandfather will be pleased to learn of it as well."

"I did nothing more than my duty to a kinswoman," he insisted earnestly. He took her hand and raised it to his lips while his green eyes twinkled down at her. "I salute you, Madame Montague. And I have every confidence that you and Dev will find happiness. The two of you are even more well suited to one another than I could have wished!"

Not at all certain what he meant by this last remark, Meghan nevertheless smiled at Charles again and allowed him to lead her back to the carriage. Jolene's Pastor Trimble had moved to stand in the doorway to the church, and he lifted a hand in farewell as the quartet set off on their way back to Shadowmoss. Marriage had been much on his mind of late, and the wedding he had just performed— though a trifle too impulsive for his taste—prompted him to consider the blessed state of matrimony with even more solicitude than before.

"Well then, I suppose I shall bid you both goodnight!" offered Linette cheerfully. She strained upward on tiptoe to give her brother a kiss, then hugged Meghan and kissed her as well. Her blue eyes fairly dancing with sisterly mischief, she cast Devlin one last significant look and said, "I daresay none of us will think it the least bit strange if you are a trifle late arriving downstairs in the morning. Of course, if not for the harvest, you and your bride would be able to go away for a proper honeymoon."

"And what makes you think a proper honeymoon may not be obtained at home?" he countered, a strange half-smile playing about his lips.

Meghan, her pulses racing wildly at his words, felt a blush rising to her face. She turned away and moved back to stand before the fireplace, while Devlin's sister laughed softly and favored him with a saucy grin.

"Touché, brother mine! Only pray, do not make the mistake of believing such things are of no consequence to a woman. I can assure you, when *I* am wed, I will not settle for anything less than a lengthy trip abroad!"

"Then you had best find yourself a man with a

great deal of money and no obligations—a rare commodity indeed." He raised the glass of brandy to his lips and drained the last of it, his eyes straying to Meghan.

"Perhaps," was all Linette would allow. With a toss of her auburn head, she swept from the drawing room, leaving the bride and groom alone for the first time since their return from the church. Charles had finally taken himself home just before nightfall, following a celebratory supper which had been served by a much subdued Naomi and a visibly delighted Jolene. Meghan had been able to eat little, but the others had displayed a healthy appetite, as well as an air of lighthearted enjoyment that belied the circumstances responsible for the event they were commemorating.

"The hour grows late," observed Devlin, his low, resonant voice bringing a renewed warmth to Meghan's cheeks. He negligently fingered the glass in his hand for a moment, then lowered it to the table. "It is time we were abed."

"No!" she blurted out, only to flush in embarrassment and look swiftly back to the dwindling blaze. "I . . . that is, I am not yet ready to retire!"

Now that the moment of truth had arrived, she realized, much to her chagrin, that her courage had fled. On one hand, she was heartsick at the thought of Devlin not wanting her; while on the other, she could not bear the thought that he did, for she told herself his desire to consummate the marriage—*if* such a desire existed—could stem from nothing more than either a lingering sense of duty or mere physical lust. Either way, she reflected miserably, she would be left unfulfilled.

But, as she was soon to learn, she had greatly underestimated her new husband . . . in more ways than one.

"Nonetheless, madam," Devlin replied with only the ghost of a smile, "I must insist." His deep blue gaze burned down into the wide, troubled depths of hers when he moved forward and took her arm in a firm but gentle grasp. "Come, Meghan," he commanded quietly.

"No, please, I cannot!" she cried, attempting to pull away. Devlin held fast, his dark brows knitting together in a frown of mingled annoyance and bewilderment.

"Damn it, woman, what nonsense is this?"

"It isn't nonsense! I simply do not wish to go with you!"

"You do not wish—" he repeated, then broke off as his displeasure grew visibly more intense. "You are my wife now, Meghan. It is your duty to obey me!"

"Duty be hanged!" she exclaimed hotly, her beautiful turquoise eyes ablaze with tempestuous emotion. "It was naught but duty that made you marry me, but duty will not make *me* do anything my heart tells me is wrong! Mayhap your precious Rosalie would have jumped at the chance to share your bed, but—"

"What the devil does Rosalie have to do with this?" he demanded as his fingers tightened about her soft flesh. His own gaze, already smoldering with passion, darkened even further.

"Everything! She . . . she is the one you love, Devlin Montague! I realize all too well that I am but a poor substitute for her in your eyes!" The pain was like a knife twisting in her heart. She furiously blinked back the hot tears gathering in her eyes and raised her head in an unconscious gesture of proud defiance.

"You are mistaken." His tone of voice, scarcely above a whisper, was one of dangerous calm.

"Mistaken? In what way? You cannot deny that you were betrothed to her—neither can you deny that you would never have married me if you had not been forced into it!" She wrenched her arm free at last and took an unsteady step backward before declaring, "I was a fool for ever believing this . . . this *arrangement* of ours could work!"

"We are married, Meghan. Nothing can change that," he decreed with unrelenting firmness.

"Yes, we are married, but in name only!" Choking back a sob, she was startled to hear herself saying, "I'm quite sure my grandfather can have the marriage annuled once I tell him—"

"There will be no blasted annulment!" he ground out, his eyes gleaming with an almost savage light. "No matter what you believe, no matter what you think of me, you are my wife and my wife you shall damned well remain!" He reached for her, but she abruptly retreated again.

"No! No, it . . . it cannot be like this!" she whispered brokenly. Without pausing to contemplate the wisdom of her actions, she spun about and raced for the doorway.

"Meghan!" Devlin's deep, authoritative voice rang out like a shot.

She drew to a halt, wavering between the desire to fly back and cast herself upon his beloved chest, and the impulse to find a secure haven in which to sort out her chaotic thoughts. In the end, she was not forced to make a decision, for Devlin suddenly crossed the room and swept her up his arms. A sharp gasp escaped her lips, and she could offer only a token resistance as he bore her purposefully across the foyer and up the stairs to his bedchamber.

He kicked open the door, then strode inside with his breathless, weakly struggling bride. He set her on her feet near the fireplace, where a comforting blaze had been started a short time earlier by one of the servants, and turned back to close the door. Sliding the bolt into place, he faced Meghan again.

"You are mine," he told her, his handsome visage forebodingly grim. "You have been mine from the first moment I tasted the sweetness of your lips aboard the *Pandora*. Deny it if you will—God knows I've tried to do so often enough myself—but the fact remains that you belong to me. And what is mine, I hold!"

"But you love another!" protested Meghan, her head spinning dizzily.

"No, Meghan," he confessed aloud for the first time. "I do not."

Her eyes grew very round as her expression became one of absolute incredulity. Surely she had not heard him correctly!

"You . . . you do not love Rosalie Hammond?" she stammered, her heart pounding within her breast.

"No," he reiterated, emphasizing the denial with a slight shake of his handsome head. He slowly covered the distance between them and raised his hands to close with gentle possessiveness about her shoulders. Gazing deeply into her eyes, he explained, "In truth, I think I've known it for some time—even before she left for England. I was reluctant to admit it to myself, however, and remained stubbornly determined to follow through with the marriage. But when I saw her again after all these months, I could no longer deny that my feelings had undergone a change."

"But you did not tell her of this, did you?" demanded Meghan. "Why? Why did you continue letting everyone believe you and she—"

"Because, blasted fool that I am, I still cherished the hope that I could somehow salvage my pride and find a way to recapture what had been lost between us."

Meghan fell silent now, her senses reeling at what she had just been told. *Devlin does not love Rosalie!* her heart sang. She waited for him to speak the words she yearned so desperately to hear—but he did not. Instead, he enveloped her with his strong arms and drew her close. She trembled as her soft curves were pressed boldly against his muscular hardness.

"So you see, sweet vixen, our marriage was of benefit to us both," he remarked in a low, husky voice that held a touch of ironic amusement. "Not only did it prevent your being irreversibly compromised, but it enabled me to escape a lifetime of being bound to a woman whose love I am convinced I no longer hold."

"I *do* see!" she agreed with surprising vehemence. Taking him off-guard, she brought her hands up and pushed at his chest with all her might. Momentarily free, she stumbled backward a few steps and stormed at him with righteous indignation, "It is convenient for you to think Mistress Hammond does not truly care for you, just as it is to your distinct advantage to believe I am so unfeeling enough as to be glad you have cast her aside without explanation!"

"And you are not glad?" he challenged curtly. "You were distressed by what you thought to be my attachment to her, so why the devil should you not be pleased to learn it no longer exists?"

Meghan could not deny the truth of what he said.

God forgive her, but she *was* glad. She was glad and relieved and flustered and wretched . . . and so many other things she could not name. Suddenly, nothing made sense. What was the matter with her? It seemed that love had reduced her to a quivering mass of feminine nerves! she thought with a self-deprecating frown. Confusion reigned supreme within her. She stared speechlessly up at Devlin, her gaze wide and clouded with her inner turmoil, her mouth opening to form words that would not come.

"I am not a man to be forced into anything, Meghan," he proclaimed quietly, his hand closing about her shoulders again. His piercing blue eyes seemed to bore into her very soul as he drew her masterfully back toward him. "I married you of my own free will."

"You did?" she breathed, stunned by his admission. Her pulses leapt crazily, and her legs suddenly grew so weak she was afraid they would give way beneath her.

"Yes. And what's more, my fiery little bride, I believe you were just as willing." He smiled softly down at her while his powerful arms gathered her close. The firelight played over the rugged perfection of his countenance and danced within his eyes. Meghan felt herself melting within his embrace. "If you are but honest with yourself," he charged as another faint smile touched his lips, "you will admit there is something between us which can neither be explained nor measured—nor denied any longer."

"But this . . . this is not the way it should be!" she faltered tremulously, referring to the fact that he had not yet declared his love for her.

"How else should it be?" he countered in a voice that was quite low and brimming with passion. His arms tightened about her, molding her so intimately against him that it seemed their hearts beat as one. "The time has come at last, Meghan. From this night forward, there will be no turning back. You are mine, and I mean to claim you for my own!"

"No! No, I—" she gasped out, only to be silenced by the pressure of his lips upon hers. She grew faint beneath the impassioned onslaught on his kiss, a kiss that was both tender and demanding. A low moan rose in her throat, and she felt her own traitorous desire rising to meet his. She entwined her arms about his neck, straining instinctively upward into the fierce ecstasy of his embrace while she returned his kiss with all the answering fire deep within her. His tongue thrust between her parted lips, exploring the sweetness of her mouth with such provocative thoroughness that she grew perilously light-headed and clung to him for support. When he finally relinquished her lips, she was left breathless and yearning for more.

"Meghan!" he whispered hoarsely, his lips roaming hungrily over her face before trailing a fiery path lower to the creamy flesh exposed by the décolletage of her gown. His hands moved downward to grasp the silk-covered roundness of her hips, bringing her into even more intimate contact with his hardness, so that she was made vividly aware of his desire. She gasped as he pressed a warm succession of kisses upon the alluring portion of her breasts which swelled above the bodice's low neckline.

Devlin, however, soon grew impatient to have more of her. His hand came round to unhook the front of her gown, his fingers performing the task with a dexterity that prompted Meghan to think he was entirely too familiar with the workings of feminine attire. She had to time to ponder her suspicions, however, for he swiftly tugged the unfastened bodice downward and sent the borrowed, floral silk gown falling into a heap about her ankles. Clad only in her chemise, she trembled in anticipation.

Then, he was stripping the delicate white undergarment from her as well. Her lush, womanly form was finally revealed to him in all its silken glory. A delicious shiver ran the length of her spine, and she blushed rosily beneath the searing intensity of his gaze as it raked over her. The fire warmed her naked skin, but it was nothing compared to the warmth created by the feel of her husband's eyes upon her. They literally devoured every plane and curve and valley of her body.

She marveled at her own boldness, to stand before him thus and not make at least some attempt to cover herself, but it seemed all her maidenly modesty had been conquered by the desire to please him—and to be pleased by him in return.

"You are even more beautiful than I'd imagined," he observed in a deep, resonant tone simmering with passion. He scooped her up in his arms again and carried her to the massive four-poster bed. Lowering her to the feather mattress, he straightened and began shedding his own clothes.

Meghan lay still and breathless, her eyes glowing with mingled fascination and desire as she watched him undress. He did so with dizzying swiftness, until at last he, too, was as naked as she. A sudden, involuntary tremor shook her, and she caught her breath upon a sharp gasp when he took his place in the bed beside her and almost roughly pulled her to him.

The sensation of bare flesh meeting bare flesh was enough to set her blood afire, for it felt unbelievably exciting and pleasurable . . . and right. So very, very

300

right. It was as though she had been waiting all her life for this moment in time, waiting for this particular man to teach her what love was all about.

Love? her mind's inner voice challenged archly. She came tumbling back to earth at the thought. Her body stiffened, and she murmured an unintelligible protest when Devlin attempted to reclaim possession of her lips.

"Meghan? What is it?" he asked with a frown of puzzlement. His arms tightened about her while his gaze searched her face in the firelit darkness. "Damn it, what's wrong?"

"I . . . I cannot do this!" she insisted, all her earlier doubts and confusion returning to hit her full force. Devlin's features relaxed into a tender smile.

"There is no reason to be afraid, wildcat," he assured her quietly. "I promise to be gentle."

"No!" She endeavored to pull away, but he was in no mood to release her.

"Come now, Meghan, you are my wife!" he sought to reason with her, his patience wearing dangerously thin as his masculine desire flared near the outer limits of tolerance. Holding her naked, delectable softness against him, it took every ounce of self-control he possessed to make himself proceed slowly.

"You don't want a wife, Devlin Montague!" she dissented hotly, squirming within his grasp. Her struggles only made things worse. "What you want is a . . . a *slave* to do your every bidding, to share your bed and ask nothing in return for the privilege of—"

"What I want, woman," he ground out, "is for you to shut up and let me make love to you as I have wanted to do every blasted time you called a halt to things! I have burned for you long enough,

301

you golden-haired witch, and I'll be damned if I'll be put off *this* night!"

Without warning, he thrust her unceremoniously back onto the bed and brought the length of his hard body down upon her startled softness. His hands seized her wrists in a firm grip and yanked them above her head, while he imprisoned both her shapely legs beneath the powerfully muscled pressure of one of his. Meghan opened her mouth to vehemently protest such rough treatment, but found herself silenced once more when his lips came crashing relentlessly down upon hers.

There was nothing gentle about his kiss this time. He demanded a response, his mouth virtually ravishing hers while his hot, virile hardness pressed her down into the mattress and seemed to scorch her wherever it touched. Keeping her wrists imprisoned with one strong hand, he lowered his other hand to her naked breasts. She suffered a sharp intake of breath when his warm fingers boldly stroked and caressed the satiny, rose-tipped globes, and she moaned low in her throat when he suddenly tore his mouth from hers and slid lower on her feverish body so that his lips and tongue could inflict their joint, exquisitely rapturous torment upon her breasts.

"Oh, Devlin!" she gasped out, her eyes closing tightly against the intense pleasure he was creating within her. His mouth closed about one of her breasts and sucked on the delicate peak, while his hot tongue flicked erotically back and forth across the nipple. His hand glided with single-minded purposefulness downward across her belly to the inviting triangle of soft golden curls at the apex of her slender, creamy white thighs.

Meghan caught her lower lip between her teeth when his gentle but insistent fingers parted the folds of silken flesh to claim the soft coral bud of femininity. Unable to prevent a faint, breathless cry from escaping her lips as he began a sensuous persuasion of her womanly flesh, she was dismayed to find her hips straining upward and her thighs parting of their own accord. She was being seduced with such swift, thoroughly inflaming mastery that she was powerless to resist what was happening to her.

Her head tossed restlessly to and fro upon the pillow as Devlin continued his wickedly delectable assault upon her body. His mouth returning to conquer hers once more, he finally released her wrists and positioned himself above her, his hard-muscled lower body between her trembling thighs. She stroked her hands almost wildly across the bronzed smoothness of his back, clutching him even closer as the ache deep within her—an ache that was strangely half pain, half pleasure—intensified to such a degree that she feared she would faint dead away.

Ultimately, it was Devlin who could bear no more. In spite of his resolve to make her want him so much that she begged him to take her, he could delay the final blending of their bodies not a moment longer. He lifted himself up a bit, seized Meghan's buttocks in a firm grip, then plunged within her velvety warmth.

She cried out softly at the sharp pain, but the discomfort quickly gave way to other sensations. Her passion spiraled higher and higher as her hips instinctively matched the rhythm of Devlin's thrusts. She clutched weakly at his broad shoulders for support, completely overwhelmed by the forceful, unbelievably potent combination of love and desire which coursed through her body like wildfire.

Her heart cried out to his in the moment of fulfillment. She felt as though she were suddenly hurtling heavenward, only to be shaken to the very core of her being when passion reached its inevitable, uniquely satisfying conclusion and sent her floating back to earth. Devlin, after tensing above her an instant later, released a long, pent-up sigh and rolled to his side on the bed. He tugged his bride's pliant softness close, cradling her beautiful golden head on his shoulder and keeping an arm flung possessively across her slender waist.

A lengthy silence rose between them, during which time they each became lost in their own thoughts. Meghan, though stunned and bewildered by what had just happened, realized that she felt a greater contentment than ever before. Indeed, she mused languidly, she felt as though Devlin had touched her very soul. She was his in every sense of the word now . . . as he had decreed, there could be no turning back.

She blushed anew as she recalled the shocking details of their first, wildly tempestuous union. She could never have imagined it would be like *that*. A complete innocent in the ways of the world she was not, and yet she'd had no clear notion of what took place when a man and woman joined together as she and Devlin had just done.

Her heart was so full of love for him that it was all she could do to refrain from giving voice to it. More than ever resolved to make her new husband feel at least a small portion of what she felt for him, she sighed softly and snuggled even closer to his hard, splendidly masculine warmth.

Devlin's thoughts, meanwhile, were also centered upon his recent claiming of his bride. Though he cursed himself again for not prolonging the sweet agony to the degree he had intended, he vowed that the next time would be different. He had never wanted to please any woman as much as he did Meghan, nor had he ever felt so completely sated as he did now. It wasn't just his body that was at ease for the first time in months, but his heart and mind as well. *And he knew the reason went far beyond the mere slaking of his physical desire.*

His eyes gleaming with mingled satisfaction and determination, he smiled tenderly down at the woman in his arms. Fate had gifted him with a good deal more than he'd bargained for that night on Andros. . . .

Chapter Thirteen

Meghan was awakened by the touch of Devlin's lips upon hers. With a soft moan, she stirred and turned into his welcoming embrace. His strong arms gathered her close, and she shivered in delight when her naked beasts swept against the hard, softly matted expanse of his bare chest. Her eyelids fluttered open, only to find that the room was bathed in darkness. Idly wondering how long she had been asleep, she glanced toward the fireplace and saw that the flames had burned down into nothing more than a few, faintly glowing embers.

"Your body would tempt a saint," her husband murmured close to her ear.

"Ah, but then you are no saint, Devlin Montague!" she retorted in a small, breathless voice, her eyes sweeping closed again as his hands set to roaming across her supple curves.

"Nor shall I ever be one," he whispered a bit hoarsely. Burying his face in the fragrant mass of her hair, he added, "Not so long as I have you in my bed!"

Meghan opened her mouth to offer another fitting reply, but found herself unable to utter anything more than a soft cry of pleasure, for Devlin's hand had suddenly closed about her breast. He rubbed lightly across the rosy peak, before cupping the ripe, satiny fullness and lowering his head to capture it with his lips.

Moments later, his fingers trailed with tantalizing unhaste down across the flat, silken planes of her abdomen to tease at the fluffy golden curls which crowned the juncture of her slender thighs. But instead of commencing with the eagerly anticipated arousal of her womanly flesh, he surprised his bride by rolling her over so that she lay facedown upon the bed.

"Devlin? What—" she started to question, raising her head to cast him a look full of bewilderment.

"This time, madam, I mean to make you pay for your torment of me!" he vowed, then proceeded to do just that.

Meghan gasped when his warm lips began a sensuous exploration of her body. Her hands clutched almost convulsively at the pillow beneath her head as he swept her hair aside so that his mouth could travel lovingly across the creamy, graceful smoothness of her neck and shoulders. Following an imaginary path, his provocatively attentive lips moved downward along her spine and the curve of her trim waist, before trailing lower to the firm, delectable roundness of her buttocks.

"Oh!" breathed Meghan, a fiery blush rising to her face as he gently nipped at her bare bottom. Her hips moved restlessly beneath his wickedly pleasurable caresses. She inhaled sharply upon another gasp when his hot, velvety tongue snaked out to lick with feathery strokes across her buttocks, before dipping lower to do the same to the silken paleness of her thighs. He did not cease the exquisite torment until he had reached the soles of her feet, at which time he urged her onto her back once more and smiled softly down at her in the darkness.

"Do you plead for mercy yet, sweet vixen?" he challenged, his low, passion-laced voice holding a discernible touch of roguish amusement.

"Yes!" she answered quickly, though without any conviction whatsoever. Indeed, her beautiful face was flushed with desire, and she was struggling to regain control of her highly erratic breathing. Her turquoise gaze, kindled with passion's fire, widened as she stared expectantly up at her husband in the darkness. She heard him give a soft chuckle.

"Denied," he murmured in a deep, vibrant tone. His eyes gleaming purposefully, he lowered his body atop hers and claimed her mouth in a searing kiss that served to further arouse her already riotous senses. She wound her arms tightly about his neck, straining upward against his lithely muscled hardness while her body filled with a veritable floodtide of love and longing.

She moaned weakly in protest when his lips suddenly abandoned hers, but she was well compensated for the loss when his mouth once again set to wandering. He first pressed a warm, leisurely succession of kisses across her face. Then, pausing briefly to linger at her ear, where his tongue dipped provocatively within the delicate cavern, his lips traveled lower along the silken column of her throat to where her pulse beat at such an alarming rate of speed. Moving lower still, he returned to her breasts, which seemed to beckon his ardent caresses. He was only too happy to oblige.

His hands glided downward to take her hips in a firm grip, his fingers curling about her enticingly rounded buttocks while his lips and tongue worshiped at her bosom. Meghan felt positively branded by his mouth, and she arched her back in an effort to offer up even more of her full, rose-tipped breasts for his moist possession.

Biting at her lower lip to stifle a cry of sheer pleasure, she grasped feverishly at Devlin's bronzed, granite-hard arms and squirmed beneath him. He groaned inwardly, his own desire raging nearly out of control, but he was still determined to bring her to such a state of arousal that she implored him to take her. It was not pride that prompted his resolve, but rather a wish to conquer the very last of her defenses and make her his, body and soul. *He would settle for nothing less.*

When he had satisfied himself that she was perilously near the limit, he left off his intoxicating torment of her breasts and scorched a path even farther downward. His hands tightened upon the firm mounds of her bottom as he bestowed a series of wildly stimulating kisses upon her silken, lavender-scented flesh. His tongue trailed evocatively across her belly, snaking down within her navel for a moment, before his lips moved lower still. . . .

"Oh, Devlin!" Meghan gasped out. Although she blushed fierily from head to toe at the bold, shocking intimacy of his caresses, she was nonetheless powerless to stop him. Her fingers traveled upward to thread within his thick chestnut hair, and she cried out softly as her passion intensified and became a white-hot flame deep within her. *No more!*

309

she thought in that small part of her brain still capable of rational thinking. *Sweet Saint Bridget, she could bear no more!*

"Say it, Meghan!" commanded Devlin huskily, sliding back up on her body while his fingers continued the rapturous inflaming of her sensitive, womanly flesh. "Entreat me to take you!"

"Devlin!"

"Tell me what it is you desire, Meghan!"

"Oh, please . . . please, Devlin . . . take me now!" she whispered brokenly, yearning for his possession with every fiber of her being.

She was rewarded for her obedience in the very next instant—though not quite in the manner she had expected. Devlin suddenly swept her up against him and rolled so that she was atop him. Before she could either protest or question his actions, she found herself being lifted a bit while his hands seized her hips in a strong grasp. He positioned her lower body so that she straddled his, then brought her expertly down upon his throbbing hardness.

A violent tremor shook Meghan as he plunged within the honeyed warmth of her feminine passage. With her luxuriant golden tresses shimmering down about her like a curtain, she rode atop her husband, meeting his impassioned thrusts while his hips tutored hers into the undulating, age-old rhythm of love. She quickly forgot all about the initial embarrassment she had felt at her position, and she reveled in the gloriously potent sensations he had awakened her to that night. Aware only of Devlin and the ecstasy they were sharing, she soared higher and higher on the wings of their mutual passion.

His hands returned to claim her breasts again, and a delicious shiver danced down her spine as she leaned forward into the splendid mastery of his embrace. Soon, they were both attaining the unequaled sweetness of completion, their passions exploding in a downpour of fiery sensations and the most overwhelming satisfaction they had ever known.

As they lay entwined together in the soft afterglow of their tempestuous loving, peace and contentment flowed between them. Their minds nearly as unified as their bodies had just been, they each smiled to themselves and gave silent thanks for whatever forces had brought them to this particular moment in time.

If her wedding night was any indication of what it was going to be like as the wife of Devlin Montague, reflected Meghan happily, then she had best be prepared to enjoy fewer hours of sleep.

Meghan stretched lazily in the bed and smoothed a loving hand across the empty place on the feather mattress beside her. Still warm, it bore the indentation of Devlin's tall frame, for he had arisen but a short time earlier and taken himself off with the announced intention of setting the harvest in motion. He had given his bride a long, wondrously stirring kiss after getting dressed. It had been with an obvious and extreme reluctance that he had left her.

Rolling to her back, she released a sigh and stared up at the brocade canopy. The room was filled with the first rosy light of the dawn—the draperies at the window having been thrown back by Devlin before taking his leave—and there was just enough chill in the air to prompt Meghan to remain snugly beneath the layers of quilted cotton. That is, until her conscience finally overpowered the temptation to idefinitely postpone her emergence from the bed.

Tossing back the covers, she slid from the massive four-poster. She shivered when her bare feet came into contact with the floor, and she wrapped her arms protectively about her naked body before padding across to where her gown and chemise still lay on the rug before the fireplace. Bending to retrieve the garments, she was made painfully conscious of the fact that her body ached in a dozen embarrassing places—some, she mused with a slight frown, she had not previously known to exist.

Her brow cleared when she recalled how her muscles had come to be plagued by this lingering soreness, and warm color flew to her cheeks as the memories of the night came flooding back to her mind. Incredibly, she and Devlin had made love a total of three times, each wildly enchanting union accomplished in a slightly different but undeniably satisfying manner than the one before. Before finally allowing her a few hours of sleep, he had made his possession of her so complete that—even if she *had* still doubted his commitment to their marriage—she would have been thoroughly convinced of their suitability as husband and wife. Surely no two people could share what they had shared and *not* care deeply for one another.

Of course, she thought with another sigh, Devlin had still not given voice to his feelings. Neither had she, for that matter. But, she told herself, the time for such declarations could not be long in coming, not if she and her devastatingly handsome husband continued to spend their nights in one another's arms. . . .

Giving herself a mental shake, she clutched the

discarded clothing to her naked breasts and hurried into the adjoining room. She was just about to ring for some hot water to be brought up when a knock sounded at the door. Quickly pulling a nightshift from the wardrobe, she donned it and made an attempt to bring at least some semblance of order to her tangled mass of hair. She abandoned her efforts as hopeless, however, and swung open the door. It was Naomi who stood smily shyly across at her.

"Jolene sent me up with this," explained the housemaid, her eyes falling to indicate the metal hip-bath resting on the floor of the landing. "She and Mary will be up with the water any moment now."

"Why, thank you, Naomi," Meghan replied with a faint blush. "It was very considerate of you and the others to . . . to think of it." She knew what else they must all be thinking—*and it was true!*

"Truly, Meg—madam, the bath was Master Devlin's idea," admitted Naomi. Though she looked a trifle ill-at-ease herself, she gave her new mistress another tentative smile and lifted the tub to carry it inside. "I'll light a fire. 'Tis likely you'll catch your death of cold without its warmth."

Meghan watched as the other woman positioned the bathtub before the fireplace and knelt to kindle the wood already stacked neatly therein. Musing with an inward smile that she and Devlin had created enough fire of their own the previous night, she was surprised to hear Naomi say, "We are all of us pleased you will be staying here at the plantation, Madam Montague. It was quite a shock at first—hearing that you and Master Devlin were to be wed—but I am glad for it and wish you much happiness in your marriage." The housemaid stood and

313

turned to face Meghan, who could read the sincerity in her brown, almond-shaped eyes.

"Thank you, Naomi," she responded warmly, her own gaze shining with gratitude for the woman's voluntary acceptance. "But please, could you not continue to address me by my Christian name?"

"Oh no, madam, I . . . I could not!" protested Naomi with a vigorous shake of her head. "Master Devlin would never allow such a thing!"

"Well then, perhaps you could call me 'Madam Meghan,'" she suggested, then added half to herself, "though it does sound a trifle odd." Before Naomi could reply, Jolene and Mary materialized in the doorway.

"Good morning to you, madam!" the cook proclaimed with her usual geniality. Mary solemnly bid her the same.

"Good morning," answered Meghan. She was relieved to see that neither of them appeared to feel uncomfortable in her presence, although they did treat her with a noticeable air of reverence. It saddened her a bit to realize that her relationship with them had been forever altered by her marriage to Devlin. Less than twenty-four hours ago, she had shared their position. And now, she mused in lingering disbelief, she was actually the new mistress of Shadowmoss. Strangely enough, fate had proven her friend instead of her enemy.

The women quickly filled the tub with the hot and cold water they had carried up from the kitchen, then hastened to leave Meghan to the privacy of her bath. Jolene, however, paused for a moment while the two housemaids went on ahead.

"I thought you'd want to know that I've already fed your husband his breakfast," the older woman

314

revealed with an understanding smile. "Once the harvest begins, it very nearly requires an act of Providence to get him inside for meals! But he charged me to tell you that his sister will see that you are kept entertained. I'll wager Mistress Linette is beside herself with impatience to begin imparting her vast knowledge of household management."

"Household management?" echoed Meghan, her eyes widening.

"Yes indeed. The duties will fall to you now. As the master's wife, it will be your privilege to give any orders you wish concerning this house, as well as any instructions pertaining to the servants. We are all ready and willing to serve you," she concluded amiably. "Now, I fear your bath grows cold, so I shall tarry no longer. If you desire anything at all, you've merely to ring for it." Her mouth curving up into one last bolstering smile, she left the room and closed the door softly behind her.

Meghan's sparkling, blue-green eyes filled with more than a touch of consternation as she stared after the cook. Pondering Jolene's words, she reflected that she knew very little about running a household, particularly one so large. As a child in Ireland, her mother had naturally seen to such details; as a young woman in London, her grandmother had done the same. There had always been servants to keep things in order, and it had been assumed that she would receive instruction in housewifely skills in due course, following her betrothal to a suitable gentleman.

A suitable gentleman, she repeated silently, wondering what her grandparents would think of Devlin. When she finally drew off the nightshift and eased her body down into the warm water, it occurred to her that they would probably be delighted with her choice of a husband. He was, after all, the owner of a highly successful plantation. And what was more, she thought as a warm flush rose to her face and her eyes took on a dreamy look, he was far superior to any of the men who had courted her back in England. *Far superior . . .*

Having bathed and then dressed in the same pink silk gown—cleaned and neatly pressed, of course—she had worn aboard Devlin's ship, Meghan descended the cantilever staircase in search of Linette. She found her in the dining room, where her new sister-in-law sat enjoying a cup of tea in anticipation of her arrival.

"Good morning, dearest sister!" the young red-head sang out when she caught sight of Meghan. Her expressive blue eyes, glistening with their usual vibrancy, narrowed a bit as she remarked with an eloquent little smile, "My, but you and Dev are up early. It is *my* opinion that he should have had the decency to wait at least until sunrise to go tearing off to his precious harvest!" She raised the china cup to her lips again while Meghan blushed faintly and took a seat opposite her.

"Truly, Linette, I did not mind."

"Nevertheless, I certainly did not expect to find myself so rudely awakened this morning. That brother of mine had the audacity to come pounding at my door before first light, merely to tell me that I was to see to you today—as if I would not have done so without his prompting. For heaven's sake, one would think 'wedded bliss' had addled the poor man's brain!"

Meghan smiled wordlessly in response, then poured herself a cup of the hot, fragrant brew from

316

the silver teapot. Though she was very much aware of the other woman's mischievous scrutiny, she assumed an air of complete equanimity and congratulated herself on keeping her hand steady.

"We have a great deal to do today, you know," announced Linette, perceptively changing the subject. Her brow creased into a pensive frown, and she released a sigh before adding, "I daresay Jolene has already begun preparations for the harvest celebration, but there will still be more than enough for the two of us to concern ourselves with. As always, the house must be put in complete order before we repair to Charlestown for the summer, and we simply *must* do something about your wardrobe!"

"My wardrobe?"

"Yes, Meghan," Linette confirmed, her voice holding a teasing note of exaggerated patience, "most definitely your wardrobe! You cannot continue to go about in things meant for *that woman*. Why, surely they must bring you at least a small measure of discomfort!"

"At first, perhaps," Meghan allowed thoughtfully. "But no longer." A well-contented glow lit her eyes, while her lips curved into a soft smile. "What care I about their intended recipient, when I am the one who bears the name of the giver?"

Linette regarded her with a look that was a mixture of humor and assimilation. She shook her titian-maned head, marveling inwardly at the transformations brought about by an emotion to which she herself had only recently been introduced.

"Nevertheless, you must have clothing of your own! We shall order you a complete trousseau once we get to the city, of course. But in the meantime I think we might be able, with one of the other wom-

317

en's help, to create an ensemble suitable for traveling. And a gown for the celebration as well," she concluded with a decisive nod.

Shortly thereafter, Naomi came in bearing a tray laden with ham and eggs, buttered grits, and freshly baked biscuits. Meghan was surprised to realize how very hungry she felt, and she proceeded to eat heartily for the first time since coming to the plantation. Linette, on the other hand, displayed an uncharacteristic lack of appetite, prompting Meghan to wonder if the other woman was preoccupied with matters of her own heart. She recalled Linette's enigmatic remark about the possibility of another wedding in the not too distant future, but she said nothing of it and instead struck up a conversation about the impending trip to Charlestown.

For Meghan and Linette, the remainder of the day was spent in the pursuit of domestic excellence. They became active participants in the spring cleaning of the main hall, neither of them inclined to sit idly by while so much was to be done. There were beds to be turned, floors to be scrubbed, rugs to be taken up, beaten, and put back down again, windows to be washed . . . the list seemed almost endless. Nor was everything to be accomplished in the space of a single day—it would require the full week's time of the harvest to finish, even with so many pairs of diligent feminine hands applying themselves to the work.

Devlin did not put in an appearance at the dinner table that afternoon, leaving his bride and his sister to dine alone again. They did not linger over the meal, however, for Linette had suddenly hit upon the idea of paying a visit to the attic, where she hoped they would be able to find something to aid them in constructing a gown for Meghan. Although she did not attach near as much importance to the matter as her vivacious young sister-in-law did, Meghan felt no reluctance whatsoever at the prospect of finally setting aside the clothes Devlin had bought for Rosalie Hammond.

Climbing the narrow staircase to the uppermost part of the house, the two of them entered the dark and stuffy confines of the attic. The gambrel shape of the roof provided a surprising amount of room, but the only openings were small windows in the gable ends. Linette, who had wisely brought along a lamp, held the light aloft as she hurried to fling open the windows and thereby allow a refreshing circulation of air to permeate the musty interior.

"There is quite an odd assortment of things up here, is there not?" she remarked to Meghan, her eyes making a broad sweep of the room. Cluttered with trunks, furniture, boxes, and other temporarily descarded—or forgotten—objects, it provided fascinating evidence of the Montagues' long, colorful history at Shadowmoss and before.

"It reminds me of our attic at Rosshaven," Meghan observed with a smile. She felt a sudden pang of homesickness at the thought, but she resolutely quelled it and wandered over to trail a light hand across the top of a leather-bound trunk.

"Rosshaven?" Linette moved to the other side of the trunk and faced her with a curious, expectant look.

"My childhood home in Ireland. Though it was not nearly so large and grand as this house, it was filled with its own wonderful memories, some of which were centuries old. It was my father's ancestral home, you see, and—" She broke off, her tur-

319

quoise gaze clouding with a sorrow she could not conceal.

"Why do you say 'was,' Meghan?" Linette probed gently. "What happened to your Rosshaven?"

"In truth, I do not know," she replied with a disconsolate sigh. "I had just learned, on the very day I was so cruelly spirited away, that it might be lost to me forever. My father had been deeply in debt when he died, and there was a woman claiming to be my stepmother—"

"Your stepmother?" interrupted Linette. "Why, I seem to recall Charles mentioning her! Let's see . . . what was it he said?" She frowned thoughtfully for a moment, before her brow cleared and her eyes lit with triumph. "Oh yes, *now* I remember! He said your stepmother is suspected of having been involved in your abduction!"

"Good heavens, are you sure?" Meghan demanded in stunned disbelief.

"Quite sure! And if she is indeed guilty, I for one hope she is thrown into the deepest, most thoroughly *vile* dungeon in all of Ireland!" the petite redhead declared with an emphatic nod.

"I have often wondered what Ambrose O'Donnell thought of my disappearance . . . dear Ambrose. I'll wager he began his own investigation before my grandfather had even been notified," Meghan theorized, half to herself. She sighed again and told Linette, "Whatever the truth, I am sure my father's solicitor will have it out soon—if he has not already done so. It is difficult to comprehend why a woman I have never even met would seek to do me such a horrible injustice. Ambrose did warn me against her, but I would never have believed her capable of perpetrating such treachery for the mere sake of what little was left to me by my father."

"Well, in any case, you are here with us now, dearest Meghan," said Linette, hoping to lift her spirits, "and I cannot deny that I am glad of it!" She gave her an impulsive hug, then knelt to open the trunk.

Easing the heavy, brass-trimmed lid upward, she set about rummaging through the tightly packed contents while Meghan held the lamp. A visible expression of delight crossed Linette's pretty countenance when her eyes fell upon a length of emerald green silk hidden away between two layers of unbleached muslin near the bottom of the trunk.

"Why, this was my mother's!" she exclaimed, rising to her feet with her prize. She unfurled the shimmering fabric and draped it lovingly across her body. "If my memory serves me correct, my father brought it back from a trip to Boston. I couldn't have been much above the age of seven then. My mother no doubt always meant to have it fashioned into something special."

"It's beautiful, Linette," pronounced Meghan, reaching out a hand to finger the lustrous folds of silk. "The color suits you perfectly."

"Does it? I think it would look much better on you." To prove her point, she held it across Meghan's taller, more well-developed form. "I was right! It will make a splendid gown for the harvest celebration. We must have you fitted for it at once."

"But I . . . I cannot accept it! It belonged to your mother, and surely she would wish *you* to have it!"

"Nonsense! You are her daughter now as well, are you not? Besides, Dev will be much more appreciative of it on you than Cha—well, than someone else would be of it on me!"

Linette obviously considered the matter settled, for she tossed the length of silk into Meghan's arms and whirled about to conduct a search in yet another trunk. By the time they left the attic and resumed their efforts downstairs, they had spent an enjoyable two hours examining the roomful of old treasures and sharing one another's company.

To Meghan, Linette had already become the sister she had always wanted, and it was obvious that the other woman felt the same. They each gave silent thanks for their compatibility, knowing full well how difficult life would have been had the opposite proven true. . . .

Night had fallen before Devlin finally returned to the house. His beautiful bride, who had by that time bathed and dressed for the traditionally late—albeit light—supper, sat curled up before the fireplace in her room with a book she had borrowed from his extensive library. It was yet another copy of William Shakespeare's plays, and Meghan had become so absorbed in it that she did not hear the door to her husband's room opening and closing.

Strangely enough, as she had discovered earlier, the door between their separate bedchambers did not have a lock. Even if she had been inclined to employ the use of one, she had little doubt that Devlin Montague would never let such an inconsequential thing as a door stand between him and whatever—or *whomever*—he wanted.

"Well, madam wife, it appears you have survived my neglect of you," Devlin remarked with a lazy grin as he stood framed in the open doorway. Meghan, starting at the sound of his voice, hastily set aside the book and rose to her feet.

"I . . . I have indeed," she stammered weakly, flushing beneath his scrutiny. She glimpsed the devilment in his eyes, as well as another emotion which set her pulses racing.

His hair was damp and waving rakishly across his head, and he was attired in nothing but an open-necked white shirt and a pair of fitted buckskin trousers. Unbeknownst to Meghan, he had washed the dirt and sweat from his body in the outside bathhouse, which featured an enclosed tub whose water was heated by fire-warmed stones carried inside and dropped into the bottom. Though an efficient means of bathing, the tub's use was, for the sake of modesty, limited to gentlemen.

"I trust my sister has been a dutiful companion?" he asked.

"Oh, much more than that!" Meghan hastened to assure him. "She is truly delightful, and I consider myself quite blessed to have such a sister-in-law!" Her heart pounding fiercely within her breast, she began to wonder if he was ever going to sweep her into his arms and kiss her as she had envisioned him doing so often throughout the day. She was sorely tempted to make the first move herself. But in spite of the bold intimacy they had shared the previous night, she realized that she still felt shy about being the one to initiate such things. *Please, Devlin!* she implored him in silence, longing for his embrace.

"To tell the truth, I had always imagined the two of you would deal famously together. You have a great deal in common."

"Do we?" Her eyes grew enormous within the delicate oval of her face as he finally began advancing upon her. His movements bespoke the easy, masculine grace with which he did everything—everything, thought Meghan with a shiver of remembered delight, except for one thing in particular. There had certainly been nothing leisurely or nonchalant about the way he had done *that*.

"You do," he affirmed, his mouth curving into a strange half-smile as he drew closer. "You are both headstrong and spirited, and damnably infuriating, but I am beginning to be resigned to my fate."

"And what fate is that?" She stared breathlessly up at him, her body atremble and her blood afire. His tall, powerful frame made her feel both incredibly small and perilously lightheaded.

"To be brother to one beautiful termagent and husband to another. And I can assure you, sweet vixen," he added in a wonderfully low and vibrant tone as he reached for her at last, "what I feel for you is not in the least bit *brotherly*." As if to prove his point, he enfolded her with his strong arms and drew her close. His gaze burned down into hers before he brought his lips descending upon hers in a kiss which, though tender at first, became fierily demanding in a matter of seconds.

Meghan's head spun dizzily, and she released a sigh of complete surrender as she melted against him. She wound her arms tightly about the corded muscles of his neck, her soft curves molding to perfection against his virile hardness while his arms held her so close she could scarcely breathe. His hot, velvety tongue masterfully plundered the willing sweetness of her mouth, and she moaned softly when his hands swept downward to close possessively about her buttocks.

"Oh, Meghan, Meghan!" he murmured hoarsely

against her ear once his mouth relinquished hers and set to roaming with sweet fervor across the silken smoothness of her face. "I have burned for you this whole blasted day, you little witch!"

"You . . . you have?" she breathed, the familiar weakness descending upon her with such swift and dizzying force that she feared she would soon be begging him to take her.

"I have, damn you!" he answered, his words more of an endearment than a malediction. Meghan drew in her breath upon a sharp gasp when his lips branded the creamy swell of her breasts.

Things would have in all probability followed their natural course right then and there, if not for the knock that sounded at the door. Meghan gasped in alarm and stiffened within Devlin's embrace, but he refused to release her. Another knock soon followed the first, and she was numbly aware of Linette's voice calling out,

"Meghan? Meghan, I should like to speak to you before my brother returns!"

"I . . . I shall be down in . . . a few minutes!" Meghan somehow managed to reply. Devlin's lips trailed mercilessly upward again to nibble along the graceful column of her neck.

"Very well," acknowledged Linette, frowning to herself on the other side of the door. "But don't be long!" She remained and listened for a moment, certain she had heard something out of the ordinary, but then gave a slight shrug of her elegantly clad shoulders and took herself downstairs.

"Oh Devlin, we—we must not keep her waiting!" Meghan gasped out reluctantly. She attempted to draw away, but he held fast.

"No, madam, it is *I* who will not be kept waiting!" he decreed, his deep blue eyes smoldering with passion.

"But Linette will begin to wonder at the delay!" she pointed out, her protests sounding woefully half-hearted even to her own ears. She swallowed hard and faltered, "And . . . and my gown will most assuredly become creased beyond repair if we—"

"Then we shall take care to prevent either occurrence!"

A startled gasp broke from Meghan's lips as she was suddenly hauled over to the large wing chair before the fireplace. Devlin, pausing only a brief moment to unfasten his trousers, took a seat on the edge of the chair and tossed up his bride's skirts.

"Devlin!" she cried breathlessly. Before she quite knew what was happening, he had seized her about the waist and pulled her forward, then down upon his lap. The firmly rounded cheeks of her naked bottom rested upon his hard, buckskin-clad thighs, while her silken limbs straddled his powerful lower body.

Her face flamed at the sheer wantonness of her position, but she had no time to ponder her embarrassment, for Devlin's hand delved purposefully between her parted thighs to begin a skillful arousal of her soft pink flesh. His other hand swept up to her back to urge her forward for his kiss, his mouth claiming hers with such captivating fierceness that she moaned low in her throat and curled her fingers tightly upon his broad shoulders.

It wasn't long at all before he was lifting her and bringing her down upon his rigid manhood. Stifling a scream of pleasure as he slid into her honeyed warmth, Meghan could have sworn he touched her very womb. Her head fell back, her eyes swept closed, and she clung weakly to him for support while his lips scalded across the tops of her breasts. His thrusts grew more and more demanding, her hips obediently following the command of his.

Finally, she cried out softly at the rapturous, explosive culmination of their passions. She collapsed weakly against Devlin, every square inch of her skin tingling deliciously while her husband tensed and filled her with his hot, life-giving seed.

Several minutes later, an increasingly impatient Linette was surprised to look up and see that Devlin was accompanying his wife into the drawing room. The petite redhead eyed the two newlyweds suspiciously.

"Why, dearest brother, I did not know you had returned already," she remarked with a saucy grin in her sister-in-law's direction. "Indeed, Dev, the reason for your wife's tardiness is now made perfectly clear to me!"

"Is it?" he retorted lazily, his gaze brimming with loving amusement as it moved back to a becomingly flushed Meghan. "It seems we are found out, madam. But the discovery suits me well, for there will no longer be any need to concern ourselves with either sisters *or* creases."

"Sisters or creases?" Linette echoed in puzzlement.

Meghan's color deepened as she gazed up at her husband, and her luminous, blue-green eyes promised later retribution for his roguish baiting of her. She left him to his brandy and crossed the room to take a seat opposite Linette.

"If you've no objections, Dev," said his sister, "I think tomorrow afternoon Meghan and I will venture outside and see for ourselves how the harvest progresses."

"Why this sudden interest in the harvest?" challenged Devlin. His fingers curling about the glass of brandy, he sauntered over to take his customary stance before the fireplace.

"It isn't sudden at all!" Linette insisted. "You know very well I have *always* been interested in everything that goes on here at Shadowmoss. It's simply that I thought the fresh air would do us a world of good."

"Are you sure it has nothing to do with the fact that Charles declared his intention of riding over tomorrow afternoon to discuss the shipment of the rice with me?" A crooked smile played about his lips, and his eyes gleamed with brotherly mischief.

"Of course not!" Linette denied a bit too vehemently.

"I should like to do as your sister suggests," Meghan intervened with a pointed narrowing of her eyes toward him. "She is correct when she claims the fresh air would do us good. We have been too much indoors of late."

"Very well," Devlin acquiesced, his heart stirring at the agreeable prospect of seeing his bride during the day. "But you may not remain for long. Charles and I have work to do, and the last thing we need is to find ourselves distracted by two young women who will invariably offer criticism or suggestions regarding our efforts."

"Why, that is completely unfair!" replied Meghan, bristling at his condescending, wholly masculine attitude.

"I think not," he disagreed with maddening calm. "It has been my experience that members of the fair sex cannot help but interfere."

"Then your experience has left you sadly misinformed!" she countered, lifting her head in proud defiance. Her eyes flashed their brilliant, blue-green fire up at him. "It so happens, Devlin Montague, that the greater majority of the 'fair sex' would not presume to interfere unless it was for a very good reason!"

"Perhaps. But the 'very good reason' you speak of occurs with amazing frequency, does it not?" Musing to himself that his wife's beauty was, as always, heightened by her anger, Devlin felt his desire for her flaring once more. It seemed that he would never get enough of her . . . the mere thought of holding her close again that night was enough to set his blood afire.

Meghan, cognizant of the fact that he was deliberately provoking, her, settled for throwing him another narrow look. Linette, meanwhile, chose that opportune moment to proclaim, "By the way, Dev, I'm *dreadfully* sorry, but I forgot to tell you that you received a letter today."

"A letter?"

"Yes, and I'll wager you will never be able to guess who it's from!"

"Blast it, Linette, where is it?" he demanded with a menacing frown. He watched as his sister withdrew the missive from her skirt pocket and offered it to him with a taunting little smile.

"It's from Rosalie Hammond!" she announced, her eyes dancing with irrepressible devilment. She turned to Meghan and remarked, "I knew she would not surrender to defeat so easily. Oh Meghan, how I wish I could have seen her face when Dev broke off their engagement!"

"I hope she was not too pained," murmured

Meghan. She experienced a sudden twinge of guilt, for she knew herself to be as much at fault as Devlin for what had happened. Still, she reflected with an inward sigh, she could not in all truth regret the fact that he had married her instead of Rosalie. And it had all happened so fast. . . .

"Pained?" echoed Linette, compressing her lips into a thin line of disapprobation. "I daresay the only pain Rosalie Hammond is suffering stems from nothing more than pride! She is no doubt livid over the fact that Dev would choose to wed another woman, and I'm sure her rage increased tenfold when she discovered *you* were to be his wife!"

Meghan, her eyes scrutinizing Devlin's face while he read the letter, did not offer a reply. She wanted desperately to know what Rosalie had written, but she dared not ask—at least not in Linette's presence. Promising herself to query Devlin about it later in the privacy of their bedroom, she was spared the trouble when Linette boldly demanded, "Well, brother mine? What does your former ladylove have to say? Is she still reeling over the fact that you married another?"

"She does not yet know of it," he startled her by admitting. Frowning darkly, he crumpled the letter into a ball and flung it into the red-gold flames dancing below the mantel.

"Oh Dev, truly?" gasped Linette.

"But," said Meghan in stunned disbelief, "I thought perhaps you had written to her—"

"No," he broke in to reveal in a voice that held a noticeable edge, "I paid a visit to her yesterday morning, at her cousin's plantation."

"Well, for heaven's sake, didn't you tell her you were marrying Meghan?" asked his sister.

330

Devlin shook his head wordlessly and looked to Meghan. He could well see that her face wore a troubled expression, and he silently cursed himself for his mishandling of the whole affair. *If only Rosalie had been willing to face the truth*, he thought, recalling the highly unpleasant scene between them.

"Why did you not inform her of your intentions?" Meghan finally demanded, her eyes full of hurt as they flew back up to meet the piercing intensity of his.

"Because, as I explained to you yesterday, I do not wish the news of our marriage to get about until a public announcement has been made in Charlestown. I would spare you as much embarrassment as possible, Meghan," he declared solemnly.

She could not doubt the sincerity of his concern. The realization that he cared so much for her feelings set her heart to soaring. With a catch in her voice and her eyes shining softly, she told him, "I thank you, Devlin, but I do not believe I could be wounded by anything or anyone now."

Staring deeply into one another's eyes, it seemed that an invisible current passed between them. It also seemed that they had momentarily forgotten Linette's presence, a condition the vivacious young redhead sought to remedy by clearing her throat a bit more loudly than was necessary and remarking, "I'm afraid Rosalie Hammond may very well seek to cause trouble for us once we are in the city." Her youthful brow creased into a frown as she questioned Devlin, "You did at least have the decency to break off your engagement to Rosalie first, did you not? I mean, I should hate to think my own dear brother was the sort of man who would keep a wife *and* a mistress—"

"Damn it, Linette!" he ground out, his blue eyes suffused with a dangerous light as he rounded on her. "You go too far!"

"Do I?" she retorted bravely. Just to be on the safe side, however, she rose to her feet and began drifting toward the doorway. "I must say, Dev, you have become something of an ogre lately. My only hope is that Meghan will somehow manage to improve your disposition!"

"I've a mind to improve your manners, you little shrew," he threatened in a low and level tone, "by turning you over my knee! *My* only hope is that Charles will take you off my hands soon." This last he spoke with a faint, sardonic smile and an imperceptible narrowing of his eyes.

Linette blushed furiously. Growing indignant, she balled her hands into fists, planted them on her hips, and confronted her brother with a resentful glare.

"Might I remind you, Devlin Montague, that it is not up to you to decide such things! You may not tell everyone else what to do, you know—least of all Charles Deverill!"

"No indeed," he agreed, ironic humor lurking in his gaze now. "That privilege falls to you. And to his mother, of course."

Meghan, certain that Linette's outrage would only increase, was surprised to glimpse an answering spark of merriment in those brilliant blue eyes that were so much like her brother's. She watched in amazement as Linette suddenly tilted her pretty auburn head back and gave a laugh of pure amusement.

"Oh Dev, you are impossible, absolutely impossible!" she proclaimed, sweeping back across the room to stand before him. "What on earth would *dear* Madam Deverill say if she knew we were speaking of her in such unforgivably irreverent terms?"

"I am quaking in my boots at the thought," Devlin quipped dryly. Sobering, he reached out a hand to take her arm in a gentle grip. "Believe me when I tell you I want only your happiness, Linette. But you must understand that I will allow no man, not even Charles, to trifle with your affections."

"Trifle with my affections? What are you talking about? Surely you don't suspect Charles—"

"I suspect Charles of nothing," he hastened to assure her, his expression softening again. "It is merely that I intend to protect you at all costs."

"You've nothing to worry about on my account, dearest Dev," asserted Linette, her hand raising to cover his affectionately. With a quick, meaningful glance in Meghan's direction, she smiled and told him, "I would say you have ample concerns of your own."

Then, stating airily that she needed to discuss something with Jolene, Linette took herself off to the kitchen. Meghan stood and wandered over to the window, where she peered outward at the darkening landscape. She was acutely conscious of Devlin's movements as he came to stand behind her, and she trembled in delight when his arms slipped about her waist and drew her back against him.

"This was always my favorite time of day as a boy," he revealed, his deep-timbred voice sending a shiver up her spine. "Evenings were as a rule reserved for doing whatever we pleased."

"And what did it please you to do?" asked

Meghan softly.

"I sat by the fire and read, occasionally challenged my father to a game of chess, or terrorized the servants by pretending to be a bloodthirsty savage in search of victims."

"You are still very good at terrorizing people," she teased. A delectable warmth spread throughout her body at the sound of his low chuckle so close to her ear.

"And you, my sweet vixen, are very good at provoking them."

"Why, how can you accuse me of that?" she countered defensively. "You have only known me a short time, and even then under the most disadvantageous circumstances!"

"I know you as well as anyone, Meghan Kearny Montague," he asserted in a resonant tone that was scarcely above a whisper. His eyes gleamed with a magnificent vibrancy, and his arms tightened possessively about her captivating softness. "Perhaps even better."

Her eyes swept closed, and she was content to lean back against him for several long moments. The heat emanating from his hard, thoroughly masculine body made her feel both secure and inflamed, and her heart was filled with so much love for him that she feared it would burst. Never in her wildest dreams had she imagined she would find herself married to such a man! He was still a stranger to her in so many ways, and yet she felt a peculiar sensation of having known him her whole life.

Indeed, she mused with an inward sigh, her happiness lacked only one thing to be complete—the certainty of her husband's love. His desire for her, while undeniably thrilling, was not enough. She desperately yearned for him to put voice to his feelings, whatever they were. *A woman needs to hear such things*, she remembered her mother saying long ago. Perhaps her father had not spoken of his love often enough. . . .

"I have been giving some thought to Linette's remark about a proper honeymoon," Devlin suddenly disclosed.

"You have?" asked Meghan in surprise, shaking off thoughts of the past. She stirred at last, turning in the warm circle of his arms so that she could look up into his face. "But I thought you said—"

"I'm afraid it will have to be postponed until after the season in Charlestown, of course. I promised Linette a full summer in the city."

"But I . . . I did not expect to go away at all!"

"Nevertheless, madam, I have decided it would suit me very well to have you to myself somewhere." A slow, tenderly wolfish smile spread across his handsome countenance, while his eyes burned down into hers. "I have heard it said that Ireland is an ideal destination for lovers seeking privacy."

"Ireland?" breathed Meghan. Her beautiful turquoise eyes sparkled with mingled pleasure and wistfulness. "Oh Devlin, *could* we?"

"I take it my suggestion meets with your approval?" he parried with loving mischief. The sight of her happiness gave him more satisfaction than he would ever have thought possible.

"Oh yes! A dozen times yes!" she answered, her face alight with joy and her arms moving up to entwine about his neck. "My childhood home near Dublin would be the perfect place for us to stay— that is, if it has not yet been sold," she added with a troubled frown.

"Sold?"

"To cover my late father's debts," she confessed sadly. "I would do anything in my power to save the estate, but I fear it is too late. I have been away so long, you see, and there is no way of knowing . . ." Her voice trailed away as her eyes clouded with renewed anguish at the memory of her beloved Rosshaven.

Devlin, his heart filling with a vengeful fury toward those who had caused her pain, gathered her even closer. His lips pressed a gentle kiss upon the top of her head, and his deep voice was brimming with emotion as he said, "I am sorry, Meghan, for ever having doubted you. I was a complete, blasted fool! I did not want to believe you. I knew that you were every bit as innocent as you appeared, but I refused to admit it, even to myself." He paused and cupped her chin with his hand, tilting her face up to his. "Can you ever forgive me, my love?" he asked softly, his midnight blue eyes holding such undeniable warmth and tenderness that Meghan felt her knees weakening.

My love, she repeated inwardly. His words echoed throughout her mind. *My love*, he had called her. A veritable floodtide of affection and longing washed over her, and she gazed up at him with all the love in her heart.

"I forgive you, Devlin," she declared tremulously, her eyes filling with sudden tears.

With her name a hoarse whisper on his lips, he brought his mouth crashing down upon hers. Meghan felt as though the world receded, leaving her alone with him in their own special realm . . . and she did not care if they ever left it.

When Linette returned from the kitchen a short

time later, she was only mildly surprised to find her brother and sister-in-law bound together in an embrace that would have been far more suited to the bedroom than the drawing room. She smiled to herself, released a faint sigh, and went back out to enter again in a much noisier manner.

Chapter Fourteen

The night of the harvest celebration finally arrived. Except for a few, last-minute preparations, all was in readiness for the most eagerly awaited event at Shadowmoss. Men, women, and children alike had done their part to make the harvest a success, and their handsome young master was anxious to see that they enjoyed their well-deserved revelry.

Throughout the long week, the rice had been cut by men wielding sharp sickles, then brought in from the fields on two-wheeled carts drawn by mules shod with special, broad-soled wooden boots to keep them from sinking in the mud. Meghan had stood beside her husband and watched as the ripened grain, poured from high platforms, was threshed with flails and winnowed by the wind.

She had been equally fascinated by the sight of the indigo dye being made—water was sent downward through a trough to the large wooden soaking vat, where the slaves beat the plants before scooping them up and putting them in the drying vat. The hard-fought process had yielded valuable cakes of the dark blue dye which could easily be transported to all corners of the world.

Idly recalling the week's events as darkness cloaked the countryside, Meghan subjected her appearance to one last critical appraisal before the mirror in her room. She owed a debt of gratitude to Mary's mother, for the woman, one of the plantation's seamstresses, had outdone herself on the creation of the emerald silk gown. It featured a deep pointed bodice onto which the skirt was gathered with numerous small pleats, a square-cut neckline trimmed with ruchings of the same lustrous fabric, and shirred sleeves with ruffles at the elbow.

Meghan could not help but be pleased with the effect. The gown's simple lines suited her to perfection, while the brilliant green color brought out the same viridescent hues in her eyes. What afforded her the most satisfaction, however, was the knowledge that the gown was hers and hers alone. She gave silent thanks once more for Linette's insistence that she have it, and she vowed to repay her sister-in-law's kindness in some way.

She lifted a finger to the narrow band of black satin about her neck, upon which was sewn the cameo Devlin had given her on their wedding day. Blissfully musing that no amount of expensive jewelry could ever compare with it, she raised her hand farther upward to tuck a wayward curl back into place. Naomi had helped her arrange her hair into a most becoming style, whereby the thick mass of golden tresses had been swept upward, tied with a ribbon, and allowed to cascade downward in the back so that they danced about the creamy smoothness of her shoulders.

Hoping that Devlin would approve of her appearance, she turned away from the mirror and gathered up her skirts to leave. Her eyes drifted toward the adjoining room as she crossed to the doorway. A sudden, rosy flush tinged her cheeks when she recalled, with shocking clarity, all the enchantment she and Devlin had shared in that big bed of his during the previous week.

Every night, after her splendidly virile and inventive husband had taken her to dizzying new heights of passion, he had held her close and pressed a tender kiss upon her brow. A variety of endearments, some wicked and some not, had passed his lips, but he had as yet to tell her what she longed to hear.

Still, thought Meghan with a sigh, she could not find in her heart to be rueful about anything that night. These past seven days had been the happiest of her life. . . .

Upon emerging into the cool night air in front of the house, Meghan was immediately greeted by Linette. The young redhead looked radiant in a gown of white satin, and her eyes sparkled with obvious pleasure as she drew Meghan aside for a moment to confide, "Oh Meghan, I am positively beside myself with joy!"

"You have seen Charles?" she asked with a soft, knowing smile.

"Yes, and what's more, he did *not* bring his mother! He has always done so in the past, you see, and when I spoke with him the other day he mentioned that she was planning to attend tonight. I do not know what could have occurred to change her mind, but I cannot deny that I am glad for it!"

"Then I am glad as well!" declared Meghan, her gaze aglow with loving amusement. She was about to say more, when she saw that Devlin was striding toward them. Her pulses quickened at the sight of him, for he looked devastatingly handsome in his black coat and breeches. He towered above the heads of the other celebrants, who were all dressed in their Sunday best and appeared to be joining in the spirit of things with great enthusiasm.

Tables laden with all manner of food and drink had been set up near the front steps, lamps had been hung from poles situated at intervals throughout the yard, and a trio of fiddlers had recently struck up a merry tune so that those who wished to dance would have ample encouragement to do so. Indeed, thought Meghan, Shadowmoss was vibrantly alive with music and laughter and the pervading sense of a job well done.

"You look ravishing this evening, my dearest bride," pronounced Devlin upon reaching her side. His eyes gleamed roguishly down at her, while his mouth curved into a crooked half-smile. "But then again, you have always looked ravishing, no matter what your attire—*or lack of it.*"

"Why, you scoundrel, you delight in making me blush!" Meghan accused with wifely indulgence, her color deepening as if on cue.

"Come, Madam Montague," he suddenly commanded. He took her arm in a firm but gentle grip.

"Where are we going?"

"It is traditional for the master of Shadowmoss to begin the festivities with a dance."

"Yes, and I must say," Linette piped up with a mischievous smile, "I am more than happy to relinquish my role as his partner. Take care, Meghan, for he possesses the uncanny ability to trod on one's toes every fourth step!"

"I shall bear that in mind!" promised Meghan, laughing softly as she allowed Devlin to lead her away.

They moved to the center of the brightly lit area designated for such activity, while the slaves gathered about in a circle. The musicians broke into the strains of a waltz, and Meghan was delighted to slip her hand into Devlin's while he held her about the waist and began twirling her around in the graceful movements of the dance. She was pleasantly surprised to discover there had been no need for Linette's warning—Devlin Montague danced as superbly as he did everything else. Applause and cheers went up from the crowd of onlookers, and several other couples now came forward to dance beneath the lamps' golden glow. The celebration had officially begun.

"Linette told me that my cousin Charles is in attendance tonight," remarked Meghan, her silken skirts rustling softly as she whirled.

"His mother left for the city this morning," Devlin revealed casually. A faint smile touched his lips, and his deep voice was brimming with humor when he added, "He seems determined to cut loose from her apron strings at last."

"I sincerely hope so, for Linette's sake as well as his own."

"Linette is too young to form a serious attachment, even if it *is* for an independent Charles Deverill."

"Why, she is but a year younger than I!" Meghan pointed out. "And you obviously did not consider me too young for marriage!"

"Ah, but then that is a different matter altogether," he insisted complacently.

"I fail to see how it is any different at all!"

"It is different for the simple reason that I proclaim it so."

342

"Because you proclaim—" she echoed in disbelief, only to break off as her eyes kindled with mild indignation. "Has anyone ever told you, my 'lord and master,' that you are quite overbearing at times?"

"I seem to recall having heard the comment before," he quipped with one mockingly raised eyebrow.

"Come now, Devlin, even you cannot decree what people will or will not feel for one another! If Linette loves Charles, and he loves her, then who are you to deny them—"

"I am her brother, as well as her legal guardian. It is for me to decide when and whom she will marry."

"But how can you possibly have any objections to Charles? He is, after all, your own friend. I, for one, think he and Linette are perfectly suited to one another!"

"What you think is of no consequence in this particular matter."

"Is it not?" she retorted, her temper flaring. Endeavoring to keep her voice down, she glanced quickly about before declaring, "If you desired the sort of wife who would bow to your every wish and thank you for the privilege, then you have married the wrong woman!"

"Be forewarned, wildcat, that I will brook no interference where my sister as concerned—not even from you," Devlin cautioned in a low, dangerously even tone, his eyes glinting like steel. His fingers tightened upon hers with almost painful force.

Meghan, however, refused to be intimidated. With a defiant toss of her shimmering golden curls, she sent her husband a narrow, proudly challenging look that left little doubt as to her own headstrong nat-

343

ure.

"Perhaps you would care to enumerate precisely what my duties are to include," she suggested with bitter sarcasm, her eyes blazing turquoise, "so that I may be certain not to overstep my bounds and risk incurring your formidable wrath!"

"Cease this nonsense, Meghan!" he commanded sharply. He, too, was acutely conscious of the fact that there were all too many witnesses to their marital discord. He leaned closer and spoke in a voice of deliberate calm, "You can storm at me all you like once we're upstairs, but for now, *madam*, you will behave as though you are enjoying the festivities!"

"Very well!" she virtually hissed in agreement. "But you have much to answer for once we are alone!" Forcing a smile to her face again, she managed to complete the dance in spite of the fact that she was positively simmering with fury and resentment.

Charles Deverill hastened forward to pay his respects to his beautiful, fiery-eyed young hostess once Devlin led her back to the bottom of the steps. Linette stood beaming beside her would-be suitor, but her happiness diminished somewhat when she glimpsed the telltale light in her brother's gaze. Taking note of the set look about his handsome visage, she glanced toward Meghan to see that there was undeniably something amiss in her demeanor as well.

"Come along, Charles," Linette said once as the usual amenities had been exchanged. "You have yet to dance with me, and I have no doubt that you will be properly dazzled by the polish I acquired while you were flirting your way across England!"

"Only London," he amended smoothly. Inclining

344

his head in Meghan's direction, he drew Linette's hand through his arm and led her away.

Although Meghan was still seething over her quarrel with Devlin, she could not help smiling at the sight of Linette and Charles dancing together. It was plain to see that love had blossomed between the two of them, she mused, no matter what the outcome of their attraction for one another. Her gaze drifted farther, her smile broadening when her eyes fell upon Jolene and Pastor Trimble. The cook's face was alight with pleasure, while the clergyman's usual somberness had given way to an expression of such delight that Meghan doubted he would remain unattached much longer at all.

"It is our duty to mingle with the others, Meghan," Devlin finally told her.

"*I* shall do so because it is a pleasure," she replied, making a pointed distinction between the two of them.

He said nothing, but merely took her arm and began strolling about the grounds to speak with the slaves. Meghan was once again struck by the fact that he appeared to know each of them very well, even the children. He was familiar with a great many particulars of their lives, and his conversations with them were surprisingly easy. Even more amazing, she marveled to herself, was the fact that he was obviously held in genuine affection and regard by the very people he owned.

Finally, they were free to dance again. Meghan, though perfectly willing to let her husband partner her for the lively reel, displayed no proclivity toward softening her anger toward him. She performed the steps with her usual skill and grace, but she remained unyieldingly silent whenever Devlin attempted to engage her in dialogue.

Heartsore at what had passed between them, she realized that she desperately wanted him to admire her for her intelligence as well as for her beauty. She had not been brought up to be a mindless decoration for her husband's arm, and her pride had been grievously wounded by his insistence that her opinion did not matter. Reflecting miserably that if was the first real disagreement of their week-old marriage, she swallowed a sudden lump in her throat and kept her face averted from Devlin's penetrating blue gaze.

She was startled when, the moment the reel ended, he suddenly seized her hand and began pulling her purposefully along with him toward the house.

"Devlin, wha—what are you doing?" she asked breathlessly. "We cannot leave the celebration!"

"We can and will!" he ground out.

Moments later, he was flinging open the door of his bedroom. He thrust Meghan unceremoniously inside, closed the door again, and rounded on her with a thunderous expression.

"Now, my dearest wife, I demand that you tell me what the devil you think you're doing!"

"What *I* am doing?" she gasped out. Hot, angry color rode high on her cheeks, while her eyes flashed up at him in outrage. "This whole thing began when you refused to lend any credence to the fact that I have a brain! Indeed, Devlin Montague, it may interest you to learn that I am entirely capable of reasoning, of making decisions—yes, and of forming opinions!"

"Blast it, Meghan, I never said you were not!" he denied angrily.

"Not in so many words, but you made it all too clear you do not care what I think or feel about anything!"

"That is not what I meant, and you damned well know it! But whatever your feelings toward me, you had no right to make them public knowledge!" His hands shot out to close upon her arms. Shaking her slightly for emphasis, he proclaimed in a low voice edged with sorely tried patience, "You are my wife now, Meghan. The mistress of Shadowmoss cannot go about spitting fire at her husband in front of the slaves!"

"I see. And would the *master* of Shadowmoss be taking his own advice?" she countered sarcastically, her Irish brogue very pronounced. Meeting his gaze squarely, she cast him a taunting little smile. "I would say your feelings were every bit as obvious as mine. You are, I believe, a man who prides himself on control, are you not? Well then, sir, I regret to inform you that you did not display the proper amount of it when we were dancing!"

"You little termagent!" he bit out. "I ought to take you across my knee and give you the sound spanking you so richly deserve!" For a moment, it appeared that he would surrender to the urge, but the thought of tossing up her skirts and baring her delightful white bottom brought him a rush of desire, not a tendency toward violence.

"You wouldn't dare!" breathed Meghan. Watching the conflicting emotions play across his face, she did not know whether to be prepared to defend herself—or give in to the answering passion which flowed through her veins like liquid fire.

"I would dare anything where you are concerned," he stated enigmatically, his deep, resonant voice sending a tremor through her.

Eyeing him warily, she was surprised when his hands grew gentle and slipped down her arms to close about her slender waist. Her breath caught in her throat, and her heart pounded fiercely within her breast as he drew her close. She looked deeply into his eyes, only to see that he was regarding her with intoxicating warmth instead of vengeful anger.

"Damn it at all to hell, woman, can you not see what you're doing to me?" he demanded hoarsely. "My life has not been my own since fate hurled you in my path! You fill my every waking thought, you haunt my dreams—I have never felt this way about anyone before!"

"And what . . . what way is that?" she challenged in a small, quavering voice. Her blue-green eyes were very wide and luminous, and she trembled beneath the intensifying pressure of his strong hands.

"I love you, Meghan," he declared quietly, finally voicing what he had acknowledged to himself a week ago. His smoldering gaze raked over her with fierce possessiveness, while his handsome features grew quite solemn. "I have loved you from the very first, though I was too blasted stubborn to admit it. I fought against it, I vowed not to lose my heart to you—but it was useless. The more I battled, the more ground I lost. My every defense was conquered by the same angel-faced little witch who raged at me one moment, only to melt sweetly in my arms the next. And since it appears I am of a mind to bare my soul to you," he added with a soft smile of irony, "you may as well know that I had planned to give you time to be certain of your own feelings before burdening you with mine."

348

"Burdening me?" echoed Meghan, her entire being flooded with such happiness that she could scarcely speak. Throwing her arms about him, she exclaimed, "Oh Devlin, I have been certain of my feelings since we were aboard the *Pandora!* I love you with all my heart! I prayed for you to return my affection, but I despaired that you ever would!" She gasped in delight when his arms crushed her against him.

"My love!" he whispered huskily, burying his face in her hair. "My beautiful, spirited little love!"

"I love you, Devlin!" she repeated, tears of joy sparkling in her eyes. "That's why I was so desperate to escape—I couldn't bear to stay and watch while you married another! And then when you told me *we* were to be wed, I was desolated to think you were making me your wife because of duty or . . . or mere physical attraction!"

"While I cannot deny I have always desired you," he allowed with soft, mellow chuckle, "that would not have been reason enough for me to marry you. Nor would duty, in spite of the fact that I have always held honor above all else. No, Meghan," he said, setting her away a bit so that he could gaze down into the glowing, upturned beauty of her countenance, "the discovery of your true identity served only to confirm what I had already come to suspect—I had fallen so deeply in love with you that I could not let you go."

"I suppose you were consumed with guilt about Rosalie Hammond!" she remarked with teasing sarcasm.

"At first. I blame myself for having become betrothed to a woman I did not truly love. She represented everything I thought I wanted in a wife."

"Indeed? Then it is no wonder you fought against your feelings for me!" Her brows knitted together in a frown of puzzlement when she asked, "But if you were so determined to deny what you felt for me, why did you insist upon keeping me with you? Once you had brought me to Charlestown, why did you not simply leave me in the care of the authorities as you had vowed to do?"

"Because, even then, I could not let you go. I told myself I was responsible for you and thus could not relinquish you into the custody of strangers. After all," he recalled with a crooked, self-deprecating smile, "I fully believed I would be a far more lenient master than you could ever hope to acquire. But the truth of the matter was that I could not endure the thought of your being sold to any other man!"

"And yet you were perfectly willing to keep me as your slave, while you retained Mistress Hammond as your fiancée!" she reminded him with mock severity, her eyes sparkling up into the loving intensity of his. "If I had not already been so desperately in love with you, Devlin Montague, I would have *despised* you for your churlish behavior toward me!"

"With ample cause," he conceded. Releasing a sigh, he drew her close again, his arms enveloping her with their sinewy warmth. "I have made many a mistake where you are concerned, my love, but I thank God I came to my senses before it was too late."

Meghan rested jubilantly within his embrace, her eyes sweeping closed and her heart soaring heavenward. *Devlin loved her!* her mind's inner voice sang. She was at last free to love him without restraint, free to give completely of herself without

350

fear of rejection. For the first time in her life, she knew what it was like to be truly loved by a man . . . a man unlike any other. Her prayers had been answered, and she knew she would never again curse whatever forces had sent her across the sea to find her destiny. No matter what she had suffered, she thought with a sigh of utter contentment, *it had all been worth it.*

Finally stirring again several moments later, she raised her head and sent her tall, handsome husband a look of purely feminine mischief.

"Perhaps now you would care to explain what you meant when you said my opinion was of no consequence?"

"My words were a damnably poor choice," he confessed, giving another quiet chuckle. "I do indeed value your opinion, but I must nonetheless follow my own counsel when it comes to Linette. However, I give you my word I will take your advice into consideration if the need should ever arise."

"Oh, it will most assuredly arise!" she insisted, then smiled hopefully and asked, "You don't consider me a mindless decoration, do you, Devlin?"

"A mindless decoration?" He responded to her smile with a slow, tenderly wry one of his own. His gaze smoldering with an irresistible combination of amusement and desire, he lowered his head and murmured just before his mouth descended upon hers, "That is something you will never be, my love—nor would I ever wish it."

Transported to their own earthly paradise once more, they forgot all about the celebration still going on downstairs. Time stood still and love reigned supreme, while the master of Shadowmoss literally swept his bride off her feet and carried her to the big, canopied bed . . . .

Elsewhere at that same moment, Linette and Charles were strolling along one of the lamplit garden paths. They had spoken of many things while dancing, though nothing in particular, and Linette had finally suggested they wander away from the celebration for a brief time. Charles had wholeheartedly concurred, so that they now found themselves alone beneath the trees. Music drifted pleasantly across the grounds, the faint sound of laughter joining the tuneful strains to be borne aloft by the gentle evening breeze.

"There is nothing quite like the smell of the country, is there?" observed Charles, inhaling deeply of the cool, sweetly scented air. "That was one of the many things I missed while I was in London."

"Oh? And what else did you miss?" probed Linette. Walking beside him with her arm through his, she flashed him what she hoped was a thoroughly captivating smile.

"The scenery," he replied without hesitation. "England's is pleasant enough, I suppose, but it certainly cannot compare with ours."

"Is there anything *else* you missed?"

"Several things. But I would not wish to bore you by enumerating them."

Linette was seized by the sudden urge to do him bodily harm. She had been making use of every feminine wile she possessed in an attempt to turn their conversation to a more personal nature, but to no avail. Every time she had endeavored to charm her reluctant suitor into a declaration of love, he had reacted by treating her as if she were nothing more than an engaging child.

But she was no longer a child! thought Linette in

growing exasperation. She had never considered Charles more than a friend, or even another brother of sorts—until recently, when her feelings for him had undergone such a change that she had been thrown into utter chaos! Although he had only been away for a few months, she had viewed him in an entirely different light upon his return.

Indeed, she recalled with an inward sigh, she had toppled head over heels in love with him that first day he had come to call, bringing with him the news of Meghan's abduction. Love had come to her in a blinding flash of realization. All that remained was to convince Charles that they were destined for one another. And that, she concluded with an imperceptible narrowing of her dancing blue eyes, was something she would do if it took all night!

"Let's have a seat, shall we, Charles?" she proposed.

Without waiting for his reply, she moved to a stone bench nestled in the shrubbery beneath a pair of massive live oak trees and sat down, arranging her white satin skirts carefully about her. Charles, his mouth curving into a crooked smile, followed her example and took a seat beside her. It was more dark than light where they sat, prompting Linette to offer, "Dear me, I suppose we are quite concealed from prying eyes here!"

"You mean from your brother's eyes, do you not?" he corrected. "I daresay he would have my hide if he knew I was out here alone with you like this!"

"But why?" she queried innocently. "For heaven's sake, Charles, it isn't as if I were in the company of a stranger! Besides," she added, inching closer to him and slipping her arm back through his, "I'll wager he is still much too preoccupied with matters of his own to take note of my absence. In fact, I would not be in the least bit surprised if he and Meghan do not come back down at all!"

"That doesn't sound much like the Dev I know. It wouldn't be at all in keeping with his character to miss his own harvest celebration."

"Ah, but you see, his character has been forever altered by his bride!" Looking very smug, she opined, "I'll wager they are closeted upstairs in his bedchamber this very moment."

"You little minx, what would you know of such things?" the attractive, raven-haired man beside her challenged in a voice brimming with laughter. Far more affected by her nearness than he would have wished, he met her irrepressibly twinkling gaze and groaned inwardly at the way his pulses took to racing.

"Far more than you think! After all, I reside under the same roof with them, do I not? One would have to be afflicted with total blindness not to see how utterly besotted they are with one another!"

"But I thought the marriage was one of convenience rather than love," Charles murmured in confusion. "It certainly appeared to be. That is, given the way it all came about. Why, Dev himself said—"

"Do you always believe *everything* my brother tells you?" Linette broke in, her tone one of exaggerated patience. "Trust me, Charles—they are very much in love, so much so that they can keep neither their eyes nor their hands from one another at every turn!"

"That does not necessarily signify love," he pointed out dryly. Fixing the vivacious young redhead with a look of fond indulgence, he elaborated

354

by saying, "While I am sure you speak the truth regarding Dev and Meghan, I have learned from experience that it is possible to . . . well, shall we say to crave 'carnal knowledge' of someone for whom you do not feel a heartfelt devotion."

"What you mean," she clarified with her usual audacity, "is that lust and love are two entirely different emotions!" She leaned closer in order to subject his face to a more exacting scrutiny. "Tell me, dearest Charles, how is it you came to be so experienced in this 'carnal knowledge' of which you speak?"

"Dash it all, Linette, you should not be asking me such things!" he protested with a stern frown of disapproval.

"Whyever not?" she retorted, settling back upon the bench with an unrepentant little smile on her face. "We are old and dear friends. It will do no harm to answer me truthfully. I know you are reputed to be a great favorite with the ladies, so who, may I ask, would be better suited to lecture me upon the 'sins of the flesh'?"

"Your brother, for one—or your brother's wife! Come to think of it, that particular duty should fall to your husband!"

"Do you really think so? I am not at all certain of that. In truth, Charles, would it not be to my great advantage to gain as much knowledge as possible about love and its pleasures *before* I am wed? It seems to me that my husband, whoever he may be, would be forever grateful if his blushing bride were not a complete innocent—"

"Where the devil did you get such pea-brained notions?" Charles cut her off brusquely. A sharp frown creased his brow, while his green eyes, usually full of good humor, darkened with intense displeasure. "I don't know who the hell has been filling your head with such nonsense, Linette Montague, but I'll be deuced if I'll sit here and listen to any more of it!"

"Why is it nonsense?" she challenged with a flash of spirit. "Do you honestly believe we women are unaware of what goes on in this world?"

"I cannot imagine *you* being unaware of anything," he allowed, a faint smile of irony playing about his lips.

"My friend Sally holds to the belief that we should become better informed upon a great many things," she remarked with a sigh.

"Your friend Sally is a flighty, forward girl who is granted far too much freedom for her own good!"

"Perhaps, but she is prodigiously well read, and her company never fails to prove enlightening. Speaking of which, have I told you of her new schoolmaster?" Linette then asked casually, though her blue eyes were aglow with a significant light.

The gentle wind teased at a silken, flame-colored curl which had fallen across her forehead, and she raised a hand to negligently tuck it back into place. Charles's gaze was drawn to the sweetly alluring curve of her breasts. Dismayed to feel a sudden fire in his blood, he shifted uncomfortably on the stone bench and tried to put a safer distance between himself and the object of his startling desire. Linette, however, determinedly closed the gap by sliding over in the pretense of rearranging her skirts.

"Now, back to the subject of Sally's schoolmaster," she pronounced with another winning smile up at the strangely silent and grim-faced man beside her. "At first, I did not credit that her rapturous descriptions of the man could be believed, but I soon discovered for myself that he is every bit as handsome and charming as she had claimed! And oh, Charles, I know you will not think it possible, but he bears an amazing resemblance to *you!*"

"To me?" he responded with a preoccupied frown.

"It is true!" she confirmed, her soft laughter sending the accursed warmth to his loins once more. "He has the same coloring, though he is perhaps a year or two older. He is a Frenchman, of all things, and he speaks with the most divine accent. All of the young ladies are in an absolute fever over him!"

"What about you?" Charles demanded with unexpected sharpness. "Are you in an absolute fever over this *divine* French schoolmaster as well?"

"I?" Her eyes grew enormous within the delicate oval of her face. "Why, Charles Deverill, surely you are not suggesting that I would ever form an attachment for a man who has no doubt seduced everything in skirts on both sides of the Atlantic?"

"Confound it, Linette, I don't give a damn how many women the man has seduced—just as long as he may not count *you* among his conquests!" His green eyes were positively blazing now.

"Why no, I daresay he will never be able to do that," she replied matter-of-factly. More and more satisfied with the progress of her scheme, she lifted a hand to her upswept titian locks again and added with a philosophical air, "But of course, who among us can predict the future? I mean, I certainly have no intention of finding myself swept away by him or any other man—I am not so naive that I do not realize the dire consequences such despicably immodest behavior would bring—but who can say for

357

certain what turn their affections will take?"

"Damn it, Linette, if I thought for one moment—" he ground out, only to break off and stand abruptly to his feet.

Linette was startled to feel herself being seized about the waist, and a gasp broke from her lips as she was yanked firmly upright before Charles. Stunned at the violence of his reaction, she blinked up into her beloved's uncharacteristically thunderous features and felt a tremor of half fear, half delight course through her body.

"Why, Charles!" she breathed.

"Shut up and listen to me!" he commanded tersely, his fingers clenching about her waist. "First of all, I forbid you to spend any more time in the company of that accursed, lecherous Frenchman! Secondly, if you ever so much as think about losing your head over a man, then it had damned well better be *me!*"

"What right have you to forbid me anything?" she shot back defiantly.

"Other than Dev, there are none who have a better right!"

"Indeed? And what, pray tell, makes you think that? You are no kinsman of mine, Charles Deverill, so I fail to see how you can possibly lay claim to the privilege of ordering me about!"

"I lay claim to it by virtue of a long and highly intimate acquaintance!" he insisted, his temper flaring while his passions flamed. He told himself he should release her, and yet he could not make his hands obey.

"Highly intimate?" Her lips curled into a soft, challenging smile, while her eyes twinkled impudently up at him. "Dear me, to think that you and

358

I have been 'highly intimate' all this time and I have not even been aware of it!" Heaving a dramatic sigh, she allowed her gaze to drift to the glow of the nearby lamp. "I sincerely hope that when I am wed, my husband will see fit to enlighten me more than you have done."

"You little vixen, I should like to *enlighten* you until you beg for mercy!" he declared impulsively.

"Truly, Charles?" Linette asked with deceptive, wide-eyed innocence. She raised her hands rather tentatively to his shoulders. "Well, do you . . . do you suppose we might begin lesson number one right now?" There was no denying the invitation of her slightly parted lips, nor the come-hither look in her eyes.

Although he was still blissfully ignorant of the fact, Charles Deverill had lost not only the present battle, but the entire war as well. He was destined for a lifetime of keeping up with the same spirited, willful redhead who had blossomed from a precocious child into an equally precocious but thoroughly bewitching young woman. To say that he would be led a merry chase for the next fifty or sixty years would be to greatly underestimate the extent of his trouble—*and* his pleasure.

For now, however, he was content to sweep Linette into his arms and kiss her as he had longed to do all evening. She thrilled to his masterful embrace, and she responded with such sweetly compelling ardor that Charles felt his senses reeling. Never again would he think of her as a child . . . .

Meghan and Devlin, meanwhile, reluctantly left the bedroom and traveled back downstairs to resume their duties at the celebration. They had been absent for a little less than an hour. Their time alone together had without a doubt proven to be the most completely satisfying and ultimately rewarding sixty minutes either of them had ever known.

The celebration finally drew to a close shortly after midnight. As the happily exhausted participants sought their beds, they gave thanks for another successful harvest at Shadowmoss. In spite of all the trials and tribulations life had sent their way, they could still be grateful for the fact that they had contributed, each in their own way, to the prosperity of one of the most magnificent plantations in all the colonies.

Meghan and Linette, lying awake in their beds, both mused that the evening had gifted them with far more than they had hoped. They looked forward to the next day with a good deal of excitement, and their thoughts were of a similarly romantic nature as they finally drifted off to sleep. There was one major difference between them, however. Whereas Linette snuggled down beneath the covers alone, Meghan did so with a devastatingly handsome rogue at her side—and a soft smile of contentment on her lips.

Chapter Fifteen

Traveling down the river, the Montagues reached Charlestown in the early hours of the afternoon. Jolene was the only servant to accompany them, the others having remained behind to look after the main hall at Shadowmoss during the next four months, although Devlin had mentioned the possiblity of sending for Naomi in the near future. Following the usual custom, the household in the city was completely separate from the one at the plantation, with a different set of servants and a markedly different lifestyle as well.

Meghan, reflecting that it seemed a good deal more than a fortnight since she had last set eyes upon Charlestown's crowded, bustling waterfront, smiled up at her husband as he assisted her from the awning-covered barge. The baggage, which Devlin had dryly referred to as a "mountainous collection of feminine finery," had been transported from the plantation in a separate boat and would soon be taken on to the townhouse.

Smoothing down the skirts of her newly completed traveling suit—a simple but fashionable gown of dark blue linen with a matching jacket—Meghan turned and watched while Devlin quickly swung his sister and then Jolene up to the wharf. The day was a warm and windy one, and the air was alive with the sounds and smells Meghan remembered clearly from her one brief, unhappy sojourn at the same location. *Had it really been a mere two weeks?* she marveled to herself in silence. *It did not seem possible that the circumstances of her life could have changed so much in a matter days* . . . .

"You know," said Linette, linking her arm companionably through Meghan's, "I suspect that even if it were not for the necessity of taking refuge from the mosquitoes which overrun the plantations every summer, Charlestown would still suffer the same deluge of humanity. If for no other reason than to pacify their wives and daughters for all the previous months of neglect, the men would, I am quite certain, continue to pack themselves and their entire families off to the city for the season!"

"From what you have told me, it does indeed offer a remarkable array of diversions," replied Meghan, smiling warmly at her sister-in-law.

"I have never before seen the like!" Jolene commented while treading carefully across the rough, salt-coated wooden planks. She held tight to her full skirts as the wind threatened to send them flying immodestly up about her ankles. "Why, there are receptions, card parties, balls, concerts—I'll wager you and master Devlin were called forth to a different house every night last year!" she observed to Linette.

"Yes, and dear Jolene was always waiting up whenever we returned home again!" responded Linette with a fondly teasing look at the older woman. "Though I doubt if she will be quite so

362

ready to press me for details of all the handsome young gallants this year. Her mind is no doubt so full of Pastor Trimble that she will require no thoughts of other men!"

Jolene merely laughed and tugged the ribbons of her cap more snugly together beneath her chin. Devlin now came forward to claim his wife, who was perfectly willing to let him take her hand and draw it through the crook of his arm. The group moved down the wharf to the waiting carriage, where Devlin handed each of the three women up in turn before taking a seat beside Meghan. After giving an order to the driver, he regained possession of his wife's hand and told her, "I'll see you to the house first, but I'm afraid I must then abandon you for the remainder of the afternoon while I take care of a few business matters."

"As you will soon learn, my dearest Meghan," Linette saw fit to interject at this point, "Dev is forever dashing off to his tiresome business whenever we are in the city!"

"Perhaps," he drawled lazily, his deep blue eyes twinkling across at his adored younger sister, "but bear in mind that it if it were not for my attentions in that particular, 'tiresome' direction, you would no longer enjoy the expensive lifestyle to which you have become so irreversibly accustomed."

"Oh, pooh!" she retorted. "You know very well that you can never tolerate being idle for more than five minutes at a time. Confess, brother dear—if you did not have your business matters and your politics to occupy your days here, you would merely find some other means of staying busy."

"What sort of business matters?" Meghan questioned her husband with a mild frown of curiosity.

It had just dawned on her that she knew absolutely nothing at all about the manner in which he spent his time in Charlestown. She could certainly see the truth in what Linette had said about his inability to remain idle . . . indeed, she mused to herself, she was familiar enough with his character to know that, if he awoke and found all his wealth vanished, he would simply set about recouping his losses—by the sweat of his own brow if necessary. Devlin Montague was in such sharp contrast to the bored, foppish young men she had known in London, and she could not comprehend how she had ever been the least bit attracted to any of them.

"The shipping line requires a good deal of my time," answered Devlin. His gaze filled with loving amusement when he added, "It may interest you to know, Madam Montague, that we have an entire fleet of vessels plying the oceans at this very moment."

"Really?" she murmured, her eyes widening in surprise. "I was under the impression that the *Pandora* was your only ship. You certainly commanded her as though she were!"

"The *Pandora* is reserved for my private use," he explained with a smile that quite took Meghan's breath away. "I had her built to my own specifications several years ago. Other than Shadowmoss, she is the possession for which I bear the most affection."

"Come now, Dev, I would venture to say you have another possession *much* dearer than that," challenged Linette, her eyes moving significantly to Meghan.

"I was speaking of material possessions—not those which belong to the heart, you little minx."

Meghan, exchanging another warm smile with him, settled back against the cushioned leather seat and turned her gaze upon the passing sights of the city. The carriage rolled briskly onward, its wheels traversing the cobbled surfaces of broad and remarkable uniform streets lined with tall, beautiful live oak trees that were draped with long cobwebs of gray moss. Azaleas were in evidence everywhere, and the breeze carried a mingling of other distinctive aromas which attested to the fact that the city was alive with springtime blossoms.

Meghan was intrigued by the houses she glimpsed, for nearly all of them featured fine, wrought iron balconies, long sweeping piazzas, and elegant walled gardens. Built in a peculiar architectural style derived from England, Barbados, and the West Indies, the mostly brick dwellings were two or three stories high, and were frequently either whitewashed or painted in an enchanting array of pastel colors. Trees and shrubbery abounded to provide shade from the often excessive heat, while the windows had been flung wide to allow the cooling air within. As was generally acknowledged to be true, the residents of Charlestown vied with one another as to who would have to coolest house—not necessarily the finest.

The city could, however, boast of its fair share of sprawling, columned mansions. Years ago, there had been those among the settlement's inhabitants who had wanted to keep it as nothing more than a summer home for wealthy rice planters. But it had nonetheless surpassed all expectations, growing rapidly into the dominant port of the Eastern Seaboard. It had survived hurricanes, deadly epidemics of smallpox and yellow fever, a succession of horribly devastating fires, and a host of other natural and man-made disasters. Still, Charlestown had flourished, and few of its visitors returned to their homes without singing praises to its charm and sophistication and overriding amiability.

Meghan's eyes were now drawn to the people she glimpsed strolling along the paved sidewalks or riding past in other carriages. There were impeccably attired ladies and gentlemen as well as men and women of the so-called "common" persuasion. Although she did not yet know it, Charlestown's population was as varied as a group as could be found anywhere else in the world. The city teemed with working people of all kinds—tanners, carpenters, shipbuilders, silversmiths, tailors, blacksmiths, shop clerks, coopers, jewelery makers, weavers, barbers, bakers, and an endless list of others whose talents combined to keep the community thriving.

While the planters were undeniably of the elite class, the merchants were only slightly lower on the social scale. They, too, hailed from nearly every background, and were not aristocrats in the truest sense. The sons of English, Irish, French, and Barbadian middle-class or yeoman farmers, they were self-made men who had built their fortunes on ingenuity and a good deal of hard work. Devlin Montague was unique in that he could claim allegiance to *both* classes.

As Meghan would soon learn, the women of Charlestown were as varied a lot as their masculine counterparts. The great ladies of the plantations and townhouses lived a number of lives, for not only were they expected to excel in the social arts of dancing and music, they were also called upon to bear children, supervise servants, oversee the preparation of great dinners, and entertain lavishly.

The women of the common class, on the other hand, usually worked alongside their husbands. They ran taverns and inns, cooked, gave lessons of every sort from singing and dancing to embroidery and needlework, and there were a number of women in the city who taught French, geography, history, English, and other "instructing" amusements. The newspaper was full of advertisements proclaiming other, more unusual occupations—upholsterers, crockery menders, livery stable keepers, shipwrights, and at least one enterprising female who made no secret of the fact that her establishment employed practitioners of society's oldest "profession."

The carriage finally began slowing down, and Meghan looked curiously ahead toward a house of positively dazzling style and proportion. A smile rose to her lips as she reflected that it would be just like Devlin to own the finest home in all of Charlestown.

"I shall be more than happy to take you on a tour of the city once we have settled in," offered Linette. "Although I'm sure everything will appear quite provincial when compared to what you are used to seeing in London."

"Not at all!" Meghan hastened to assure her. She met Devlin's warmly affectionate gaze. Faint color tinging her cheeks, she turned back to her sister-in-law and said, "As a matter of fact, I have no doubt whatsoever that I will soon come to prefer Charlestown to virtually any other place on earth—except for Shadowmoss, of course."

"Yes, and it requires very little in the way of intelligence to guess why!" Linette countered with a saucy grin just as the driver pulled the horse to a halt.

Meghan's eyes widened in delight at what they beheld. The townhouse, a superb example of what was familiarly termed a "double house," was situated a short distance back from the street and reached by way of a tree-shaded walk surrounded by a wrought iron fence. Constructed of English-type brick laid in Flemish bond, it was roofed with tile and featured a portico supported by four columns and divided to form a balcony on the second floor.

"My father began the house when I was still a boy," Devlin informed his wife while assisting her down from the carriage. "The completion did not take place until two years later, but I have always considered the results worth it."

"Oh Devlin, it's lovely!" Meghan pronounced in genuine pleasure. Thrilling to the pressure of his hands about her waist, she smiled happily when he swung her down. A tiny shiver ran the length of her spine as he held her a moment or two longer than was necessary, and she cast him a glance of mock reproval before moving determinedly away so that he would be forced to remember his duty to Jolene and Linette. Those two ladies, once alighted, swept through the gate and down the walk, considerately leaving the newlyweds alone to say their good-byes.

"I hate like the very devil to take my leave of you so soon, but I will return before nightfall," said Devlin. His mouth curved into an irresistibly rougish smile when he added, "In any case, you can be certain I mean to observe the traditions followed by my father and grandfather before me."

"And what traditions are those?" Meghan asked a trifle breathlessly, for the look in his eyes could best be described as tenderly wolfish.

"The first one I will demonstrate for you now," he announced as he suddenly bent and scooped her up in his strong arms, "but the second will have to wait until we are alone together."

"Devlin!" she protested with a laugh, blushing rosily while he turned and began carrying her down the walk. She glanced swiftly about, only to be made all too aware of the curious, sternly disapproving stares being directed their way by the well-dressed men and women strolling nearby. "For heaven's sake, Mister Montague, what will our neighbors think?" she whispered.

"Whatever they damned well please," he replied unconcernedly. "Should they be inclined to think of us at all, they will no doubt speak of your great beauty—and my great wisdom in having captured you for my own."

"Will they indeed?" Laughing softly, she soon found herself deposited just beyond the threshold of the front doorway. Devlin paused to bestow a quick kiss upon her lips before striding back down the walk to the carriage. Meghan watched until he was out of sight, then released a faint sigh and closed the door. Tugging the ruffled satin bonnet from her head, she pivoted about to see that Linette was regarding her from the center of the long, flagstone-paved hallway that separated the interior house into two even halves.

"Come along, if you please, I am anxious to get unpacked!" She breezed forward to link her arm companionably through Meghan's once more. "I hope you will like the house. It is quite small compared to the one at Shadowmoss, but it is very comfortable!"

Musing to herself that there was no possible way

she could help liking the house, Meghan allowed herself to be led away by her perennially energetic sister-in-law. She managed to catch a glimpse of the downstairs drawing room to the left of the wide hall, as well as the library and study to the right. Climbing the mahogany and pine stairway beside an amiably chattering Linette, she learned that the dining room, located at the rear of the house on the lower floor, was reserved only for the family's use—it was the custom for dinner parties to be held in the great drawing room upstairs.

Reaching the upper landing, she found that a large portion of the space was taken up by the drawing room of which Linette had spoken. The corresponding space to the right was given over to domestic arrangements. Although there were a limited number of bedrooms, they were designed to be airy and spacious.

The carriage house and servants' quarters, almost as notable as the house itself, were situated in the midst of the garden behind the main building, where a double flight of stone steps led down to a courtyard ending in a rounded newel of brick. There was a flagstone porch on the north end of the house, where, according to Linette, Devlin liked to sit with his coffee of a morning.

"And *this*, my dearest Meghan, is your room!" announced Linette, throwing open the door of the bedchamber at the farthest end of the landing. Meghan obediently stepped inside.

"Why, it's perfectly charming!" she opined with a smile. Her eyes traveled appreciatively over the azure blue satin window curtains, the gilt-trimmed, blue and cream wallpaper, the polished mahogany furniture, and the canopied four-poster bed. The bed was not quite as massive as the one in Devlin's room at Shadowmoss, Meghan observed to herself as her thoughts took a decidedly wicked turn, but it was still longer than most.

"I saw no necessity for you and Dev having separate bedrooms," the petite redhead explained with a knowing little smile, "so I gave the order for your things to be brought up here." Her brow suddenly creased into a frown of puzzlement. "Our trunks should have arrived by now. Perhaps I'd best go and see what is causing the delay. I shall soon return!" With that, she took herself back downstairs, leaving Meghan to smile indulgently after her and wander across to the open window.

She was pleased to find that the room overlooked the garden. Inhaling deeply of the sweet scent given off by a profusion of magnolias, roses, jasmine, and the seemingly ever-present azaleas, she felt such an overwhelming sense of peace and contentment that her eyes swept closed and her thoughts drifted back to the joyous revelations of the previous night. On the heels of her newfound inner tranquility, however, came a sharp and sudden feeling of uneasiness.

But why? she wondered, frowning to herself. Her turquoise gaze clouded with bafflement, as well as a touch of apprehension. The foreboding sensation was too strong to be ignored.

" 'Tis not wise to be inviting trouble," she murmured aloud. Resolutely attempting to push the troubled thoughts from her mind, she turned away from the window and headed downstairs to join Linette in her quest for the baggage.

The remainder of the afternoon passed in a dizzying whirl of activity for the two young women. Meghan met with the servants and gratefully accepted their words of welcome, then set about learning everything she could about the particular customs and management of the household. She discussed the week's meals with Jolene, contributed to Linette's plans for a dinner party to be held at the townhouse in five days' time, and finally returned to her new bedroom upstairs to unpack her woefully inadequate trousseau.

She was in the process of hanging her emerald green ballgown in the tall, mirrored wardrobe when she heard Devlin's voice echoing up from the center hallway downstairs. The sun had set a good quarter of an hour earlier, but she was not in the least bit inclined to scold him for his tardiness. Her heart leaping as it always did whenever he was near, she quickly put the gown away and hastened to check her appearance in the mirror.

"Mistress of the house!" Devlin called out in a playfully gruff tone as he climbed the stairs. "Come, woman, and greet me like a proper wife should!"

Meghan laughed softly at his words. Gathering up her skirts, she flew to the doorway, arriving just as he reached the landing.

"Faith, sir, must you bellow at me like a ship's captain?" she scolded teasingly, her blue-green eyes twinkling across at him while he advanced on her at an easy, unhurried pace. "That may well serve on board the *Pandora*, but it will simply not do here!"

"Will it not?" he retorted, his own gaze full of splendid devilment. From the look on his handsome face, it was apparent that he meant to make amends for his neglect of her. "I expect complete obedience from my bride as well as my crew, madam, so bring yourself forward at once and kiss me!"

"It may surprise you to learn, my dearest lord and master, that I bestow my favors on no man unless *I* wish it!" she told him with a saucily defiant toss of her golden curls. At the sudden, menacing gleam in his eyes, she whirled about and fled back into the bedroom.

Devlin gave chase, striding inside to kick the door closed with the heel of his boot. Meghan immediately took refuge behind a chair, where she stood facing him with a boldly challenging smile on her lips and the assurance of sweet passion in her eyes.

"I give you fair warning, my love," he proclaimed in a low, vibrant tone laced with both humor and desire. "Come here or face the consequences!"

"Is that a threat—or a promise?"

"Both!"

Delighting in the game, Meghan remained securely behind the barrier. She squealed in alarm a moment later, however, as Devlin suddenly closed the distance between them and seized hold of the chair to thrust it easily out of the way.

"Surrender now and I will be merciful," he offered with a rakish grin.

"Never!" Meghan replied, laughing.

Darting past him, she scurried around to the other side of the bed. Her breasts rose and fell rapidly beneath her low-cut bodice, her beautiful eyes were aglow, and there was a becoming rosiness to her cheeks. The sight of her fired Devlin's blood, as did the seductive playfulness with which she resisted him.

"If you think to put me off with such missish conduct, you little vixen, you'd best think again!" He moved slowly toward her, his sun-bronzed features bearing an undeniably predatory expression.

373

"Heed the words of a boastful man!" she taunted while she searched for the best avenue of escape.

"Heed them well, my love!"

Rounding the bed at last, he lunged for her, but she eluded his grasp once more and went scrambling across the embroidered coverlet of the four-poster. Her feet had no sooner touched the floor again when Devlin moved with surprising agility and swiftness to catch up with her. A breathless little cry of defeat broke from her lips when his hand shot out to tangle within the gathered folds of linen which formed the back of her skirt. She was startled to feel herself toppling unceremoniously forward to her hands and knees upon the braided rug as her husband gave a forceful tug upon the fabric.

"Why, you devil!" she protested, inhaling sharply when he suddenly clamped a powerful arm about her waist and hauled her off the floor. Almost before she knew what was happening he had taken a seat on the edge of the bed and yanked her facedown across his knees. Her eyes flew wide, and she raised her head to demand breathlessly, "What on earth do you think you're doing?"

"I warned you, did I not?" he drawled, giving what sounded to Meghan's ears like a chuckle of thoroughly wicked enjoyment. Without further ado, he tossed up her skirts, thereby exposing the pale, satiny roundness of her derriere to his appreciatively burning gaze.

"Devlin, please!" Her cheeks flaming, she struggled and pushed against him in an effort to free herself, only to cry out—more in shock than in pain—as his large hand suddenly descended with a loud smack upon her bare bottom. *"Devlin!"* she gasped.

"It comes to mind, madam, that I still owe you for your defiance of me last night!" His midnight blue eyes gleaming with roguish intent, he brought his hand down upon her squirming backside again, using just enough force to promote a warm stinging of her flesh.

"Stop it at once!" Meghan commanded indignantly. "Let me go, damn you!"

She was rewarded for her impudence with yet another hearty slap upon her bottom, and her struggles had begun to grow quite earnest when Devlin finally ceased his halfhearted punishment and turned her over. His arms imprisoned her there upon his lap. Her eyes flashed their brilliant turquoise fire up at him, but he merely chuckled quietly once more and decreed, "Henceforth, Madam Montague, you shall obey your loving husband in all things!"

"Loving husband indeed!" she retorted, her countenance stormy and her color still much heightened. "You have behaved in a cruel and ungentlemanly fashion, Devlin Montague, and if I were a man I should not hesitate to repay you in kind!"

"Ah, but if you were a man, none of this would have happened," he pointed out wryly. "I will own up to the ungentlemanly part, but not to the charge of cruelty, for you know as well as I that the only thing I have wounded is your pride!"

"Untrue!"

"Then I will have to set about soothing your pain—in the best way I know." His arms tightened about her, and his gaze filled with such impassioned tenderness that she could not find it in her heart to remain annoyed with him any longer.

"Well, perhaps you *could* make atonement," she

conceded with a dramatic sigh, her eyes softening while a provocative little smile played about her lips. "Of course, I'm quite certain the entire household will become suspicious if we do not soon put in an appearance downstairs."

"We've already settled the matter of my sister's suspicions, and I for one do not give a damn about the others!" he murmured. His lips had already begun a slow torment to her senses by nibbling along the slender column of her neck. In the next instant, his hand slipped beneath the bunched-up folds of her skirt and petticoat to glide soothingly over the shapely mounds of her bottom, which still bore the faint, reddened marks of his playful chastisement.

"You are an impossible man," whispered Meghan, her fingers curling upon his shoulders while a delicious shiver ran the length of her spine, "but in truth, I would not have you any other way!" She shivered again as his hands moved to the hooks on the front of her bodice, and a gasp of pleasure escaped her lips when his warm fingers delved within to close upon the thinly covered fullness of her breast.

Soon, Devlin's kisses and caresses provoked such a white-hot blaze of desire within them both that they could not even think of denying themselves the most perfect release known to man—and woman. Swept away, they did not even bother to dispense with their clothing, a fact which did not appear to impede their efforts in the least.

Meghan was shocked to discover that her beloved apparently meant to take her while she was facing the "wrong way," but her stunned bewilderment quickly gave way to profoundly delectable enlightenment when he settled her upon her hands and knees, tossed up her skirts again, and plunged into her feminine passage from behind. She cried out softly and strained instinctively back against him, while his hands reclaimed their gentle yet possessive hold upon her breasts and his warm lips trailed a searing path across the silken curve of her neck and shoulder. Their rapturously tempestuous union sent their passions soaring higher and higher, until together they achieved a fierily explosive oneness that only the truest of lovers can ever know.

Afterward, as they lay entwined upon the bed and floated back down to earth, Meghan smiled up at her splendidly virile husband and sighed, "Oh Devlin, will it always be this way between us?"

"Indeed it will, my love," he replied softly, then added with an endearingly crooked smile of his own, "Even better."

"In that case, I don't know how I shall bear it!" she remarked with a laugh of pure delight. Snuggling closer to him, she released another contented sigh and lightly traced a repetitive path along the deep V of his white, open-necked shirt. "Devlin?" she asked at a sudden thought.

"Yes?"

"What is the second tradition of which you spoke?" she questioned, referring to what he had told her before taking his leave of her earlier that same day. He knew immediately what she meant, and he gave a low chuckle while his eyes gleamed with wry amusement.

"As a matter of fact, sweet bride, I have just demonstrated it for you."

"Indeed?" Raising up on one elbow, she peered closely down at him. "What do you mean?"

"Exactly what I said." His gaze dropped with a

bold significance to her wildly disheveled attire before returning to her face. He watched as the warm color crept up to her cheeks.

"Good heavens!" she breathed, her blue-green eyes filling with startled realization. In the next instant, however, she eyed Devlin suspiciously and demanded, "How on earth could you know such a thing about your own father and grandfather? I find it difficult to believe *this* to be the sort of tradition which could ever be spoken of so readily between a father and son!"

"You underestimate the Montague men, my love," he countered with a roguish grin. "Not to mention the Montague women."

"But how could you know?" she stubbornly persisted, still disbelieving.

"Quite simply, I was told. It seems the first night in any new abode was always reserved for intimacy between the master and his wife—a unique and undeniably enjoyable method of 'breaking in' the domicile. And in a house such as this one, it is difficult for anything to take place without the other inhabitants being privy to it."

"Devlin Montague, you are making the whole thing up!" accused Meghan. "And even if you were not, you told me yourself that your father did not even build this house until after you were born, so it would therefore have been impossible for your grandfather to have brought *his* wife here to—"

"Ah, but I did not lay claim to the fact that my grandfather had established the tradition in this particular locale," he answered smoothly. "Suffice it to say that it matters not where the tradition is upheld—so long as it is." He reached up and drew her head back down to rest upon the loving cradle of his

378

arm. "I have every intention of passing it along to *our* son when he begins to display an interest in such matters."

"You most certainly will not!" she protested, pushing herself upright again. Her eyes flashed down into his rugged, visibly amused features. "That is not at all the sort of thing I would wish him to know!"

"And why not?"

"Because . . . because it seems highly improper for anyone to be aware of such intimate details concerning their own parents!"

"You think our children will not be aware?" challenged Devlin with another quiet, resonant laugh. Meghan gasped as he suddenly and quite masterfully pulled her atop him. "No, wildcat," he decreed, his gaze holding hers while his arms tightened about her, "our feelings for one another shall not be a secret from them. They will grow up with the evidence right before their eyes, for I mean to love you well and often—though I will, of course, reserve the more amorous tokens of my affection for the privacy of our bedroom."

"I should hope so!" she retorted, still not at all certain she liked the idea of having her children know so much about what she and their father did whenever they were alone together.

What children? that small, inner voice reminded her. She had never given much thought to the matter before now. It struck her that having Devlin's sons and daughters would be to celebrate their love in a way unlike any other, a way that suddenly seemed both natural and wondrously fulfilling.

"Pray, sir," she queried him as her mouth curved into a rather impish smile, "how many offspring do

379

you foresee being present to witness your tokens of affection?"

"As many as you please. I should like at least two of each gender—after that, you may feel free to decide."

"How very generous of you!"

"I agree," he murmured. His hand sweeping up to entangle within the tangled mass of golden curls streaming down her back, he urged her head downward so that he could give her one last passionate, utterly breathtaking kiss. Then, he reluctantly rolled her to her back once more and released her. "I would like nothing better than to remain and kiss every square inch of your beautiful body, madam wife, but I fear Linette would never forgive me if I abandoned her to her own devices our first night in town."

"But I thought you said the 'tradition' was wellknown," Meghan pointed out teasingly. She watched while he rose from the bed and turned back to face her with a mock frown of reproval.

"We must practice at least some small measure of self-control, my love. Else it will be all over Charlestown that Devlin Montague is an ogre who never allows his poor bride a moment's respite from her duties in bed." His brow cleared, and a wolfish smile played about his lips when he added, "Of course, those who say it would not be far from the truth. And once they have seen you, they will of a certainty know why!"

Heaving a sigh of mingled disappointment and acquiescence, Meghan sat up and slid from the bed as well. She hurried to change into another gown and restore order to her coiffure, while all Devlin had to do was fasten his breeches again and rake a hand through his tousled chestnut hair. He stood leaning negligently against the wall, his arms folded across his broad chest, while his wife flew about the room in her efforts to look presentable and tossed him a speaking look every now and then.

Once downstairs, they passed a very pleasant evening with Linette. The three of them enjoyed an intimate family diner in the dining room, after which they strolled outside to gaze overhead at the stars and speak of long-ago memories brought to mind in the peaceful beauty of the cool, lamplit garden. The faint strains of music and laughter drifted to them on the wind, for the city was a lively place during the summer, and Meghan was content to sit beside Devlin on the flagstone porch while he and his sister talked of the happy times they had known there throughout the years. When pressed for memories of her own childhood, she had dwelt only upon those which were pleasant, but neither Devlin nor Linette had failed to glimpse the shadow of pain crossing her face when she spoke of her home in Ireland.

Since a veritable deluge of invitations had already been delivered to the townhouse—word of the Montagues' arrival had spread quickly among their peers—Linette turned the conversation to social engagements. It was decided that they would attend the ball at Lord and Lady Westerfields' the very next night, but Devlin refused to so much as consider taking his wife and sister to a performance at the Dock Street Theatre until the end of the week.

He also left little doubt as to his negative feelings regarding Linette's proposal that he escort them to one of the concerts sponsored by the Saint Cecilia Society, which bore the distinction of being the first musical group in the colonies to support a paid orchestra. Devlin, unimpressed, maintained that he would under no circumstances allow himself "to be dragged into a roomful of women who have nothing better to do than sit about commenting on how superbly a group of pompous young dandies play their French horns and bass violins." Both Meghan and Linette adamantly protested this narrow-minded, wholly masculine attitude, but he remained unrepentant.

By the time the three of them retired for the night, Linette was blissfully looking forward to seeing Charles again at the Westerfields' ball, Devlin's mind was full of plans to expand the shipping line, and Meghan was more than a trifle apprehensive at the prospect of being presented to Charlestown society as the new Madam Montague. She took comfort in what Devlin had once said about no one daring to cast dispersions upon her name once she was married to him, but she was nonetheless facing the season with some trepidation.

The last thought on her mind before she drifted off to sleep in her husband's arms was, strangely enough, of Rosalie Hammond. . . .

Devlin took himself off to the waterfront shortly after breakfast the following morning, leaving his wife and his sister to spend the day in the pursuit of beauty, knowledge, and sisterly fellowship. The first item on Linette's full agenda, as it turned out, was a visit to the dressmaker's.

"We must have you fitted for a complete wardrobe, my dearest Meghan," she pronounced, "and I have every confidence that we will be able to find a

382

gown for you to wear to the ball tonight."

"But I had planned to wear the emerald—"

"No indeed!" said Linette. "It is very becoming, to be sure, but you must have something much more elegant. As Devlin's bride, all eyes will be upon you, so we will simply have to procure you the absolute finest in dresses, hats, gloves, shoes—everything!"

"I cannot deny that the sound of it is like music to my ears!" Meghan admitted with a laugh. "Please accept my deepest gratitude in advance, dear sister, for applying yourself so diligently to improving my appearance!"

"You are most welcome, but I am afraid I cannot take credit for it all," the young redhead disclosed with a dimpled smile. "Truly, it was Dev's idea. In fact, he practically threatened me with bodily harm if I did not see to it at once!"

Meghan's heart soared at the news, and her eyes glowed with a soft radiance as she silently vowed to repay him for his thoughtfulness when they were next alone together.

The visit to the dressmaker's lasted most of the morning, but both women deemed the time well spent. They were rewarded for their efforts with a vast array of boxes, as well as the promise of more to come. Meghan had met with success in finding an exquisite ballgown to wear that night—it had fortunately required only a few minor alterations—and she had patiently submitted to an endless amount of measuring, dressing and undressing, and pinning before she had finally escaped outside to the welcoming sunshine again, weary but triumphant. Linette, not to be completely outdone, had commissioned a number of things to be made for herself as well, though she had giggled and remarked that

Devlin would in all likelihood threaten to pack her off to a convent once he received the bill.

Next, Linette made good on her promise to take Meghan on a tour of the city. Climbing back up into the carriage, she ordered the driver to take them to Bay Street.

"I know you have already seen the waterfront area, but I think it the best place to begin," she explained to Meghan. "It is, after all, Charlestown's very center of commerce. I daresay that, within its environs, one could purchase nearly anything and everything available for sale."

"My first impression of it was that it appeared to be one of the liveliest places I had ever seen. I shall never forget the sight of all those ships and wharves and people . . . so very many people," recalled Meghan as the carriage rolled on its way. "Except for Dublin, I had never seen such a busy and crowded port!"

"I have yet to travel farther from Shadowmoss than this," Linette confided. She heaved a rather wistful little sigh. "Dev always manages to put me off with one excuse or another. But," she said, her face brightening, "I still mean to spend my honeymoon abroad!"

"And does Charles share the same desire?" asked Meghan with a smile.

"If not, I have every confidence that I can bring his mind into accordance with my plans!" She did not add that she had as yet to convince Charles Deverill to marry her—he had been perfectly willing to kiss her that night when she had led him away from the harvest celebration, but he had balked when she suggested they exchange wedding vows without delay. He had insisted that she needed time to know her own mind, and he had obstinately refused to let things progress any further.

Musing that Charles had always been impulsive, displaying a devel-may-care sense of adventure which had frequently gotten him into trouble, Linette was perplexed by his sudden prudence. Indeed, she thought with an inward sigh of disgruntlement, even though he had admitted to being in love with her, he had not asked her to be his wife. She could only suppose that his reluctance to do so had something to do with his mother, who had never really liked her and would no doubt faint dead away if told that *she* was the woman Charles had chosen to marry. . .

"Linette?" Meghan repeated. Watching as her sister-in-law's gaze cleared, she said gently, "I believe the driver is awaiting further instructions."

"Oh, dear me, of course!" exclaimed Linette. She hastened to correct the situation, telling him that they wished to drive along Bay Street to Broad Street, then down Broad Street past Union, Church, and Meeting Streets. With a wordless nod of his head, the man hastened to comply, obediently guiding the horse around the corner. It was no easy task to avoid the horses, cats and dogs, other carriages, and people crowding the avenue that was the life-blood of the city, but the Montagues' driver was well accustomed to such obstacles and therefore managed to perform his duty without incident.

"That is the Exchange Building," Linette announced a short time later, pointing out the large, impressive stone building standing guard on the corner of Bay and Broad Streets. "It was just completed last year. The lower level is where customs business is transacted, while the Great Hall above is used for dancing assemblies and civic meetings. Dev can often be found upstairs whenever one of those tiresome political debates is called into session. You know, there is actually a dungeon underneath the building!" she revealed proudly, her eyes sparkling with excitement at the thought. "Would it not be a terribly splendid coincidence if *your* pirate was eventually captured and imprisoned in *our* dungeon?"

"I am certain the likelihood of that is quite remote," Meghan replied, shuddering involuntarily as The Wolf's sinister image rose in her mind.

"Stranger things have occurred," Linette offered airily.

Meghan was relieved when her irrepressible companion did not pursue the subject. She had not thought of her former captor much since the day Rosalie Hammond had confronted her in the drawing room at Shadowmoss, and she now found herself praying that the man would never be heard of again.

"There you see St. Phillip's Church," Linette proclaimed soon thereafter. She drew Meghan's attention to the handsome, towering structure which rose in such steepled prominence above the houses and trees on Church Street. "It is the Church of England, of course, and it was built some fifty years ago."

"It looks remarkably similar to a good many of the churches at home."

"That is not at all surprising, considering that its congregation actually dates back to among the earliest in South Carolina. And Charlestown was, of course, terribly British before it began to develop a unique character all its own."

Traveling a short distance farther, they arrived at the intersection of Broad and Meeting Streets. In the very middle of the street stood a colossal statue of William Pitt, the great English statesman. Its subject was presented in a classically draped attitude of vehement speech, and Meghan could not help thinking that his expression was perhaps a bit too severe for the repose of art.

"It may or may not interest you to know that this statue, the first erected in America, cost more than seven thousand pounds," the vivacious redhead beside her remarked. With a pleasant trill of laughter, Linette added, "Though it has been six years now, I remember what a stir it created. Why, even Dev said that we were spending an awful lot of money for something that might very well frighten children for generations to come!"

"Oh, I would not consider it frightening," Meghan opined, eyeing the statue thoughtfully. "I suppose the artist thought it entirely suited to the feelings of those who ordered its creation."

"Well, you are much more diplomatic in your opinions than I!" Linette freely admitted. Turning her head, she went on to declare, "Over there is St. Michael's Church, which is the oldest such building in the city. I was told that it follows the architectural form of the Wren-Gibbes churches of London. The first services were conducted there a good ten or eleven years ago. The bells were imported from England—naturally—and the steeple is more than one hundred and eighty feet in height."

Following Linette's direction, Meghan's gaze moved up the magnificent structure which could not easily be mistaken for anything other than the church it was. Her eyes, returning earthward, were next drawn to the market on the northeast corner of the intersection, where one could buy the popular sweetgrass baskets made by slave women. On the northwest corner, Linette went on to inform her, was a public building, while on the southwest corner stood the Guard House or Watch.

"If we but had the time, I would suggest we pay a visit to Mister Thomas Elfe's workshop," Meghan's willing guide remarked. "He is one of our most renowned craftsmen—as a matter of fact, he made some of the furniture in our townhouse. But since I should like for you to see White Point, we will save the remainder of Charlestown's more intriguing sights for another day!"

The carriage rolled along the cobblestones toward the sea now. Meghan watched as they approached a glaring white expanse of sand and bleached oyster shells. Here there was a seawall built of brick on a foundation of Bermuda stone and faced with palmetto logs. The wall was about five feet in height, and there was a shell walkway running alongside it.

"It is easy to see why this is called White Point, is it not?" offered Linette. "Over there is what remains of Battery Broughton." With a nod of her auburn-maned head, she indicated an old fortification with wooden platforms on top for guns which had never been fired or even mounted. "And there, of course, are the White Point Gardens," she said, waving her hand toward the tree-shaded collection of foliage and wrought iron benches which provided a lovely setting to view the harbor. "When I was but a child, Dev would bring me down here to watch the gulls diving for fish and listen to the sea crashing against the wall. I must say, I found it all very exhilarating!"

"As would I," Meghan responded with a rather wistful smile. Devlin's handsome face swam before

388

her eyes when she thought about what an exceptional brother he had always been to Linette. She could not help feeling a small twinge of envy—both for the fact that she had never been blessed with such a companion as a child, as well as for the wish that she could have known Devlin her whole life. *But then*, her inner voice theorized, *he would have in all likelihood paid you no notice at all.*

"Well, I suppose that will have to suffice for now!" pronounced Linette. Requesting that the driver take them home again, she leaned back against the leather seat and told Meghan, "We have a great deal to do before the ball tonight. And I would not be at all surprised if we should receive a horde of callers this afternoon, for nearly everyone must be in town by now!"

"Do you think it possible that Mistress Hammond will be among those who call?" Meghan questioned on sudden impulse.

"Rosalie? Why, I should certainly hope not!"

"I quite agree," she replied with a soft smile of irony, "but I have the strangest feeling that we shall see her again soon."

"Sooner than I would wish," muttered Linette, her eyes darkening at the thought. "She will no doubt be in attendance tonight, for Lord Westerfield and her father are partners in some sort of business venture—at least from what I have heard." She suddenly grinned mischievously and remarked, "I'll wager Rosalie behaved like an absolute *pea goose* when those pirates attacked your ship!"

"From what I recall, none of us felt terribly brave," Meghan answered quietly, shuddering again at the awful memory. Her eyes grew visibly clouded, prompting the young woman beside her to frown and slip an arm about her shoulders.

"Oh Meghan, forgive me! I . . .I should not have spoken of it at all!" Her youthful countenance displayed such heartfelt contrition that Meghan could not refrain from smiling warmly at her.

"Truly, Linette, it is of no consequence," she assured her. "It's simply that I wish to put all thought of that behind me now."

"Of course you do! And I have every intention of helping you," insisted Linette. Her eyes shone with renewed excitement. "I am nearly mad with impatience for Charles to see me in my new ballgown, you know, and I am quite certain Dev will declare you an absolute vision in yours!"

"I hope you are right," said Meghan, her spirits lifting once more.

Traveling homeward beside a happily chattering Linette, Meghan was treated to a description and brief family history of some of the people she could expect to meet at the ball that night. And though she knew she would never remember it all, she was nonetheless grateful for the information.

Chapter Sixteen

Arriving at the home of Lord and Lady Westerfield shortly before nine o'clock, Devlin assisted first his wife and then his sister down from the carriage. Meghan shook her skirts out gently in an effort to remove any creases, while Linette did the same beside her.

"Have I told you yet, my love, that you look exceedingly well this evening?" Devlin remarked with a crooked smile as he gallantly offered Meghan his arm.

"Yes, dearest husband, you have, but you may say so as often as you like!" Her eyes sparkled beguilingly up at him. Curling her slender, gloved fingers about his arm, she added, "Linette said you would proclaim me an absolute vision."

"For once, she spoke the truth," he quipped, unscathed by the mock glare of reproach he received from his sister. She took his other arm, and the three of them moved together up the front steps.

Meghan's apprehension increased as they drew nearer to the wide double door, but she took comfort from the knowledge that she looked her best. The ballgown she had purchased earlier that same day was fashioned of the palest shade of robin's egg blue satin, its fitted bodice closing in front and its low, rounded neckline an interesting concoction of scalloped white lace caught in each curve with a pink velvet ribbon. The full, three-quarter-length sleeves ended in several layers of lace and pink satin ruffles, which were deeper in back so that they hung gracefully, and the skirt was of plain satin to match the bodice.

Around her neck, she wore a gleaming strand of pearls presented to her by Devlin just before they left the house. She had left her thick golden locks unpowdered, though she knew the majority of the ladies at the ball would follow the usual custom of either wearing a wig or having their own hair dressed with sticky pomatum and then powdered white. Coiffures were as a rule of absurd heights with extravagant decoration, but she had never ascribed to that particular mode of fashion. Thus, on this particular occasion, she had chosen to arrange her long tresses in a simple style whereby she swept them up in the back, threaded a black velvet ribbon through the curls which cascaded down her neck, and softened the severity of the effect about her face with a few "escaping" tendrils at her forehead and ears.

She took a deep breath of determination as she gathered up her skirts and ascended the immaculate brick steps. Devlin's strong, wonderfully steadying hand was at her back, and she cast him a rather tremulous smile before preceding him into the house.

The Westerfields' home was in actuality one of the elegant mansions she had glimpsed earlier. A sprawling white structure, the house was three stories high, with four massive columns in the front and a preponderance of trees, shrubberies, and ornate wrought iron flourishes. Guests had begun arriving nearly half an hour earlier, so that the equally impressive interior was already brimming with light and music and laughter.

To Meghan, it all seemed at once familiar and strange. She had attended more than her fair share of such gatherings back in England, to be sure, yet she was not at all certain what to expect from her first ball in the colonies. *America is your home now as well*, she reminded herself, musing that she would have to leave off referring to her new homeland as though it were in some way inferior to her old one.

The next thing she knew, she was being introduced to Lord and Lady Westerfield, who stood waiting to greet their guests just within the tiled, brightly lit entrance foyer. Devlin kept a possessive hand upon his bride's arm when he presented her to their hosts, who spoke to her with such warm cordiality that she felt truly welcome.

"Thank you, Lady Westerfield," Meghan responded earnestly. She smiled up at the tall, bewigged older woman whose lofty bearing and undeniably expensive attire belied the merry humor in her eyes.

"Not at all, my dear. I am glad to see that someone has managed to lead young Montague to the altar at last. He has been the despair of those of us with marriageable daughters for entirely too long!"

"Perhaps if you yourself had been available, madam, I might have succumbed even sooner," Devlin drawled teasingly as he raised the woman's gloved and diamond-becked hand to his lips.

393

"Rapscallion!" she scolded fondly.

He smiled unrepentantly and moved forward to exchange a few words with her husband. Linette's gaze took to wandering, prompting Meghan and their hostess to glance at one another in mutual understanding.

"If you are by any chance looking for young Mister Deverill, dear child," Lady Westerfield told the petite redhead, "then I suggest you search in the ballroom. The last I saw of him, he was doing his gallant part to consume as much of our rum punch as humanly possible."

"How did you know it was Charles I sought?" asked Linette, her mouth curving into a guilty little smile. She had followed Meghan's example and chosen to wear her flame-colored tresses unpowdered, while her slender curves were encased in a delightfully ruffled gown of primrose silk.

"Because he happened to inquire after *you* some two minutes after his arrival!" the older woman revealed, laughing softly. "Now run along, all of you, and enjoy yourselves." With that, she turned to dutifully greet another group of well-dressed ladies and gentlemen who had just that moment crossed the threshold.

Taking Devlin's arm again, Meghan headed toward the Westerfields' exquisite, music-filled ballroom with him while Linette followed behind. They paused in the doorway, gazing upon the bustle of social activity for a few brief moments before suddenly finding themselves besieged by a throng of friends, acquaintances, and those who merely wished to get a closer look at the new Madam Montague.

Meghan weathered it all admirably. She soon lost

count of how many people she had been introduced to, and it was very difficult to keep straight which names accompanied which faces, but Devlin remained protectively at her side throughout her initiation into Charlestown society. His deep blue eyes gleamed with noticeable pride each time he presented her to someone as his wife, and she knew she would never forget the way he smiled at her whenever the romantic haste and secrecy of their wedding was commented upon.

As he had predicted, however, no one dared to breathe one word about her former position as an indentured servant. Discovering that the announcement of their marriage had appeared in *The South Carolina Gazette* that very day, she wondered why Devlin had not told her of it. But she was nonetheless pleased to learn that she had been listed as the granddaughter of Sir Henry Claibourne of London, a deceptively minor detail for which she would soon have even greater cause to rejoice.

Finally, Devlin led her out onto the dance floor. Charles, having caught sight of his heart's desire in the midst of the crowd near the doorway, was only too happy to take charge of Linette.

"Damn it, woman, I thought I would never get you to myself again!" Devlin growled while he swung his radiantly beautiful wife around in the movements of the dance. "I had forgotten I knew so many blasted people!"

"Come now, my dearest husband, you would not wish to appear churlish in front of your friends," countered Meghan, tossing him a smile of saucy challenge.

"Look at me like that again, madam," he threatened in a deliciously vibrant undertone for her ears alone, "and you will find yourself taken upstairs!"

"Will I really?" she retorted, her eyes sparkling up at him.

"Tempt me not, vixen!" he warned with an imperceptible narrowing of his own smoldering gaze. He gave a low, appreciative chuckle when she merely tilted her chin farther upward in a gesture of playful defiance. "If only I had you alone at this very moment, my love," he murmured with a soft smile.

"You know very well we cannot leave yet, Devlin Montague," she told him with wifely indulgence, "if for no other reason than the fact that your sister needs the company of her own friends after so many months in the country."

"It appears to me that she is determined to enjoy no other company save Charles's," he observed. His gaze now traveled significantly to where Linette and her reluctant suitor were standing alone in the far corner of the ballroom, deep in conversation. Meghan glanced their way as well, and she frowned to herself when she saw the troubled expression on Linette's usually cheerful features.

"Oh Devlin, do you suppose he is preparing to break her heart?" she wondered aloud.

"If so, I will not hesitate to call him out."

"*What?*" she gasped, her eyes flying back up to his face. She was both relieved and annoyed to find that he was merely jesting. "Impossible man! Can you not be serious at a time like this?"

"At a time like what?"

"Your own sister stands on the very brink of womanhood, and all you can do is make light of the situation!"

"What the devil do you mean?" he demanded,

sobering at last. He looked back to where Charles was now taking Linette's hand and slipping an arm about her waist to dance. "Has he spoken of his intentions yet?"

"No, not that I'm aware of. But Linette has left little doubt as to her own."

"Hers do not matter."

"And why not? Sweet Saint Bridget, Devlin Montague, are you after keeping her a child forever?" Meghan challenged with a spirited flash of her eyes.

"Must we have this same blasted conversation every time we dance?" he parried, his sun-kissed brow creasing into a dark frown while his fingers clenched about hers.

"I suppose we must, since you refuse to believe the evidence before your eyes! Linette is a woman now and will no longer suffer being treated like an adorable little girl who—"

"What would you have me do? Sell her to the highest bidder?" he demanded with a faint, mocking smile.

"I would have you allow her to choose for herself!" she answered, her voice full of sorely tried patience. "She will know when she is ready to wed, just as her heart will guide her to the right man."

"And did your heart do the same?" he asked unexpectedly. His gaze softened while it caressed her flushed, rather stormy countenance, and his arm drew her closer. "Did it, Meghan?"

"You know it to be so," she replied, her eyes shining with all the love in her heart while her body trembled at his nearness. "I think, my dearest 'Master Devlin,' that we are well and fairly mated." She cast him another look of such captivating warmth that he growned inwardly and felt his desire for her, always smoldering just beneath the surface, flaring upward once more.

"By damn, I *will* take you upstairs!" he vowed in a low, wonderfully vibrant tone.

"No indeed, sir, you will not!" she dissented with a soft laugh. "But I give you my word you may do as you please once we are safely home again!"

Devlin's magnificent blue eyes gleamed fiercely down at her. He was given no opportunity to reply, however, as the music suddenly ended in a dazzling crescendo and the crowd on the dance floor began to disperse. He led Meghan across to where Linette and Charles stood catching their breath alongside the far, respendently mirrored and gilt-papered wall. The two men went off to fetch refreshments, affording their partners a few moments of private conversation.

"Is Charles's mother not in attendance tonight?" asked Meghan, musing that she would have of a certainty remembered meeting anyone with the name of Deverill.

"No, thank goodness!" sighed Linette. "It seems she claimed to be upon her very death bed to keep Charles from coming as well. He defied her, I am happy to say, but . . . there is something troubling me, Meghan." Her delicate auburn brows knitting together in a frown, she glanced toward the refreshment table.

Even if it had not been for the superior height of both Charles and Devlin, it would have been easy to spot them in the crowd, for they were among the few men present who had refused to don wigs for the occasion. Add to that the fact that the two of them affected a much more restrained style of dress than the other gentlemen, and it was easy to see why so many feminine hearts were set to fluttering at their undeniable masculinity.

"What is it, Linette?" Meghan probed gently, her eyes full of concern as they settled back upon her sister-in-law.

"I made a terrible mistake," she confessed miserably. "I grew angry when Charles once again refused to discuss the possibility of our marriage. Dash it all, but I told him that if he would not speak to Dev right away, I would set about flirting with every man in sight!"

"I see. And how did he receive your threat?"

"He said that if I was so incredibly fickle-minded that I could not keep faith with him for a few months' time, then he could not help but think his concerns regarding my youth and inexperience were even more well founded than he had originally believed!" She compressed her lips into a tight, thin line while her eyes fairly snapped with displeasure. When she spoke again, it was obvious that her anger was beginning to turn more in Charles's direction than her own. "He is being thoroughly pigheaded! How is it possible that I could have fallen in love with a man who infuriates me to such an extent?"

"It occurs more often than you think," said Meghan, a wry smile tugging at her lips as she thought of her own situation.

"Does it?" Linette released another highly expressive sigh. "All I know is that I seem to have been waiting my whole life for him to take notice of me as a woman."

"But do you truly think it wise to try and push him toward marriage?" asked Meghan in an attempt to reason with her. "After all, he has only just returned from several months abroad, and it may be possible that he is not yet ready to settle down. Perhaps you should follow his direction and wait until—"

"What reason is there to wait? I love him and he loves me, so what else is there to consider? No Meghan," Devlin's sister concluded with all the wisdom of her seventeen years, "I am meant to become Charles Deverill's wife, and if need be, I shall not hesitate to employ drastic means in order to accelerate his courtship of me!"

Meghan felt a sharp twinge of dismay at Linette's words. She had no time to question her further at the present, however, for not only did Charles and Devlin return with the punch, but a number of other guests chose that moment to come forward and draw the foursome into a discussion of the horse races planned for the following day.

Eventually, Meghan and Linette managed to extricate themselves from the group and go in search of the room designated for the evening as the "Ladies' Retiring Chamber." They climbed the magnificent, sweeping staircase up to the second floor, where they followed a uniformed housemaid's direction to the correct door. Stepping inside, they were pleased to find they had the spacious, beautifully decorated bedroom to themselves for the time being.

It did not take long for them to repair the little bit of damage suffered by their coiffures during the dance. An adjoining room, attended by a young female servant, provided the necessary "conveniences" with which to answer nature's indiscriminate call. Subjecting their appearance to one last critical inspection in the gilded oval mirror, they swept forth again and headed back downstairs to rejoin Devlin and Charles.

"Oh Meghan, there is Tallie Raymond!" whispered Linette as they approached the staircase. She drew to a sudden halt. Meghan stopped as well and looked ahead to where two young women were moving up the carpeted steps toward them. "And she is with that horrid Eustacia Peacock! Would you mind terribly going on without me?" she requested, her hand giving Meghan's a quick, conspiratorial squeeze. "I simply must have a few words with Tallie—she has been after Charles for years!"

"Of course," Meghan agreed with a bemused smile. She gathered up her skirts and continued on her way, nodding politely at the two dark-haired ladies who favored her with a barely civil response as she passed them.

Once downstairs again, she was preparing to return to the ballroom, when a sudden movement to her left drew her attention. She turned her head and looked toward the doorway which led into the drawing room. Having caught a glimpse of the room's interior on her way upstairs a short time earlier, she wondered idly why the doors were now closed. She would have given the matter no further thought, if not for the fact that she could have sworn she saw one of the doors being eased open the merest fraction of an inch while she hesitated at the foot of the staircase.

Still puzzled, she nonetheless turned away and crossed the bright reception hallway to seek out Devlin in the crowded ballroom. She did not catch sight of him immediately, however, and it was while she stood just within the wide doorway that she heard an all too familiar voice address her by name. Whirling about, she was dismayed to find that the

401

evidence of her eyes confirmed what her ears had already told her.

"Good evening, Mistress Hammond," she spoke with a cool formality that belied the tumult of emotions within her.

"We meet again at last, Mistress Kearny," the haughty blonde replied, her wideset gray eyes glittering with undisguised rancor. She looked as elegant and aristocratically striking as ever. Every strand of powdered and plumed hair was in place, every nail manicured to perfection, while her impeccable figure was attired in a superbly fashioned gown of deep green watered silk.

"It is 'Madam' now," Meghan corrected her, taking a certain amount of perverse pleasure from it. She recalled quite vividly the way Rosalie had treated her in the past—not only that day at Shadowmoss, but on board the servant ship and as fellow captives of the pirates afterward. " 'Madam Montague,' to be precise," she added. "But I suspect you are aware of that by now."

"I am aware of it!" snapped Rosalie. "Just as I am aware of how you lured *my* betrothed to your bed and then trapped him into marriage!" She made no effort to lower her voice. Fortunately, however, the music's benevolent strains prevented her accusations from being overheard by anyone else.

"Lured and trapped?" Meghan smiled faintly and denied, "No, that I did not do. But if it pleases you to think so, then I am quite certain nothing I say will make you believe otherwise."

In spite of her intense dislike of the woman, she could not help feeling compassion for her. After all, she told herself, even if there had been no true love between Devlin and his former fiancée, Rosalie had

402

believed for a period of several months that *she* would be his wife. Her disappointement must have been acute, reflected Meghan with yet another twinge of guilt. She consoled herself with the thought that anyone as wealthy and beautiful as Rosalie Hammond would attract a swarm of suitors.

"Devlin does not love you," the other woman declared with icy composure now. "He loves me, and he always will. Why, he told me so himself on the very day you were wed!"

"That cannot be true," insisted Meghan, a dull flush of anger staining her cheeks.

"Oh, but it is! Did you not know that he came to see me?" Rosalie challenged with a triumphant smirk.

"Indeed I did. But I also happen to know that the sole reason for his visit was to end his betrothal to you."

"So he would have you believe!"

"And I do believe him, Mistress Hammond!" countered Meghan, doing her best to control her rising temper. "While I am truly sorry for any 'discomfort' you have suffered as a result of your broken engagement, I will *not* stand here and listen to any more of your baldfaced lies and loathsome insinuations!" She started to move away, only to draw up short with a startled gasp when Rosalie suddenly moved to block her path.

"I have not finished with you yet, *Madam Montague!*" the other woman hissed viperously. Her features, already sharply defined, took on a furious intensity that made her look anything but elegant or beautiful. She spoke in a low, unmistakably malevolent tone when she said, "I do not care who your grandfather is—the fact remains that you were nothing but a slave in the Montague household before Devlin married you, and I will never be convinced that he made you his wife willingly! No, he was forced into it, and I will not rest until he has been persuaded to abandon you and come back to me!"

"Then you'll be having a good many sleepless nights ahead of you!" retorted Meghan, her turquoise eyes ablaze. "Now, either you remove yourself and allow me to pass, or else I shall be faced with no other choice but to make you!"

"Are you actually daring to threaten me with physical violence, you little strumpet?" Rosalie demanded indignantly. Hot color rose to her face while her eyes widened in disbelief.

"That I am. If you force my hand, it will in all likelihood cause untold embarrassment for us both, but that is a risk I am willing to take!"

Rosalie Hammond knew she was beaten—at least for the moment. Surrendering with an ill grace, she gathered up her skirts and flounced stiffly to one side.

"You will not be so superior when I am done with you!" she warned, her eyes narrowing into mere slits of scornful fury. "My father has many well-placed connections in Charlestown, and I intend to see to it that both you and your *devoted husband* are made to pay for everything!"

"I thank you for those words, Mistress Hammond," Meghan shocked her self-proclaimed adversary by responding. She smiled mockingly and explained, "Now that I have heard you express a desire to avenge yourself against Devlin, I know that what he said is entirely true—there could never have been any love between you."

With her head held proudly erect, she swept past

404

a speechless Rosalie and into the ballroom at last. Devlin came forward to claim her for another dance before she had traveled far inside the room. Grateful for the support of his arm about her waist, she was also relieved that he had intervened in time to rescue her from a group of matrons who were descending upon her yet another round of questions about her life in london.

"What did Rosalie say to you?" Devlin demanded with a frown immediately after the musicians struck up a waltz.

"You saw us?" asked Meghan in surprise. She performed the steps with an inborn grace, her free hand holding the fullness of her satin skirts at the perfect angle as she whirled.

"If your 'conversation' with her had lasted an instant longer, I was damned well going to put an end to it." His eyes darkened, while his hand tightened about hers. "I blame myself for this!"

"You are no more at fault than I!" she protested. "But in truth, how can anyone choose where to love?" She released a sigh and shook her head. "It was not nearly so unpleasant as it could have been. Were it not for the fact that Mistress Hammond cares so much for appearances, she might have created a scandalous scene indeed. As it was, she merely claimed to be in possession of your heart and predicted that you would forsake me for her."

"The devil she did!" he ground out, his eyes filling with an almost savage light.

"Devlin, please!" whispered Meghan. Her wide, anxious gaze moved hastily about the room full of avid onlookers before she cautioned him, "It would not do to have people think us quarreling over your former betrothed!"

405

"Maybe not, but I'll be damned if I'll let her speak to you like that ever again!" he vowed fiercely, all of his protective instincts rising to the core.

"Truly, it does not matter," she hastened to assure him. She managed a smile, and her eyes silently implored him to pursue the subject no further. "Such things are best left between women, my dearest husband. It is only through the interference of men that trouble arises!" She was pleased when his features relaxed into an answering smile of wry amusement.

"It seems to me, madam wife, that you are at times wise beyond your years. And there are other times when you display incredible naiveté." His eyes, aglow with tender admiration and love, stared deeply down into hers while he remarked in a voice only she could hear, "You are a beautiful woman-child, Meghan Kearny Montague, and the prospect of growing old with you gives me the greatest of pleasures."

"Surely not the greatest?" she challenged with a smile of purely feminine mischief. A delicious tremor coursed through her body at the sound of his low, resonant laughter, and her heart stirred with delight as his gaze traveled possessively over the flushed, upturned smoothness of her face.

"You have a wicked tongue," he scolded teasingly.

"As do you, sir!" she retorted, her blush deepening when he suddenly looked as though he would like nothing more than to literally devour her.

The waltz ended soon thereafter, and Devlin led his bride dutifully over to where their hostess had motioned to them with a graceful nod and uplifting of her gloved hand. A newly arrived gentleman stood at Lady Westerfield's side, but Meghan did not spare him so much as a passing glance until the older woman drew her insistently forward.

"My dearest Meghan," said Lady Westerfield, "I should like to introduce you to one of the city's charming, much too infrequent visitors."

Her mouth curving into a polite smile as Lady Westerfield turned to indicate the man beside her, Meghan looked his way at last. The smile froze on her face while her eyes widened in horrified disbelief.

Dear God, no! she cried inwardly. *It is not possible!* She battled a wave of panic as she felt the color draining from her face.

"Madam Montague," their hostess went on to perform the introductions, "may I present Mister Barrett Wolfe, who hails from Barbados. I believe he and your husband are already acquainted with one another."

"We have met," allowed Devlin with a curt nod at the other man.

"How do you do, Madam Montague?" Barrett Wolfe inquired smoothly. His attire was that of a dandy, his coat of white satin embroidered with gold and his blue satin breeches fastened at the knees with ornate metal buckles. Covering his own hair was a powdered wig which featured a long pigtail in the back, while about his neck he wore an elaborately arranged neckcloth of snowy white linen with a stock of black silk.

Meghan was still too thunderstruck to resist when he took her hand and raised it to his lips. Her stunned, blue-green gaze fastened upon the elegantly dressed man before her, and she told herself that she could not be mistaken. The sinister, swarthy features were the same. His voice—she could never forget that voice. But most of all, she mused dazedly, she recognized those eyes, the same heavy-lidded dark eyes which had filled with such a harsh, menacing light when she had dared to defy him.

The Wolf! her mind screamed. The last time she had seen him, he had been wearing a shoulder-length black wig and eyepatch, but she knew with a certainty that the suave gentleman before her and the evil pirate who had held her captive were one and the same. *By all that is holy, they are the same!*

She stood as if transfixed, her mind racing frantically as she tried to decide what to do. The matter was seized from her hands when Lady Westerfield suddenly took possession of Devlin's arm and decreed with a firm, undeniably maternal air, "Meghan, you shall bestow the honor of this dance on my friend, Mister Wolfe, while *I* shall steal your husband away to humor a few old women who are dying to hear more about his whirlwind courtship of you!"

Devlin, given no choice but to go along with their hostess, tossed a quick glance back at Meghan over his shoulder. He had not failed to notice the way she had stiffened upon being introduced to Barrett Wolfe, but he told himself that it was no doubt because she had felt uneasy beneath the man's damnably hawkish stare. He himself had taken an instant dislike to that particular gentleman several years ago. Thinking of Meghan in Wolfe's arms, even if only for the duration of a dance, he realized that his dislike had suddenly intensified into near hatred.

Meghan, still in a state of shock, was only dimly

aware of Barrett Wolfe claiming her for the dance. Her eyes flew back up to his face when he slipped an arm about her waist and clasped her hand with his, and alarm shot through her as she watched his dark gaze fill with derisive amusement. Shaking off her numbness at last, she looked for Devlin, but could not see him.

"Is something troubling you, Madam Montague?" her partner inquired with a faint smile. He held fast when she tried to pull free. "The dance has already begun. Surely you would not want Lady Westerfield and her guests to think ill of you?" His words, though spoken with nonchalance, held an undercurrent of a darker meaning.

"Do you truly think me deceived, Mister *Wolfe?*" she demanded in a furious undertone that was scarcely audible above the music.

Moving stiffly about in the steps of yet another waltz, she felt her entire body begin to tremble with the force of her emotions. It was all she could do to refrain from tearing herself away from her detestable partner and taking flight straight into Devlin's comforting arms. But something made her stay, something deep within which warned her not to involve Devlin or anyone else just yet.

"Deceived?" echoed her partner, feigning mild bewilderment. "I do not know what you mean."

"I cannot comprehend why you did not at least see fit to choose a vastly different name for your alter ego! But I suppose it affords you a great deal of amusement to flaunt yourself so boldly among polite society!"

"Ah, but I have no alter ego. I have always been known as Barrett Wolfe. And I happen to be a member of 'polite society' myself. Indeed, my name is well known throughout the city, for I have made it a point to visit these fair shores as often as possible."

"Although you have somehow managed to conceal your true nature from the good people of Charlestown, *I* know you for who and what you really are!" she declared bravely, her eyes blazing up at him.

"And what is that?" he challenged, his lips curling into another sardonic half-smile.

"A man entirely without conscience, a man who does not hesitate to take what he will from others, regardless of the considerable pain and suffering his greed causes! It is beyond me how you have escaped detection thus far, though I daresay no one—until now—has connected Barrett Wolfe, a foppish gentleman from Barbados, with a notorious buccaneer who calls himself The Wolf!"

"I haven't the vaguest notion what you're talking about, my dear Madam Montague. Who is this buccaneer of whom you speak?" he asked with deceptive innocence, though his eyes glittered dangerously down at her. The touch of his arm about her waist and hand upon hers made her experience a sharp twinge of revulsion, but she forced herself to continue with the dance.

"Come now, did you think you would never be exposed? Even if I had not recognized you, there is still Mistress Hammond! I am certain she cannot fail to remember the man who dared to hold her for ransom!"

"I have already shared a delightful conversation with Mistress Hammond this evening," he countered with a triumphant chuckle. "She does not, I am happy to report, suffer under the same delusion as yourself. You are a very beautiful woman, you

410

know, but a very foolish one."

"She . . . she did not recognize you?" Meghan stammered in wide-eyed disbelief.

"Oddly enough, I had never been given the pleasure of meeting the charming young lady before tonight. Our paths must have crossed quite frequently, and yet we were only formally introduced by Lady Westerfield a short time ago."

"I do not believe you!"

"It matters not what you believe," he replied, his swarthy features tightening now. "If you persist in confusing me with this pirate of yours, then you had best be prepared to offer up proof to support your ridiculous claim!"

"I require no other proof than what my own eyes and ears have given me!

"Yes, but will anyone else put their trust in your young and overly imaginative senses? I think not, Madam Montague. I think not," he repeated with an ill-disguised sneer. "I find it very difficult to believe that the 'good people of Charlestown' would ever be tempted to take the word of a newcomer—an Englishwoman at that—over a wealthy Barbadian planter whose presence has long been accepted here and whose reputation has remained untarnished by the slightest hint of scandal for all these years."

"My husband will believe me!" insisted Meghan, still refusing to accept defeat. "And you can be certain he will make others believe me as well!"

"Your husband, *my sweet,* had better remain ignorant of your hysterical rantings, or else you will very likely find yourself widowed long before fate intends!"

Gasping sharply, Meghan felt her heart twisting in very real alarm. Her eyes filled with horror as she stared up at the man who had once cruelly assaulted her and vowed to take her by force. There was no denying Barrett Wolfe's threat—if she revealed his true identity, she would be endangering Devlin's life.

No! she cried in anguished silence. *Dear God in heaven, no!*

"You cannot mean that!" she tried reasoning with him, though she could not keep a note of desperation from her voice. "If you ever dared to harm him in any way, I would see you hanged!"

"Would you?" he drawled mockingly. His soft, contemptuous laughter burned in her ears while his predatory gaze raked over her body. "Once again, dear lady, there is the matter of your lack of credibility, as well as my impeccable standing in this community. And even if you *were* able to convince anyone of my guilt, it would not serve to bring Devlin Montague back from the dead."

"No!" she choked out, shaking her head in benumbed denial.

"No indeed," he concluded as another slow, scornful smile spread across his darkly attractive features, "I have every confidence that you will do as I bid and keep your pretty mouth shut. You see, there are those under my command who would not hesitate to serve me in any way I wish. And if your husband's welfare is not enough to persuade you, then rest assured I have other methods of dealing with you."

"Other methods?" she repeated hoarsely. Her mind was full of terrible, heart-rending visions of Devlin lying dead or injured, and she knew without a doubt that she would give her own life to save him.

"I shall offer you an example," he proclaimed as

412

though he were making idle conversation instead of cold-blooded threats against another person's life. "You have a charming young sister-in-law, do you not?"

"Linette!" breathed Meghan, her stomach churning in awful dread. "Surely even you would not—"

"If I am the bloodthirsty pirate you believe me to be, then I daresay I would do anything to get what I want. And if I am none other than Barrett Wolfe, then you have no cause to worry."

It was obvious to Meghan that he took perverse pleasure from the game of cat and mouse he was playing with her, just as it was apparent he meant to continue the game for as long as necessary. She could bear no more of it!

"Very well, Mister Wofle," she told him, capitulating at last. She continued to glare venomously up at him, however, and the proud, unconsciously defiant angle of her head provided evidence of her dauntless spirit. "You have given me little choice!"

"I knew you would be reasonable," he murmured smoothly. As if by arrangement, the members of the orchestra signaled the end of the waltz just then, stilling their instruments to enjoy a well-deserved respite from their efforts.

Barrett Wolfe led Meghan from the dance floor. It required every ounce of self-will she possessed to refrain from jerking her arm away when he drew it through his. She prayed fervently that she would be able to conceal her distress from Devlin, for she knew him well enough to be able to predict his response if he had the slightest suspicion that the other man had insulted her in any way. *Dear God, what am I going to do?* she beseeched silently.

They were nearing the spot where Devlin stood

413

virtually surrounded by Lady Westerfield and her cronies. Meghan's heart pounded in her ears, and she was dismayed to feel hot, telltale color staining her cheeks. She waged a fierce battle to master her emotions and regain her composure, while the man beside her merely smiled. The smile did not quite reach his eyes, which were glittering coldly and full of a silent warning as he favored her with one last hard look.

"Ah, Meghan, my dear!" proclaimed Lady Westerfield, her face alight with pleasure when she caught sight of the approaching couple. "Your husband has been regaling us with the most delightfully *wicked* tales of his exploits at Oxford!"

"Has he?" Meghan replied with only a faint unsteadiness to her voice. Avoiding Devlin's gaze, she forced a smile to her lips and added, "I have not yet been privy to such information myself."

"Well then, you must demand to hear all about it at once!" one of the other women said with a laugh. "You can, of course, claim the privilege of a wife to know everything about her spouse!"

"Yes, but do you not think that particular privilege brings with it far too much responsibility in other areas?" another middle-aged matron opined thoughtfully, setting up a discussion of the merits and limitations afforded married women in the current society. Lady Westerfield and the others became so caught up in their mutually commiserative deliberations that they temporarily forgot about the younger members of their group.

Meghan breathed an inward sigh of relief as she was finally released by Barrett Wolfe, who exchanged another wordless nod with her husband. She moved immediately to Devlin's side, unable to prevent a slight tremor from shaking her when his strong fingers closed about her arm.

"What is it, my love?" he asked quietly, his brow creasing into a sudden, worried frown. "Are you unwell?"

"No, I . . . I am fine, Devlin!" she hastened to assure him. She still could not bring herself to look at his face. When she realized that her former captor apparently intended to remain close by, she began to fear that she would not be able to carry the whole thing off.

But she soon received assistance from a most unlikely source—Rosalie Hammond. The arrogant blonde swept forth to join the other three, her gray eyes full of disdainful humor as they lit upon Meghan. She slipped her arm through Barrett Wolfe's with an undeniably possessive air, while her mouth curved into a smile of almost feline satisfaction.

"Is it not odd, *dearest* Montagues, that Mister Wolfe has been coming to Charlestown all these years and never managed to get himself introduced to me before this very night?" she remarked with a significant arching of her eyebrow.

At least a portion of her words were true, thought Rosalie with an inward laugh of malicious amusement. She had not met Barrett Wolfe during his many previous visits to the city—at least, she could not remember having done so—and they had indeed only become "formally" acquainted with one another that evening. But, she recalled with a shiver of purely sensual delight, she had come to know him as The Wolf only a short time ago. . . .

"Do you not think he looks vaguely familiar, Madam Montague?" she challenged Meghan. Her

415

smile broadened in spite of the fact that she felt her pirate lover's arm stiffen in barely controlled fury beneath her hand.

"No, I do not, Mistress Hammond," Meghan answered calmly, refusing to rise to the bait. It was now made clear to her that the woman and Barrett Wolfe were in complete accord with one another regarding the secret of his identity. Although she could not understand why Rosalie Hammond had agreed to remain silent on the matter, she sensed that there was a good deal more to their relationship than she had previously believed.

"My wife has also just recently made his acquaintance," Devlin pointed out. His piercing, deep blue eyes fastened upon his ex-fiancée with angry intensity, for he was thinking about her earlier offensive behavior toward Meghan.

"But of course," countered Rosalie with a triumphant, knowing look at the other woman. She turned her gaze upon Devlin again and cast him what she believed to be an irresistibly alluring smile. "Do you not think you should dance with me, Devlin? After all, if things had followed their rightful course, *I* would have been attending this affair as your bride."

"I am sorry, Mistress Hammond, but I have already agreed to partner my wife in this next dance," he lied easily.

Though her own emotions were still in utter turmoil, Meghan found it necessary to suppress a smile as she watched Rosalie grow visibly enraged. All traces of humor vanished, however, when her eyes were drawn back to Barrett Wolfe. He had turned his hawkish gaze upon her again, and she caught her breath on an inward gasp as she glimpsed the same burning, rapacious light with which he had regarded her the last time she had faced him alone. But she had been a prisoner in his island fortress then, she reminded herself in an effort to gather her badly shaken courage about her once more, whereas now she was protected by dozens of witnesses.

"If you will please excuse me," Meghan suddenly became aware of Devlin saying. Managing a weak smile up at him, she felt almost giddy with relief when he led her away from Rosalie and the man who called himself Barrett Wolfe. *This cannot be happening*, she mused dazedly once more. Remembering the strange premonition she had experienced the day before, she realized that she would never have guessed it could owe its origin to the presence of the black-hearted villain who had intended to make her his captive mistress. . . .

"Tell me, Meghan—what is troubling you?" Devlin commanded her once they had joined in the dancing again. "Damn it, there's no use in denying it any longer, for I am neither blind nor dim-witted!"

His deep, resonant tone was both gruff and caring, and she found herself sorely tempted to tell him the truth. But a warning signal sounded in her brain, followed immediately thereafter by the unbidden memory of Barrett Wolfe's murderous threats. She knew that, just as she had admitted to Wolfe a short time earlier, she had no choice. Revealing the truth to Devlin could result only in disaster. And no matter how fervently she wished to see justice done, she could not endure the prospect of placing either him or Linette in danger. *God forgive her, but she could not expose The Wolf for what he was—she could not!*

"Is it Rosalie?" probed Devlin, scowling darkly.

"Because if it is, I swear I will not hesitate to—"

"No! No, Devlin, I am not troubled by Rosalie!" she denied honestly. Meeting his gaze at last, she felt hot tears sting her eyes. Her heart was so full of love for him she feared it would burst, and she could not prevent herself from shuddering at the horrible thought of him falling prey to The Wolf's treachery.

"Then it must be that overly primped and powdered bastard you were just dancing with!" he ground out, his eyes filling with a dangerously savage light.

"No!" Meghan denied a bit too emphatically. When she saw that he was peering down at her with a mixture of concern and suspicion, she hurried to think of a way to steer him away from the truth of his accusations. "I . . . I did not find Mister Wolfe at all to my liking as a partner, to be sure," she told him with downcast eyes, "but he is not to blame for my present state of . . . of disquiet."

"Then who or what the devil *is* to blame?" he demanded in growing impatience.

"I must admit that I did not speak the truth a short time ago when I denied feeling unwell," she answered, feeling sick indeed at the lie she now found it necessary to tell. "I am terribly sorry, my love, but it seems I have developed a headache of unusual severity. I—I thought perchance it would go away, but it has only intensified."

"I will make our apologies to Lord and Lady Westerfield at once," he declared without hesitation, his expression softening as he escorted her solicitously from the dance floor.

Within minutes, Meghan found herself leaving the Westerfields' house with Devlin's strong, lovingly supporting arm about her shoulders. Linette fol-

418

lowed closely behind, striving to conceal her acute disappointment at having to bid goodnight to Charles while things were still so unsettled between them. She was, however, genuinely concerned about her sister-in-law, and she reached over to press a comforting hand upon Meghan's once they were seated in the carriage and on their way home.

"I do hope you will be recovered enough to attend the horse races with us tomorrow," said Linette. She smiled impishly, her eyes fairly dancing beneath the soft golden glow of the street lamps while she rearranged her lace shawl about her shoulders. "Imagine—Dev has actually agreed to tear himself away from his precious business long enough to take us!"

"I have agreed to take the matter under consideration," Devlin corrected her with a wry half-smile. He grew solemn again as he looked back to Meghan, his arm drawing her even closer to him on the cushioned leather seat. "Would you prefer that we traveled the remainder of the way with the top up, my love?"

"No, thank you, Devlin," she murmured. Her eyes swept closed while she rested gratefully against his warm hardness.

"Perhaps we should summon a physician once we are home," suggested Linette, her eyes clouding at a sudden thought. "It might not be a simple headache, you know. Indeed, it might very well turn out to be something far more serious—"

"No, really, I'm quite certain I shall be fine come morning!" insisted Meghan. Her heart twisted anew when she recalled Barrett Wolfe's veiled threats concerning the young redhead. She gave Linette a tremulous smile and added, "It is no doubt from having consumed too much of Lady Westerfield's rum punch."

Devlin and his sister exchanged quick frowns of worriment on her behalf, but they said nothing else. The carriage rolled to a halt in front of the town-house a short time later, whereupon Devlin, disregarding his wife's protests, carried her upstairs and tucked her into their bed with such incredible tenderness that she very nearly gave in to the temptation to dissolve into a flood of tears. Instead, she closed her eyes and tried valiantly not to think of Barrett Wolfe.

But his dark, sinister features haunted her dreams that night, and the memory of his warning returned to hit her full force when she awoke the next morning.

Chapter Seventeen

Horse racing during the summer season in Charlestown never failed to prove popular as a spectator sport among the members of polite society—even more popular than cockfighting, Linette had informed Meghan with a giggle, for the simple reason that ladies could attend the races along with their husbands. A track had been established nearly forty years ago, although the present track, called the New Market Course and located just north of the city, had only been in existence for a short time.

"The Carolina Jockey Club offers purses up to a thousand pounds!" Linette went on to reveal excitedly as they waited inside the townhouse for Devlin to arrive. "Oh Meghan, I am so glad you decided to come after all! Why, nearly everyone we know will be there, all of them in their new fashions and handsome coaches. I daresay even the servants will be decked out in unsurpassed finery!" She spun away from the window and began to pace restlessly about the downstairs drawing room. "I do wish Dev would hurry!"

"Perhaps he has been detained at the shipping office," offered Meghan with a soft smile of indulgence.

"He is always more concerned with business than anything else!" Linette complained with an audible sigh of disgruntlement. She virtually threw herself upon the sofa beside Meghan.

"Come now, you know that is not true."

"I know, but I am nearly overcome with impatience for us to be on our way! Charles will of a certainly be there by now."

"And does his mother attend today?" asked Meghan.

"I doubt it," Linette answered with an expressive twist of her mouth. "She rarely exposes herself to sunlight, you see. She claims it 'saps her strength.' I daresay she has never accepted an invitation unless it was for an event to be held indoors. She can be dreadfully trying at times! Good heavens, to think that she will be my mother-in-law once I have married—" She broke off all of a sudden and leapt to her feet again, resuming her vigilant stance at the window. Seconds passed, and yet there was still no sign of Devlin.

Meghan's brow creased into a frown of puzzlement at Linette's rather odd behavior, but she found her thoughts being forced in another direction when Barrett Wolfe's face swam before her eyes again. Her pulses quickening in renewed alarm, she wondered if he would be at the races as well. She was filled with dismay at the prospect of seeing him again, and she mused unhappily that he would no doubt be in attendance at many of the same events as she and Devlin and Linette. He was apparently a favorite among the city's elite. Indeed, she thought bitterly, he would seem the perfect guest to any hostess, for he was wealthy and attractive and—more importantly—unmarried.

Or was he? she suddenly asked herself, realizing that he could very well have a wife somewhere, or even a dozen of them throughout the world. She knew nothing about the man, other than the fact that he was a notorious pirate who masqueraded as a gentleman whenever it suited his fancy to do so. A faint smile of irony tugged at her lips as she recalled that Devlin had carried out the same masquerade, only in reverse, that night on Andros . . . .

"He has arrived at last!" exclaimed Linette. She went flying from the room to open the front door and greet Devlin with a sharp, sisterly word of rebuke for his vexing tardiness.

Meghan rose to her feet and gently smoothed a hand over the gathered fullness of her new, pale lilac muslin gown. Like the white lawn dress Linette wore, it was a fashionable *sacque*, with an embroidered stomacher exposed by the edges of the bodice in the front. The low, squared neckline was set off by a delicate tippet of lace ending in a knot just below the shadowed valley of her breasts.

Devlin, evidently unscathed by his sister's verbal chastisement of him, strode into the drawing room and greeted his wife with a warm embrace and a long, lingering kiss. Linette rolled her eyes heavenward before declaring that she would take herself out to the carriage to wait. Since there was no response forthcoming—truly, she had not expected one—she followed through on her announced intentions and marched briskly outside.

"Are you certain you're feeling well enough to go?" Devlin asked Meghan quietly, his deep blue gaze holding both tenderness and desire as he released her with obvious reluctance.

"I am completely recovered, my dearest husband," she replied a trifle breathlessly. She smiled at him, then added on a teasing note that belied her growing trepidation at the day's excursion, "If I had not been, I daresay the touch of your lips upon mine would have done the trick!"

"Saucy wench," he murmured with a soft chuckle. He gave her a mock scowl of ferocity and took hold of her arm. "Damn these social obligations! I can think of a number of better ways to spend my time."

"I am sure you can, but your sister will no doubt be eternally grateful for your indulgence."

"I'll wager she has talked of little else but Charles the whole blasted morning." His frown this time was genuine.

"She is a young woman in love, my dearest husband," Meghan ventured to remind him as they began moving toward the front door. "And Linette is too much like you to accept defeat easily. Take care, Devlin—if you order her to feel or behave a certain way, she will in all likelihood do the opposite!"

"It seems, madam, that you have come to

understand a good deal about the Montague temperament," he observed wryly. "Perhaps *too* much."

"You need have no fear upon that score." Her eyes sparkled winningly up at him as he opened the door. She preceded him across the threshold into the crisp brightness outside, tossing an affectionately mischievous look back at him over her shoulder when she said, "I am convinced that it will require at least fifty or sixty more years' acquaintanceship with you to be truly knowledgeable!"

"Granted," he concurred with another irresistibly crooked smile.

Meghan's heart was considerably lighter by the time they arrived at the racetrack. She and Linette were both enthralled at the sights before them. It appeared that half of Charlestown had turned out for the event, as there were people and carriages and horses everywhere.

The races afforded yet another opportunity for the ladies to impress one another—and the men, of course—with their latest finery, while the gentlemen were glad of the chance to try their luck at predicting the outcome of the competition on the track. As always, they were willing to wager with one another as to whose choice would prove the fastest; vast sums of money were won and lost, usually without the knowledge of wives, mothers, and sweethearts. The difference between the sexes was here, as everywhere else, clearly delineated. Unbeknownst to their male counterparts, however, the ladies enjoyed their own brand of gambling, though the stakes were more often than not a new hat or fan, or even a week's use of a much valued servant.

"How shall I ever find Charles in this crowd?" Linette wondered aloud. Many of those gathered to watch the races remained seated in their carriages for a better view, while others strolled about the grassy, gently rolling grounds to visit with friends. Whatever the case, most of the spectators had brought along woven hampers packed with food and drink, and the area was almost like a sea of broad-brimmed bonnets as the ladies sought to ward off the undesirable effects of the sun upon their complexions.

"I've no idea," Devlin drawled lazily while he assisted Meghan down from the carriage, "but if we trust in Charles's sense of direction we may very well be spared his company."

"Devlin Montague, what a perfectly horrid thing to say!" his sister accused hotly. "I seem to recall that Charles Deverill is your closest friend, so how in heaven's name can you stand there and abuse—"

"I meant no abuse, Linette," he interrupted in a low, conciliatory tone. "As you said, Charles is my friend. That is precisely the reason I feel free to make light of his presence—or lack of it." There was only the ghost of a smile on his lips when he reached up to lift her down, but Linette could not fail to glimpse the light of devilment in his eyes.

"Oh Dev!" she sighed, her stormy features relaxing into a begrudging little smile. "It is not fair to tease me so, for you must know by now that I . . . well, that I have quite lost my head over him!"

"You may have lost your head, you little minx," he replied softly once her feet had touched the ground, "but you are far too young to lose anything else."

His gaze now held an unmistakable warning, and Linette colored rosily before pulling away. She turned toward Meghan, but her eyes were drawn a short distance past to where two young women and an older gentleman sat conversing amiably with one another in the comfort of their carriage.

"If you've no objections," said Linette, "I should like to go and speak to Tallie and Eustacia. Please feel free to take a turn about the grounds without me, for I will no doubt be kept more than adequately entertained in your absence. Oh, and if you should happen upon Charles—"

"I will direct him immediately to your side," avowed Devlin, favoring her with a mocking little smile. Meghan sent him a look of wifely reproach after Linette left them alone.

"Devlin Montague, you are the most provoking man!"

"That I am, but you know you would not have me any other way."

She could not resist smiling up at him, and his eyes twinkled roguishly down at her as he offered her his arm. They set off at a leisurely pace, spending the next quarter of an hour in dutiful conversation with various friends and acquaintances. By the time the first race began, they had made their way around to the opposite side of the

427

track, where they stood within the cool shade of the trees and watched the running of the horses.

Meghan found the sight exhilarating, and she was in the process of telling Devlin about the races she had once attended in the countryside near London when Rosalie Hammond and Barrett Wolfe suddenly intruded upon their privacy. Her face paling and her eyes clouding with dread, Meghan moved instinctively closer to her husband.

"Good day, Devlin," purred Rosalia. She spared a brief, haughty glance for Meghan, but refused to observe even the barest civilities by bidding her hello.

"So we meet again," observed Wolfe, tipping his hat gallantly to Meghan. "I trust you are well, Madam Montague?"

"Yes ... thank you," she forced herself to respond, though her voice was scarcely audible. She was only dimly aware of Devlin speaking to the loathsome couple, as she was waging a fierce battle to control her emotions. Her conscience screamed at her to do something, to tell Devlin and everyone else the truth, but her heart forbade it.

"My father is here as well," Rosalie informed Devlin. Her gray eyes glittered vengefully while narrowing up at him. "He swears he will never forgive you. But as you will no doubt recall, he never believed you worthy of my hand. I should have listened to him!"

"Come now, my dear Rosalie," Barrett Wolfe intervened suavely, "you must not harbor a grudge against Mister Montague. I am certain he had his reasons for . . . shall we say, 'transferring his affections,' " His dark gaze was full of malicious amusement—and something else she dared not name—as it lit upon Meghan. "Far be it for any of us to question a man's choice in such a matter."

"This particular matter is none of your concern, Mister Wolfe," Devlin pointed out in a deceptively low and level tone. His own eyes reflected an intense annoyance with Rosalie and a growing animosity toward her foppish, overly bold companion. He tucked Meghan's hand in the crook of his arm again and announced coldly, "If you will please excuse us, my wife and I must return to our carriage." Favoring Rosalie with a curt nod, and sparing only a hard look for Barrett Wolfe, he did not wait for a response before leading Meghan away.

"Oh Devlin, I am so glad to escape their presence!" she confessed once they were safely out of earshot of the other two. *Sweet Saint Bridget,* she added in chaotic silence, *how I am I going to continue with this charade if I must face The Wolf at every turn?*

"I find they are remarkable well suited to one another," Devlin remarked with a scowl of displeasure. "I cannot believe it possible that I was ever tempted to marry her. And as for Barrett Wolfe," he went on to declare, the rugged planes of his face tightening while his eyes darkened in jealous rage, "if he ever dares to look at you that way again, I will damned well beat him to a bloody pulp!"

"Dear God, no!" gasped Meghan in sudden

429

dismay. Her eyes were very wide and full of near frantic entreaty as she gazed up at him and cautioned, "You must never think of doing such a thing! Please, Devlin, promise me you will not!"

"I will give no such promise." He studied her face closely and demanded in a voice that was whipcord sharp, "What is it, Meghan? Why should the man's welfare be of such concern to you?"

"Because I . . . I cannot abide the thought of you in danger!" she answered honestly.

"Danger?" he echoed in disbelief. "From that frilled-up bastard?" His handsome features relaxed into a smile of wryly appreciative humor. "No, my love, you need have no fear on my account. I have every confidence that I could best him with one hand tied behind my back."

"Appearances are often deceptive," she murmured. "There are those who are not at all what they seem." Her heart pounded as she offered the subtle warning, for she wanted so desperately to say more.

"Perhaps. Whatever the case, I will allow no man to insult you—even if it is with his eyes alone."

Although she normally would have found such a statement touching, Meghan could not be anything but alarmed by it under the present circumstances. She wondered just how long things could go on this way before something occurred to change them—for better or for worse.

They reached the carriage a short time later, following the completion of the second race, and were surprised to discover that Linette was nowhere in sight. Devlin handed Meghan up into the carriage, then strode away to question Tallie Raymond about his sister's whereabouts. When he returned, his face was suffused with a dull, angry color, while his eyes smoldered with a dangerously savage light.

"Oh Devlin, what has happened?" asked Meghan. His forebodingly thunderous expression struck fear in her heart. "Where is Linette?"

Without a word, he climbed abruptly up into the carriage and bit out an order to the driver. The whip cracked above the horse's head, causing the carriage to lurch forward and roll away from the track at an unusually brisk pace.

The Montagues' hasty departure prompted a good deal of speculation among those who witnessed the event, though it was generally agreed upon that the reason was without a doubt a good one. Devlin Montague was known as a mature, responsible young man who was not given—at least not in recent years—to impetuous behavior unless it was called for.

Meghan clutched breathlessly at the side of the leather seat. Her eyes were very round and glistening with bewildered worriment as she looked at Devlin.

"Devlin, what is it?" she demanded once more. "Where are we going, and why are we leaving without—"

"Read this!" he ground out, thrusting her the piece of paper he had crushed in his hand. Meghan took it from him and unfolded it, her eyes

431

hastily scanning its contents while the carriage sped back toward Charlestown.

Dearest brother, Linette had written, *I know you will be angry with me for what I am about to do, but I also know you will forgive me once you have accustomed yourself to the notion. I have gone away with Charles, and I shall be his wife before day's end. Do not try to stop us, Dev. I know that what I am doing is truly for the best. I shall contact you once I am the new Madam Deverill. Your loving sister—Linette Montague.*

Meghan raised her wide, luminous gaze to her husband again. Her head spun dizzily as she pondered what she had just read, and she faltered in stunned disbelief, "Dear God, she . . . she has—"

"She has eloped with Charles!" Devlin finished for her, his deep voice edged with white-hot fury.

"But how could this have happened?"

"She and Charles obviously had it all planned, damn them! They knew we would never suspect an elopement, just as they must have realized we would be conveniently occupied while they carried out their blasted, idiotic little scheme!"

"Good heavens, Linette gave me no indication that she intended to do anything so dras—" Meghan remarked dazedly, only to fall silent when it occurred to her that Linette had indeed declared only the night before that she would employ *drastic means* if necessary.

But, Meghan then asked herself in confusion, who could have guessed those means would turn out to be anything so foolhardy and irreversibly

432

damaging as an elopement? And who could have predicted that Charles Deverill, who had stubbornly refused to even so much as discuss marriage, would participate in such a dishonorable scheme?

Perhaps Linette was lying about that as well, her mind's inner voice suddenly suggested. She did not want to face the possibility, for it hurt her deeply to think that her sister-in-law had been deceiving her all along. No, she was convinced that the elopement was every bit as impulsive as it appeared, and she was determined to reserve judgment on the matter until all the facts were known.

"What are you planning to do?" she asked Devlin quietly, her heart aching for him as well as for the misguided lovers.

"First, I am going to find them," he vowed grimly. "And then I am going to make Charles Deverill wish he had never been born!" Viewing the murderous gleam in his deep blue eyes, Meghan had very little doubt that he was capable of throttling Charles with his bare hands. She knew she had to try and make him see reason.

"They may not be able to find anyone willing to perform the ceremony," she offered hopefully. "Linette requires your consent to wed, does she not?"

"Theoretically, yes. But such a minor detail will hold little significance outside of Charlestown. Once they have traveled to an area where our name is not so well known, they will no doubt meet with success."

"Oh Devlin, perhaps . . . perhaps you should

433

not try to stop them at all." Aware that she stood a good chance of incurring his wrath with such a remark, she was not at all surprised when he turned a narrow, scorching look upon her.

"What the devil do you mean by that? Linette is my sister, Meghan, and I'll be damned if I'll stand by and do nothing while she sets about ruining her life!"

"But she may not be ruining her life at all! If she and Charles love one another so much that they are willing to risk public condemnation—not to mention *your* formidable temper—then it may well be that they should be together! After all, you and I were married in haste, were we not?" she reminded him.

"The situations are entirely different," he replied tersely, his gaze becoming unfathomable.

"But Devlin, surely—" she started to protest, only to be cut off when his hand shot up to close about her arm in a firm, authoritative grip.

"No more, Meghan," he commanded in a tone that made it clear he would hear no further argument on the subject. "Whether or not they love and deserve one another is not the issue here. The fact remains that my sister has defied me. She is little more than a child. Charles Deverill, however, is old enough to be aware of the serious consequences of his actions. I would not have thought him capable of—" He broke off and muttered a savage oath, then released Meghan's arm. A long, heavily charged silence fell between them.

She watched as several conflicting emotions

played across his face. Though her heart stirred with compassion for his obvious disquietude, she felt a sharp twinge of resentment over his continued refusal to lend credence to her advice. She certainly could not deny that Linette and Charles had acted improperly, but neither could she deny that they were entitled to the same happiness she and Devlin had found together. Love complicated things terribly sometimes, she mused to herself, settling back against the seat with a sigh and a trouble frown.

She was surprised a short time later when they pulled up in front of their own townhouse. Before she could question Devlin, however, he had climbed down from the carriage with swift agility and reached back up for her. His hands closed about her waist, and he swung her down to the sidewalk but did not immediately release her.

"You will wait here," he decreed solemnly. "I intend to find them, Meghan, no matter how long it takes. I may not return before nightfall, so do not worry if the hour grows late."

"But how will you even know where to begin your search?" she asked, her eyes full of mingled concern and perplexity as she gazed up at him.

"They cannot have traveled far yet. And it may be possible that someone saw them. My guess is that they have headed northward." He lowered his head and brushed her forehead with his lips, then set her firmly away from him. "Go inside, my love. I will fetch a mount from the stables, for I stand a better chance of overtaking them if I give chase on horseback." With that, he left her, his long, purposeful strides leading him toward the narrow strip of unfenced yard between the buildings.

"Oh Devlin, please have a care!" Meghan called after him. Watching until he had disappeared around the corner, she gathered up her skirts and moved disconsolately down the tree-shaded walk to the house.

She had no sooner stepped inside than Jolene came bustling toward her down the long center hallway. Since it was not at all the cook's usual custom to meet anyone at the door, visitors or otherwise, Meghan knew immediately that something was amiss.

"There is someone waiting for you in the downstairs drawing room, Madam!" Jolene informed her in a conspiratorial whisper.

"Who is it?" asked Meghan with a mild frown, instinctively following the other woman's example and keeping her own voice low.

"He would not give me his name!" replied Jolene, darting a quick glance toward the room which held the man in question. "But he is an older gentlemen, quite distinguished looking, and he proclaimed he has a matter of much importance to discuss with you. I told him you and Master Devlin would not be returning for at least another hour or two, but he insisted upon waiting!"

"How very odd!" murmured Meghan. It suddenly occurred to her that the man, whoever he was, might have information regarding Linette and Charles. "I will speak to him, Jolene," she announced. Giving the cook a faint smile, she took off her bonnet and hastily smoothed a few loose tendrils of hair back into place, then headed for the drawing room.

Once there, she paused in the doorway, her gaze seeking out the mysterious caller. She frowned to herself when she caught sight of him, for he was standing near the fireplace with his back toward her. Apparently sensing her presence, however, the tall, bewigged man spun about to face her. In that moment, Meghan's eyes filled with startled recognition and her face lit up with profound joy.

"Grandfather!" she breathed. She flew across the room and into his welcoming embrace. His arms gathered her to him, and he held her close to his heart as though he would never let her go.

"Thank God I have found you at last!" he exclaimed in a hoarse voice brimming with emotion. "I feared you were dead, my dearest child!"

"Oh Grandfather, I . . . I can scarcely believe you are here!" she faltered tremulously, her eyes glistening with sudden tears.

She was content to remain in his embrace for several long moments, her body trembling and her mind awhirl with all the cherished memories evoked by the reunion. It was a reunion for which she had prayed these past several months. Though her hopes had faltered at times, her heart had remained strong in the belief that it would come to pass, and she gave silent thanks as she rested against the solid strength of the man who had been both father and grandfather to her these many years.

Finally, Meghan raised her head and looked up at him. Her eyes traveled lovingly over his chiseled, aristocratic features while her mouth curved into a smile of tender warmth.

"But how on earth did you find me?" she asked in mingled happiness and confusion. "You couldn't possibly have received my letter in time! And where is Grandmother? Did she not come with you?"

"Your grandmother was not feeling well enough to make the journey," he answered. Glimpsing the sudden anxiety in her eyes, he hastened to assure her, "The doctors insist it is nothing serious, but they advised against such a lengthy trip. And I was uncertain as to whether my efforts would yield anything at all, for I had only the unreliable information given me by your late father's wife to act as my guide."

"Then she . . . she was involved with my abduction after all?"

"I am afraid so." His thick gray brows drew together in a scowl while his green eyes glittered with a harsh, vengeful light. "You can rest assured that she shall be made to pay for her treachery! The vile creature confessed to everything. She had involved her own brother in her nefarious scheme, and it was by questioning him that Ambrose O'Donnell and I were able to trace you to the *Bristol Packet*. Once I discovered that the ship was bound for South Carolina, I wasted no time in giving chase."

"I wrote to you as soon as I could, but the letter was only sent a few days ago." Her eyes grew very wide as something else suddenly dawned on her. "Have you not yet learned of what misfortune befell the *Bristol Packet* on its way here?"

"Misfortune?" he echoed, frowning in bewilderment. "I have heard nothing of that accursed vessel! I arrived in Charlestown only this morning, intent upon enlisting the help of the authorities to search for you. If I found you at all, I expected it to be as an indentured servant, for I knew you had been sold into bondage." His eyes blazed again at the thought. "You can imagine my surprise when I was apprised of the fact that my granddaughter had recently become the wife of a Mister Devlin Montague! I would never have believed it, but the evidence was put before my very eyes—there, in the newspaper for all to see, was a notice of your marriage. After inquiring after this Montague fellow's address, I came straightaway here and have been waiting for nearly an hour to ascertain if his bride was indeed my Meghan, or merely an imposter!"

"Oh Grandfather, I have so much to tell you!" she pronounced with a heavy sigh. She drew away and led him over to the sofa. He took a seat beside her, his hand retaining possession of hers while she sought for the best way to begin her unbelievable tale of captivity, rescue, enslavement, and finally, marriage.

"Now please, hear me out before you threaten to run my husband through!" she requested, casting him an ironic little smile before sobering again. "I love Devlin Montague with all my heart, dearest Grandfather, and you must realize that, given the circumstances, he fully believed that he was acting in an honorable manner."

439

"I do not like the sound of this, Meghan," Sir Henry Claibourne warned, scowling again.

Meghan felt her pulses leap in apprehension, just as they had been wont to do when she was a child facing him with the shame of some misdeed, but she was determined to make him understand. She took a deep, steadying breath, then set about relating to her stern-faced grandfather all that had happened since she had defied him and gone to Ireland to see her father buried. She was careful to avoid any mention of the scandalous fact that Devlin had required her to share his bedchamber at Shadowmoss prior to their marriage, and also of the equally shocking truth of her own willingness to love a man who was at the time betrothed to another.

Upon finishing, Meghan waited anxiously to receive her grandfather's opinion about what she had told him. He sat in pensive silence beside her, his countenance inscrutable and his eyes narrowed while he digested the startling information. Finally, he rose to his feet and wandered back to the fireplace, where he stood regarding her solemnly from his great, intimidating height.

"I cannot say that I approve of the way Montague has treated you, my child, but I owe him my undying gratitude for spiriting you away from those swinish cutthroats! And I suppose it does not signify how your marriage came about, so long as it *did!*"

"I knew you would understand!" Meghan cried happily, leaping to her feet and crossing the room to embrace him again.

"Not entirely," he murmured gruffly. He then gave her a smile of fond indulgence and said, "You have a good deal more to explain. I want to hear more about this husband of yours. And you do realize, of course, that your grandmother will demand to approve him for herself as soon as possible?"

"I have every confidence that she will love him as much as I do!"

"No, my darling Meghan, not as much as you." He lifted a hand to cup her chin affectionately, his eyes softening as they stared into the sparkling turquoise depths of hers. "I should have to be blind not to see how deep your affections for this hotheaded American run." His arms enveloped her once more, and he hugged her close while silently repeating a heartfelt prayer of thanksgiving for her deliverance from evil.

Seconds later, the front door flew open with a crash. Meghan pulled hastily away from her grandfather and whirled about just in time to catch a glimpse of Linette racing down the hallway in tears. Devlin and Charles entered the house close on her heels, and Meghan was startled to see them disappear into the library across the hall and close the door. Musing that apparently none of the three had caught sight of either her or her grandfather, she stared toward the doorway in dazed confusion.

"Which one of those gentlemen was your husband?" Sir Henry asked dryly.

"What?" gasped Meghan, turning back to him at last. She colored beneath his penetrating gaze, and she looked uncomfortably preoccupied while

441

declaring, "Devlin was the taller and more handsome of the two."

"I see. And who, might I ask, was the distraught young lady?"

"My sister-in-law, Linette." *Linette.* Something was obviously very wrong! "Please, Grandfather," she asked, her eyes pleading with him for a bit more indulgence, "will you excuse me for a few moments? I must see to her at once!"

"Of course. I shall be here when you return," he assured her with a faint smile.

Meghan gathered up her skirts and hurried from the room. Climbing the stairs to the upper floor, she paused in the hallway outside Linette's room for a moment, her heart twisting when her ears detected the pitiable sound of the other woman's sobs. Knocking on the door, she called out to her sister-in-law, but received no response. She eased the door open and peered inside, only to see that the petite redhead lay sprawled facedown across her bed, weeping as though she would never stop.

"Oh Linette!" said Meghan, her voice full of sympathy. Stepping into the room, she closed the door behind her and moved swiftly to the bed. She took a seat on the edge of the feather mattress and placed a comforting hand upon Linette's trembling shoulder. "What is it? What happened?" she probed gently.

"My . . . my life is . . . is at an end!" Linette choked out between sobs, her face buried in her arms.

"But why? What happened, Linette?" Meghan asked once more. "How did Devlin manage to find you and Charles so soon?"

"He found us because . . . because there was no
. . . no elopement!"

"No elopement? But your letter said—"

"I know, but things didn't . . . .didn't turn out
the way I had expected!" bemoaned Linette. She
finally managed to compose herself somewhat, and
she raised a lace-edged linen handkerchief to her
reddened eyes as she turned upon her side and
confessed to Meghan, "It was all my fault, truly!
I . . . I wrote the letter this morning, after I had
hit upon the idea of an elopement. I did not know
if I could carry it off or not, but as God is my
witness, Meghan, I never intended to . . . to cause
such trouble! I just wanted to be with Charles,
and he . . . he would not listen to reason!"

"Do you mean to say that Charles did *not* agree
to this ill-advised scheme of yours?"

"He did not," Linette admitted reluctantly, her
miserable, watery gaze falling beneath the inquisitive brightness of Meghan's. "I knew Charles
would be in attendance at the races today, you see,
and so I decided that it would be the perfect
opportunity for me to slip away with him. Once
you and Dev had set off about the grounds, I went
looking for Charles. He arrived late, and I was
able to intercept him before he had a chance to
talk to anyone else."

"But how on earth did you ever persuade him to
take you away alone with him in his carriage?"

"I . . . I lied and told him I had suddenly taken
ill, and that I could not find Dev but had left
work with Tallie Raymond that he, Charles, would

see that I got home safely. He was naturally hesitant at first, but I remained insistent and he finally gave in. If I had not been able to persuade him, I would simply have reclaimed the letter from Tallie and waited for another day."

"And when, if ever, did you inform Charles Deverill that he was eloping with you?" asked Meghan with a faint smile of irony. Scarcely able to believe what she was hearing, she shook her head in wonderment at Linette's bold deception.

"Not until we had traveled back to the city. I told him of the letter I had left for Dev, and he became furious. He did not even have the decency to let me explain!" Linette recalled, her eyes flashing in renewed indignation. "I tried to make him see that this was the perfect way for us to get around *his* mother and *my* brother, but he refused to listen! The worst of it is, Dev happened to pass us on our way here, and he blames Charles for everything!"

"Perhaps not for long," Meghan remarked consolingly. "They are closeted together in the library at this very moment."

"Yes, but you know how very unreasonable Dev can be when he is angry! Why, he might very well challenge poor Charles to a duel!" Her expressive blue eyes widened in horror at the thought, and she came bolt upright in the bed. "Dear God, I had best get down there right away!"

"No Linette, that is the one thing you should *not* do," advised Meghan firmly. "Neither one of them will thank you for your intervention, and you may very well risk wounding Charles's masculine

444

pride if you set yourself up as his defender!"

"But I cannot simply remain up here and do nothing while the two of them—"

"You have no choice but to do precisely that! Devlin is your legal guardian as well as your brother, and it is up to him to decide what is to be done. He will of a certainty be angry with you, but you know as well as I that he will forgive you, just as he will forgive Charles."

"Forgive Charles? For what, pray tell?" demanded Linette, rising to her beloved's defense.

"For not believing your love for him to be genuine in spite of your 'youth and inexperience,' " replied Meghan. Her eyes twinkled across at the other young woman, and she smiled softly before adding, "I have every confidence that if you love Charles as you say you do, and he loves you as well, then the two of you will be together. But you cannot force the issue, dearest sister. I am not all that well acquainted with my cousin Charles yet, but if he is anything at all like Devlin, I suspect he will not be pushed where he does not want to go!"

"Indeed," the redhead with an audible sigh, "I suppose they are alike in that respect." She frowned as Meghan suddenly stood and prepared to leave. "Where are you going?"

"You'll never believe what else has happened, Linette! My grandfather has just arrived from England, and he is awaiting my return in the drawing room downstairs!"

"Your grandfather? For heaven's sake, why did you not say so before now? Oh Meghan, how

445

selfish I have been, going all to pieces while you have such wonderful news to share! Give me but a few moments and I shall be down to meet him!"

She gave Meghan a quick hug, then bounced off the bed and hurried to set her appearance to rights. Meghan smiled at her friend's ability to recover so quickly from the brink of despair, and she breathed an inward sigh of relief as she left the room and returned downstairs.

True to his word, her grandfather was exactly where she had left him. He welcomed her back with a smile, his hand holding a half-empty glass of her husband's brandy. She rang for tea, then was pleasantly surprised when Jolene brought it in right away.

Though Sir Henry was too much of a gentleman to pry into the reason for his granddaughter's temporary absence, she felt compelled to offer some explanation. She was in the process of telling him that Linette had suffered a disappointment of the heart, when Devlin and Charles suddenly emerged from the library.

Excusing herself once more, Meghan stood and hurried out into the hallway. She saw that both Devlin and Charles wore solemn expressions, and her worriment increased as she viewed the unfathomable glow in her husband's eyes. Charles greeted her with a polite smile, while Devlin's hand closed about her arm and drew her to his side.

"I am sorry, my love," he apologized quietly, "that I did not seek you out before now. As you no doubt know, Charles and I had a matter of great importance to discuss."

"Have you spoken to Linette?" asked Charles in obvious concern. "Is she . . . is she well?"

"She is quite well, Charles," Meghan assured him. "She should be down any moment now." She turned back to Devlin, her face alight with pleasure. "There is someone in the drawing room who is desirous of meeting you, my dearest husband."

"Who is it?" he demanded with a mild frown.

"Someone whose name is all too familiar to you!" she replied evasively. She then told Charles, "And to you as well, I believe!"

Refusing to say anything further, she led them across the hallway and into the other room. Her grandfather stood near the window now, and he cast the two younger men a stern look while his gaze flickered briefly over each of them in turn.

"Devlin Montague and Charles Deverill," said Meghan, "I should like to present my grandfather, Sir Henry Claibourne."

"Your grandfather?" echoed Devlin, frowning down at her in surprise.

"Sir Henry?" seconded Charles.

"How do you do, Mister Montague?" asked Sir Henry, coming forward now to offer his hand to the newest member of his family. Devlin accepted the proffered hand and shook it firmly.

"It is an honor to meet you, Sir Henry," he responded sincerely. "My wife and I had not expected to see you for quite some time yet." He cast Meghan another questioning look, but she merely smiled, her eyes full of pride as she read the approval in her grandfather's.

"So I have been given to understand." The older

man smiled broadly and pronounced, "I shall allow my granddaughter to explain how I came to be here." He turned to Charles now, who shook his hand as well. "I understand we are kinsmen, Mister Deverill."

"Yes, Sir Henry, it seems we are," replied Charles, his own features relaxing into a disarming grin. "I discovered the connection when I was in London visiting my uncle recently."

"Meghan has told me how you acted in my stead to protect her reputation."

"Really, sir, it was nothing, for Dev would have done right by her even if—" he blurted out, only to break off in discomfort while a dull flush crept over his attractive young features.

"You need not worry, Mister Deverill, for I am already aware of the 'unusual' circumstances surrounding my granddaughter's marriage." He turned back to Devlin, who had the grace to look a trifle guilty.

"I have offered Meghan my deepest apologies for rejecting the truth of her plight," he offered with a fierce gleam in his eyes, then added stubbornly, "But I refuse to express remorse for the fact that I have made her my wife."

"Indeed, young Montague, I did not ask for any," Sir Henry countered with another faint smile. His own eyes twinkled across at Meghan, and she laughed softly before moving to resume her seat on the sofa. Her grandfather sat down beside her, while Charles chose the chair opposite them and Devlin sauntered over to pour himself a much-needed drink.

448

Before anyone could speak again, Linette appeared in the doorway. The smile froze on her face when she saw that Charles and Devlin were in the room as well, and her eyes grew round as saucers as they moved anxiously back and forth between them.

"Grandfather, this is my sister-in-law, Mistress Linette Montague," announced Meghan calmly. Sir Henry rose to his feet, while Linette swept forward and murmured a polite response to the introduction. The older man raised her hand gallantly to his lips.

"It is a pleasure, Mistress Montague. My granddaughter has told me how very fond she is of you."

"Meghan is very special to us all," Linette declared earnestly. She could not help smiling when she glimpsed the merry humor in his eyes, but she blushed uncomfortably when she turned her head and met Charles's gaze again. He, too, had stood when she came into the room, and he experienced a sharp pang of regret when he saw the faint, telltale redness that still rimmed her eyes.

"As luck would have it, Sir Henry," Devlin suddenly announced, "you have arrived just in time to celebrate my sister's betrothal to Mister Deverill."

"*What?*" gasped Linette, visibly thunderstruck by his words.

"Oh Devlin, do you mean—" Meghan started to question.

"Yes, my love," he cut her off with a tender smile. "I have given my consent for Charles and Linette to become engaged—a very *long* engage-

449

ment."

"My dearest, dearest brother!" exclaimed Linette, whirling about and flinging herself upon his chest. She hugged him tightly, her eyes alive with a mixture of gratitude and jubilation. "You have made me the happiest of all women on earth!"

"No, you little minx, that duty falls to your future husband," he dissented with a wry grin. "And do not think your crimes will go unpunished, for I shall of a certainty think of an appropriate penance." He brushed her cheek with his lips, then released her and bestowed a firm, brotherly smack upon her saucy backside. "*I* am not the one you should be favoring with these unladylike bursts of affection," he pointed out, his amused gaze moving significantly to Charles.

Linette needed no further encouragement. Oblivious to the fact that there were others in the room to witness her shocking behavior—including a titled English gentleman—she threw her arms about Charles's neck and pressed a kiss of delightfully innocent fervor upon his mouth. He was only too happy to reciprocate, until such time he deemed it advisable to put an end to the delectable torture. Setting his vivacious redhead away from him, he kept her possessively at his side while the two of them received congratulations from Sir Henry and a warm embrace from Meghan.

Much later, after Charles had finally taken his leave to go home and tell his mother of his betrothal, and after Meghan's grandfather had been made comfortable in the bedroom across the hall from Linette's, Devlin led his bride into the privacy of their own room. They were soon entwined together beneath the covers of the canopied four-poster, with Meghan's fingers spread lovingly across the bronzed, hard-muscled expanse of Devlin's chest and her luxuriant golden tresses cascading in glorious abandon about them both. She raised her head from where it had been resting upon his shoulder, and her lips curved into a soft smile when his arm tightened about her waist in silent protest of her stirring.

"You have not yet told me why you agreed to the betrothal," she determinedly reminded him in the candlelit darkness.

"Must we speak of this now?" he grumbled, his handsome brow creasing into a mock scowl of intimidating ferocity.

"Indeed, you maddening rogue, we must! I have related everything pertaining to my grandfather's arrival here, so it is now your turn to enlighten me about Charles and Linette!"

"Very well," he capitulated with an ill grace. "I can see I shall have no peace until I tell you whatever it is you wish to know!"

"You know very well what I wish to know!" she retorted, her voice full of wifely exasperation. "Why did you relent and allow them to become betrothed? After all, you have persistently maintained that Linette is too young to know her own mind, and you were so very angry over their intended elopement—"

"Angry? I damned near wrung both their necks when I first came upon them!" he recalled. "Once

451

I spoke to Charles, however, and once I realized that my dearest sister would be impossible to live with unless something was done, I decided a betrothal might be just the thing. You see, I will now have poor Charles's help in keeping her under control—not to mention his mother's!" He gave a low chuckle while his eyes filled with wry amusement. "The next year promises to be an interesting one."

"Then you do believe their love for one another to be constant?"

"I do," he admitted, though his deep tone brimmed with reluctance. "You tried to warn me, sweet vixen, but I would not listen."

"I only told you what I suspected to be true," she allowed generously. "It was simply that I knew myself to be so deeply in love, and I could well imagine how Linette must have felt. But at least Charles Deverill did not belong to another!" Her eyes flashed down at him in loving reproach.

"I never belonged to Rosalie," he denied, sending shivers up her spine when his warm fingers trailed lightly down to her naked hip.

"Do you truly expect me to believe, Devlin Montague, that I am the only woman you have ever—"

"You are the only woman I have ever loved," he cut her off with a significant, endearingly crooked smile.

A soft gasp escaped her lips as his hand closed with firm possessiveness upon the bare, shapely mound of her bottom. His other hand smoothed across her back to set up a slow, tantalizing caress on the side of her naked breast. Meghan's turquoise gaze sparkled with passion's sweet glow, and she could see that her beloved's midnight blue orbs smoldered with an answering flame.

" 'Tis a bold one you are, sir!" she remarked in a voice full of mingled laughter and desire, her Irish brogue quite pronounced.

"It takes a bold man to tame a wildcat like you," he murmured in a low, vibrant tone that sent a delicious tremor through her.

"And do . . . do you really consider me tamed?" Her eyes issued him a silent challenge, while her lips seemed to invite the warmly demanding pressure of his.

"Not yet." He pulled her masterfully atop him before adding in a husky whisper, "Nor do I expect to meet with success in this lifetime!"

Meghan was given no opportunity to reply, for he urged her head downward and claimed her mouth in a fiercely intoxicating kiss that soon rendered them both incapable of rational thought for quite some time to come.

Two days after Linette's impulsive, initially disastrous scheme had resulted in her ultimate success, she and Meghan returned to the dressmaker's for additional fittings. They were both excited at the prospect of the dinner party to be held at the townhouse the following night—a dinner party which would now also serve as a celebration for Linette's betrothal to Charles—and they had been extremely pleased to receive word that the new gowns they had ordered were nearing completion.

Sir Henry Claibourne, meanwhile, had announced his intention of remaining in Charlestown for the space of a week before sailing home to England, and Meghan was anxious that he should approve her performance as a hostess. Of course, it was Devlin's approval which mattered the most to her, though he had assured her teasingly that she could "damned well dress in rags and serve boiled boot leather" and still find herself completely adored by him. Although she had thanked him very nicely for the sentiment, she had then declared him a typical male who required domestic perfection but did not wish to be bothered by the many details which made it possible.

Meghan and Linette remained closeted with the dressmaker and her assistants for the better part of an hour. The gowns had, once again, surpassed even their fondest expectations, so that both young women emerged with their spirits high and their eyes alight with youthful vibrancy.

"I know we've so very much to see to at home, Meghan, but do you suppose we might spare the time to pay a visit to Charles's mother?" Linette asked unexpectedly, drawing on her gloves while she and Meghan waited outside the shop for the carriage to return and collect them.

"To Charles's mother?" Meghan echoed in surprise. "Why, I thought you had sworn to avoid the woman until tomorrow night!" Settling her bonnet upon her bright locks, she raised her face gratefully to the sun's warmth while tying the ribbons beneath her chin.

"I had." Linette frowned and released a highly expressive sigh. "But dash it all, I can't very well avoid her forever, can I? Charles let it be known that she expects me to call again right away, in spite of the fact that he took me to see her only yesterday morning."

"Well, you *are* going to be her daughter-in-law within a year's time."

"Must you remind me?" the redhead complained playfully. She sighed again, her gaze making a broad sweep of the surrounding area. There were few people to be seen about on the side street where she and Meghan stood. "I wonder what is keeping the carriage? I know I said we should be finished within the hour."

"I'm sure it will be along soon. At least we have been favored with pleasant weather while we wait." At a sudden thought, she smiled and suggested, "Perhaps we could stop by Devlin's office on our way home. I have not yet seen the place where he spends so much of his time, and I—" She broke as Linette suddenly grabbed her arm.

"Good heavens, Meghan, look there!" her sister-in-law bid in a breathless voice.

Meghan's eyes swiftly followed the direction of the other woman's wide, troubled gaze. She saw a coach careening wildly down the street toward them as the driver whipped the pair of horses pulling it into a frenzy.

"What on earth . . . the man must be out of his mind!"

"Whether he is or not, *I* do not intend to stand here and face the possibility of being run down!"

Linette proclaimed quite adamantly. She began tugging Meghan back toward the door of the shop. "Come, we must get inside!"

Meghan was not inclined to argue, for she suddenly felt her heart gripped by fear. She sensed that something other than the obvious was not quite right, and her uneasiness grew with each passing second. But she and Linette had just turned about to seek refuge in the shop when the driver jerked on the reins and brought the coach to an abrupt halt alongside them. Without warning, two men burst from the enclosed conveyance and swooped down upon the alarmed, totally defenseless young women.

A scream broke from Meghan's lips as one of the men caught her up in his arms. She fought him as best she could, but he was a veritable ox of a man. Before she knew what was happening, he had tossed her over his shoulder and borne her away to the coach. He thrust her roughly inside before following after her and clamping his hand across her mouth while his other arm held her like a vise about the waist and threatened to cut off her breath.

His partner, meanwhile, had seized Linette and kept her out of the way—no easy task, given the fact that she fought him like a tigress—until Meghan disappeared inside the coach. Then, apparently in obedience to the orders he had been given, he abruptly released her and darted away to resume his own position in the black vehicle. The driver cracked the whip, and the horses snorted loudly in protest before lunging forward and hauling the coach down the street in a flight even more perilously swift than before.

Linette staggered to her feet from where she had been flung down against the brick wall of the dressmaker's shop. She jerked her sadly crushed bonnet from in front of her eyes just in time to see the coach rounding the corner ahead.

"Dear God, *Meghan!*" she breathed in horrified disbelief.

Several people now hurried forth to offer the young redhead their belated assistance, but she numbly shook her head at them, her mind racing to think of what she should do. Finally, oblivious to the fact that a gentleman announced that he had summoned the watch, she gathered up her skirts and fled from her would-be comforters.

Linette went flying down the sidewalk toward the nearby waterfront, her only thought to get to Devlin and tell him what had happened. Praying that he would somehow be able to think of a way to save Meghan from whoever had taken her, she blinked back hot tears and fought down the panic rising within her.

Chapter Eighteen

A low moan of frustration welled up deep in Meghan's throat as she struggled in futile desperation against her bonds. She lay with her hands bound behind her back, her ankles shackled together with a rough length of knotted rope, and a dirty gag tied across her mouth.

Rolling over until she was perched on the edge of the hard bunk, where she had been flung a few minutes earlier, she threw her legs forward and attempted to stand. But she lost her balance and toppled to the bare wooden floor below, the breath knocked from her body and hot tears filling her eyes at the painful contact.

It took her a moment to reclaim her strength again, but she finally managed to climb to her knees. Her eyes aglow with a renewed burst of determination, she braced her elbows back against the bunk and eased herself slowly upright, until she stood beside the narrow bed at last. She looked toward the porthole, only to see that night had fallen.

Sweet Saint Bridget, where am I? she wondered, her eyes making a rapid sweep of the small, dark

cabin in which she was imprisoned. That she was
aboard a ship was readily apparent, but she had
no clue as to the location and identity of the
vessel.

The events of the past several nightmarish hours
flashed through her mind again. Following her abduction by the two men in the coach, she had been
rendered unconscious by a forceful blow to her
chin. She was uncertain as to how long it had been
before she awoke again; by the time she became
aware of masculine voices nearby, she had been
tied up and blindfolded. One of her captors had
carried her inside a building somewhere and locked
her inside an airless, musty-smelling room. Just
when she had feared she would faint again from
the lack of fresh air, she had been snatched forth
and taken aboard the ship where she was now a
captive below decks.

Desperately wishing her bonds had been removed
at the same time the blindfold had been jerked
free, Meghan sank back down upon the bunk. Her
chin throbbed painfully, while her wrists and ankles felt raw from the chafing of the ropes. The
worst of all, however, was the gag, for its foul-
tasting bulk made it difficult for her to swallow
and caused her throat to burn from lack of moisture.

Suddenly, the door was unlocked and flung
open. Meghan jerked her head about and staggered
hastily to her feet again, her eyes wide with alarm.
The man whose immense frame filled the doorway
was the same black-bearded villain who had seized
her earlier. He held a lamp in one hand, and he

raised it higher in order to get a better look at his beautiful young captive.

Meghan felt the color drain from her face while her heart pounded in very real terror. She trembled in spite of her resolve to be brave, and her mind reeled dizzily as panic threatened to overwhelm her.

"Rest easy," the man growled, his coarse, ugly features twisting into a malevolent grin as he advanced upon her. "I've come only to loose your bonds." He lifted the lamp to a shelf above the bunk, his gaze raking over Meghan in bold, lustful appreciation of her womanly charms.

She instinctively recoiled when his hands reached for her, but he merely laughed and spun her roughly about. He cut the ropes at her wrists and ankles with his knife, then unfastened the gag about her mouth. She drew in a deep, ragged breath and whirled to face him again.

"Who are you?" she demanded hoarsely. "Why have I been brought here?" Her proudly defiant manner belied the wild dishevelment of her appearance and the utter helplessness of her position. She brought a hand up to impatiently sweep the tangled, streaming golden curls from her face while she glared up at the dark giant looming over her. "Answer me, damn you!"

" 'Tis easy to see why you've been chosen," he remarked with a rasping chuckle. "He likes his women with spirit! I'll wager you'll last a goodly while."

"What are you talking about? Dear God, did someone pay you to—"

"You'll be brought food and drink thrice a day.

but you'll not be allowed up on deck. And if you give us any trouble, you'll be bound again." He laughed banefully again before adding, "We've orders to see you're made comfortable for the voyage, Madam Montague. No one will touch you—of that you may be sure!"

"Voyage? But where . . . where are we going?" she faltered weakly.

"Never you mind." He turned about as if to leave, but Meghan clutched at his arm in desperation.

"Will you not at least tell me who has issued these orders of which you speak?" she pleaded, her show of bravado tumbling in the face of her mingled dread and confusion. "Whoever it is, you—you must not listen! No matter what you have been promised in the way of payment, it cannot be enough for you to risk imprisonment! My husband will not rest until I am found, and he will see to it that all those responsible—"

"Your husband will do nothing," he declared scornfully. His ugly face split into another wide grin that revealed a set of yellowed, rotting teeth. "He'll not know where to search for you. We're weighing anchor now, and we'll be well away before morning. There's no need to worry just yet—you'll not be meeting your new 'bridegroom' until we reach our destination. So rest easy," he reiterated, turning his back on her. His boots clumped noisily on the floor as he moved to the door again. "You'll find everything you need here in the cabin. The Wolf never fails to provide generously for his women." With that, he was gone, closing the door

461

and locking it behind him.

"The Wolf!" gasped Meghan, her legs giving way beneath her so that she was forced to grasp at the bunk for support. She sank down heavily upon the hard mattress and raised an unsteady hand to her throat.

No! her mind screamed in horrified disbelief. *Please God, not again!* It could not be possible that The Wolf held her in his clutches once more, she thought dazedly, it could not!

Your new bridegroom, the bearded giant had said. His mercilessly taunting words echoed throughout the turbulence of her mind. She realized now that he had been speaking of The Wolf. Indeed, she reflected as the awful truth dawned on her, the man who had arranged her abduction was none other than the same cunning pirate who had held her prisoner before. He had paid the men to seize her and bring her aboard the ship, a mysterious ship bound for an equally mysterious destination where he planned to join her.

But why? she asked herself, her eyes clouding with anguished bewilderment. She had not revealed the truth of his identity to anyone, nor had she given any indication that she intended to do so. Why had he suddenly decided to take her captive again? From what she had been able to tell, Rosalie Hammond was the recipient of his evil affections at the present. Why then was he going to so much trouble to possess a woman who was married to another, a woman who would be able to expose him for the fiend he was?

The frantic questions ran together in her mind,

462

causing her head to ache terribly while a wave of nausea shook her. None of it made any sense to her, she mused through a haze of pain and trepidation, but neither did it matter. Whatever The Wolf's motives for his contemptible scheme, she was his prisoner once again. Fate had tricked her by giving her all the love and happiness she could ever want, and then cruelly snatching them away. . . .

"Oh Devlin, Devlin!" she whispered brokenly.

Meghan buried her face in her hands and prayed with all her heart and soul that her beloved would somehow manage to find her before it was too late. She could not bear the thought that she would never gaze upon his face again, that she would never again know the feel of his arms about her or the sound of his voice in his ears. It took every ounce of self-will she possessed to keep from surrendering to the hopeless despair which threatened to overtake her.

But she could not hold back the tears. Crumpling upon the narrow bed, she felt herself beseiged by the effects of her ordeal. She wept as though her very heart were breaking, and she did not stop until she lay physically and emotionally drained in the lamplit darkness of the ship's cabin.

Night gave way to morning as the sun rose slowly above the horizon and awakened Charlestown with its benevolent radiance. For Devlin Montague, however, the coming of the dawn meant only that precious hours had gone by without

463

yielding up any trace of Meghan.

Meghan. He would never have believed it possible to love anyone as much as he loved her . . . her face haunted his every thought, while the memory of her voice burned throughout his brain. His soul cried out to God in raw, bitter torment. Offering up yet another silent prayer for her return, he pleaded for guidance in knowing what course of action to take next.

He had been like a man possessed ever since he had received Linette's terrifying report of how Meghan had been taken. Wasting no time, he had immediately begun a search for her. He had turned both his savage fury at her abduction and his heart-stopping alarm for her welfare into action, investigating every possible lead and threatening to tear the entire city apart if need be.

The authorities were doing what little they could. However, with such a crippling lack of evidence, and literally millions of acres of rivers and swamps and densely forested countryside to explore, their efforts were doomed to proceed at an excruciatingly slow pace. Though no one had dared to voice the analogy in Devlin's presence, it began to look as though his bride had simply vanished into thin air. Other than a much-shaken Linette, there were no witnesses to identify the two assailants or the coach they had used to carry out their treachery, nor was there anyone who could offer an opinion as to which direction the coach had gone after disappearing from Linette's view.

Devlin had thus far concentrated his own efforts—and those of his crew—along the waterfront, for he had correctly surmised that Meghan's kidnappers would be more likely to try to spirit her away from the city by sea. But there was such a vast area to cover and an endless number of people to question, not to mention the fact that nearly a hundred ships passed through Charlestown's harbor every week. Neither he nor his men gave a thought to their own increasing exhaustion as they set about combing the warehouses and other buildings on the wharves. They did not pause to sleep; and so it was that the darkness of the long night surrendered to the light of a new day. . . .

It was not until midafternoon that Devlin finally returned to the townhouse. He was hoping that perhaps Meghan's grandfather had heard something, though he had given strict orders to have any messages brought to the shipping office without delay. Since no messages had been waiting for him when he had stopped by there a short time earlier, he had decided to return to the house. He knew how worried Linette and Sir Henry must be, and he also knew that his body needed nourishment in order for him to continue his search for Meghan.

Linette met him at the door. Her bright eyes held an unspoken question as she peered up into the dully glowing intensity of his gaze, and she felt her hopes plummet as he shook his head wordlessly in response. Flinging her arms about his neck, she tried valiantly not to cry.

"Sir Henry has gone out to see what else may be done," she stated in a small voice as he briefly returned her embrace. Upon being released, she hooked her arm through his and cast him a worried frown as the two of them moved into the drawing room. "Oh Dev, you look dreadful! Why don't you try and get a few hours' sleep before—"

"Has there been any news?" he demanded grimly, though he already knew the answer.

"No, I—I'm afraid not." She left his side and hurried to ring for food and drink to be brought in, then turned back to him with a weak smile. Her own eyes were swollen and red-rimmed, and her usually glowing features were quite pale. "Charles has notified all of our friends, of course, and they have promised to do everything in their prower to help. Surely, Dev, with so many people searching for her, Meghan will be found!" she sought to reassure him.

"I can only hope you're right," he murmured, his manner one of restive preoccupation. He bent his tall frame into the wing chair near the fireplace and raked a hand through his thick, dark brown hair. "Damn it all to hell, if we only had a clue, one blasted clue—" he ground out, only to break off and mutter a blistering curse. Rising abruptly from the chair, he strode across to the window and turned his fierce blue gaze outward, as though by simply willing it he could make something turn up.

Devlin spun away from the window and moved back to the fireplace, bracing a hand against the mantel while his eyes fastened unseeingly upon the ornate brass andirons below. He was scarcely aware of Jolene bringing in a tray of tea and sandwiches, and it was only with extreme reluctance that he heeded Linette's pleas for him to have something to

466

eat.

The bell at the front door rang just as he was lifting one of the sandwiches to his mouth. He tossed it back down to the plate and moved hurriedly to answer the door, jerking it open in the hopes that the visitor would be someone with word of Meghan. His mouth compressed into a tight, thin line of acute disappointment and anger when he saw that it was Rosalie Hammond who stood there.

"Devlin, I must speak to you at once!" she insisted, looking uncharacteristically distraught.

"In the event you have not heard, Mistress Hammond, my wife has been abducted!" he informed her tersely, his eyes full of a harsh light. "Damn it, I've no time for your—"

"This is about Meghan!" She brushed past him and into the house.

Devlin closed the door and followed swiftly after her. Determined to hear her out for no other reason than Meghan's name had crossed her lips, he battled the urge to throw her out. He strode back into the drawing room, eyeing his former fiancée mistrustfully while Linette bristled at her presence in their house.

"What are *you* doing here?" she demanded. She balled her hands into fists at her sides and fought down her own violent impulses.

"I have come to speak with Devlin!" answered Rosalie, raising her head in angry defiance. "Leave us alone at once, for what I have to say is for his ears alone!"

"Leave you—" Linette started to echo in wrathful indignation, only to be effectively cut off by her brother's low, commanding voice.

"Please Linette, do as she says." His face was forbiddingly solemn, while the look in his eyes gave unmistakable evidence of the dangerous state of his temper.

Linette's gaze filled with furious resentment as it darted back and forth between Devlin and Rosalie, but she bit back the scathing retort which rose to her lips and swept from the room. The door which led into the garden could be heard opening and closing as she took refuge outside.

"You have something to say regarding my wife's disappearance?" Devlin prompted impatiently.

"I do," confirmed Rosalie. She glided forward to take a seat on the sofa, quickly arranging her peach-colored muslin skirts about her before raising her eyes to Devlin's once more. That she was greatly troubled about something was obvious to him, for he knew she would never have dared come to his house otherwise. "First of all, I want your word that you will not seek revenge against me!" she unexpectedly proclaimed.

"Revenge? What the devil have you done, Rosalie?" he demanded, stalking forward to seize her arms in a bruising grip. He yanked her up from the sofa, his eyes blazing savagely down into the wide, frightened gray depths of hers. "You know something about Meghan's abduction, don't you? What is it, damn you? *What is it?*" His fingers clenched about the soft flesh of her arms until she cried out sharply at the pain.

"Let go of me!" she gasped out, her eyes flooding with tears. "I—I will tell you everything I know!"

Devlin released her as though the contact burned him. She sat heavily back down upon the chair, withdrawing a fine lawn handkerchief from the pocket of her skirt and raising it to her eyes. Composing herself as best she could, she swallowed hard and looked apprehensively up at the man who towered menacingly above her. Devlin Montague had become a stranger to her, and she sensed that he would not hesitate to carry out the silent threat contained in his smoldering blue gaze.

"Where is Meghan?" he demanded harshly.

"I . . . I can only tell you where I believe her to be." She trembled beneath the thunderous expression crossing his handsome face, and her profound alarm caused her to blurt out, "Barrett Wolfe has taken her!"

"Barrett Wolfe?" His hands closed relentlessly about her arms again, hauling her back up before him. "What reason do you have to accuse him?"

"He sailed for Barbados this morning!"

"That proves nothing!"

"You do not understand! He is not what you think, Devlin! You see, he—he is not truly a stranger to me, nor to your wife!"

"What the bloody hell are you talking about?"

"Meghan and I were both acquainted with him! He is The Wolf, Devlin!" she finally revealed, the tears streaming down her hotly flushed cheeks. "He is the same pirate who attacked the *Bristol Packet* and took us captive!"

"If that is true," Devlin replied in a voice of

deadly calm, "then why didn't Meghan tell me? Why would she conceal such information from me?"

"Because he threatened her! Because he threatened us both! He warned Meghan that he would have you killed, while he vowed to tell everyone of my . . . my indiscretion with him if I dared to expose him!"

"How do you know he has taken Meghan? Damn you, Rosalie, do you expect me to believe he told you of his plans and then left you behind to put me on his trail?"

"He did not speak to me of his intentions!" she denied, shaking her head emphatically. "But he was always talking about Meghan, always taunting me with his desire for her! It was almost as if he had become obsessed with her, Devlin, and I am certain he is the one responsible for her disappearance! I would not have suspected it myself, if not for the fact that he left Charlestown so unexpectedly. When I heard he had sailed homeward, without bothering to say good-bye and within hours of Meghan's abduction, I could not help but think he was behind it all!"

"You say he spoke of his desire for Meghan?" he ground out. A murderous rage gripped him at the thought of her in The Wolf's clutches, but he knew he must keep a cool head about him if he hoped to get her back.

"Yes, damn him!" seethed Rosalie, her own eyes glittering with renewed outrage. "Even when he and I were . . . were together, he praised her beauty and her spirit. He seemed to gain some perverse pleasure from wounding me thus, and yet he promised to take me with him when he returned to Barbados. Barrett Wolfe promised that I would be his wife!'"

Her hands came up to clutch at the front of Devlin's shirt, while her aristocratic features grew contorted with vengeful fury. Her eyes, wild and full of desperate entreaty, met the narrowed blaze of his.

"That is why I have come," she explained, "why I have told you all I know! I know he has taken her, I know it! Oh, I've no doubt he took pains to ensure he would not be connected with her disappearance, but I *know* he has her! He has betrayed me, Devlin! He has betrayed me and must be made to pay!'"

Having heard more than enough to convince him of Barrett Wolfe's guilt, Devlin sprang into action at last. He thrust Rosalie away from him with a savage oath and stalked from the room, his long, furiously purposeful strides leading him out into the garden where Linette waited.

Rosalie Hammond, meanwhile, staggered back against the chair. She sank numbly down into it again while her gray, tear-filled gaze remained fastened on the doorway through which Devlin had just disappeared. Cursing him as well as her pirate lover, it never occurred to her that she herself was to blame for the misfortune which had befallen her. Devlin Montague had stolen her pride, but Barrett Wolfe had stolen much, much more. . . .

471

The next several days passed in a blur of terrible anticipation and heartache for Meghan. She alternated between determined hope and ever-encroaching despair, though she did her best to hold fast to the belief that Devlin would somehow find her.

He filled her every waking thought. His beloved image entered her dreams at night when she fell asleep from sheer emotional exhaustion. Because of him, she was able to be strong. Whenever she began to panic at the thought of what was waiting for her at the end of the voyage, she managed to reclaim her flagging courage by recalling how Devlin had single-handedly rescued her from The Wolf's fortress on Andros. He had achieved the impossible then, she would staunchly remind herself, and there was every reason to believe he would do so again.

But it was becoming increasingly difficult for her to keep the faith. Just as her bearded captor had warned, she was never once allowed to leave the cabin. Her only source of fresh air was the porthole, which she kept open whenever the weather permitted. She attempted to while away the long hours by reading the tattered old Bible she had found at the bottom of the sea chest, and by making use of the needle and thread she had found beside it to repair the considerable damage done to her gown during her struggles. There was also a copy of Chaucer's bawdy *Canterbury Tales* for her pleasure.

A good deal of her time, however, was spent gazing out at the rolling swell of the sea. She felt a strange surge of hope whenever she caught a glimpse of some unknown island in the distance, and her own spirits soared, at least for a few brief moments, whenever she sighted birds diving for their food in the dazzling, aquamarine depths surrounding those nearby shores.

Devlin. Her heart cried out to his again and again. She wondered where he was, what he was doing . . . if he had any idea what had happened to her. She could not allow herself to think about the fact that he had no reason to suspect Barrett Wolfe of anything; nor could she permit the memory of The Wolf's cruel embrace to enter her mind. Day after day, she struggled to keep her mind occupied and her youthful vitality intact.

Finally, after nearly a week, the sound of a man's voice raised in a shout drifted down to Meghan in the early hours of the dawn. She was certain she had heard him proclaiming their anchorage to be in sight off the port bow. Flinging back the covers, she slipped fully clothed from the narrow bunk and hurried across to the porthole, her pulses leaping in mingled excitement and dread as she peered outward. She was disappointed to find she could see nothing but a vast expanse of water sparkling beneath the rising sun, and she muttered an oath of frustration as she spun away from the salt-streaked glass.

A few minutes later, her bearded captor unlocked the door and ducked inside. He gave a chortle of derisive humor at the sight of her, for she was standing near the porthole in defensive readiness, the light of battle in her blazing turquoise eyes while she courageously brandished a broken chair

473

leg in her hands.

"Put away your weapon, Madam Montague, else you'll find yourself going ashore like a trussed-up turkey," he warned.

Although Meghan would have liked nothing better than to knock him senseless and make a run for it, she knew such tactics would prove futile, since she was aboard a ship with God only knew how many other men to prevent her desperate flight to freedom. She relinquished the chair leg with visible reluctance, lifted her head proudly, and preceded the foul-smelling giant from the cabin.

Soon, the ship had dropped anchor and a boat was lowered to take the beautiful prisoner and a handful of the men to shore. Meghan was grateful to breathe the air and feel the sun's warmth on her face again, and her eyes moved curiously over the nearing landscape as the boat was rowed toward a sandy, waveswept coral beach.

The coast, tranquil and protected in the lee of the northeast trade winds, was lined with towering palm trees and lush patches of tropical greenery. From what Meghan could see, the topography appeared to be rather flat, though there were gently rolling hills and dales rising just beyond the shore. She remembered what the coastlines of the Bahamian islands of Andros and New Providence had looked like, and she surmised that the mass of land before her, while undeniably similar in climate, did not belong to quite the same geographical area.

" 'Tis Barbados," her black-bearded escort supplied in a gruff tone, answering the unspoken question in her mind.

"Barbados?" she echoed breathlessly. Of course, she then mused, her gaze filling with renewed fire, Barbados was where The Wolf played out his role of gentleman planter.

She knew that Barbados, with its charming seaside villages and English country churches, was the most easterly of the long chain of Caribbean islands. The small, pear-shaped island had been colonized by British settlers nearly a hundred and fifty years ago, and had become known for its tobacco, cotton, and sugar cane plantations. The sugar was used in the manufacture of rum, a highly prosperous local industry. Meghan recalled something she had once heard regarding the colony's large slave populations—unlike other islands to the north, there had as yet been no bloody slave uprisings on Barbados. It seemed the slaves there were treated relatively well in comparison to others.

She would be the The Wolf's slave now. She wondered if anyone on the island knew that Barrett Wolfe was also a notorious, bloodthirsty pirate who terrorized the seas and preyed on helpless women. How was it he had been able to guard the secret of his dual life for so long?

The question still burned in her mind as she was lifted from the boat and set on her feet. Her legs felt perilously unsteady, for it was the first time in many days that she had stood on solid ground. Although she was not bound, her burly captor maintained a firm grip upon her arm while he set off with her across the beach. He urged her impatiently along a well-worn path through the trees to an open field a short distance away. Once there, she was virtually hauled up a steep incline, then through a dense forest of casuarina and calabash trees, before finally emerging into yet another spacious clearing.

Meghan pulled to a sudden halt, her ungallant "escort" scowling down at her but nonetheless allowing her a brief moment's scrutiny of her new home. Her eyes widened in astonishment at what they beheld, for she had not expected to find anything so grand.

The house before her was a large, two-storied white structure built in the typical Barbadian plantation style—an intriguing mixture of Caribbean and British architecture—with covered verandas on three sides and half a dozen supporting pillars in front. Surrounded by a profusion of flowering shrubberies and tall, gently swaying trees, the main house stood in the very center of the compound and stood guard over a number of outbuildings.

Looking farther, she glimpsed vast fields of sugar cane growing beneath the sun's perennial radiance. She took note of the black slaves toiling in the fields, before her gaze was drawn back to the immediate yard. Since she was already well aware of the fact that white bondservants were much in demand on Barbados—indeed, she recalled having heard several discussions of the matter while aboard the *Bristol Packet*—she was not surprised to see more than a dozen young, mostly fair-haired men and women going silently about their morning chores. None of them appeared to pay her any

476

mind, and she could not help but wonder if the arrival of a new "slave" was perhaps an all too frequent occurrence.

"Come," growled the man at her side. "It's time we were inside." He moved to seize her arm again, but she jerked it free. Though his dark, coarse features tightened in anger, he did not stop her as she gathered up her skirts and began walking proudly toward the house. His long strides enabled him to overtake her, however, so that he was the first to reach the front steps.

A stout, silver-haired woman dressed completely in black met them at the door. She spared only a passing glance for Meghan. Her face wore a strangely impassive expression, and she spoke thickly accented English as she exchanged a few words with the man.

"Please, you must help me!" implored Meghan, disregarding the minatory glare sent her way by her bearded captor. "I have been brought here against my will, and—"

She was silenced by the brutal pressure of the man's hand upon her mouth. Helpless against his superior strength, she could do nothing more than squirm in his forceful grasp and scream in protest against the almost suffocating pressure of his fingers. He easily bore her up a winding staircase to the second floor of the elegantly furnished house, where he carried her inside a room and tossed her unceremoniously upon a bed. She scrambled up to her knees on the mattress just as he went lumbering back out to the corridor, slamming the door behind him and turning the key in the lock.

Meghan's eyes made a rapid sweep of the dimly lit room in which she was imprisoned. Like the rest of The Wolf's house, it was tastefully decorated, its furniture of carved mahogany and its walls covered with expensive paper of a stenciled design. There were lace curtains at the window, and the canopy of the bed was also of delicate, snowy white lace.

Her gaze lighting upon the window, she slid from the bed and hurried across the room in an effort to peer outward. Her vision was obstructed by a louvered wooden shutter on the outside, however, through which only a minimal amount of air and sunlight could make their way into the room. She attempted to pry the slats farther apart, but succeeded only in pricking the skin of her fingers on the splintered wood.

"There must be a way to escape—*there must!*" she murmured aloud, striving to hold back the panic which threatened to defeat her. She spun away from the window and ran to the door. Pressing her ear against it, she listened for any sound of human voices, not at all certain what she meant to do if she heard them.

It was not a voice she heard a moment later, but rather the sound of the key being turned in the lock again. A sharp gasp escaped her lips while her eyes widened in alarm, for she realized that it might very well be the The Wolf who was about to enter the room. She backed away in benumbed terror, her eyes darting frantically about in an effort to find something with which to defend herself. Her hand had just closed about the lamp

478

beside the bed, when the door flew open to reveal not The Wolf, but a woman.

"So, you have come!" she spat at Meghan, her brown eyes shooting venomous sparks. She was a very pretty young woman, with fine Spanish features, long ebony hair cascading down about her face and shoulders, and skin of a creamy, deep golden hue. Clad in a frilly, lace-trimmed negligee of pale blue satin, she had apparently just tumbled from her bed.

"I will mark that face of yours!" she suddenly proclaimed, her voice rising on a shrill note. "Your beauty will tempt him no more!"

With that, she launched herself at Meghan. Her fingers curled into talons as her dark eyes narrowed into mere slits of vindictive fury.

Meghan, her own gaze full of stunned disbelief at what was happening, acted on impulse to defend herself. The lamp fell to the floor with a crash as she brought her hands up to ward off the unwarranted attack. She succeeded in grabbing the woman's wrists before those long, sharp nails could inflict any damage, but it took all her strength to hold the rancorous shrew at bay. The two of them struggled with one another in the center of the room, blazing turquoise eyes locked with brown in a combat of wills.

"You will not take him from me!" the woman hissed, her black hair streaming wildly across her face.

"If you are speaking of The Wolf, I do not *want* him!" gasped out Meghan. A soft, breathless cry of alarm broke from her lips when her unidentified adversary gave her a mighty shove backward. The two of them went toppling down to the floor together in a furious tumble of skirts and petticoats and shapely limbs.

Meghan immediately rolled so that she was atop her fiercely battling opponent, but she found herself temporarily outmaneuvered when the woman's hand shot up to entangle within her thick golden tresses. Hot tears stung her eyes and she drew in a ragged breath of pain as the woman yanked brutally on her hair. Never one to surrender without a fight, however, she reciprocated by grabbing hold of the mysterious assailant's ebony locks and jerking her head to one side.

While the other woman screamed in mingled pain and outrage, Meghan pulled free and staggered to her feet. She stood beside the bed, her breasts rising and falling rapidly beneath her square-necked bodice, and her own hair a tangled mass of burnished gold about her face and shoulders. Eyeing The Wolf's jealous paramour—for that was what she had by this time judged the woman to be—with a mixture of analysis and vengeful ire, she declared hotly, "If you're after making me pay for what you foolishly believe to my enticement of your lover, then you'd best think again! Fly at me once more, mistress," she warned in a low voice edged with intent, "and I shall not hesitate to render you completely bald!"

Fortunately, the woman was never given the opportunity to test the validity of Meghan's threat. The noise of their confrontation had not gone unnoticed. In the next instant, the black-bearded giant materialized in the doorway. He muttered a foul curse before storming into the room to lay hands on the dark-eyed beauty.

"Let go of me, you filthy whoreson!" the young spitfire commanded at the top of her lungs. "Let me go, damn you!" She fought him tooth and nail, but he merely dragged her forcibly from the room and closed the door after them. The lock was set in place again, and the sound of the woman's shrill, screeching voice could be heard echoing throughout the house as she was borne away to the quarters she shared with her master down the hall.

Meghan released a long, pent-up sigh and sank wearily down upon the bed. Her head spun dizzily as she pondered all that had just taken place. She recalled how she had once wondered if perhaps The Wolf was married—while she did not believe the Spanish wildcat to be his wife, it was obvious that the woman had some claim upon his affections.

Good heavens, she mused at a sudden, horrible thought, *did the blackguard plan to establish a harem on Barbados as well?* She shuddered in revulsion, her skin crawling at the possibility.

But she was given little time to indulge in such turbulent reverie, for within minutes, the silver-haired housekeeper unlocked the door and came marching silently inside. She had brought up a tray of food and drink, as well as a pitcher of water for bathing. Setting the things down atop the carved mahogany chest of drawers in the corner, she turned back toward the door to leave.

Meghan leapt to her feet in desperation and

481

hurried forth to try reasoning with the older woman again. She blocked the housekeeper's path, her countenance full of entreaty and her eyes glistening with tears of helpless frustration.

"Please, in the name of mercy, will you not help me? I am Meghan Montague, and my husband is Devlin Montague of Charlestown! The Wolf arranged to have me abducted and—"

"The Wolf? I know of no such person," the woman denied coldly. She started to brush past, only to find herself detained once more when Meghan's hand closed insistently upon her arm.

"I am speaking of Barrett Wolfe! This is his plantation, is it not?"

"It is. But I know nothing," the housekeeper reiterated with a sharp frown. Pulling her arm free, she moved back out into the corridor, the skirts of her black silk gown rustling quietly as she went.

Locked in again, Meghan stared despondently at the door. Devlin's face swam before her eyes, and she dropped to her knees on the floor as she buried her face in her hands.

In the midst of her darkest hour yet, she could have sworn she heard the sound of her beloved's deep voice, calling her name . . . telling her that she would soon be with him again.

Chapter Nineteen

The day wore on. Barrett Wolfe's impending arrival was on the mind of nearly everyone at the plantation—particularly Meghan's.

Having long since bathed and forced herself to eat something, she paced restlessly about the room as the late afternoon sun blazed down upon the lush tropical landscape outside. Her nerves felt raw and strained to the limit from the many hours of waiting, and she began to suspect that it might very well be days before her dreaded encounter with The Wolf finally took place.

Unfortunately, her suspicions proved incorrect. She whirled about at the sound of the door being unlocked, expecting to see either the housekeeper or the dark-eyed virago who had attacked her earlier. But it was a man who sauntered inside the room and closed the door behind him . . . a man whose familiar, sinister features struck fear in

Meghan's heart.

"You!" she breathed in startled dismay, her eyes growing very round and her face turning ashen.

"At your service, Madam Montague," Barrett Wolfe retorted sardonically, his lips curling into a sneer. "My apologies for not calling upon you sooner. I arrived last night, you see, but I found it necessary to spend the better part of the day in Bridgetown." As it had been in Charlestown, his attire was that of a well-to-do gentleman's. But Meghan knew his heart was that of a vile, unscrupulous brigand's who would stop at nothing to get what he wanted.

"Last night?" she echoed dazedly. Her mind raced to think of a way to save herself. *Dear God, help me!*

"My own ship is a good deal faster than our black-bearded friend's," he observed in a voice brimming with malevolent humor. "I must admit to considerable impatience where you are concerned, my sweet. We have both waited too long as it is. The moment has come for you to have a taste of what your new life will be like."

He began slowly advancing upon her, his dark, hawkish gaze full of lustful intent. Meghan fought down a renewed surge of panic and backed instinctively away from him.

"Why—why have you done this?" she demanded with as much bravado as she could muster. "Why did you have me brought here?" When he did not answer, she swallowed hard and raised her head in a gesture of proud defiance. "My husband will kill you if you touch me!" She inhaled sharply as her hips came up against the bed.

"From this day forward, you have no husband."
He gave a soft laugh of triumph as he reached for
her.

"Wha—what are you saying?"

"Only that *I* will now be your lord and master.
The first time I set eyes on you, I decided that I
must have you. My plans were thwarted then, but
there is no one to save you here. Scream and
complain all you like, but bear in mind what I
told you once before—you will be made to pay for
your resistance!"

"*No!*" Meghan cried hoarsely. Vowing never to
surrender, she made a desperate attempt to prevent
the inevitability of his embrace. Her hands flew up
to strike out at him, but he seized her wrists in a
brutal grip and forced them ruthlessly behind her
back. She gasped as he yanked her against him,
her breasts making repulsively intimate contact
with the lean hardness of his chest.

"You are mine at last, you fiery-eyed little
bitch!"

"I will never be yours!" she denied hotly, struggling in vain against him.

"Ah, but you will! You escaped me once, but
never again! It may interest you to know that I
have been planning this 'reunion' ever since I returned to Andros and learned you were gone!" he
snarled, his voice charged with mingled fury and
desire. He jerked her arms farther upward so that
she cried out sharply at the pain, while his eyes
seared down into the wide, blazing turquoise
depths of hers. "Resign yourself to your fate, my

sweet! You will never see Devlin Montague again! You are mine now and will remain so until I tire of you!"

"No! By all that is holy, you shall have no pleasure of me, *Mister Wolfe!* I swear I will kill you myself if you dare to . . . to force your repulsive affections on me!"

"Will you?" he taunted. She gasped as he suddenly ground his lower body into hers and spoke in a low, derisive tone, "If there were not other matters requiring my attention, I would exact a penance for that foolish threat here and now! As it is, I am entertaining guests tonight—very distinguished members of our quaint island society," he added with a contemptuously mocking smile. "Therefore, much to my own regret, I am afraid I've time for nothing more than a brief 'demonstration' of what is to come once those guests have departed!"

"What about your paramour?" charged Meghan, frantically employing another tactic. "You can have no need of me, not when you already have a woman who is obviously more than willing to—"

"She is no concern of yours!" he bit out. His eyes kindled with a dangerously feral light. "Besides, if you prove as amusing to me as I anticipate, I might very well banish Consuela and install you in her place. Think of it, my sweet—you could be mistress of this household! I am a rich man, a highly respectable planter here on Barbodos. The elite class includes *me* among its ranks!" he informed her with a derisive chuckle. "You could have everything your heart desires. I will teach you a hundred different ways to please me, but first you must be taught to obey!'"

"Never!" Meghan defied vehemently.

A scream rose in her throat as she read the intent in his dark eyes, but she was silenced by the cruelly demanding pressure of his mouth upon hers. She shuddered as a powerful wave of nausea washed over her, and hot, bitter tears of rage stung against her eyelids while she squirmed helplessly within The Wolf's brutal, possessive grasp.

He kissed her with such punishing force that she tasted blood, and she writhed violently against him when his hot tongue suddenly stabbed between her lips. Overcome by a combination of revulsion and fear, she felt herself growing faint, her senses reeling beneath the merciless onslaught of his embrace while very fiber of her being cried out to God to make the torment stop.

Finally, Barrett Wolfe's mouth ceased its forboding ravishment of hers, and he flung her roughly to the floor, where she landed so hard that the breath was knocked from her body. Then, with cold, studied equanimity, her sinister captor straightened his immaculate white neckcloth and sauntered back to the door. He paused before leaving, casting Meghan a disdainful glance while his lips curled into another sneer.

"You will not be so proud when I have finished with you," he vowed smoothly. "No indeed, *Madam Montague*, you will soon learn that I am not a man to be crossed." Opening the door, he delivered his parting shot in a voice laced with sadistic amusement. "I bid you farewell—until tonight!"

Darkness fell, the moon chasing the sun from the sky while the hot winds of the day gave way to a cool evening breeze. The deceptively calm tropical night held a good deal more in store than anyone had reason to suspect. . . .

As always, Barrett Wolfe played his role of host to perfection. The six guests, all of them gentlemen who had been invited for a few pleasant hours of male fellowship—namely, drink and cards—assembled at the plantation shortly after eight o'clock. They had been acquainted with their host for a number of years, their wives having found him a delightful dinner guest, while their daughters still considered him a prime catch. These particular men represented the most prestigious group of settlers on the island, since they held not only wealth, but also good connections back in England.

There was, however, an unexpected visitor among their ranks that evening. He was not a resident of Barbados as they were, but rather an English gentleman only recently arrived. It seemed that he had called upon a longtime acquaintance of his immediately upon docking in Bridgetown earlier that same day, and had expressed a singular interest in meeting Barrett Wolfe—though he was very evasive as to the reason why. He would say only that he had a matter of business to discuss with Wolfe.

His friend, a financier by the name of Gerald

Ralston, had generously offered to take him along to Wolfe's plantation so that he might achieve his goal that very night. Ralston's invitation had been accepted, though the English gentleman had insisted upon supplying the transportation.

And so it was that Gerald Ralston climbed the front steps of Wolfe's house in the wake of the other guests and presented his tall, bewigged companion to a coolly smiling, impeccably attired Barrett Wolfe.

"I say, Barrett, I knew you wouldn't mind if I brought along an old friend of mine from my salad days in London!" said Gerald with a hearty laugh. In deference to the title of the man beside him, he addressed him first while performing the introductions. "Sir Henry Claibourne, I should like for you to meet our host, Mister Barrett Wolfe. Mister Wolfe, may I present Sir Henry Claibourne."

Sir Henry forced himself to take the other man's hand in a firm, steady grasp. Barrett Wolfe's eyes narrowed imperceptibly up at him.

"Sir Henry Claibourne," he repeated, giving him a slight nod before releasing his hand. "I bid you welcome to my home." His gaze flickered rapidly from Sir Henry to Gerald and back again before he added with a faint smile, "Your name, Sir Henry, has a familiar ring to it, though I cannot place the occasion upon which I heard it."

"Indeed?" the older man responded with what appeared to be condescending aloofness. "Well then, Mister Wolfe, perhaps your memory will improve over the course of the evening."

Barrett Wolfe's gaze darkened at that, but his

489

mouth curved up into another ghost of a smile. He turned and led the way into the drawing room, where the other guests had already gathered to converse with one another over their brandy and cigars.

Sir Henry Claibourne glanced surreptitiously up toward the bedrooms on the second floor as he went. For a fleeting moment, his gaze filled with a fierce light, while his expression became one of barely controlled rage. He schooled his features to inscrutability once more, however, before he moved into the smoke-filled drawing room on the heels of the man he fully intended to destroy—if Devlin did not do so first—once Meghan was safely away from the island.

Upstairs at that precise moment, Meghan sat alone in the candlelit darkness and pondered her next course of action. She had heard the carriages drawing up in front of the house a short time earlier, and her mind raced to think of a way to use the arrival of the Wolf's guests to her advantage.

"There must be something . . . some way!" she murmured aloud, rising from the bed again and folding her arms tightly across her breasts. She began to pace restlessly about the room as her brow creased into a deep, pensive frown. Her eyes lit with triumph when she hit upon an idea. "Of course!" she whispered to herself in satisfaction. "The candle!"

She would set the curtains and bedclothes afire! The smoke would alert everyone else in the house to her plight. When the servants came bursting into the room to put out the blaze, she would rush downstairs and make her presence known to The Wolf's guests. If they were as distinguished and respectable as he had boasted, she mused, then they would of a certainty agree to help her!

She sprang into action at last. Taking up the candle, she held her other hand protectively about its flame while she hastened across to the window.

"Now, Barrett Wolfe, you shall learn that I am a *woman* not to be crossed!" she vowed, her eyes flashing with dauntless spirit as she recalled his similar warning to her. Offering up a silent prayer for the success of her daring scheme, she raised the candle toward the lace.

The door behind her was eased cautiously open just as the flame ignited the lower edge of the curtain. A man peered inside, his eyes gleaming in mingled triumph and relief when they fell upon Meghan. Wasting no time, he entered the room and closed the door quietly behind him.

"Meghan!" he called to her in a resonant undertone.

Starting in alarm, she dropped the candle and whirled about. Her eyes grew enormous within the delicate oval of her face as they filled with recognition.

"*Devlin?*" She stared at him in profound incredulity. "Oh Devlin, thank God you have come!" she then breathed as the reality of his presence sunk in. Her whole body trembled with exaltation, and her head swam dizziliy.

Devlin was across the room in an instant, his strong arm catching her about the waist while at the same time he jerked the curtain free and flung it down to the floor. He quickly smothered the flames with the heel of his boot, doing the same to the candle before allowing himself the luxury of wrapping both of his arms about Meghan. Clinging to him in breathless joy and relief, she buried her face gratefully against the warm, broad expanse of his chest.

"Blast it, woman, what were you trying to do?" he demanded in a vibrant whisper close to her ear. Meghan could hear the loving amusement in his voice, and her eyes filled with tears of happiness at the sound.

"I was trying to escape!" she retorted. Quickly sobering again, she gazed anxiously up at him, but could scarcely make out his beloved features in the darkness. "The Wolf has . . . has not yet conquered me, Devlin!" she hastened to inform him. "But he is planning to return as soon as his guests depart!"

"We shall be well away from here by then, my love!" He set her purposefully from him and took her hand in a firm grasp with his own. "Come. We must hurry! Your grandfather no doubt grows impatient by now!"

"*My grandfather?*" she echoed in shocked disbelief. "But I do not—"

"Later!" he reiterated with a brief, enigmatic smile. He urged her along with him to the door, slowly opening it again and glancing about to make certain the hallway was still deserted.

"The man who brought me here usually guards the door!" whispered Meghan. "He is very large, with a black beard, and—"

"We will not be bothered by him!" Devlin confidently assured her.

Meghan's eyes moved apprehensively about as she and Devlin headed back along the same route he had followed while sneaking inside. Before they had traveled more than a short distance from the room, however, the sound of a woman's piercing scream alerted the entire household to the fact that something was amiss.

Devlin pulled Meghan with him back against the wall. She watched in dismay as the stout, silver-haired housekeeper went bustling down the interior staircase to tell Barrett Wolfe of her awful discovery—the unconscious form of Meghan's guard lying at the far end of the corridor.

"Dear Lord, what do we do now?" gasped Meghan.

"We proceed downstairs to join your grandfather," he answered calmly. Although he had hoped to get Meghan safely away from the plantation without The Wolf's knowledge, he had recognized the need for an alternate plan. It was that alternate plan which he now set into motion.

"But we—we cannot go down there!" protested Meghan, her eyes full of bewilderment and alarm. "The Wolf will see us for sure!"

"That he will," Devlin startled her further by agreeing complacently. "But you must trust me in this!"

With that, he scooped her up in his arms and carried her down the winding staircase. Meghan, her head awhirl with confusion and lingering trepidation in spite of Devlin's masterful assurances, looked down to where Barrett Wolfe and his guests had just come rushing out of the drawing room with the intention of conducting an investigation into the housekeeper's frantic claim of a dead man's body.

The masculine group assembled at the foot of the staircase stared in surprise at the unfamiliar, beautiful young woman being conveyed downstairs by an equally mysterious gentleman.

But there was more than surprise contained within the dark, hawkish depths of Barrett Wolfe's gaze. He was not a man to suffer defeat easily.

"Ah, Meghan, my dear!" proclaimed Sir Henry. He stepped forward to meet them as they reached the last step. "I am sorry to see you are not feeling any better."

"Grandfather!" Meghan responded in a small, tremulous voice. She read the silent warning in his eyes, and her wide, perplexed gaze darted toward a strangely silent Barrett Wolfe. Paling beneath the hard, burning look he gave her, she instinctively tightened her arms about Devlin's neck.

"Gentlemen, I am afraid my granddaughter requires medical attention at once," Sir Henry went on to announce.

"Your granddaughter?" repeated Gerald Ralston in complete bafflement. "But I thought you said—"

"I will explain it to you later, my friend," answered Sir Henry with a faint smile. "But for now, we must be on our way back to Bridgetown!"

Meghan could scarcely believe it, but she found herself being spirited away beneath The Wolf's very nose. He was powerless to stop them—if he dared to try, he risked having his own deception exposed. Sir Henry Claibourne's word would hold enough weight to convince the others of his duplicity. Thus, he could do nothing but stand and watch in silent, simmering fury while Devlin bore Meghan outside to the waiting carriage.

"Good evening, Madam Montague," the young footman said quietly as he opened the door to the hired conveyance. Meghan was startled to see that it was Peter Hobbs who stood smiling across at her in the moonlit darkness. Her eyes flew up to the driver's seat, only to discover Malachi Flynn's craggy features grinning broadly down at her.

"We'll soon have you feelin' better, my lady!" the burly seaman guaranteed.

Devlin settled her gently upon the seat, then gave her a quick, bolstering smile before moving away. She watched as he strode around to mount the horse Peter had retrieved from behind the main house. Sir Henry climbed up into the carriage to take a seat beside his granddaughter, slipping a protective arm about her shoulders and drawing her close. A much confused Gerald Ralston sat down opposite them.

With a vigorous crack of his whip, Malachi Flynn guided the carriage away from Barrett Wolfe's plantation and along the road leading back to Bridgetown, the island's bustling main port. The *Pandora* was anchored at the quay there, and her crew waited in readiness for their captain's return.

Devlin rode behind the carriage, his eyes moving

warily about to make certain the group's progress would not be impeded by any of The Wolf's men. Musing that the bastards were no doubt well on their way to roaring drunkenness in the comfort of Bridgetown's taverns by that time, he turned his head slightly and caught one last glimpse of the leader of the pirates standing on the front steps of the house.

Soon, you blackhearted son of a bitch! Devlin promised silently, his deep blue eyes smoldering with deadly intent. He would make the man pay with his life once they had Meghan safely away from Barbados. Her welfare was his primary concern, but the desire for revenge burned deep within him. *Soon . . .*

Barrett Wolfe's own eyes blazed with cunning madness. His obsession with Meghan, as well as his burning refusal to let himself be bested in anything, drove him to uncharacteristic rashness. Hot, murderous rage filled him as he watched the carriage roll out of sight. Oblivious to the fact that there were a number of influential gentlemen waiting for him to enlighten them about the recent, ~artling events, he muttered an evil obscenity and ~rned his steps in the direction of the stables.

There was little opportunity for talk as Malachi Flynn urged the horses to a breakneck pace across the rolling countryside. Meghan clung tightly to her grandfather while the carriage's wheels bounced along over the rough dirt road. Devlin maintained his vigilance as he rode close behind; like his men, he was armed and ready to fight should the need arise.